Nerine served all three norns as handmaiden. And Nerine would choose the new materials required for this day's weaving.

She would need pale peach for the baby born to a king, blood red for a battle between Sparta and Athens, gold for a hero's bright deed. And if she failed to watch the images unfolding in the Well of Destiny, she would not know the other threads to choose for the day's work.

She had to know.

So Nerine watched, but her heart ached, and memories from her past overlaid the flowing images on the waters of the well.

Altairos as a curly black-haired boy, laughing, his eyes crinkling in that way that only he had.

Altairos as a gangly youth, earnest and passionate, reciting poetry to her.

Altairos as a young man, strong and sure, pressing a first kiss upon her willing lips.

Who but she would lay out the symbols of his death? She, the handmaiden of the fates. She couldn't bear it – to lose him so.

Also by J.M. Ney-Grimm

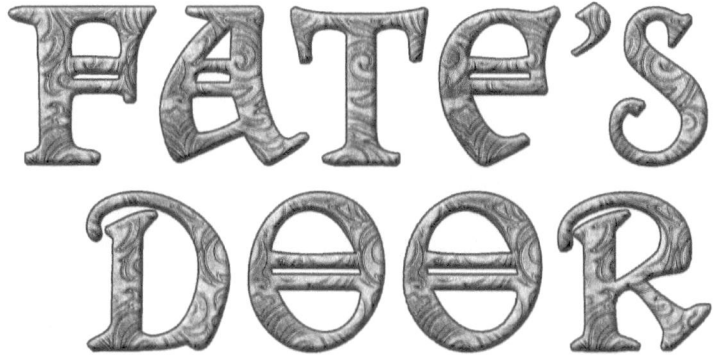

FATE'S DOOR

A MYTHIC TALE

by J.M. Ney-Grimm

Wild
Unicorn

ISBN-13: 978-0692583654
ISBN-10: 0692583653

Designed by JMNG

Cover art:
"Spring Blonde" by Dmytro Konstantynov / Dreamstime.com
"Wave Crashing" by Tatiana Morozova / Dreamstime.com

For Rachel

With thanks to Dean
for all I've learned from him
and for his utterly essential advice
regarding *Fate's Door*

Table of Contents

The Well of Destiny

The Middle Sea

The Tapestry of the World

Appendices

The Well of Destiny

1 ~ Salt of Sea and Tears

A LONG GREEN COMBER rolled the man's body, flaccid and pale in the water.

Nerine could almost smell the tang of the ocean, hear the roar of surf on an unseen, but nearby shore, taste the salt air on her lips. Or was it merely the salt tears running down her cheeks?

She'd stepped up behind her mistress. Well, Nerine answered to all three, but Tynghed was kindest.

Above them, the rooks cawed in the winter-bare branches of the World Tree. Did the birds see visions in the well of destiny? Sense the dooms meted out there?

The shrouded norns had first watered the Tree, dipping from the spring's chill outflow. Now they posed beside its deeps, meditating on the images they saw reflected. What did they see? Did they see Altairos, the island-prince of Zakynthos? Did they see what Nerine saw?

She steadied her quivering lip and felt Tynghed's hand, stealing from within the fate's dark cloak, slipping behind her to clasp Nerine's hand.

Ah, blessings, it could not be! Altairos drowned in the waves of his beloved ocean? And yet she knew it was. The breath of life would pass from him this day, and she would lay out the blue and green silks with which the norns would weave his fate. "I won't. I won't do it," she breathed. But she would. The Shuttle-catcher, the Patterner, and the Weaver commanded her obedience. How could a stranded sea nymph defy them?

"I must!"

Tynghed's fingers pressed Nerine's hand.

Nerine bit her lip. She possessed a role in this morning's seeing.

The leafless branches of the World Tree loomed over them on the rise, while its massive twisting roots clawed the lichen-spotted rocks and pockets of moss where it grew. One root crawled down the low outcrop overhanging the well to wrap the far side of the water. Dark water, not reflecting the gray sky, but holding a translucence that suggested it went down and down to the ice at the world's heart.

Orroch, bent and old under her dark cloak, the Weaver of Fate, would translate the well's visions into a tapestry of events. She was grouchy, was Orroch. Did it bother her that she doomed thousands to die every day?

It must.

Eowys, tall and stern within her black mantle, the Patterner of Fate, would use the well's visions to select and draw the heddles of the loom that gave Orroch her textile canvas. Eowys was almost prissy in her demeanor. Did it spill over from her duties at the loom? She had to be so precise in the strings she pulled. One mistake, and someone innocent would suffer for it. How did Eowys bear the responsibility? Nerine was glad it was not hers.

The Shuttle-catcher of Fate, Tynghed, hidden by her somber cloak, but beautiful and smiling within it, would send the weft threads across the loom to Orroch's hand, and catch the shuttle again when Orroch tossed it back. Tynghed was the youngest of the norns. Would she grow finicky like Eowys as she grew older? Or crotchety like Orroch? Nerine hoped not. Fervently hoped not. She couldn't bear it here in the north without Tynghed's warm kindness.

Nerine served all three norns as handmaiden. And Nerine would choose the new materials required for this day's weaving.

Take heed, Nerine. That was the meaning in Tynghed's pressing fingers. Nerine would need pale peach for the baby born to a king, blood red for a battle between Sparta and Athens, gold for a hero's bright deed. And if she failed to watch the images unfolding in the well, she would not know what else to choose for the day's work.

She had to know.

So Nerine watched, but her heart ached, and memories from her past overlaid the flowing images on the waters of the well.

Altairos as a curly black-haired boy, laughing, his eyes crinkling in that way that only he had.

Altairos as a gangly youth, earnest and passionate, reciting poetry to her.

Altairos as a young man, strong and sure, pressing a first kiss upon her willing lips.

Who but she would lay out the symbols of his death? She, the handmaiden of the fates. She couldn't bear it – to lose him so. And yet . . . had she not lost him years ago, when she came north to this place?

A rook cawed.

The mossy smell of cold rock wrapped her round.

And Tynghed's hand pressed hers again. It was time.

The visions in the well were complete, but the norns would stay to pursue a rite too secret to share with their handmaiden. Nerine would leave them, returning home to review the threads in the dozen shuttles and the silks rolled on flat sticks, strewn across the tray at the front of the loom. Were they right? Did any need to be refilled or removed?

Nerine would walk along the many shelves filled with reel upon reel of threads. Some wool, some flax, some silk, a few spun of feathers. Every color and texture were present. She would choose the right ones and ready them, perhaps changing the heather blue wool in one shuttle for a bright aqua flax, perhaps adding a dull bronze silk to the palette on the tray.

Today, she would seek a porcelain plaque enameled with violet flowers and a small gold key to be sewn into the tapestry.

Today, she would choose the green and the peacock blue and the turquoise that would draw Altairos down into the depths to drown. Blessings, no!

Tynghed's hand pressed hers a third time. Nerine was lingering, and she mustn't. She bowed her head in a courtesy that the norns saw not and felt Tynghed's cool fingers release hers.

The path down the slope was narrow and uneven, descending in abrupt jolts, and curving around the hillside. A jinking route, but familiar. Nerine had climbed this hill every morning for five years. She knew its every quirk. And still she tripped as she descended today. She had fallen into an older habit, flowing swiftly down as though she were swimming, then forgetting that she moved on land, not through water. She stumbled over a thick hump of root, but recovered her balance without falling. Walking would never be as comfortable as swimming, but it was more interesting. Different. And differences still attracted her, even after five years of them.

The damp earth felt cool on her bare feet. No ferns grew in this late winter to tickle her ankles as she picked her way, but the wet hem of her black cloak slapped her skin.

The cold, damp north was so different from the warm waters in which Nerine had spent her childhood. She'd grown accustomed to the change. It had been easier at the beginning, when everything felt new and exotic.

Now . . . even while reveling in the less familiar, she missed the warmth of home, the welcome of home.

But these were perilous thoughts. She was here. Better to forget the past, dwell in the now.

At the hill's base, the path leveled out and passed through a cluster of holly trees, threading between clumps of hawthorn, elderberry, and hazelnut. The shrubs were pretty when in bloom. Or in leaf. Or in fruit. But their gray tangle in winter spoke of dearth and death.

Nerine shivered.

Beyond the scattered shrubs lay the norns' cottage, its back pressed against a low, sheltering bluff, its front stoop looking out across a diminutive meadow. The grasses, mashed flat under old snow – long melted – lay rank and matted, a dull tan.

The cottage had seemed quaint, even charming, when Nerine first set eyes on it in autumn. The flame-red leaves of sweet-smelling twinflower clung to its rugged stone walls, peeking in through the open window casements and sprawling across the steep, thatched roof.

The window casements – diamond-paned with translucent horn, not glass – were open now, as were the shutters. The norns considered the days of late winter, about to turn to spring, to be mild ones and they enjoyed the fresh air. Nerine . . . had grown to accept the practice after enduring five years of it.

But the cottage in winter – gray-veined stone, slot-like gabled porch, and dingy thatch – possessed a brooding presence it doffed in spring. The winter cottage was indeed the home where dooms were born.

～

Nerine wiped her feet on the rag mat on the porch. It held a lot of old mud and felt gritty underfoot. The space was dim beneath its steeply slanted roof, and the hard narrow benches on either side, perpendicular to the cottage, did not invite lingering.

Nerine threw back the hood of her cloak, pulled the latchstring on the lower half of the door – soon the norns would have the upper half open, like the windows – and pushed on the door's gray-weathered wood.

Inside, the mood was cheerful, despite the small windows, which admitted little light, and the thick walls – their inner surface formed by the dark black-brown of ancient, squared, pine logs. A vivid red-orange door quilt and four window quilts, pushed aside from the openings, brightened the space. An oval rag rug of turquoise, indigo, and grass green softened the pine boards of the floor.

Nerine usually smiled upon entering the cottage. She loved that rug. It reminded her of home. Today she shuddered. It was too like the silks that would doom her beloved.

She paused before the banked fire in the massive stone hearth to warm her chilled hands and feet. In the evening, at the end of the day's work, she would throw new logs on the coals to kindle a fresh blaze. But this room would be untenanted, once the norns had broken their fast at the round table before the hearth. The coals must stay banked, for now.

Nerine drew her cloak off and hung it on one of the hooks beside the front door. Her gown beneath the dark outer garment was brighter, a greeny-gold felted wool that matched her long wavy hair, and brought out the deeper hazel green of her eyes. The white fichu around her neck, covering the skin left bare by the low neck of her gown, was also fashioned of felted wool.

The norns, embracing chilled air, wore linen. But they had learned, when Nerine caught cold in her first winter with them, that she was not so hardy.

All of her winter garb was woolen now. This particular gown was a gift from Tynghed, created during the norn's free evening hours. Nerine touched the soft material at the waist, drawn in by back lacings from hip to shoulderblades. Vicuna wool was the softest fiber in the world, softer even than the silks Altairos had once brought her.

She crossed the front sitting room and passed through the doorway into the weaving room, stumbling on the threshold plate. Would she always forget to pick her feet up when she was preoccupied?

The weaving chamber was a large space, with a pitched ceiling higher than all the rest of the rooms in the cottage – showing the underside of the thatch roof. Six generous windows pierced the outer walls, letting in a flood of cool, gray light through their open casements.

Every other scrap of wall boasted cabinets with doors and drawers along the lower half, and shelves filled with reels and reels of thread along the upper.

The rich scent of raw silk and dyed wool mingled with the cool freshness of the air from the outdoors. It smelled like . . . home – this place that had become her home, even though it smelled nothing like her old home in the Middle Sea.

The jumble of color had bewildered Nerine when she first saw it. Now she knew the location of every item in the cabinets or on the shelves: each color and texture of thread, each coil of floss, each needle, each handheld beater, everything.

It was her job to know.

But the magnificent loom occupying the center of the space still amazed her. Still terrified her. And always would.

It was a draw-loom, stretching from the front of the room toward the back, eighteen feet long and as wide as Nerine was tall. At its center, nearer the front than the back, rose a scaffolding like a small tower. Nerine had not understood what she was looking at when she first arrived. She knew only small ground looms and simple vertical looms, comfortable devices signifying comfortable domesticity.

This loom . . . was a monster, but more powerful than any kraken or gorgon. Those monsters slew by the dozens. This one eventually slew every living creature born.

Nerine repressed a shiver each time she entered its presence. Was she foolish?

At the front of the loom, wizened and gray-haired Orroch's bench awaited her. A tray, directly abutting the woven fabric, held silks wrapped around flat spindles. And a bronze mirror below the fabric gave Orroch a glimpse of its finished right side.

Orroch rarely looked at the mirror. She seemed to know what she was producing just from the patterns on the wrong side of the cloth, where she did her work, passing a spool of pink silk through six warp threads, another spool of silver silk through a dozen. Or calling for Tynghed to throw the shuttle of dusty green wool across the whole breadth of the tapestry, and then tossing it back to her.

Orroch would weave Altairos' death today. The bubbles rising through the water from his last breath as his body sank toward the sea's floor. The fishes that nosed him as he descended, down and down. The crabs that awaited him, hungry to nibble his dead flesh.

Nerine's breath caught in another sob.

No, no, he could not die!

Was there any way Nerine could stop Orroch? *Make* her weave differently?

Oh, blessings! Orroch was the most powerful of the norns, the eldest, the one who bent others to her will. Orroch commanded Nerine. Not the other way round.

Nerine pressed her fingers to her lips, stifling more sobs.

What of Eowys? Queenly, black-haired Eowys, who would sit atop the scaffolding tower. There, her small seat perched just below the thatch, with a canopy of plain cream silk spreading under the rests for her feet, present to catch any falling dirt, before it could touch the vital threads below.

The leashes which lifted the threads of the world's tapestry hung just before Eowys' hands, like long streamers of ribband seaweed. The heddles, these leashes were called. And Eowys listened for Orroch's coded call – "eighth draw, noose ring, kittle kettle" – to know which of them to pick and pull. By pulling the heddles, Eowys created the pattern across which Orroch passed her spindles of thread.

Could Nerine persuade Eowys to pull the wrong set of heddles? Create a pattern that raised Altairos to air, there to breathe and live?

Just yesterday, Eowys had made an error and pulled the wrong heddles. The look of shock on her patrician face when she realized it – that look had shocked Nerine. Eowys was always so sure of herself, so stately. She prided herself on her perfect memory of the thousands of codes that Orroch might call, that directed Eowys in her picking and pulling. She prided herself on the accuracy of her hands.

Eowys would never pull the wrong heddles deliberately. Not for Altairos, so dear to Nerine's heart. Not for Nerine herself. Not even for Orroch, were Orroch to order such an unthinkable thing.

Nerine clenched her fists.

She stood at the center of fate itself, beside the loom that governed the past, the present, and the future. How could she be so powerless? There had to be some action she could take to save her beloved.

Grim Orroch and haughty Eowys would take no such action. But what of Tynghed?

Kind, chestnut-tressed Tynghed would occupy a stool on Orroch's far right, ready to send any one of a dozen shuttles across the warp threads. Ready to catch the shuttle when Orroch sent it back. Tynghed would help Nerine, if she could.

If she could.

There was the rub. For what could Tynghed do? Refuse to throw the shuttle when Orroch commanded it? Toss the wrong shuttle?

Even if Tynghed could bring herself to fail her sacred duty, Orroch would merely insist that the Shuttle-catcher correct her mistake. That was what she had done yesterday, with Eowys' error.

Paying no heed to Eowys' distress, Orroch had merely repeated her instruction: "No, Patterner. Trill shawl seven, not thrill paw eleven."

And they'd gone on, weaving the cloth of the world.

Orroch and Eowys and Tynghed – the Weaver, the Patterner, and the Shuttle-catcher – would, or could, do nothing to preserve the prince of Zakynthos.

If Altairos was to be saved, Nerine must do the saving. She *must*.

But how?

⁓

Nerine's fingernails dug into her palms, so tightly did she clench her hands, as she studied the monstrous loom before her, determined to wrench Altairos' salvation from it. Somehow.

The loom on which the norns wove the destiny of the world possessed two mysteries more alarming than all the rest of it.

Normal cloth on a normal loom had a beginning and an end.

The weaver measured her warp threads – the long ones – and cut them. The warp threads fed off a cylinder at the back of the loom, passed over the vast length of the loom like a table, through the heddles in the middle, and became fabric at the front of the loom where the weaver wove.

But the world cloth . . . had no ends, or none that Nerine could see.

She'd been under the loom.

Whenever Orroch needed an ornament attached to the face of the fabric, she sent Nerine to hold it in place, while Orroch sewed or knotted the crossing weft strands that would keep it there forever.

Under the loom was scary, a shadowy cave beneath the warp threads and the forming fabric, with the sense of an abyss looming at Nerine's feet. Where a normal loom would have its roll of woven cloth, this one possessed merely a bar to keep the fabric of the world – hanging free – away from Orroch's knees.

From there, the tapestry fell into darkness.

The worst thing was the lack of a definite brink.

Beneath Nerine were the hard pine boards of the floor. Below the fall of tapestry was only dark space. And where the secure floor gave way to dark nothingness was entirely unclear. Nor did Orroch minimize the danger.

Each and every time Nerine crawled under the loom, Orroch cautioned her, "Move slowly, feel thy way. Set neither hand nor knee nor haunch without testing the surface. The abyss is known to move!"

Nerine suspected Orroch and Eowys knew what – or who? – awaited the world cloth in the abyss. But Tynghed didn't. Nerine had asked her straight out. And Tynghed would never lie. She might smile kindly and refuse to answer, but she would tell only the truth.

The back of the loom of destiny was even more terrifying.

On an ordinary loom – a loom used to weave cloth for garments or household linens – the warp threads unrolled from a cylinder.

But the world loom had weighted threads that came up from the abyss – a void similar to the forward abyss, but feeling even more fraught. From the abyss, the threads passed over the back beam through the raddle, a series of pegs that kept the threads separate and untangled.

Twice, the ring-weight on the end of a warp thread had emerged from the abyss. And twice had the norns followed a careful procedure to return that weight to its origin in darkness.

Eowys had washed her bare feet thrice and donned special silk slippers. Then she'd climbed up onto the side frame at the back of the loom, and leaned over to grasp the weight hanging from the end of the thread.

Only after the weight came into Eowys' hand and she had turned to sit on the side beam, did Orroch and Tynghed huff sighs of relief.

Perched there, Eowys had untied the old thread from its weight, and then spliced the old thread to the new, spinning the fibers together with her fingers.

Then Tynghed began to unspool the new thread, looping the lengths around Orroch's outstretched arms. Around and around. How could one small reel hold so much? This was the magic of the fates.

Orroch's arms trembled with the weight of it, and still the thread unspooled.

The norns laid the heavy loops carefully on the floor, and began a fresh set of loops.

Eowys waited quietly, sitting on the frame where before she had squatted to retrieve the weight. No one spoke. Nerine, watching, had hardly dared breathe.

Orroch and Tynghed laid the second set of looped thread on the floor and began a third. They reached the thread end at last. Eowys tied the weight – an ancient, rust-corroded ring of bronze – onto the end of the new thread. Then she maneuvered herself into a squatting position and began to lower the weight into the abyss.

Tynghed paid out the thread to Eowys, painstakingly ensuring that it came off the loops without tangling. Down and down went the weight, the thread following after, disappearing into the dark.

When the last interval of that long, long strand came into Eowys' fingers, she set it between the proper two pegs of the raddle and let it go. Her legs were shaking. Tynghed and Orroch helped her down from the loom and supported her steps away from it.

"Well done," muttered Orroch.

"You know you'll need to let me try it sometime," said Tynghed.

Orroch had merely pressed her withered lips flat and shaken her head. "Not yet. Not yet." She'd looked away from Tynghed, her wise old eyes piercing Nerine's wide gaze. "Fetch the blackthorn cordial, girl. And one glass."

Nerine had tripped over the threshold plate in the door to the front room she'd moved so fast.

Orroch herself had held the thimble glass to Eowys' lips. And then they'd returned to weaving. A day's inches could not be stinted, no matter the stress and strain of adding to the length of a spent warp thread.

That day, after their labors of returning the warp weight to the abyss, they'd worked late into the night.

This day would hold nothing so strenuous . . . for the norns at least.

Sobs crowded Nerine's throat.

The loom of destiny held no answers for Altairos.

～

2 ~ Secrets, Wise and Unwise

BRUSHING HER TEARS ASIDE with the back of her hand, Nerine readied the green silks and the aquas that would weave Altairos' doom. She measured the proper length of each from the reel, snipped it, and wound it around the flat rods used by Orroch for the small patterns.

She had a job to do: readying the materials for the day's weaving. It had to be done, Altairos or no Altairos. But, oh, her fingers were heavy as she worked.

When she stood before the tray at the front of the loom, she hesitated.

What if she didn't lay down the necessary threads? What if she put them back on the shelf? What if she dropped them down into the abyss?

Without the threads, the doom could not be woven. Wouldn't Altairos be safe then?

She imagined the bright silks disappearing into darkness, the loose ends trailing, glimmering in the last hint of fading light.

She shivered.

No, Altairos would fall into darkness with them, his fate more dreadful than even the drowning meted out to him.

Another tear spilled from Nerine's eye, its track down her cool cheek hot. She drew in a long, slow breath, steadying herself. She couldn't subtract from Altairos' destiny. Could she add to it? Add safety, add blessing, create a different outcome? She would try. She had to try. This was her only avenue for changing his fate.

What addition might do what she wanted?

She thought over the contents of the many drawers: beads, brooches, bones. Every kind of trinket. What if she set out the lump of petrified wood? Might Altairos cling to a floating spar of his riven ship? Or what if she chose a fishhook? Would a fisherman pull Altairos from the sea before he drowned?

A knock on the door of the cottage interrupted Nerine's calculations.

She started, lost her balance, caught it, and hurried into the front room to open the door.

A red-cheeked young woman with shiny black hair and a wide smile waited on the porch. A white and blue kerchief covered her head. Her sturdy arms emerged from her blue wool cloak to hold a large basket.

Linnea was assistant to the cook who provided the norns' meals. She nodded to Nerine and stepped across the threshold.

"I found a crock of starflower honey hidin' behind the jug of beet kvass!" announced Linnea. "Himinlaeva" – that was the cook – "scolded me, but your porridge'll taste a sight bit better with it. *And* there's limpabread and summer sausage, too. Oh, and there's blackberry leaf tea."

Linnea was unloading her basket onto the round table as she spoke – teapot, covered serving bowl, covered platters – smiling at Nerine all the while.

Nerine forced a smile back at her.

She'd spent many a free morning with Linnea in the cookhouse, learning how to bake biscuits and how to ferment cabbage. Land foods were so utterly different from sea foods: breads and meats and pickles instead of fish and water plants and mollusks. And *northern* land foods were just as different from *southern* land foods. Learning about baking and roasting was fascinating, and Linnea was kind and generous to share her knowledge.

But Nerine was glad she didn't have to do regular meal preparation. Cooking for fun was . . . fun. Cooking all day long would be drudgery. Although Linnea didn't seem to find it so.

And Linnea didn't deserve the cold shoulder now, just because Nerine was scared witless about another – vital – matter. She moved to the wall cupboard and started stacking bowls to take to the table. Linnea joined her, clattering the bread plates and tea mugs.

Just as they laid the spoons at each place, crotchety Orroch came through the front door with Eowys and Tynghed behind her.

"Ye've discussed it enough," insisted Orroch as she hung up her cloak, her voice scratchier than usual.

"Indeed, yes," answered Eowys, cool and stately. She turned from the cloak hooks to address Linnea. "You've breakfasted, child?"

Linnea bobbed a curtsey. "Yes'm. Cook's expectin' me. We'm startin' the pressed *sylta* today, so luncheon and supper'll be plain, if your venerableness permits?"

"Of course, child. Run along with you and tell Himinlaeva that we're appreciative of all she provides, the simple as well as the ornate."

Linnea bobbed another curtsey and whisked herself out the door.

Tynghed followed her sister norns to the table, seating herself with a troubled expression on her lovely face. "Don't you think talking about it –"

Orroch interrupted her. "No. Talking pays no toll. Done is done, and what must be, must be. Hold thy tongue!"

Orroch never raised her voice. Her authority as the eldest and most senior of the fates held without any extra effort on her part. And stress just made her tone scratchier, not louder. But it was louder now. What *could* they be arguing about? They never argued.

"I will not be silenced, elder sister." Tynghed's voice sounded musical even when she was stirred. "Sometimes talking leads to better solutions. Or, at least, more understanding and greater acceptance."

Nerine drew up her own chair at the table between Tynghed and Eowys, and began pouring the blackberry leaf infusion from the teapot into the mugs, while Eowys served the porridge. The fragrant aroma of cooked oats mingled with the fruity scent of the tea, but Nerine's stomach felt tight and sick. Between the quarreling norns and her anxiety for Altairos, food held little appeal.

Orroch sat across from Nerine, but her attention focused on Tynghed. Thank the blessings! Nerine certainly didn't want her attention at this moment.

"Tynghed." Orroch's voice had quieted, but all the force of her personality sounded in the name. "Choose, and choose carefully. Will ye pack thy belongings and go? Or will ye stay and be mute in this affair?"

Nerine felt shock punch her belly. She held very still. Such an ultimatum was unprecedented. Could a norn really be deposed from her post?

∼

Tynghed stared at Orroch, her breath sounding loud through her nostrils. She looked angry, not scared. Perhaps thinking? She picked up the honey crock and drizzled honey onto her porridge, then took up her spoon and ate a bite, still saying nothing.

Orroch nodded and sipped her tea. "We've a big day before us. Did ye get all the silks laid out and the new blue for the weft wound on a spindle, Nerine?"

Nerine felt herself blushing. *Had* she finished her work before Linnea arrived? Before she started pondering ways to save Altairos?

"Yes, eldest, I did."

Had she? Really? She had no idea.

"Good." Orroch lifted the cover from the summer sausage, took the small knife from her belt, and started cutting slices of the meat. "The earlier we start, the more likely we'll finish before dark."

Abruptly, Nerine had an idea.

"There was one item I couldn't find in any of the drawers." Delay would be good, wouldn't it? If she could put off Altairos' death long enough, maybe it wouldn't arrive at all. "It was for . . . for the shipwreck."

Orroch's wizened face didn't change at all, but Eowys' eyebrow lifted as she murmured, "Indeed?" And Tynghed hissed.

So. They'd been arguing about Nerine. Nerine and her reaction to Altairos' fate.

Nerine stilled the impulse she felt to shuffle her feet. She wasn't going to admit she knew that they knew. She'd stand no chance of saving Altairos if she did. She would be innocent and unknowing, focused on her job.

"What couldn't ye find, Nerine?" Orroch's words were almost gentle, despite the rasp in her voice.

"I don't know. I didn't get the certainty that I usually do." She made herself meet Orroch's gaze, her own eyes wide and guileless. "Remember that time I needed a thimble for the wisewoman of Messina. The thimble didn't come clear at the well. It wasn't until I looked in Tynghed's workbasket and saw it, that I knew."

She allowed herself to blink once, naturally. "I think the thing I need for the shipwreck is in my bedchamber, but I don't know what it is." That last was true. She didn't know what might avert Altairos' death. But neither did she know it lay in her bedchamber – that was a lie – and the saving of the prince went specifically against the vision shown in the well of fates.

She didn't care. She would save him if she could.

A strange expression passed across Orroch's face. Nerine didn't know what it meant. What was Orroch thinking? Something . . . devious? Maybe.

"Eat fast and light, then. Ye can search while we three partake more fully." Orroch glanced to the side and down, then back up to study Nerine.

Nerine shook her head. "I'm not hungry. I'll go now."

Tynghed's protest burst out. "Orroch!" – angry. "Nerine!" – concerned.

"Your choice," Orroch reminded the youngest norn.

"I'll just finish my tea." Nerine spoke fast, to beat Tynghed to whatever further protest she might make. "I'll be fine. Really I will."

She grabbed her mug, sloshing some of the liquid over the side, and gulped. The sweet berry flavor spread across her tongue, and the infusion soothed her throat. She hadn't realized she was thirsty.

Tynghed huffed, but said nothing further.

"I'll be as quick as I can." Nerine shoved back her chair to hurry away.

Orroch's bony hand shot out, seizing Nerine's wrist.

"No. Do it right. Find the proper item. We'll light as many candles as need be, if we must weave after sundown." Orroch's eyes looked grim.

Nerine found herself bobbing a curtsy as though she were Linnea, a mere serving girl, instead of handmaiden and fate-in-waiting. "Yes, ma'am. I'll be thorough."

"Good." Orroch turned back to the table.

As Nerine passed through the doorway into the weaving room, closing the door behind her, she heard Eowys say, "Perhaps a few more words wouldn't come amiss, now that our handmaiden is absent?"

And Orroch's fierce answer, "No, now less than ever."

Then the door was closed, cutting off anything more.

～

Nerine scanned the brackets, where the shuttles rested on the right side of the loom, as well as the front tray with Orroch's pattern silks.

A sigh of relief puffed out of her.

She *had* finished the preparations for the day's weaving. She hadn't lied to Orroch. At least, not about that. What a mistake that would have been. Orroch was . . . adamant in her choices, in her adjudging.

Nerine shivered, hearing again Orroch's tone in her correction of Tynghed. Nerine never wanted to hear that tone when Orroch addressed *her*.

Off the short hallway beyond the weaving room lay the bedchambers, the linen cupboard, and the stillroom, as well as the small back door by the bluff behind the cottage.

Nerine's bedchamber was second on the right. Its door – like the others – was formed of plain pine planks, darkened to a blackish brown. She pulled the latch string and crossed into the warmth awaiting her. Ah . . . it welcomed her in like salt water under the noonday sun, limpid and soothing and beautiful as only the sea could be.

Nerine paused inside the door, taking in this space that was hers. Taking in its warmth, both corporeal and spiritual.

Built-in cabinetry formed the left wall. Her narrow bed jutted out from the right. The outside wall, with its two casement windows – their diamond panes cut from translucent horn – stood opposite her.

Adorned by a swirling mosaic in varying shades of aquas and blues, the round tile stove in the far right corner, beyond her bed, was the source of the physical warmth. The norns permitted Nerine to keep it lit year round. No, they insisted on it, even while their own chambers went unheated from the day that winter's snow melted. Just as they decreed that Nerine's windows remained closed until the heat of summer arrived.

Between the two windows hung a mirror of polished bronze, one of the few items she'd brought with her from home. Below the mirror and the sills of the windows lay a long, narrow shelf holding the other trinkets. From her little sister Agnippe, a hinged mussel shell protected a ring carved of nacre – the sea's opal. It had been her parting gift. Next to it stood a miniature portrait of her mother created from inlaid agate. She had the same green-gold hair of her daughters, but her eyes were gray, not hazel like Nerine's. The fan of wafer-thin jade panels came from eldest sister Eilidh.

But most of Nerine's trousseau had been ordered from the nymphs of Mount Helicon.

The ways of the sea were so different from the ways of the land. A boar bristle brush, needed for her hair, lay on the shelf beneath the mirror. Ribbands and brooches filled the drawers of the small chests resting below each end of the shelf. A padded bench, its cushion of turquoise and silver brocade, sat before the mirror. All these were things of the land, unneeded beneath the waves of the sea.

Would one item amongst them save Altairos?

Nerine stepped past the washstand, just inside the door, to sit in the padded chair at the right of her bed. Its cushions, covered with the same turquoise and silver brocade of the bench under the mirror, received her cozily, their support firmer than water, but welcome nonetheless. Air was so thin in its essence, barely noticeable against one's skin unless blown by a storm gale.

She nestled into the cushions, resolved not to waste the comfort that had stolen into her upon entering her room. She would consider her possessions in the quiet of her mind, rather than flailing through drawers and chests and cupboards in a panic.

Her narrow bed was useless. She already knew that.

The aqua silk of its quilt, knotted with silver thread and embroidered with rose arabesques and pale green diamonds, kept her warm through the northern nights. As did the fall of heavy rose silk from the hook driven into the planks of the ceiling. While she slept, the circular curtain hung to the floor around the bed, but she'd gathered it together and pushed it aside when she awoke.

The firm mattress and soft coverings were familiar to her now.

During her first night of attempted slumber on land – on Mount Olympus, not here – sleeping couches seemed utterly alien. She'd wondered where was the mass of sponges to lie upon and where the laval brazier to warm the water. Except there was no water. She'd not slept a wink that night.

But pillows and quilts and fine linen sheets were far too large to incorporate into the world tapestry. Her eyes passed onto the nightstands at either side of her bed.

Candlestick, bowl of lily-of-the-valley potpourri, ewer of water, empty glass, rondel of embroidery she was sewing for Tynghed.

No, no, no, no, no, and no. Likewise the washstand with its pitcher, basin, knob of soap, washcloths, and hand towels. No.

The chest at the foot of her bed held more sheets and pillowcases and extra woolen blankets.

Built into the wall beyond, a niche held a tapestry woven by Eowys, depicting children playing in a wood. A white-gowned girl sat on a garlanded swing while two little boys rolled hoops around her. Nerine loved that picture. It reminded her of her youth, when she'd believed that only adventure and the exotic awaited her on land.

Below the niche, six drawers held possibilities. She would consider them momentarily.

A built-in wardrobe to the right of the niche-and-drawers held her gowns of linen and silk. She no longer wore the silk ones fashioned by the southern nymphs. Orroch, Eowys, and Tynghed all wore linen in soft colors, and Nerine felt more comfortable fitting in, which the vivid silk assuredly did not. In the wardrobe on the left hung her wool gowns – for the cold months; so many cold months in the north – and the linen shifts she wore under them. Not all her woolens were so soft and free of scratchiness as the vicuna wool of today's frock.

What was in the single drawer, with its pair of hanging bronze drawer pulls, under the lefthand wardrobe? She never used it and couldn't remember.

～

3 ~ Broken Bronze

NERINE UNFOLDED FROM her chair, crossed the room, and knelt to grip the two hanging drawer pulls. The drawer stuck when open a crack. She shifted it to the side, trying to unstick it, but wedging it even more firmly. A tug to the opposite side did nothing. She pulled harder.

The right pull broke entirely away from the drawer at its hinge points, while the drawer itself shot out of the cabinetry onto her lap.

It was heavy, weighed down by some sort of massive wrought iron tongs lying on the bare drawer bottom: vast wide calipers, substantial round handles, ferocious picks at the end of the calipers. What in the sea –?

She had seen them before, five years ago when Tynghed first guided her into this room. What had Tynghed said they were? Assuring Nerine that they could be stored elsewhere.

Ice tongs. That was it. For manhandling great heavy chunks of ice.

Nerine hadn't needed the drawer, so the tongs had never been moved.

She looked at the drawer pull loose in her hand. Good thing she didn't need that drawer. It wouldn't be useable until old Eindred made his twice yearly visit to fix things. Sighing, she placed the pull – and the two broken bolts that had held the pull – next to the tongs and nudged the drawer shut.

Still on her knees, she moved over to the built-in drawers between the two wardrobes. The bottom drawer slid out smoothly, full of drawing parchment and charcoal sticks and pastel chalks. She'd taken up drawing that first year here, fascinated by an art impossible under the sea, but frustrated by her ineptitude. She still enjoyed drawing, but did less of it – ironically so – now that she had more skill and was better pleased with her creations.

The next drawer up was full of embroidery hoops, needle packets, and floss. Necessary supplies, since the norns set her regular assignments to learn and master all the skills she would need one day, when it was her turn to add stitches to the tapestry of the world.

She turned over the jumbled contents impatiently, looking for inspiration. A small bell rattled in one corner. She took it up, listening to the sweetness of its chime once the clapper swung free. No. This would help Altairos not one iota.

She shoved the drawer shut, conscious that her sense of peace was unravelling.

The third deep drawer contained her sand supplies: tightly woven linen bags of sand – pure white, soft cream, warm ecru, pale pink, and clean gold – as well as clear blown-glass jars, and boxes of dainty seashells and polished agate.

She'd filled a jar to give to Eowys on Othinn's Day, with layers of white and cream and pale pink, intersected by lacy fans of peach coral. The gift sat in the back corner of the right wardrobe, hidden until the feast day.

The northern feasts were different from the southern celebrations. At home, instead of Othinn's Day, they'd be preparing for the Festival of Zeus, which didn't feature gift giving. And they didn't honor Loki's Madness at all. Thank the blessings!

Nerine shivered, even though she wasn't cold, and rose to her feet. She stared at the top three drawers, all shallow, and didn't bother opening them. Her pantelettes, camisoles, fichus, and handkerchiefs weren't going to save Altairos.

Except – what about the handkerchiefs? Hadn't warriors of land kingdoms worn them as a sign of their ladies' favor when they went to war? Could her handkerchief serve as Altairos' favor? Could it save him?

She bit her lip in frustration. This was impossible.

When she sought a curio in response to the visions in the well of fate, she always had a notion of what was needed. Or, at least, a feeling of rightness to guide her. Now . . . she was going directly against the well, and she had nothing.

Or did she?

What if she pondered the wreck – blessings, it felt awful – and tried to sense wrongness, things that would impede the working out of destiny? Could that work?

◡

She opened the left wardrobe with her lovely warm woolen gowns, most of them woven by Gwenedd and sewn by Briallyn, the neighbors who supplied the norns with clothing and linens. Gowns of turquoise, of aqua, of burnt umber, of seaweed green, and more, crowded the wardrobe, along with shifts of fine white linen. They were signs of her welcome in the cottage, her welcome in the north. This was her home and her community now.

She swung the doors closed. No feelings of wrongness there.

What about the other wardrobe? The one full of her summer gowns and her outmoded ones.

The rightmost door stuck a little, and she had to jiggle the bronze catch to open it.

Linen gowns of willow green, of apple green, of clear yellow, and varying hues of cream, draped neatly on their hangers. Silk gowns – long unworn – of peacock green, brilliant chartreuse, and sapphire, billowed. The jar of layered sand for Eowys squatted behind their colorful hems.

What would she give Orroch? The embroidered medallion for Tynghed – depicting two clownfish peeking out from a sea anemone – would be finished soon. But Orroch was so hard to choose for. So hard to give to.

Nerine lost her balance – and caught it – as she banged the wardrobe doors shut. Nothing for Altairos there.

She could feel her heartbeat speeding up.

Would there be what she needed amongst the fripperies of the shelf that served as her dressing table? Unless she counted the basket hamper on the other side of the door from the washstand – and she didn't – the shelf and its two chests of drawers were all that was left.

She stepped over to the chest at the far right, near the tile stove.

The bottom drawer held a tangled mass of ribbands. She'd worn her hair in braids tied with ribbands during the many moons of travel from the Middle Sea to the northern cottage of the norns, and for a few months after. Then she pinned her hair up for a while. Now she wore it loose and hanging.

Ribbands would work well in the tapestry of the world. She could tie them together, wind them around a flat rod, and place it on the tray in the right place. Orroch would never question her, simply weaving the strand into the pattern of the wreck. But would it help Altairos?

An image of seaweed in the current surged before her mind's eye, its waving tentacles reaching out to grab Altairos and drag him down. Blessings, no!

She slammed the ribband drawer shut.

She checked the drawer above it, even though it was pointless. There was the jar of the sticky unguent she'd used on her skin underwater. She still smoothed it onto her feet, here on land, and sometimes on her hands, when they grew chapped in winter. But she preferred the lighter honey almond cream for her arms and legs, and the still lighter aloe lotion for her face.

Something rattled in the back of the drawer as she closed it. She jerked it open again. What was that?

Her hand dived in and came up with a small vial, once full of perfume, now empty. Oh! Altairos had given it to her before she bade him her last farewell. She'd dabbed it on her wrists and neck every day for a year. And saved the vial.

She closed the drawer more carefully and set the vial next to the fan of thin jade on the shelf above the chest.

There were three shallower drawers in the chest under the left end of the shelf, near the summer wardrobe. In the bottommost, on a white satin cushion, reposed her favorite jewelry from her days under the sea: a belt and pectoral set, fashioned of gold scales, adorned with diamonds and peridot. She wasn't sure why she'd brought it with her, except that the luster of the gold, the white fire of the diamonds, and the delicate green of the peridot all spoke to her of liquid warmth and familial love. Both pieces fit her form too exactly to go over dresses. And even if they could, they'd look ridiculous.

But she drew out the drawer to admire their beauty whenever she grew homesick, which was more and more, lately.

The middle drawer featured all the hairpins she'd needed when she'd been wearing her hair up. Here were pins set with opals, with pearls, with agate, plain silver pins, plain gold pins, as well as a few necklaces of pearl, peridot, and jade.

The top drawer held brooches: an opal carved in the shape of a rose, simple silver depicting a starfish, another fashioned as an oak tree. And here was the one she loved the most: the slim auger with its spiraling pattern from base to point, like a narwhale's horn, replicated in plain gold. She wore it nearly every day. Why hadn't she worn it today? Or yesterday? Or the day before?

Would the well of fate have shown a different destiny for Altairos, if she had?

No, that was ridiculous. History emerged from the clashing of choice and chance and serendipity, to be seen in the waters of fate, and secured by the weaving of the world cloth. The wearing of a brooch – or the failure to wear it – was mere superstition. She'd learned that from Altairos, if not from her own family.

She took the auger seashell from the drawer and pinned it at the neck of her gown, just below her right collarbone, where rested the knot of the white fichu covering her neck.

Biting her lip, she slid the last drawer closed.

She'd looked in every drawer. Well, every drawer except the one beneath the summer wardrobe. That one was filled with the modest cases and pouches that she'd traveled with.

She'd reviewed all her possessions. And none of them spoke to her in any way relevant to saving Altairos.

Some small voice inside of her wept at her failure. But around the weeping spread a vast calm, like the eye of a hurricane: still air, still water, breathless waiting. Her answer lay in this heavy hush.

A tap sounded on her door.

～

4 ~ Mother Holle's Three Questions

NERINE EXPELLED a spurt of air – a small sound at the back of her throat.

This would be Eowys, come to see what was taking her so long. Or – better – Tynghed, sneaking in that talk forbidden by Orroch. Whichever of them had knocked, the rap had dispelled Nerine's sense of an answer drifting forward on heavy silence.

She bit her lip.

She crossed to open the door, readying herself to say, "I'm almost ready," if it were Tynghed. Or, "Tell Orroch I need a moment more," if it were Eowys.

Orroch stood on the other side of the door.

Without saying anything at all, Nerine stepped back, allowing Orroch to move across the threshold.

"I can't find it," blurted Nerine.

Orroch sat in the armchair and gestured for Nerine to sit before her on the bed. "I was the Patterner before I sat to weave," she said, her old face very still. Was Orroch the eye of a hurricane?

Nerine nodded. "Before I arrived?"

Orroch didn't answer for a moment. She shifted her hands, clasped on her knees. "No, child, your arrival was not the moment when I left pattern-making, although it was the moment when Eowys ceased to catch the shuttle and climbed to the top of the loom to draw the heddles. And when Tynghed rose from handmaiden to norn."

Oh. Nerine's lips moved silently.

Orroch continued. "But I was the pattern-maker for many years. And before that, I was the shuttle-catcher. And in the beginning, I was the handmaiden who chose the silks and the wools and the ornaments."

Nerine's belly tightened. Did Orroch suspect what Nerine was attempting? Did she know that Nerine aimed to subvert the well of fate?

Nerine rushed into speech – anything to divert Orroch. Only – how foolish was that? Diverting Orroch! As though anything could. Orroch was the granite of the mountain. The gale in the storm. The cold of winter ice. "Did you always know which item was needed?"

"No."

Nerine's eyes widened. Orroch not knowing? It seemed impossible. As impossible as Orroch failing to guess Nerine's current scheme.

"You've been with us five years," stated Orroch.

Nerine nodded.

"You've never chosen the wrong silk, the wrong wool, the wrong bibelot."

Nerine didn't dare nod at that, although it was true.

"You're very gifted, child. Did you not know?"

Nerine opened her lips to speak. Closed them. Then tried again. Her voice was very small. "No. I didn't know."

"Did not Tynghed tell you?"

"Tynghed . . . always made me feel good about my progress, but –" the next words came in a rush "– Tynghed makes everyone feel good about everything."

Orroch's smile was very dry. "Yes. She does."

They both sat in silence for a moment.

Orroch leaned forward slightly. "When I was handmaiden, I made mistakes."

Nerine couldn't quite believe that, even though she believed Orroch without question.

"I made mistakes. Once it took me an entire morning to find the sewing scissors in Mother Holle's basket that were needed to save a goodwife fighting for her child's life. We wove until midnight that day."

Nerine bit her lip. "Was Mother Holle the weaver then?" She had the feeling Mother Holle was even more formidable than Orroch.

"Mother Holle was the weaver and she managed without a shuttle-catcher."

Nerine could see this long-ago weaver in her mind's eye, tall and statuesque, her long hair coiled atop her majestic head and adorned with bright holly berries. A queen. No, an empress. No, a goddess. Beautiful and utterly unapproachable.

"Did she chastise you? When it took you an entire morning?"

"No. She told me what I am going to tell you."

∼

Nerine sat a little straighter on her bed. She'd been hunching, almost without realizing it.

Orroch leaned forward from the armchair, her voice compelling.

"There are times when the right thread is not present. Or only the wrong color comes to hand. Or the proper article exists only in some far-off time in the past or the future. Too far to fetch it, the way some of our tools are obtained."

This was a morning for shocks.

The past and the future mingled with the present? She'd suspected it, because some of the trinkets were so . . . unexpected. And the cottage itself was so . . . unusual. Altairos' palace had no horn-paned windows, only unshielded or latticed openings, but this cottage did. And her own sea home featured only chests, no drawers, which were commonplace here. But . . . still. She was shocked.

Then there was infallible Orroch's confession of past errors. Her promise to dismiss Tynghed, if Tynghed failed to be silent. The vision of Altairos drowning in the well. And now this: learning that the fates wove wrongly, on occasion. Nerine felt dizzy.

"Did you ever fail to find the right thread or the right article?" Nerine still couldn't quite believe it.

"No. But I needed to know it was possible. Just as you do."

Sudden tears moistened Nerine's eyes. "But I mustn't! I can't. Not this time!"

Orroch leaned further forward and actually took Nerine's hand. Orroch's gnarled fingers felt dry and cool and strong. "Before you come to that defeat – and it is a defeat," acknowledged Orroch, "there are questions you must ask yourself."

Nerine gulped. Orroch had an answer. Even though her answer would contravene the integrity of the fate that she was sworn to uphold. Nerine listened with all her heart.

"First. Did you ignore the still small voice of inspiration, because you feared the outcome?"

Oh, Nerine feared the outcome all right. But she'd ignored nothing. She shook her head.

"Second. Did you feel only wrongness and, if you did, what is its opposite?"

Nerine had felt wrongness too. The handkerchief that would become an entombing sail. The ribbands that would drag Altairos down. Her failure to find anything at all, the failure that would seal Altairos' doom. What was the opposite of a handkerchief or a ribband? What was the opposite of doing nothing at all? Something. She must do something. Or anything. Anything at all. But what?

Nerine shook her head.

"Third. Did anything unusual happen while you searched? If so, something connected with that happening will yield what you need."

Nerine frowned. There'd been something. Hadn't there?

"I can't remember," she burst out. "What if there's nothing? Do you have another question?"

"There are three, and no more, that Mother Holle taught me. Come, child. Let us be aweaving."

Orroch stood and moved toward the door.

"Please!" gasped Nerine. "Just before you knocked, there was something coming. I could feel it."

Orroch looked at her, her gaze very steady.

Nerine felt as though her very insides must be visible, along with every criticism she'd ever made of Orroch in the privacy of her own mind. Along with her intention to change the wreck of the *Astiphílaka*.

"If you felt an answer coming, then one exists. And you must learn what it is." Orroch's gaze stayed steady, but Nerine sensed a question in it.

She volunteered: "I . . . felt something inevitable, something heavy, like fate itself, settling, looming, approaching. Something momentous, and engulfing."

Orroch nodded. "Then you must seek that feeling again, child. Come when you have it." And she closed the door behind her.

Nerine sank back on her bed, lying across it with her feet still on the floor, her knees pointing at the chair vacated by Orroch, her head near the foot.

She'd earned a grace period. A chance to cultivate that heavy sense of calm with destiny approaching. A destiny different than shipwreck for Altairos. One different – perhaps – for herself.

Was that the scary part? That another life might await her?

She'd wanted adventure when she was little. She'd longed to explore the utter unknown of the land above the sea, an entire world she'd never seen.

What had happened to that longing? Had it ebbed away entirely? Or merely gone into hiding?

She could remember the first time she'd gratified it.

She'd been very young, maybe eight, lingering in the garden below the waves that were her home.

～

The Middle Sea

5 ~ Seeking Adventure

NERINE LOVED THE GARDEN just outside the nursery.

She loved its bright colors – the scarlet of the wrinkled fire coral, the vivid yellow of the cluster anemones, and the clear green of the ruffled sea lettuce on the low dike surrounding the irregular space.

She loved the strange textures and shapes – porous pink tube sponges shaped in tall columns, fans of waving lace coral, pillows of pale vase sponges, and the black spikes of spherical sea urchins.

But most of all she loved the neverending movement of the garden and the sense of freedom it promised. The silver flash of a school of lookdowns turning. The dart of dark triggerfish. The ripple of the sea plants as the pulsing water waved them to and fro.

The murmur of the everflowing tides and the beams of sunlight shining down through the translucent water like columns of glory, the only ceiling the surface of the water far overhead, made her feel like anything could happen. Something spectacular might dive upon her from above. An adventure might hurtle over the dike.

Or – perhaps – *she* might slip over the dike to seek the adventure that failed to come to her.

But on the morning that Nerine was destined to find adventure, she was anything but reveling in the wonder of her favorite place in the sea.

Baby Agnippe had touched the fire coral and was screaming from its sting, her eyes squinched tight with the spiracle openings between them and above her nose gaping, and her mouth open wide, yelling. She was angry more than sad. And furious that everyone was ignoring her.

Eilidh and Tyr – Nerine's older sister and brother, thirteen and twelve years old, respectively – perched on the dike amidst the sea lettuce and argued about who would get to visit the deeps below the reef face.

"I'm the eldest," announced Eilidh self-importantly. "Of course, I'll go first." She tilted her head to look down her nose at Tyr, but her long wavy green-gold hair rather spoiled the effect by drifting across her mouth.

"Hah!" retorted Tyr. "But I'm a boy! Of course, Father will take me first!" His bronze hair was shorter and curlier and stayed out of his face, but he wasn't trying for dignity. His cheeks were flushed enough to look almost pink in the sunbeam crossing his skin.

Who-would-do-what-first was an old argument. Nerine didn't know why it had acquired fresh heat, but she was sick of hearing it.

Xianthe, only two years older than Nerine, was turning backward somersaults right over the wrinkled sheets of fire coral and yelping occasionally when she misjudged and stung her toe or her knee. Since her long hair – longer even than Eilidh's – enveloped her curled up body completely, Nerine didn't see how she could judge anything at all. Apparently it was a challenge.

But Agnippe's screams, the quarreling voices of Eilidh and Tyr, and the excited shrieks of Xianthe utterly squelched any sensation of the adventurous wonder Nerine usually felt outside. This was all so mundane and ordinary.

She pushed off from the patch of sand where she'd been hovering, diving up with her hands overhead, then sweeping her arms down as she undulated her torso and legs. The sea water, warm and fluid, caressed her bare skin as she glided up. She felt it rushing in through the spiracles just to the inside of her brow ridges and above her nose, then along the channels beside her nasal passages and down. Down through her throat, down over the gills beneath her ribs and out, bringing fresh energy to her limbs.

She paused there, overhanging them all, a good twenty feet from the sea floor, but still far below the surface.

Her brother and sisters were just as loud. Noise carried through water too well. But removed from their emotions by even a small distance, she could notice other sounds. The singing of a maid cleaning the nursery chamber. The low vibration of her father conferring with one of his counselors. The soft tink of a craftsman cold-forging a lantern-globe bracket. Even the echo of gentle waves slapping the lagoon face of the reef.

She flexed her operculi – the cartilaginous flaps over her gills – pulling more water in through her spiracles and her nostrils, enjoying its clear warm briny scent and the faintly spicy aroma wafting off one of the plants below.

Her hair drifted above her head, a diffuse cloud of green-gold wavy tresses created by the firm stop to her upward dive. One tendril at the nape of her neck tickled the skin there.

This was her garden, the place were chances beckoned and anything might happen.

Then another irate voice joined the cacophony that she'd just succeeded in ignoring.

"Eilidh! Tyr! You're supposed to be watching your sister. Xianthe, stop that twirling this instant! You nearly kicked little Agnippe!" Nurse bustled out in a plume of bubbles stirred by her movement and caught Agnippe in her arms. Her voice changed to a soothing murmur. "There now, precious. Nurse has you, you'll be just fine, little sweeting."

Eilidh and Tyr stopped arguing, but didn't look particularly abashed. Nurse's scolding was stronger than her displeasure, and each of them had been the recipient of her partial defense as often as they'd borne her reproofs.

Agnippe roared louder, now that she'd secured some sympathy.

It didn't work.

"No, no, you're not hurt, sweeting," averred Nurse matter-of-factly. When Agnippe brandished her slightly pink finger and toe, Nurse scolded her. "Just a bit of a sting. What did you go poking fire coral with? You know better than that."

Agnippe did know better, too. She was the youngest, so they all thought of her as a baby, but she was four.

Nurse started shooing them indoors. "Tyr and Eilidh, you've both got lessons. Xianthe, *stop* that spinning! You've left sand and shell fragments all over your niche, and *you* are going to tidy it up, *not* the maids."

Only when Nurse paused in the nursery doorway – Tyr and Eilidh already inside – and glared at Xianthe once more did she stop somersaulting and come along. Just before Nurse closed the door, she glanced up at Nerine, nodded ambiguously, and went in.

What did that mean?

That Nerine wasn't naughty? That Nerine had finished her chores? That Nerine had the rest of the day to do as she wished?

What did she wish?

～

Nerine looked beyond the garden dike, following the brightly quilted slope down into a shallow vale and up the opposite hill to its crest. What lay over that crest? She'd never been outside the immediate environs of the castle – the gardens, kelp groves, sand courtyards, artisan work yards, and the dolphin summoning post – all located on the lagoon side of the coral reef that was home.

Perhaps . . . perhaps . . . perhaps . . .

Without anything so clear as a decision or a goal, she ghosted through the water above the dike and the vale, swimming in a leisurely way up the slope bounding her horizon. What would she see when she got to the top?

More of the same, as it turned out: an undulating carpet of sponges, soft corals, sea lettuces and sea grapes, and ribband-like greenery in various hues and configurations – stretching away into the blue tint in the distance. A tower of stony coral stood on the farthest ridge. That must be the nearer guardtower her father mentioned at times.

If she swam to it, would she see the farther guardtower? Perhaps she would do just that.

She strengthened the stroke of her arms and quickened the beat of her kick. It was exciting to be moving through unfamiliar waters. The schools of fish were the same, and the creatures of the seafloor were the same, but they formed new combinations against unusual outcroppings of rock.

The water felt cooler and tasted saltier. It lacked the spicy sweetness of the palace garden, with a wilder aroma that hinted of surprises.

She reached the guardtower more quickly than she had expected. She was faster and stronger than when she'd been a baby like Agnippe.

Beyond the tower, the seafloor leveled out and gave way to meadows of sea grasses, strand upon strand of tall, clear green filaments with glimpses of sand between. Two manatees – massive, but placid creatures with wrinkly gray hides – grazed in the meadows.

Nerine swam closer to them, reached out a hand to touch one. Its belly felt silky smooth, but its side was rough. The creature ignored her, and she swam onward.

A ridge of rock, rising from the level meadows, came into view in the distance. The farther guardtower – a natural formation in the rock, rather than a coral growth – perched on one end of the ridge.

Nerine swam over the grasses.

A new sound vibrated in the water, the echo of a rhythmic roar, like an angry sea lion. And the taste and smell changed too, more mineral, less plant-like.

Gliding around the end of the ridge, she saw white sand extending under the waves, with ever varying ripple patterns of light and shadow passing across it. Oh! It was nothing like the densely grown and colorful terrain around the reef.

Nerine dove down to the sand and scooped up double handfuls. She let the grains sift through her hands, forming a glittering fall through the water.

To her right, the seafloor sloped gently downward and away to the deeper blue of the sea on the reef face at home. The deep! If she swam that direction, she could visit the deep even before Tyr and Eilidh!

But the land interested her more. To her left, the sandy floor sloped shallowly up. *That* was where she would go!

As she swam the water grew shallower and shallower. Just an arm-stretch or two above her head was that translucent, but reflective surface that marked where the water gave way to air. One moment it was clear and close. The next it was farther and more blue. Up and down it heaved. In just another stroke of her arm, another beat of her kick, she would be able to push her hand through it! Nurse had always warned her that it was dangerous. But Father said that one day she would pass through that surface and experience the air for herself. Although Mother reminded him – and Nerine – that Nerine's first sojourn out of water would happen only under their aegis and only when she was ready.

But Nerine felt ready now. Excited and thrilled and eager.

Ahead of her the water was a froth of white bubbles and sand.

The next instant she was in it.

The water seized her like a god's hand, tumbling her over and over in a powerful confusion of up and down, flinging her legs around and over her head, twisting her hands behind her.

Her spiracles and nostrils tightened to exclude all the sand mixed with the turbulence.

Her gills ached for water and the air that it carried.

The water tossed her up on a peak of itself and then slammed her down against hard, wet sand. The blow to her ribs knocked the last remnants of water from her gills, and ground sharp shell fragments into her knees and palms. The airborne sunlight – brighter than she had ever seen it – blinded her and she could not breathe.

Black spots gathered in her dazzled vision as she fought to open her closed spiracles, to pump the operculi covering her gills, anything to get air.

A sharp cramping knotted in the base of her throat and, right next to it, a sharper ache of something stretching as it had never stretched before. As it was never meant to be stretched. Ah! Was she dying?

An instant later, she coughed wrackingly, inflating the lungs that had rested quiescently behind her gills for all eight years of her life. Air rushed into them, hot and dry and smelling of strange scents – dusty scents and sweet scents and piercing scents. It was incredible!

One breath.

Another breath.

She had air!

And then another breaker arrived, seizing her and tumbling her, flooding her mouth and nostrils. Her lungs spasmed in an agony of stinging pain, but each cough that expelled the surging water brought another mouthful in.

Ah! Ah! This was the drowning that Nurse talked of.

Nerine was dying.

～

Someone's thin, bony arm locked around her ribs, under her arms, and dragged Nerine up.

"Egó tha sas glitósi!" yelled a boy's voice.

And then she was in the air once more, coughing and coughing as he dragged her through the surf, stumbling when a fresh breaker hit his legs, but pulling her to safety even though his arm was no bigger than hers.

He stopped where a thin skimming of water ran hissing over the sand, surging up with each new wave, flowing away after.

He crouched down before her, his black eyes bright with excitement, his mouth smiling wide in a grin. "I kimatomorphés ínai megáli! I palírria ínai pou érkhetai." His face was tan and framed by black curling hair.

Nerine stared at him panting.

The sun hurt her eyes. The sand felt strange under her too-heavy limbs. Everything felt wrong except his face. His face was a beacon of friendliness and happiness.

But she couldn't understand a word he said.

Another wave fizzed across the sand.

The warmth of it around her tucked legs and over her hands, where she supported herself, comforted her. The air felt cool on her skin. She had coughed the last of the water out of her lungs, and all the intriguing aromas of land came in with each unfamiliar breath.

She gazed into the boy's delighted, crinkling eyes.

"This is – this is wonderful!" And it was, now that she wasn't drowning.

A faint line in the tan skin just over the boy's snub nose and between his eyes appeared.

So he didn't understand her any better than she understood him.

Still grinning, he stood up, gesturing her to follow him.

Eager, she pushed with her hands, gathered her legs under her. And pitched face first into the wet sand.

She heard the boy laughing. Not meanly, the way Tyr would have, but joyfully, as though even falling were fun.

Then he was helping her, his hands under her armpits tugging her upward.

But it didn't work.

He wasn't strong enough to lift her, and they both pitched forward under her weight.

He laughed again. But he seemed to grasp the problem, because he pushed himself up onto his hands and knees, all the while looking hopefully at Nerine.

She tried to copy him, getting her knees, not her feet, under her and then pushing with her hands.

It felt very, very odd. So utterly different from the feel of water buoying her body. But she could do it!

She balanced there on hands and knees, swaying, and laughed.

He moved one of his arms forward, placing his palm a little ahead of him and transferring his weight to it.

He waggled his head at her and widened his eyes.

She grinned at him and moved her hand. Yes, she could do this, too. It was unfamiliar – nothing like swimming – but she could do it.

He moved his knee on the opposite side.

She moved hers.

His already bright eyes, brightened still more.

Then they were crawling up the beach together, laughing wildly.

She fell when they hit the soft sand. It was hot, blazingly hot. She yelped.

The boy patted her shoulder, gestured with his hand, and then raced off at speed across the hot, yielding beach.

She gasped, and set off after him. Hand, knee, hand, knee.

It was harder, keeping her balance over the uneven, shifting surface. And speed was essential, because of the heat it held. But it was fun, too. Almost like racing Tyr and Eilidh and Xianthe under the waves. She was racing this boy across the sand.

The slope of the beach leveled out, the sand grew even softer, but cooler, and clumps of short shore grasses appeared. Nerine and the boy passed a small log of gray driftwood and then fetched up at a larger one, its middle section curving up off the sand, and a dense thicket of grasses behind it, waving gently in the moving air.

The boy helped Nerine to sit on that arching middle section. The sand immediately below it, in shadow, was much cooler, even pleasant.

"Periménete edó," the boy told her. Then he made gestures here and gestures there, smiling, but a question in his eyes.

Nerine nodded, because he seemed to want her to.

He scampered off, on his feet this time, clearly comfortable with this mode of moving.

Following him with her eyes, she wondered if she would ever be able to run like that.

He jogged along the shore, the white line of the surf and the blue, blue sea – stretching far out to the blue, blue sky – on one side of him. Low dunes and shore grasses backed by a craggy cliff on the other side.

He reached a square patch of gleaming yellow with a squodgy brown sack and a round container woven of reeds resting on the yellow.

He bundled the yellow square up into a wad in his arms – along with the sack and the reed container – then turned around, and jogged back to her.

He set the yellow bundle and the reed container on the sand at the far end of the log, and pulled a stopper out of the narrow neck of the brown sack. He tipped his face up to the sky and tilted the sack toward him. A clear, clear arch of water streamed into his mouth. He gulped it down and lowered the sack. Then he moved it toward her, his eyebrows lifted.

She nodded, tipped her head back, and opened her lips. That clear, clear water arched into her mouth, cool and sweet – *ah!* all the way down her throat. She could feel it cold and heavy in her stomach.

The boy straightened the sack and pointed to her knees and hands. They were covered in small cuts from when the wave had slammed her into the land, and they were very sandy.

Shyly, Nerine held out her hands, while the boy rinsed them. Ah! It stung a bit, but it felt good, too.

He rinsed her knees, stoppered the bag and slung it over his shoulder by a strap, and then gestured her to scoot along the log.

She wasn't sure she could. It felt very precarious, up away from the sand, with only air around her torso. The air was so thin. It felt like nothing at all, even while it tickled her bare skin and flowed rhythmically in and out of her lungs. The air didn't hold her the way water did. She was balancing all by herself, with no watery support.

The boy stepped closer and slid his hands under her armpits again, urging her.

Very well, she would try.

She pushed against the smooth driftwood with her palms while he lifted up and over. She moved only a handspan, but she was moving. Again she pushed, and he lifted. And again. The fourth or fifth time, she realized she could push with her feet as well, and then she moved much farther.

When she reached the end of the log, the boy spread the yellow wad into a square again right below her feet. He helped her lower herself to sit on it. It felt smooth and silky and warm. Almost like water, but firm, because of the sand under it.

The boy sat beside her, and they looked at one another.

His tan face and neck and arms and legs were so different from her paleness. And unlike her, he was not bare. A somewhat rumpled, matte blue covering hid his upper arms, his shoulders, chest, hips and upper thighs.

He smiled at her and touched his hand to his covered chest. "Al-tai-ros," he said. He sounded a lot like Tyr, but with a crispness to his syllables, instead of the melodic flow of words that she heard from her family and all their people in the reef.

She touched her collar bone with her hand and smiled back at him. "Ne-rine," she told him.

"Nuh reen," he repeated.

"Al tye ros," she said.

He grinned and reached for the reed container, lifting a lid from it. Small bundles wrapped in cream coverings – similar to the blue covering he wore – reposed within. He set them out on the yellow square, and then pulled out a small bronze cup that he filled with water from the leather sack.

He unwrapped one of the bundles, revealing three withered lumps of purply brown. He bit into one and chewed, exuberance lighting his eyes. He offered one of the unbitten lumps to her.

She accepted it, turning it over in her fingers. It's skin felt velvety, but also sticky. It was soft, but not soft like the fringes of seaweed. Soft like a clam, with resilience.

She put the morsel up to her nose and sniffed. Ah! Sweet, slightly musky, slightly floral.

She bit into it, and flavorful sweetness filled her mouth. It was delicious.

"Fig," said Altairos.

"Thank you!" said Nerine, when she'd chewed the sticky mouthful and swallowed.

He offered her the remaining fruit.

She bit her lip. Then her smile flashed out, and she used her fingers to pry the fruit apart into two halves, one for him and one for her.

His contagious grin – his eyes crinkling the way they did – matched her smile as he accepted his half.

Her fingers were sticky, really sticky. But she licked them clean.

There were other strange and delectable foods in the other bundles. A salty, white curdlike substance with a strong, strong taste she couldn't place. "Cheese," said Altairos. Small purple globes with thin skins that burst on juicy sweetness. "Grapes." Dry, chewy brown stuff with a strong peppery overtone to its savoriness. "Sun-dried beef." And tiny yellow spheres in a yellow sauce flecked with red that burned her mouth with its spice and yet still tasted good.

She had to swallow many gulps of water from the cup they shared, and even that didn't soothe her tongue until Altairos offered her more of the cheese.

"Chana massala – chickpeas," he explained.

When they'd eaten their fill, Altairos repacked the basket, neatly rewrapping the leftover food, and folding the empty cloths. Nerine's stomach felt full and comfortable. The moving air felt good against her bare skin. And she was getting used to holding her torso erect without support.

She looked around them, taking in the low dunes and the shore grass, the rocky bluff some distance away, towering up to the blue, blue sky. The land was beautiful, more beautiful than she'd ever guessed.

∼

The roar and crash of the waves on the beach sounded rhythmically, just like the breath in her lungs. And the water was bluer than she'd ever seen when she was under it. It went on and on forever. How far away was that thin line where water met sky?

This was wonderful! More wonderful than she'd ever dreamed it could be, all those times she wished she could visit the land.

Altairos touched her shoulder.

She turned her gaze to him – all sun-browned and rosy, with his shining black eyes and his wild, curly black hair. He was wonderful, too!

He stood up, then sank back down to his haunches, gestured at her, and stood again.

Did she want to stand?

Ah, yes! She wanted to stand just like that: balanced and steady on her feet the way he was.

He crouched again, very close to her, and put his hands under her armpits.

She got her feet under her and watched his legs. When his calf muscles flexed, she pushed with her legs, and they rose together, Altairos keeping her balanced.

It wasn't that she was weak. She was strong. And it wasn't that she was uncoordinated – like a baby flailing before it could swim. She was graceful. But she'd never had to balance her body with each portion aligned above the other, and all her muscles keeping that alignment. She just didn't know how to manage it. Even with Altairos helping her, she swayed, and then toppled, thumping down on the blanket.

Altairos sank beside her, controlled in his descent, his face anxious.

She couldn't help laughing.

"I'm not hurt," she told him.

He grinned. That bright, happy grin with the crinkling eyes. He might not understand her words, but he did understand.

"I want to try again," she said, getting herself into position for that push to her feet.

Altairos nodded and got himself ready to help her.

Up they rose. The flex in her legs felt so different from the kick of swimming, and the weight of her body, pressing down through neck and waist and knees and ankles felt utterly different too.

For an instant, she balanced. Just an instant. And then she tumbled down once more.

"Again!" she insisted.

They did do it again. And again and again and again.

The very last time, she stood for long enough to count to thirty. She knew, because after she'd balanced for a few moments without toppling, she started counting. "One, two, three . . ."

Altairos must have realized what she was saying, because he joined her chant: ". . . téssera, pénte, éxi . . ."

When she reached "twenty, twenty-one, twenty-two," he slowly loosened his hold on her.

". . . íkosi pénte, íkosi éxi, íkosi eptá . . ."

". . . twenty-eight, twenty-nine . . ." She was standing unsupported!

". . . triánta!"

She gave a little skip in her excitement. And toppled right over.

They both dissolved into giggles.

Altairos scrubbed his brow with his hand. "Prépi na páo tóra."

What?

He pointed at the cliff. The shadow had crept out from its base, nearly to the edge of their very crumpled blanket. He tapped his chest and gestured at the top of the cliff. "Aftí ínai i dikí mou patrída."

Nerine could just make out the sharp white corner of a tower, there at the clifftop, partially obscured because it stood back from the edge. Was it a guardtower to *his* father's castle? Had he run past it, just as she'd swum past *her* father's guardtowers?

"You must go home?" Nerine guessed, touching his chest and waving at the strangely regular tower on the cliff.

Altairos nodded. "Ikía."

Nerine bit her lip and turned her head to observe the sea. The water was closer to them than it had been, but the waves looked and sounded gentler. Could she get into the sea more easily than she'd gotten out of it?

"Tha sas vithísoume?" Altairos tapped his chest, tapped her collar bone, and gestured at the sea.

Oh, yes! He would help her. Just as he'd helped her to stand. Just as he'd helped her when she was drowning.

She shivered. Would she drown when she went back? How was that possible? She'd always lived under the sea. She *belonged* there. And Mother and Father had planned to do this visit to the air with her. And back again to the sea. Of course she wouldn't drown. But she felt nervous.

Altairos got up and started tugging on the blanket. She shifted, so that he could pull it out from under her, fold it, and lay it atop the leather water sack and the basket of food.

When he knelt down to his hands and knees, she got onto hers, and they raced toward the water, laughing. It felt cool, compared to the warm air, and so very wet, so very *right*. Altairos stopped her in the shallows, before they reached the line where the waves broke. With his hands, he made a wave flowing toward shore and then breaking. He did it twice more.

She nodded.

Next he showed her the hand wave moving toward shore with a finger standing there – Altairos himself – waiting for it.

She nodded again.

Next came the hand wave moving toward the waiting finger Altairos, and just before the wave broke, finger Altairos dove through it. Could she do that?

Could she? She'd managed to stand on the yellow square, where no water pushed or pulled her. But she wasn't good at it. Could she stand here? What if she fell?

Well, then she'd fall. And maybe be tumbled. Which was awful. But Altairos was here. He'd help her.

"I'll try," she decided, nodding.

Altairos grinned – she loved his grin – and crouched.

With his hands under her armpits, they rose. He moved closer to her and slipped one arm around her back, steadying her that way. She focused very hard on balancing. The push of the water surging up from the breaking waves wasn't so bad. But the drag of it ebbing back into the sea was strong. Without Altairos' arm, she would have fallen instantly.

Altairos gestured his free hand, making the wave: coming in, coming in, coming in.

"Éna." He made the wave.

"Dío." He made the wave.

"Tría." He made the wave, but he also made the finger Altairos diving.

"Yes!" She nodded.

He gestured out to sea, to a wave rippling shoreward, and followed it in with his hand. It broke just before them. " Éna!"

That was the first one.

"Dío!"

That was the second one.

Nerine staggered in the undertow, sand and broken shell fragments scraping her ankles and calves as the water hurried. Somehow, Altairos kept her on her feet.

"Ekí! Ekí!" That was the third one coming.

"Tría!" Altairos' arm urged her forward, and she dove with him.

Her arms lengthened over her head, her body tilted forward, and her legs bent and sprang. She cleaved through the back of the wave cleanly, just as though she'd dived up from the sea bottom at home, all fluid grace and ease.

～

6 ~ Home Consequences

THE WATER ENFOLDING HER felt good, good, good. This was where she belonged. This was her home. She relaxed into it, taking a stroke with her arms, giving a kick with her legs and body almost without realizing it.

Her spiracles opened, and a sharp cramping knotted in the base of her throat along with that impossible opening that she felt when she left the sea the first time. This time, it didn't hurt as much.

And then water was flowing over her gills, while her lungs expelled their last air and compressed to await her next visit to the land. Ah!

She glanced to the side. For a moment longer, Altairos swam by her, his cheeks puffed out to hold air in his lungs, but that wide grin on his lips nonetheless.

Nerine smiled, touched her collar bone and gestured back toward shore. She would come again.

Altairos nodded, and then turned away and up.

She paused to watch him. What a splashing he made, there atop the water, his arms and legs churning. But he was fast. As he approached the white foam of the surf, his legs came down and he ran. Ah! So that was how to go ashore. She would remember.

As she followed the sea floor down, the clear transparency of the water changed to the bluer translucence of early evening, with the closing down of the visual distance that came when the sunlight slanted at an ever greater angle.

The farther guardtower on its rocky ridge was a blurred deeper blueness within the blueness of the sea. The nearer guardtower, with its more irregular outline, was nearly indistinguishable. And then the glow of home shone out, softly golden light winking from the many latticed window openings in the castle reef.

Nurse had closed the nursery door – a screen of woven chitin – but not locked it. Nerine slipped through it, a slight chill abruptly present in her stomach. She was very late in returning. Later than she'd ever been. Would Nurse scold? She was used to that. Scolding and loving were almost one and the same with Nurse. But what if Nurse had told Mother? Even worse, what if Mother had told Father? Not that Father's reprimands were too bad. He always seemed to have a laugh behind his eyes, even when correcting his children. But Mother's rebukes were much worse once Father got involved. She seemed to feel she must be more severe to make up for his mildness.

The nursery was empty, except for all the usual nets full of toys, the scattered sponge cushions, Eilidh's shell collection, and Tyr's rock collection. Round openings at different heights on the curving walls gave access to the private niches where each child slept. No one occupied the niches either. Too early for that.

Nerine wasn't sure whether she should feel relieved – no one to see just how late she was – or more nervous – was Nurse already on her way to alert Mother and Father?

She glided into the hallway beyond the nursery, a generous passage through the center of the reef. Its smooth white walls – clouded with the rippling and bubbled pattern of fossilized coral – stretched high overhead, slanting inward near the top to meet in an arched point. It was so strange that the same distance up always seemed more moderate outside, and so much farther inside.

A faint murmur of conversation traveled through the water from the right. She swam along the hallway, ignoring all the doorways that opened at different heights, giving access to the highest chambers in the reef as well as the lowest.

She moved past the bedchambers and informal withdrawing rooms, then the private dining rooms and their service pantries, and then the formal salons and reception rooms. The voices were growing louder. The feasting hall and the ballroom fell behind her. Father's voice boomed in a tone Nerine had never heard before – truly angry. Then Mother, sharp and insistent. And then Tyr, defensive and speaking fast.

What in the sea could they be arguing about?

Nerine quickened her pace, streaking past the state reception rooms and the throne room to emerge in the front hall, a vast white space ringed by knobbly columns and featuring two great portals onto the deepening blue of the evening sea; one on the lagoon side, the other onto the deeps.

Nerine braked abruptly.

～

Her family floated just above the smooth white floor near its center. Father wore his bronze pectoral with its breastplate and his bronze belt and loin piece. He always looked more formidable in his war gear than he did in the jewel-laden things he donned for the throne room or the council chamber. Shaking his spear, as he was now . . . Nerine shrank back into the arch of the hall. Was Father really threatening Tyr?

No, maybe not.

"Did you take a spear? A gladius? A trident? Do you even know how to use them, should the kraken rise for you?" Father roared, his thick curls – bronze like his armor – whipping through the water like squid tentacles.

Tyr hunched, shame-faced.

Mother entered the fray. Her golden-green hair couldn't lash like father's. The long wavy locks were gathered atop her head in her favorite platinum and diamond net that matched her platinum and diamond pectoral and belt. But she was just as angry. Her finely carved nostrils pinched in to whiteness, and her gray eyes were cold.

"The kraken?" she cried, her voice as cold as her eyes. "It rises when provoked, which isn't often. But the tide flows every day! They could be far into the Ionian Sea by now, if you hadn't found them first!"

"I'm a stronger swimmer than that!" protested Eilidh. "I could rescue Tyr and still beat the tide!" Eilidh had clasped her hair – greeny-gold and wavy like Mother's – in a gold mesh band at the back of her head. It flowed out like shrimp antennae behind her.

Nerine was beginning to understand what must have happened. She wasn't the only child to sneak out. But where had Tyr and Eilidh gone?

"Only a fool believes herself stronger than the sea," Mother declared.

Father was nodding. "True, Ionia, true." – Ionia was Mother's name; Father was Meren – "We of the watery realm feel its might in our hearts, and we know." His gaze sharpened as he gazed at his eldest daughter and his only son. "Or . . . we should know. You, apparently, did not!"

Tyr's head came up. "But I wanted to see the deeps, and you were going to make me wait until I was fourteen!"

Oh, wrong thing to say. Even Nerine – young as she was – knew that.

Mother drew herself very tall in the water, looking down her aristocratic nose.

"You are a child and our son. That alone should command your obedience. Furthermore, you are subject and vassal to the sovereign of the Middle Sea – your father. How dare you contravene his will?"

Nerine scooted a little farther back into the hallway. She was scared when Mother got like this.

But apparently Tyr was not. Bunching up his face in rage, he flung back: "A king serves his people, not the other way round. Or, he *should*!"

Mother seemed to grow even taller. "Your father and *king* is the wisest being I know. You are privileged to live under his governance and should be proud to obey his decrees."

"Yeah! Well I'm not you!" spat Tyr.

Nerine bit her lip. Oh, this wasn't going well. She wondered if she should swim back to the nursery and pretend to have been there all along. Except . . . Tyr would be unbearable if this ended the way it looked to. She wanted to know whether she should avoid him for the next few days. Or whether it would be safe to tease him for treats as usual.

Father touched Mother's wrist, and she merely gave Tyr a withering look, instead of blistering him with stronger reproofs.

"Tyr," began Father. Then he looked at his own hand, noticed he still held his spear, and pinched the clicker shell on his belt. *Click!* A guard emerged from the vestibule adjacent to the portal onto the deeps, swam across the vast front hall, and accepted the spear. "Thank you, Corydon," said Father.

Corydon bent to indicate his respect and carried the spear back to the guard chamber.

Tyr started to renew his tirade. "You're unrea –"

Father interrupted him. "Tyr."

Eilidh butted into the momentary lull. "I'm nearly fourteen, but all you say is to wait. Tyr's right. You are unrea –"

Father just looked this time, but it was enough to silence Eilidh.

"Tyr is right that the best of rulers serve their subjects. But, Tyr." Father's eyes conveyed that calm, warm strength that seemed unique to him. Weighty, but accepting. Nerine loved that look, but her brother squirmed under it. Father kept looking until Tyr stopped squirming. Then he turned to Eilidh.

"Eilidh." He gave that same weighty cadence to her name. Eilidh raised her chin, but said nothing.

Mother had relaxed, a small smile on her lips. Father smiled back at her. Then he continued. "A king serves his subject's true interests, not their whim or their caprice. Can you tell me truly that in visiting the deeps with your sister, and no one else, you have acted responsibly?"

It was amazing how fast Tyr could shrivel, when someone said the exact right thing to him. He bent his head and muttered, "No, Father."

Father reached out, lifted Tyr's chin, and smiled. "Tell me again." His voice was kind. Tyr brightened and unhunched to meet Father's eyes straightly.

"No, Father, I was not wise."

"Good lad." He flicked Tyr's cheek. "What should your consequence be?"

"I'm confined to the castle for a *déka*-day, and then I must tell Nurse before I go anywhere." Tyr winced at his own words, but he was trying to be brave and fair.

This was the Tyr that Nerine loved and often begged for treats. Like towing her – with her hands on his shoulders – when he dived into the swift current that raced through the crack in the giant's boulder in the lagoon. The speed of their passage made her giddy with delight. Maybe she would ask him tomorrow.

A movement at the edge of Nerine's vision caught her attention. Oh! Nurse had been floating beside a column all this time – the white of her *nålbindning* knitted hose and bodice blending with the white of the coral reef. She was nodding now, a genial expression on her face. Nurse liked how Father disciplined his children. She never had enough good things to say about him.

Father laughed. "I have a better idea."

The beginnings of a smile were turning Tyr's lips.

"You'll have your mornings free. For lessons, as well as play," he added as Tyr grinned. "But your afternoons shall be spent with me, watching how I rule my subjects. And teaching you how I touch the *numina* of the tides, the waves, and the currents of the sea. Hey?"

"Oh, yes! Thank you, Father!" Tyr was bobbing with excitement.

"And the day following the morrow, you shall see the deeps in company with me and my warriors."

Tyr's eyes were shining, but Eilidh's were not.

"Oh!" she burst out. "So Tyr gets rewarded, because he's a boy. But I do not, because I'm a girl! Even though I'm the eldest!"

Mother, composed and listening, stiffened at this. But Father chuckled. "I have not pronounced your sanction, my daughter."

"No, but Tyr gets a reward, and I get a sanction! How is that fair?"

"Listen first, Eilidh, and then you shall tell me." He looked aside at Mother, tilting his head. She nodded, and he turned back to Eilidh. "While your brother is following in my wake all the afternoon, you shall be following your mother."

Eilidh started to protest, and then looked thoughtful.

"You have a place as handmaiden to Hera herself awaiting you, you know."

Eilidh nodded.

"It will be well for you to be preparing for that exalted station."

"Yes, I know, and I like that very well, Father, but –"

Father held up his hand. "And on the morrow, *you* will go with me to the deeps."

Eilidh's cheeks flushed. "Really? Really, truly? Oh! Thank you, Father!"

Nerine edged over to Nurse. Seeing Eilidh grateful and overflowing with it was decidedly odd. She was usually on her dignity, and never gushed. *Huh.* She must not have believed Father ever meant to let her visit the deeps. Which was silly. Eilidh constantly said Tyr got more privileges and more leeway because he was a boy. But Nerine hadn't seen it. Now if she'd said *Agnippe* got more attention and spoiling . . . well, Nerine could agree with that, but Eilidh hadn't.

Nurse looked down and stroked Nerine's hair back from her face.

Mother was saying, "Really, Meren, you spoil them," but her body was relaxed, and she still smiled.

"But you agree with me on this," Father answered, sliding an arm around her waist.

Mother grimaced. "Indeed. It was too serious for mere punishment and correction."

They drifted toward Nerine and Nurse, Tyr and Eilidh giggling and murmuring before them.

"Hey, and here's my good little girl," boomed Father in his normal merry tone. He scooped Nerine into a big kraken-hug.

The platelets of his pectoral pressed uncomfortably against her cheek, but his chest felt warm and solid and comforting, his arms, powerful and safe. Nerine nestled against him. Often the clasp of the sea around her felt like Father's embrace, but today it had not. She needed this.

Father was talking with Nurse and Mother while he cradled Nerine – arranging schedules for tomorrow, who would be where and doing what.

Nerine listened to the rumble of his voice not bothering to comprehend the words. Her eyelids started to droop. She was drowsy, really drowsy.

Father transferred her to Nurse, and then Nurse was swimming with her along the hallway to the nursery. She could feel the beat of Nurse's kick, even while Nurse's arms held her secure. And then Nurse was laying her down on the cushion of sponges in her niche, clipping the mesh covering over her, and setting the laval brazier nearby. As heat from the brazier rolled over her, Nerine's eyes slipped shut.

"Sleep sound, my sweet," whispered Nurse.

"Mmm," murmured Nerine. And then sleep swept around her, warm and welcome as a lazy current bearing gifts from the shore, its flow singing of delight and celebration.

⁓

When she awoke, the sunlight brightening the waters of the nursery flooded into her niche, warming her to her bones, but with a more buoyant character than the heavy heat of the laval brazier, which had burnt out in the night.

She nuzzled the sponge under her cheek, luxuriating in its fuzzy softness and enjoying its pale green hue. Her gaze drifted over the creamy strands of the silken mesh covering her, to the small apron of white floor between her sleeping circle and the round opening onto the nursery, and then to the pale amber corrugations of the bubble that was her niche.

Mother said the inside of coral was always white. It was only the surface, harboring different algae, that took on color. The floor of Nerine's niche – and, indeed, of all the floors in the castle – were white because they'd been rubbed flat and smooth. Some of the walls, like the central hallway, were white because they'd been carved from the inmost core of the reef. Only the natural pockets, which retained their rough original surface, were amber or rose or lilac.

Nerine loved her niche and its cheerful color.

She started unhooking the mesh that held her within her sleeping circle.

The shadow of Nurse's profile eclipsed Nerine's hands.

"Did you have your sleep out, sweeting?"

Nerine smiled and stretched her arms over her head, shrugging her shoulders. She felt fine.

Nurse set a covered tray within a small hutch on the floor and carried on with the mesh hooks where Nerine had left off. "I've brought you conch, *thali*, and lettuce to break your fast. Your brother and sisters have already started their lessons."

Nerine must have slept very late. Her stomach gurgled, and she was abruptly hungry. The mild sweetness of conch flesh was the best flavor in the world to wake up to, but she only liked the crunchy, peppery pods of *thali* sometimes. Nurse insisted they were nutritious, so Nerine had to eat them more often than she wanted. But the fresh taste of the sea lettuce would help her choke down the *thali*. And Nurse wouldn't have served more than three of the pods.

As Nerine floated up from her sleeping circle, Nurse hooked its mesh back in place.

"Need the surging closet?" she asked.

"Not yet. I'm hungry!"

Nurse chuckled. "Well then." She took the covered tray back out of the hutch and removed its domed lid. There was the white flesh of the conch, the blue pods of *thali*, and the green sheaves of lettuce, each in its own glass globe complete with spout.

Nerine anchored her toes in the edge of her sleep mesh and lifted the globe with the conch, removing the plug just before she placed the spout between her lips. She sucked, forcing sea water out of her mouth and down toward her gills, then taking a bite of the conch protruding from the spout. *Mmm*. It was delicious. This was one of the times when she was glad her father and mother were king and queen of the Middle Sea. She knew that poor folk ate their food right out of the water. Only royalty and nobility served their dishes in proper eating globes. Nerine didn't care about the properness – in spite of Nurse's lectures on good manners – but she thought the tastes were clearer when they weren't drowned in the sea.

"Nurse?"

"What is it, sweeting?"

"Father is a good father, isn't he?"

"Indeed, yes. The best I've ever seen."

Nurse's answer was exactly what Nerine expected, but that wasn't what she really wanted to know.

"Is he a good chooser, too?"

"Good at choosing what, sweeting?"

Nerine wished she could say what she was thinking as easily as she could think it. "Tyr's going to rule the Tyrrhenian Sea when he's big. Under Father. Like Mother rules the Ionian Sea."

"Are you worried about that, love?" *Nurse* looked worried.

Nerine shook her head. "I think Tyr will *love* it."

Nurse's face lightened. "Exactly so. Your father *is* good at choosing."

"And Eilidh is going to Queen Hera," continued Nerine. "Mother says she is very proud."

"And so is your sister proud, sweeting."

Nerine's next words came slower. "Mother is cousin to Queen Hera."

"Which is why your sister is offered this honor."

"But Father chose it?"

Nerine took her first bite of *thali* pod. Its peppery flavor filled her mouth, pleasing after the sweet mildness of the conch. This was going to be one of those times she liked *thali*. Good.

"You know your mother and father work together in your rearing,"

Yes, Nerine knew that. But she trusted Father more. A lot more.

"Is Mother good at choosing things?"

Nurse paused a moment, and Nerine crunched on the next *thali* pod. It didn't taste as good as the first one had. Stronger peppery flavor, and also bitter. Maybe she did like *thali*, but she liked it exactly perfect. Too strong, a little bitter, or tough: *ick*. Delicately crisp, mildly peppery, and fresh: *mmm*.

"Your mother is *very* good at deciding and choosing, but she's not as –" Nurse hesitated "– she's not as friendly when she *explains* her choices."

Nerine felt relief sliding through her. It was as nice as the water sliding over her gills. She'd felt what Nurse said, but she'd not been able to even think clearly about it, let alone find words for it.

"Where will they choose for Xianthe?" Now Nerine was getting closer to the heart of the matter.

"That's not decided yet. Your sister likes salt water, but she's . . . turbulent, and not steady. She wouldn't be happy ruling a domain. But there's time yet."

"You mean she wouldn't be good at it."

Nurse smiled. "Probably not. But the right opportunity will turn up," she added comfortably. "The sea's a big place, and Xianthe's full young."

"Am I full young?"

"To be sure, sweeting. You're naught but a fingerling yet." Nurse's gaze sharpened. "Were you worried about this? What your father and mother would choose for you? Whether they would choose well?"

Nerine choked down the last *thali* pod. It was even more bitter than the second one. Oh! she hated *thali*. Yes, she did. Why had she thought she might like it? The good ones came once in a dozen bad ones!

Nurse continued her reassurances. "Your mother and father will talk with you as you grow older. And they'll notice what you like and what you don't. They won't just decide one evening and then tell you in the morning."

More relief slid through Nerine, loosening the tightness she'd felt in her chest. She trusted Father. She trusted him all the way down to the bottom of the sea. But Mother . . . well, Nurse thought she could trust Mother, too. And Nurse was probably right. She was right about most things. Except . . . what Nerine liked most was seeing new things. Like yesterday, when she'd visited land for the first time ever. Was there a post for her where she could go new places always, seeing more and more strange things?

Nerine took a bite of sea lettuce. *Mmm.* Compared to the *thali*, it tasted almost sweet, its clean clearness washing away the bitterness on her tongue.

She wriggled her toes free of her sleeping mesh and flicked a foot to push her toward Nurse, leaning her head into Nurse's shoulder.

Nurse stroked her hair. "You were worried about it, weren't you, sweeting?" She pressed a kiss on Nerine's brow, just above her spiracles. "Do you feel better now?"

Nerine nodded. She did feel better. A lot better. But what would Father and Mother find for her? Now she was curious. Would she journey from shore to shore in a chariot drawn by dolphins? How did the land people travel?

"Nerine?" Nurse stopped stroking Nerine's hair to put a gentle hand under her chin, turning Nerine's face up. "Your father knows you're a good child. Not willful like Eilidh. Not wild like Xianthe." Nurse patted Nerine's cheek. "Not in a rush like your brother. Nor fussy like little Agnippe."

Nerine felt her face heating. It was lovely to have Nurse praising her, but embarrassing to listen to her strictures on all Nerine's siblings.

"Your father knows it. Your mother takes it for granted, but she knows it. And I know it, sweeting."

Where was Nurse going with this? She was usually preoccupied with all the little things that needed doing. Pulling shells out of Agnippe's hair. Making sure the nursery meal didn't have urchin roe in it, because Eilidh was allergic to it. Making Xianthe do her lessons. Making Tyr sit still long enough to actually eat something.

Why was Nurse indulging Nerine with this long conversation, instead of hurrying her onward from breakfast?

"You wondered yesterday why I made you free of the afternoon, didn't you?"

Nerine nodded. She had wondered. Usually Nurse had notions about what she and her siblings should be doing at every moment of the day. Even if her notion was just that they should play in the garden.

"I trust you, sweeting. You're a sensible little fishie, not likely to do rash things."

Nurse nodded decisively, but Nerine felt terrible. Nurse had *trusted* her yesterday, and Nerine had let her down. Nurse would never have agreed that visiting the land alone and unsupervised was anything but rash. Oh, no!

"Indeedy, I think you need a spell of freedom! A chance to explore what you like best. How else can your Mother and Father know what to seek for you?"

Nerine wasn't listening anymore. Instead she wrestled with her conscience. Should she confess to Nurse what she'd done? But if she did . . . oh, blessings! What would Nurse do then? Stop her from going. And Nerine knew, even amidst her guilt, that she would visit the land again. Today, if she could, if Nurse gave her the freedom to go. No, Nerine wasn't telling. But she felt bad.

Here was Nurse saying she was good, when in fact Nerine was not good at all. Not the way Nurse imagined she was.

"Go on with you, now," Nurse was returning to her normal bustle. "You're late to lessons, but I told your tutor that I wanted you to have your sleep out. No harm done. But time's awasting!"

In the schoolroom, Xianthe was struggling with tides and how the configuration of the seabed affected them, while Tyr studied the biomes of the Erythraean Sea. Why did he need to know that? The Erythraean Sea was a long way from the Tyrrhenian. Eilidh was practicing oratory, which seemed to suit her. And little Agnippe was learning her letters, pressing her stylus against a sheet of copper foil with her chubby fingers.

Nerine bent her concentration to her own work, arithmetic, which she found dull. It was hard to focus on memorizing how many units made four groups of eight, and how many made five groups of eight. She kept seeing the surf on the edge between sea and land, and Altairos' crinkling eyes, instead of the columns of numbers on her own sheet of copper.

After lessons were done and luncheon eaten, Nerine almost forgot to breathe – not that drawing water in through her spiracles was anything she needed to think about. Would Nurse ask her to amuse Agnippe in the afternoon? Or say she needed to help Xianthe tidy her sleeping niche?

⁓

7 ~ Ashore in the Sun

Tyr and Eilidh were already swimming off to their respective appointments with Father and Mother. Xianthe was exhorting Nurse to come outside and throw the diving hoops so that Xianthe could race through them as they soared through the water. And Agnippe was begging for an excursion to the Sedes Fountain, a spot in the lagoon where fresh, unsalted water bubbled up through a crack in the sea floor.

Nurse nodded smilingly at Nerine. "Whatever you please, sweeting. This afternoon and every afternoon."

Oh! She *could* visit the land again. And maybe this time she'd learn to balance while upright there and move at the same time!

She gave Nurse an impulsive hug and darted for the nursery door, never noticing Nurse's look of surprise. Or the outcry of protest from her sisters.

She dove out into the garden and across its dike, then over the quilted brightness of the reef. There was the nearer guardtower. She swam around it and across the meadow of sea grasses where the manatees grazed. There was the farther guardtower. Beyond it, she reached the expansive sands beneath the waves rolling shoreward.

She could see the frothy water where the breakers slammed the land. Would they knock her down this time? Tumble her?

Perhaps if she swam very fast, she could get ashore just the way Altairos did.

She quickened the stroke of her arms and the beat of her kick. Faster. Faster. And now! The turbulent water dragged at her arms.

She slammed her feet downward and felt the shock of the land travel up through her legs.

Her head and shoulders burst from the surface.

She surged forward, running, coughing fluid out of her lungs and feeling that strange cramping and stretching sensation deep in her throat. The water billowed around her hips. A wave broke just ahead of her and she leapt over it splashing into shallow white foam. She fell to her hands and knees, gulping air into her newly re-opened lungs as her gills settled to quiescence.

She'd done it! Made it to land by herself! Her success felt sweet.

She raised her head to look around her.

The sky was that same deep, hard blue it had been before. There were the cliffs beyond the sands, rising in rough crags with the smidgeon of a tower visible at the top.

The long stretch of beach to her left was bounded by those same cliffs. To her right, the shore went on and on in a gentle curve that disappeared in the distance. Behind her, the choppy sea reached all the way to the far horizon. It was windier today, and whitecaps dotted its surface.

Yet where was Altairos? Nerine had been so sure he would be there, but she didn't see him anywhere. Not running on the beach, not swimming along the surface of the sea the way he did, not sitting on a square of yellow and eating strange foodstuffs.

She gathered her feet under her and pushed upward, stood balanced for an instant, wobbled, and then lurched forward, catching her fall with a step and then another. On the third, she stumbled and went down, just at the edge of the wet sand. But she'd done it! She'd moved on land the way Altairos did.

What if she surprised him? Met him on her feet when he arrived? She still felt sure he *would* arrive. She'd just gotten here first, was all. And the idea of surprising him appealed to her.

She shoved to her feet again, moving quickly, powering forward with the muscles in her thighs.

One, two, three, four, five, six steps – the loose sands hot under her soles – and then she tripped on an exceptionally uneven bit and slammed to her hands and knees. Ouch! The sand burned too much to stay still. She set off – hand, knee, hand, knee – aiming for the cooler slope where the dune grasses grew. The sand felt almost silky there, finely sifting beneath her palms.

She practiced standing and stepping.

It was harder on the slope. She thought about going back to the wet sand, but that meant crossing the hot dry sand again. What if she slowed down, pretended she was doing an undersea dive in reverse, but in slow motion?

She tried it, and it answered very well.

Diving cleanly and swiftly required the most precise alignment. So, apparently, did upward land diving: ankles over heels, knees over ankles, hips over knees, each spinal knob atop the other, chin level instead of tucked, and crown pressed high.

It felt good. It felt stable. *She* was in control, rather than the force which pressed her down. She could feel her muscles relaxing into this new configuration, creating a set point just the way they had when she'd gotten good at sea diving.

She stood there, letting it sink in, letting it grow to feel natural. It was natural for Altairos. It would become natural for her, too.

A flash of color – bright green – on the cliff caught her eye.

Ah! The bluff wasn't sheer, just steep, with a winding path that descended to the beach. A black-haired boy wearing a green covering ran down it. Altairos! Altairos ran like that. It was he!

She waited, smiling to see what his reaction would be when he saw her.

He reached the bottom of the cliff path, turned toward her, and kept running. A moment later he was close enough that she could see the grin on his face.

"Nerine, íste ipérokhi!" he called from fifty paces away.

"I can do it, Altairos! I can do it!" she called back.

And then he was right before her, grinning and talking and gesturing. She couldn't understand the words, but she understood what he meant. He thought she was wonderful, and he thought her standing was wonderful. She basked in his approval the way she'd basked a moment before in the act of standing.

Then a flicker of mischief stirred in her.

She laughed, tapped the green covering on his shoulders, and took off running.

Her long, slow moment upright had changed something within her. The stride of her legs and the shock traveling up through them felt right. The balance of her torso, secure. The pumping of her arms, exhilarating. It was as though she were swimming through the air, strong and able, meant to move across the land just as she was meant to move through the water.

She heard pounding footsteps behind her.

"Ekteléste grígori, Nerine!"

Altairos was catching up!

She swerved toward the sea as he came abreast of her and grabbed her hand. Together they plunged through the surf to finish their race in the waves. She held her breath, not wanting to reactivate her gills, and then surfaced, churning her legs to keep her head above the water.

Closer to shore than she, Altairos yelled, "Tha ímai philí sas píso!" and spurted back toward land.

Nerine laughed. In the sea, she was far faster than he. She gulped another lungful of air and dove, power in the stroke of her arms and the double beat of her kick. At the surf line, she jerked her feet down to strike the sand and dashed through the breakers, side by side with her friend.

Altairos took her hand again and slowed their pace.

Slower was harder, but his clasp steadied her, and she didn't fall.

He led her along the water to where the cliffs met the sea in a series of rocky ledges, each pocked by tide pools filled with different creatures than lived on the reef. Green anemones, purple-shelled limpets, rusty brown scales of sea plants, and small scuttling crabs.

She and Altairos traded words.

"Crab."

"Kavoúri."

"Rock."

"Pétra."

The tide pools were beautiful, and the words were, too. Although some of them sounded very peculiar to Nerine. She laughed from sheer joy of the adventure, and Altairos laughed with her.

"Asterías!" What a gorgeous word for starfish!

She was more mindful of the passing time than she had been on her first visit. When the shadow of the cliffs lengthened, approaching the dunes, but not yet engulfing them, she straightened from watching the antics of a trio of lizards gamboling on the rocks. She didn't want to return home so late as yesterday. Although . . . she wished she didn't have to return home at all. Not just yet.

Altairos was much more fun to play with than her brother and sisters. They squabbled almost constantly, while Altairos just tugged her toward the next new thing and said, "Kitáxte to! Kitáxte!" *Look at this! Look!* And she loved looking. But the later she came home today, the more likely that she couldn't come again tomorrow. Or maybe ever, if her secret visits were revealed.

"I have to go," she said.

Altairos' happy eyes turned somber. "Gnorízo óti tha prépi na prokhorísete." *I know you must.*

"I'll come again tomorrow."

His eyes lit, and he leaned forward to brush a kiss on her cheek. His lips were warm and dry, their surface very soft. Nerine smiled and led him away from the tide pools toward the sands. She needed to be farther from the rocks and the surf pounding them, if she was to enter the sea safely.

Shyly, just before she plunged into the water, Nerine stepped close to Altairos and pressed her cheek against his.

Then she was away, diving through the base of a breaking wave and following the seabed down.

∽

She reached home in time for dinner, which she didn't eat in the nursery as usual.

Mother came to fetch her before the food arrived. Floating poised and queenly within the archway to the hall, she issued an unusual invitation. "Nerine, darling, you're younger than Eilidh was when your father and I deemed her ready to dine at our table, but your manners are much better. Come with me!"

Nerine glanced back as she left the nursery. Nurse was nodding and smiling. Agnippe was cuddling her knitted clownfish toy. But Xianthe shot a look of pure hatred at her next youngest sister.

Nerine gave an extra flick of her feet to swim away faster. Would Xianthe hold a grudge? She didn't usually, but . . . seeing Nerine get two treats in the same day might change that.

Mother took Nerine to her dressing room, where she pulled a small, trailing ribband of vivid aqua from a hinged scollop shell. "It would be improper to array you in belt and pectoral," she stated.

"I'm almost nine," protested Nerine.

Mother smiled graciously. "Yes, you will be nine in a *déka*-day. And when you are thirteen you will don the raiment suitable to your station."

"Eilidh is thirteen, but she still swims bare!" Nerine wasn't sure why she was arguing, but she didn't like Mother emphasizing how young she was.

"And Eilidh will receive her belt and pectoral as soon as the artisan has completed them." Mother touched the tips of her first two fingers below Nerine's chin. "But! You must not swim bare within our formal dining parlor, and so you shall be clothed." She spread the aqua ribband with both hands, and Nerine could see that it was two separate lengths of *nålbindning* knitting, one shaped as a triangle, the other, a long and wide sash.

Mother tied the narrow end of the triangular piece around Nerine's neck. The wide part wrapped around her ribs and tied in back. The sash wrapped twice around Nerine's waist, secured in an elaborate knot in front, while the generous tail from the knot passed between her legs and ended in an equally elaborate knot at the back.

Mother turned Nerine to face the large bronze mirror. "There! See how grown up you look."

Nerine stared. The bodice and sash gleamed almost like jewelry. Their aqua hue brought out the green tints in her flowing gold hair, as well as the green within the golden brown of her eyes. She looked elegant, and she felt *very* grown up.

"Thank you, Mamma." Her old name for her mother slipped out. It was a special thing that Mother had given this gift with her own hands and dressed Nerine as well. Queens normally delivered such tasks into the hands of their retainers.

Mother's eyes warmed. "You are ready. Let us go."

Dinner was served in one of the smaller staterooms – not the vast feast hall, nor an intimate family parlor. Streamers of white and silver adorned its fuchsia coral walls. The table – faced with mother-of-pearl – was large enough to accommodate twenty: Father at its head, Mother at its foot, a few of Mother's handmaidens and several of Father's ministers along the sides. Eilidh and Tyr were placed next to one another near Mother's end. Nerine was across from them.

She was very, very careful to use her best manners. Her toes gripped the bronze loops in the floor at her place. It wouldn't do to drift around the way she often did in the nursery. She fastened her eating globe back into its bronze clip on the table, whenever she chose a bite from a different one. How embarrassing it would be, if one of her globes slipped into the space of the lady on her left side. Or the high minister on her right.

She was so preoccupied with justifying her mother's trust that she barely noticed what she ate, and the talk passed her by entirely until the very end of the meal.

"Your Majesty," said the minister on Father's right hand, "the strengthening of the current through the Pillars of Herakles has wrecked five ships of the landwalkers this summer. The prayers of their sailors' wives and children acquire fresh poignancy."

Father's lips tightened, but he said nothing.

The minister on his left replied instead. "Great Poseidon grows restless, and the World Ocean beyond the Pillars tosses with his energy."

The lady beside Nerine joined the conversation. "The poor innocents!" she cried. "They call on Poseidon, who answers not. Could not *you* do so, King Meren? As the *numen* of the Middle Sea, you have power in this realm."

Father's eyes softened. Nerine bet he would have patted the lady's hand, if she'd been nearer to him. "Worry not, Philena. I hear all the prayers to the essence of the sea, even those directed to my liege, Poseidon. I will act." He turned a sterner glance to his ministers. "These are matters for my council chamber, Rhaxmus. Spiro. Not for the dining hall where tender ears listen." A shift of his eyes indicated exactly which ears he meant: Eilidh, Tyr, and Nerine.

"Yes, Your Majesty."

"Pardon, Your Majesty."

Father nodded. So interesting that Mother's nods were always slightly haughty, while Father's – even when he was displeased – seemed warmer, as though he understood and accepted one's mistake. Nerine loved Father best. And Mother didn't seem to mind. Grown ups were strange sometimes.

Later, she thought about angry Poseidon while she lay in her sleeping circle with its mesh pulled over her, waiting for sleep to come. Why was Poseidon so angry? Always angry? It seemed whenever the grown ups talked of him, they used words like wrathful, jealous, mighty, and vengeful. She imagined the waves mounting higher and higher in the World Ocean, until they poured between the Pillars of Herakles, wrecking ships as the current raced to the Middle Sea.

The lord of the World Ocean must be an unreasonable ruler. How did Father manage being his vassal? Father was so reasonable. So approachable. *Father* was a good ruler. Nurse said so. Everyone said so. The ministers, the nobles, the artisans, the common folk. Nerine was glad she lived in the Middle Sea. What if Poseidon had been her father, instead of Father? She shuddered. What a horrible thought. She wouldn't think about Poseidon any more. She'd think of Altairos and her day.

Altairos was wonderful. Almost like Father, but more lively and more smiling. Had Father been like Altairos when he was a little boy? She bet he had.

Altairos had taught her so many words today. She had taught him words, too, but he had a harder time pronouncing her words than she did his.

Mother said the sea folk spoke in the "language of the gods." Nerine wondered if that was because Hera and Zeus and all the other gods on Mount Olympus spoke it, or because their tongue was so musical and flowing. She hadn't realized just how melodic her own words were until she heard Altairos speaking them in the more punctuated way that his language sounded.

Nerine giggled softly. He did sound so funny. But he refused to give up.

She wondered what they would do tomorrow. It would be new and fun. Of that she was sure. There were surely as many adventures to be had on land as there were in the sea. And Altairos would lead her to every single one.

As the days, and then the *déka*-days, passed, Nerine's anticipation of the delights to be found in Altairos' company proved exactly right. They raced in the sea and on land. They visited the rock pools, where the inhabitants changed with each coming and going of the tides. Altairos showed her how to make boats from driftwood and float them atop of water. They found a long strand of braided grapevine hanging from an overhanging tree on the cliff, and Altairos pushed Nerine high and higher as she swung on it.

Always they traded words: his word for a thing or an action, and hers.

～

8 ~ Complications

ONE MORNING, SOON AFTER Nerine's first appearance at the formal table where her parents and their retinues dined, Father met her outside the schoolroom, just as lessons were finishing. He smiled, and his eyes were alight.

"How is my good little girl today?" he greeted her. "Did you mind your tutor and learn well?"

Nerine nodded shyly, wondering why Father floated in the schoolroom archway instead of consulting his ministers in his cabinet chamber as was usual for the late morning.

"I have something to show you," he said, seeming to guess her unspoken question.

"Is it a surprise?" she asked. Father loved bestowing unexpected treats on his children, and he looked exactly like he always did right before he produced something fun.

He winked, but didn't answer her, saying merely, "Come along."

Tingling with anticipation, she followed him.

They threaded their way through the reef palace and out one of the lagoon doors into a kelp forest. The great leafy columns stretched high overhead, glowing green where the sunlight passed through them and casting a dappled shade on the sand of the sea floor below. Father swam around one of the giant plants and between two others, leading Nerine onward. A school of silvery lookdowns drifted by.

The heart of the grove was magical. Beams of light angled down through the water like blessings from Apollo's chariot, and the fronds of the kelp rippled like tangled lace. Its scent – warm and woody – wrapped around Nerine like an exotic veil.

She loved the kelp forest, but surely Father's treat was something more than a visit there. She looked at him for clues. He widened his eyes and gestured toward a gap in the foliage.

She heard the pulsing sound of a strong and muscular creature swimming, and then the sleek and shining gray form of a dolphin surged into the upper reaches of the clearing. It was Kriy, the matron of her pod and teacher to the dolphins who towed the vessels of the sea people.

Kriy curved past the tousled pillars of kelp, spiraling down and around. Her eye was bright and dark, and her mouth smiled in the manner of her kind.

Nerine watched her, marveling at the dolphin's strength and grace. Dolphins were special. She still missed Pheep, her first dolphin friend when she was only a little older than Agnippe. Then Nerine saw that Kriy was not alone. A young one, perhaps half Kriy's size, hugged her far flank.

Oh! He was splendid! With the same deep and limpid eye, and the same gentle smile on his mouth as his elder.

Kriy swept by Father and Nerine, and the young dolphin peeled off from her side to circle Nerine, letting Nerine's hand flow over his smooth flank.

Oh! He was handsome!

But not small, despite his youth. From snout to tail fin, Kriy herself was almost twice Father's height. The young one was a bit longer than Nerine was tall.

"This is Mai'ip," said Father.

Mai'ip dove toward the sand below them, pried up the flat disk of a coin urchin shell, and brought it to Nerine in his mouth. She accepted it, and he jigged in front of her, almost bouncing.

Nerine laughed. "Father, he wants to play!"

"So he does. Do you know how to toss the coin shell? It's flat shape makes it tricky."

Nerine shook her head and handed the shell to Father.

"Like this," he said, holding one edge with his wrist curled inward, and then flinging the shell by straightening his wrist as he swung his arm.

The coin shell flew through the water across the clearing.

Mai'ip darted after it, catching it in his mouth, and streaking back to them, offering it again to Nerine.

Father helped her position her fingers and her wrist. Then she swung her arm and let her fingers release as her wrist straightened. The shell flew outward, although not as far as Father's cast, and Mai'ip caught it, again racing back to Nerine.

Father uttered something in the squeaky language of the dolphins and Kriy, circling above, left them.

Mai'ip played catch with Nerine for a few more tosses, and then nudged her to spiral around him while he spiraled around her in a dance. Nerine felt fizzy with the fun of it, and then dizzy with all the spinning.

She stopped to regain her equilibrium.

Father's hand came to rest on her shoulder. "Nurse tells me that she's allowing you to roam the lagoon in your free time, Nerine."

Nerine tensed. Nurse never asked where Nerine went on those gorgeous afternoons she spent ashore, but Father might be more inquiring. What would she say, if he asked her? She'd not known Nurse assumed she stayed within the lagoon. Would father take Nurse's word for it? Or would he probe more? Nerine didn't want to share her secret. Its secrecy was part of what made it special.

"I think she's right to allow you more freedom," continued Father, "and the lagoon's a safe stretch of water, but I'd feel more comfortable, if you weren't completely alone. Dolphins are clever, and Kriy has indicated that Mai'ip is ready for more interaction with people."

Mai'ip nudged Nerine's hand at this, a bright look in his eye, and Nerine scratched the base of his flipper gently.

"I'd like you to accept Mai'ip as your companion when you wander. He's Pheep's sister's son, you know," stated Father.

Nerine's fear for her secret, and her guilt over swimming far beyond the lagoon, changed into a feeling even more undesirable – sadness and fury combined. When she was very young and went everywhere with Nurse, Pheep had gone with the nursery party as a protector. His big, looming presence had made her feel so safe, while the rushing rides he gave her, as she clung to his dorsal fin, caused her to shriek with delight. She'd loved Pheep, and when he died of old age – she was six – she knew she'd never be happy again. Father had assigned a different dolphin to guard Nurse and the children, and attempted to comfort Nerine with the platitude that the only thing to do when you lost a cetacean friend was to find another.

"How can you?" she'd screamed. "Pheep was *Pheep*, and *no one* can replace him!"

She couldn't remember what had happened to Pheep's successor, or why Father had consented to the nursery party coming and going without a dolphin guardian, but now he was trying to replace Pheep again.

Her old grief for Pheep's death and her outrage at Father tore through her with renewed strength.

She swallowed hard, trying to swallow the uncomfortable emotions.

"You couldn't replace Pheep when I was six," she bit out, "and I won't let you do it now!"

Father sighed.

Grinning his dolphin grin, Mai'ip dove around her.

"Nerine, love," – Father's hand squeezed her shoulder – "Pheep himself will never be replaced. He lives still in my heart. But others may fill his role. I think you misunderstood my words, when we lost him."

"You said I should make a new friend," she accused.

"I did, for only love can comfort loss. But perhaps, in my own grief, I suggested it too soon."

Father looked sad, and Nerine's rage drained out of her.

"Mai'ip will never replace Pheep," he said, "but his presence with you would relieve my anxiety. Will you not accept Mai'ip for Mai'ip himself?"

Mai'ip butted Nerine gently in the stomach and then raced away, inviting her to chase him.

The last of her resistance melted. She flung her arms around Father, and he folded her close.

"I'm sorry," she whispered. "And I will accept Mai'ip."

From then on, whenever she swam out of the reef palace, she found Mai'ip waiting and eager to go with her, whether she stayed within the lagoon or went outside it. He seemed unperturbed when she went ashore, busying himself in the waves until she returned to the sea. When Altairos joined them in the water, he played with both of them.

Nerine learned more of the dolphin language, realizing as she did so that the lower register – the part that her ears could hear – was but a fragment of their full range, more a system of signals than complete communication. Kriy and the other dolphins might learn from Mai'ip where Nerine went, but Father and Mother would not. Her secret was safe.

As time passed, her affection for him grew ever stronger.

～

One day Altairos led her inland over a low point in the bluff. The dune grasses gave way to a quilted pattern of plants – similar to the variegated texture of the reef – but all in shades of green and scented with spicy aromas that reminded her of the land foods.

Dusty gray greens, deep greens, soft minty greens, vivid greens, yellow greens. She'd not realized how many greens there were in the world until now. And just as many textures: fine needled, round and frilly, smooth and fleshy, prickly. It was a paradise amidst smells of pepper and mustard and savory musk and sweet honey.

She stopped a moment, closing her eyes and inhaling deep into her lungs. Sea smells were subtle. Land smells were intense.

Altairos grinned at her pleasure, then tugged at her hand.

"Come! Come! It's better farther on," he urged her.

The meandering path through the scrub twisted around a low hillside studded with a few wild olive trees, their small leaves flickering in the slow movement of the air.

The sea breeze had died, and the air was very warm, but not still.

The path dipped to cross a shallow gully and emerged beside a low wall. It was built of dry-laid stone, and on the other side of it lay a colorful garden. A garden of the land people, just as the spot outside her nursery was a garden of the sea people!

Altairos guided her to a break in the wall guarded by a black, latticed panel that reminded Nerine of the chitin-latticed doors in the palace. Altairos pushed it open to usher her through. Ah! It was a half door.

"Gate," said Altairos.

Inside, small trees displayed fruits of brilliant yellow and orange on their branches.

"Lemon. Tangerine."

Mmm. Their smell was both tangy and sweet.

And all across the dusty earth were clumps of flowers: soft lilac, bright pink, burning orange, cheerful yellow, and cordial white.

Altairos pointed beyond the flowers to where a heavy vine clustered with fuchsia blooms, and a delicate vine bearing a froth of dainty white petals, climbed a smooth white wall, much taller than the rough wall around the garden.

"My old nosokóma lives here."

Nerine looked more closely at the dwelling. Its lines were so straight, nothing like the curving and sometimes jagged outline of the reef palace. And it was so very white, blocks of whiteness like teeth, with a terrace between them where more vines grew from pots, twining up posts to cover open beams above with their leaves and blossoms.

A woman appeared on the terrace.

Her hair was white, like Nerine's nurse, but coiled smoothly atop her head, and her skin, very wrinkled. Also like Nerine's nurse, but tanned and leathery, not soft and pale. She wore a tunic, similar to the garment Altairos always wore, but white and much longer, falling in elaborate folds and draperies to her ankles.

The instant her eyes fell on Altairos, her whole face lit up and her arms reached. "Agoraki mou! Come let me see you!"

Altairos scampered onto the terrace and into the offered embrace. "Mana mou, I want you to meet my new friend!"

Nerine followed him, feeling a little shy. Altairos was the only land person she'd ever met. Would this lady be as friendly as he? What would she think of Nerine?

But the woman's attention was all for Altairos at first. She and he spoke too quickly for Nerine to follow it. Something about liking his new mother and wasn't his *mana mou* right, and blessings but it had been so long since she'd seen him.

Nerine waited while Altairos submitted to having his hair stroked and his height exclaimed over. This woman had to be his old nurse. She was too old to be his mother, but she loved him. Finally she patted his cheek and turned to meet his friend.

Her face lost all its light and affection, turning stern and forbidding. Nerine shivered. How had she ever thought her own mother stern. Her mother was dignified, regal. Formal. This woman was . . . condemning.

"Mana mou, this is my friend, Nerine." Altairos was looking at Nerine. He hadn't noticed the abrupt change in his nurse's demeanor, and his voice held only joyful excitement. "Nerine, this is my old nosokóma" – his nurse – "Calla."

"Mana mou –" he tipped his gaze up and stopped.

"She is naïáda, a numen of the sea," said his nurse.

Altairos' brow wrinkled, then smoothed as his irrepressible grin burst out. "She is *wonderful*, mana mou, and she is my *friend!*"

Calla shook her head. "Man to men, numen to numina. No good can come of this!"

Altairos put his arm around Nerine's shoulders and hugged her to his side. He felt very warm and solid. "Why not?" he challenged his nurse. "Good has already come of it. I have a friend to play with!"

"No. You do not. The naïáda are heartless." Calla's face darkened further.

"Callitsa, you are wrong. Nerine will prove you wrong." Altairos' chin lifted. "If you give her a fair chance."

Calla's face softened, and she sighed.

Nerine felt her own sigh puff out of her. It was scary to be disliked by someone on sight. Especially when that someone was a friend's dear old nana. Might Calla change her mind? Why was she so convinced sea people were heartless? Nerine thought of her own nurse – sensible and loving – and of her father, so warm and understanding. Calla was wrong. Even Father's warriors smiled kindly when not on guard duty.

Calla held out her right hand, and Nerine took it hesitantly.

"Yasas, Nerine. I bid you welcome to my home." Calla nodded.

Nerine inclined her head, just like Mother would. "I give you greeting, Kyría Calla, and thanks for your welcome." There. She'd managed that *just* like Mother. Except the words were a mix from her own language of the sea and Altairos' *Ionikós*.

A gleam of humor passed through Calla's eyes. "Well, then, I'll fetch you some lemonáda and you shall both tell me all about it."

She led them over to a white ledge built out from the wall, its surface inlaid with bright bits of glass – scarlet and turquoise and jade. Altairos sat, drawing Nerine down beside him. "You'll see, mana mou, that Nerine is caring and gentle. And fun!" He squeezed Nerine's hand.

Calla shook her head as she went back into her dwelling, but she smiled.

Altairos bumped his forehead gently against Nerine's. "My mother was very ill when I was born, so Calla was my mother. She . . . she does not like the ocean. It makes her sick!"

"It makes her sick?" How could the sea make anyone sick? The sea was home!

"She went on a boat when she was little. To get from Libúa to here. The boat going up and down made her wretched."

Nerine puzzled on that. She knew what he meant about boats going up and down. She'd seen how the toy floats they made bobbed on the waves. How it could make someone sick escaped her, but she could imagine how someone who hated the sea might also hate the people who lived in it.

"She'll like you after she feeds you," Altairos assured her.

Now *that* made sense. Her own nurse always liked people better after she fussed over them. The tension in Nerine's shoulders ebbed a little, and still more when Calla came rustling back with three pottery mugs on a tray.

Nerine sipped the liquid in hers. It was cool, tangy, and sweet. And very strong. Were all the flavors of land stronger than those of the sea? No wonder she had longed to visit the shore.

Altairos gulped his lemonáda and started telling Calla about how he had rescued Nerine from the surf that first day, so many moons ago, but soon shifted into describing their favorite racing game – the one where he tapped Nerine and ran until she tapped him. Where upon she ran, and he chased her.

"She always catches me in the sea, she's so much faster," he complained, laughing. "And she's gotten so much steadier on land that she catches me there, too!"

It was true. Her strides on land were quicker than his. It was only her uneven balance that still slowed her at times.

Calla smiled, almost reluctantly. "Ah, you've no brothers your own age. I see it's a happy thing to have a playmate with only ten years. How old are you, child?"

"I am nine." Nerine studied Calla a moment. Sitting beside Altairos, his nurse had relaxed back against the wall and abandoned her earlier formality. Was it worth taking a chance? Abruptly Nerine made up her mind. She looked Calla in the eye. "I'm not heartless!"

Calla's eyebrows flew upward. Then she sighed. "No, you're not, child. You're not."

"Why did you say it then?" probed Nerine.

Altairos looked curious too.

Calla just shook her head. "Never you mind, child. Never you mind."

It seemed Altairos was right that his nurse mellowed after feeding her guests. She mellowed still further in the *déka*-days after this first visit. Altairos and Nerine visited her cottage regularly, sometimes spending the entire afternoon there in the very hottest or windiest weather. Altairos liked carving animal figurines out of driftwood while Calla spoiled them with sweet drinks, dried figs, and almond pastries.

Nerine tried carving, but the sharpness of the knife made her nervous. So Calla taught her how to make ribbands doing *nålbindning* knitting. That was really interesting, because the land dwellers used such different materials. The sea people harvested fibers that didn't absorb water: their own hair – with its thicker strands, filaments of wiry sea jute, or lengths of the linked spines of sea urchins.

The rolls of silk or flax that Calla provided were so much softer and satiny.

Nerine made hair ties for herself, which was fun. She learned to braid her hair with the ribbands interwoven in the plait and wondered if she dared show off the new style underwater at home. She knitted a blue-and-white striped sash for Altairos. And then created a shawl of knotted ribbands for Calla herself.

Calla got teary-eyed when Nerine presented the garment to her. It was an openwork rectangle of blue and aqua and cream silk, adding elegance to a tunic without adding weight or heat. Calla had thought Nerine to be making it for herself, and never guessed that Nerine was making it for her.

"What a little love you are, mikroula!" she exclaimed.

For Calla had thawed completely, treating Nerine much the way she treated Altairos, scolding – did all nurses scold? – praising, directing, and suggesting.

Once Nerine had mastered the *nålbindning*, Calla initiated Nerine into the intricacies of her ground loom. It was called a ground loom, and Calla said that such looms were usually located on the floor. But Calla's rested on a tiled, raised section of floor in the middle of her weaving room. She said it saved her back, not having to stoop so low.

Nerine learned how to set up the long warp threads, the ones that reached all the way from the front of the loom to the back. She learned how to send the shuttle with the weft threads across smoothly and surely, laying down the thread nice and straight for easy beating into the fabric. So this was how the coverings that Altairos and Calla wore were made!

After the linen was removed from the loom, Calla gave Nerine a sharp needle – not dull like the thicker one used in knitting – to embroider designs onto the edges of the fabric.

All of these games with textiles fascinated Nerine, seeming part and parcel of the magic that imbued the land. Sea people wore jewelry or abbreviated garments that hugged the body. The generously flowing robes and gowns available to land people were so beautiful! When Calla gave Nerine a gown – gleaming cream with white flowers embroidered along its hems – Nerine burst into tears and flew into Calla's open arms.

"Mana mou! Thank you!"

Calla patted Nerine's shoulders, looking troubled as she did at times – still. "There, there, mikroula. There, there."

⁓

Soon after Nerine passed the tenth anniversary of her birth, her father and mother declared that it was past time that she and her older siblings made their first visit to the air.

What an odd way to put it, thought Nerine. When *she* visited the air, she was visiting the land. And Altairos. Would her parents have her and Eilidh and Tyr pop their heads above the water without actually going ashore? She remembered how the waves tumbled her the first time. Maybe it would be wiser to skip that part.

Mai'ip was not part of the expedition. Neither was Xianthe, and she was much more vehement about it than was the dolphin.

Father and Mother – and even Nurse – had each explained on separate occasions why Xianthe needed to wait. Evidently her aversion to fresh water went hand in hand with slight physical differences. If she attempted to breathe air at the normal age, it would be much more painful than if she waited a few more years.

Xianthe had protested after each explanation.

When Mother and Father arrived to collect the three who were going, Xianthe pitched a fit, grabbing Nerine's arm and yelling, "Nerine's two whole years younger than me! If I'm not breathing air, then she isn't either! It's not fair!"

Xianthe's face scrunched up, and her grip on Nerine's arm pinched.

"Let go, Xi," gasped Nerine. "That hurts." It did, too. Xianthe's nails were digging into her skin.

Xianthe turned away from their parents to face Nerine. "You think that hurts? What about this?!" And she aimed a kick at Nerine's stomach.

It didn't connect.

Father's hand encircled Xianthe's ankle, like a kraken's tentacle whipping around its prey, and stopped his daughter cold. He was quick, and he was strong.

"That's enough, Xianthe." How did he sound so firm without getting angry?

Xianthe's yells changed to sobs, and she let Nerine's arm go, knuckling her eyes. "I know she's good and I'm bad, but I want to go, too."

Nerine stared at her unhappy sister. This was strange. Xianthe always taunted Nerine for being young and for being obedient, letting her know that neither of those things were admirable. She'd never given any indication that she thought ill of herself.

Father drew Xianthe into his arms. "Hush, now, acushla. You'll be strong enough to rival Tethys herself when you're grown, but you must await your season."

Xianthe hiccuped. "Really?" Her face held a surprised, vulnerable look that Nerine had never seen before.

Father kissed her brow. "Really. Now apologize to your sister."

"I'm sorry I pinched you, Nerine." Xianthe actually sounded like she meant it, for a wonder.

Nerine nodded, but couldn't quite manage to say, "I forgive you." There were a lot of pinches and name calling before this that Xianthe hadn't said sorry for.

"Meren," prompted Mother, "if we wish to catch the slack tide, we must leave."

Nurse made shooing motions with her hands. "Go, go. On with you, now."

Tyr was through the door to the garden before Nurse spoke, and Eilidh followed him. Neither swam bare anymore. They weren't yet grown up, but they weren't children either. Tyr affected a bronze breastplate like Father's – even though his skill with a spear wasn't much – and a belt and loin piece to match. Eilidh liked color, lots of color, and she wore a mother-of-pearl pectoral and belt adorned by a confection of pink and blue and purple quartz. Nerine closed her eyes every time Eilidh swam in front of her. She really didn't want to follow her too close.

"Nervous?" inquired Father as he urged her forward.

Well, she was nervous. Just not about what he thought she was. She smiled, shook her head, and swam outside.

Mother overtook Tyr and Eilidh, leading them into the lagoon, the exact opposite direction that Nerine took when she visited Altairos. That was a relief. She didn't know what she would have done if they'd gone the other way. Pretended she didn't know her land friend? No, her secret would have come out. It still might, if her parents realized that she'd been breathing air for nearly two years already.

The lagoon waters were very calm and warmer than the rolling seas off Altairos' shore. The reef sheltered the lagoon, which was why Mother and Father felt it would be the best place to practice the transition from water to air.

Really, I should have thought of that, thought Nerine. She'd been silly and thoughtless, just swimming off toward shore two years ago without planning at all. But it had worked out. The real question was: would it work out this time? Wouldn't Mother and Father suspect something when Nerine poked her head out of the water with not one choke or cough? Should she try to fake discomfort?

Ahead of her, Eilidh's gaudy jewelry flashed, and Eilidh prattled like she was three instead of fifteen. "I'm going first, because I'm the eldest. When my lamellar pharynx closes, I won't be scared at all! And I won't cry when my tracheal pharynx opens either. So what if the first time hurts!"

Nerine snorted. Eilidh was boasting because she *was* scared. That's what Nerine thought.

Nerine would have been scared two years ago, if she'd known more about it. As it was, her ignorance had protected her from fear, while it endangered her life. If Altairos hadn't been there . . . but he'd saved her.

Nerine glanced at Father, swimming beside her. He grinned. "Your body is designed to do this," he reassured her.

Yes, she knew. She barely gave it a thought when she emerged from the water onto Altairos' beach.

Tyr slowed to allow them to catch up. "I still don't see why I can't go first," he grumbled. "I'm the boy. Boys always face danger first."

Father chuckled. "But this is not dangerous, Tyr. It can be alarming the first time. For some, not for everyone. I think we'll spare your sister's dignity."

"Hah!" Tyr sounded suddenly satisfied. "I'll bet she cries."

They stopped in a small dell in the lagoon floor. The normal colorful reef plants and creatures encrusted its sloping sides, but a clear bit of bare sand filled the bottom. The water was shallow, with air waiting above at perhaps twice Father's height. At one end of the dell, a steep bluff went up to yet shallower water. If Nerine stood there, she'd be in the air from her chest up. Which was the whole idea.

The surface was very, very still. Nerine doubted there were any waves at all. The lagoon was always placid, but they'd hit the slack tide precisely.

Eilidh went first, as she'd boasted she would.

Nerine and Tyr waited at the bottom of the dell, while Mother and Father accompanied Eilidh up the bluff to the top.

"Stay low," Father cautioned his eldest daughter. "And get your feet under you."

"I *know*," said Eilidh. "I've practiced it over and over again at home."

"But this is real, not practice."

Eilidh huffed impatiently.

Tyr sniggered and poked Nerine's stomach. "Even you'll do it better than she will."

Father's head turned. "Be quiet, Tyr."

Tyr hunkered down, but didn't apologize. Nerine wasn't surprised. Tyr and Eilidh insulted one another constantly, but they were close in spite of it. Maybe because of it.

Father's attention was back on Eilidh. "On my count of three, you will rise and break the water. Your mother and I will rise with you. Be sure to stay standing once you emerge."

Eilidh nodded.

"One."

Nerine could see Eilidh's leg muscles tensing.

"Two."

Now Mother and Father looked ready.

"Three!"

And the trio straightened, thrusting their bodies into the air.

Almost instantly, Eilidh crouched down again, returning to the water and crying. "Oh! No, no, no! It's too dry, it's too warm, it *hurts*!"

Tyr prodded Nerine again. "*Told* you." He kept his voice low enough that neither Father nor Mother heard him. They had resubmerged, but were preoccupied with comforting Eilidh.

It took some while to persuade Eilidh to try again.

Tyr turned a somersault and then straightened into a handstand. When he swayed over into a backbend, he urged Nerine to swim through the bridge made by his body. She humored him, and they amused themselves with all the different ways to make swimable arches – bending backward, bending forward, through the legs, through the arms, through an arch made with one leg and one arm.

But when Eilidh finally gathered enough courage to try the air again, Nerine stopped to watch.

This time, Mother had her hands under Eilidh's armpits, while Father held Eilidh's waist. They rose together, and Eilidh couldn't dodge back down. But she did fling her arms around her mother and sob violently. Nerine could hear her, even though the sounds were muffled by originating in the air.

"What a crybaby," scoffed Tyr.

"She's always been more sensitive, like Agnippe," said Nerine. "Nurse says."

"Agnippe has an excuse. Mother says she takes after our great grandmother, the river numen. That's why the sea's a bit too salty for her."

"Mmm." Nerine thought Tyr was too hard on Eilidh, but she wasn't going to argue with him.

Eilidh seemed to have calmed down. She'd released her frantic clutch on Mother and was standing straighter. Her whole body began to acquire the queenly stance that was typical of Eilidh.

Father resubmerged and swam down to Nerine and Tyr.

"Your turn, son."

"Hah! Wish me luck, Nerine!"

Nerine grinned. "Enjoy the air, Tyr."

"I will!" Unlike Eilidh, who'd been nervous, Tyr was excited.

Nerine hoped he'd manage better than Eilidh had. Eilidh never remembered when she was less than stellar. She seemed to change her memories to suit her notions of how things should have been. But Tyr would be embarrassed forever, if he screamed or cried. Also . . . if Tyr did well, maybe Nerine's comfort in the air wouldn't seem so odd. She didn't think she could pretend to more than a little agitation.

She watched – anxious – while Father counted to three and her brother rose into the air.

Tyr coughed wrackingly, his whole body bending forward, but he kept his face clear of the water and his legs straight. Eventually his coughs subsided. Nerine could see his operculi flattening tight to his ribs to cover his quiescent gills while his lungs took air in and out, moving his ribs rhythmically.

Mother, Eilidh, and Tyr moved to make room for Nerine.

Father swam down to fetch her.

"You'll be more like Tyr than Eilidh," he said.

Nerine nodded, trying to conceal just how nervous she felt. Then it occurred to her that she shouldn't try to hide her nerves. Father would think she was worried about how hard breathing air might be, rather than about how easy it would be. She nibbled her lip and let her eyes widen.

Father gave her a quick, one-armed hug.

"Up with you now."

Atop the bluff, Tyr stepped forward to pat Nerine's shoulder, then retreated to give her room.

Then Mother and Father were crouching with her.

"Would our touch help you, Nerine?" asked Mother. "Or do you prefer to rise without our assistance."

Nerine's teeth were chattering. "I c-c-can do it myself."

"Good girl." Father smiled at her. "On my count, then."

Nerine gathered her feet under her. The sand felt silky smooth against her soles.

"One."

Nerine tensed her leg muscles.

"Two."

Nerine straightened her arms, holding them just a little out from her body.

"Three!"

Nerine shot into the air. Her spiracles closed to mere dimples, while her operculi pressed the last water out of her gills. The deep shift in the base of her throat went forward – the lamellar pharynx that fed water to her gills closing, and the tracheal pharynx that fed air to her lungs opening. She coughed once. It sounded fake to her ears. And then she was breathing, the air moving in and out of her lungs as naturally as water passed over her gills in the sea.

She cast a scared look at Father.

He was smiling. "Well, well, we've got a natural here, Ionia."

Nerine glanced at Mother. Mother looked quietly pleased. "Nerine is good at all she attempts. I had every confidence in her."

Tyr was jumping up and down. "Wee hee, Nerine! You were awesome!" he shouted.

Now *that* felt good. Tyr teased more than he complimented. Nerine grinned back at him. Then she asked Father, "Can we wade to shore now? Walk on the beach?"

The land was not far off, perhaps a hundred strides. It was quite different from the beach where she visited Altairos. The strip of sand was narrow and there were no dunes. Or cliffs. A slope of scrub mixed with thickets of wild olive trees and cork trees stretched away to the sky. Nerine longed to go explore.

"Whoa, sea lions!" exclaimed Father. "Just breathing air is enough for today. Walking is another skill completely. One thing at a time!"

Nerine winced. What had she been thinking? If she walked along the beach while Tyr and Eilidh fell down and fell down again – her secret *would* be out. Thank the blessings Father had said no!

He tapped her cheek, approving of her eagerness. "We'll get to it. Not next time. Or even the next. The transition from water to air will become easier rapidly. When it feels natural to you, then we'll try walking ashore."

Eilidh sniffed. "You *said* we were naturals, Father." She'd already forgotten her grand fuss. "After all, we're *your* children." She turned to their mother. "Will you teach us to walk on shore as regally as you swim?"

Mother seemed to be repressing a smile. "I'm sure a regal carriage will come quite naturally to you, Eilidh, but I'll certainly assess the fine points. Your grace will please Hera, be sure."

Eilidh's chin lifted, and she looked satisfied.

Neither Tyr nor Eilidh had much trouble returning beneath the water. Nerine remembered that it had felt very natural her first time, too. Her comfort now drew no attention from anyone. Which was good.

As they swam home, Tyr and Eilidh returned to bickering, arguing about who would walk on land first. Tyr grew so angry that his cheeks showed pink. And Eilidh was just as mad, her nostrils and spiracles pinching inward and whitening. Nerine had a sudden revelation: they *liked* being furious. How odd! She hated it when someone raged at her – usually Xianthe – and she hated feeling anger herself even more. But Tyr felt powerful. And Eilidh felt superior. And *that* was why – yet another realization surprised Nerine – *that* was why Tyr hadn't mentioned Eilidh's poor showing in trying the air. He liked brangling, but he didn't actually want to hurt Eilidh.

Nerine blinked and glanced at Father, who winked at her. Had he known this all along? Was that why he rarely intervened?

He did interrupt them as they neared the palace. He was tired of hearing them, maybe. *Nerine* was certainly tired of listening to their endless taunts, even though none were directed at her.

"You'll practice walking in shallow water, and all three of you can do that at the same time. No need for any one of you to wait on the others," he informed them.

Nerine thought back on all her falling and getting back up again with Altairos' help. She'd done almost everything wrong. Going ashore in rough water. Doing it alone without help, and nearly drowning because of it. And trying to walk with only air around her, instead of waist-deep in water, which could support her.

She felt stupid. And yet, she didn't regret any of it. It had been an adventure, the best one of her life.

Her next adventure happened the very next day.

～

9 ~ Palace Gallivant

THEIR TUTOR GRANTED the children a respite from lessons. Nurse said that he needed the break as much as they did, which was probably true. Eilidh liked to tell him he was wrong about court etiquette. Tyr protested all the reading and reciting, demanding more practical exercises. Xianthe yelled, whenever she didn't want to bother learning something, which was often. And Agnippe cried. Really they were pretty awful!

But Nerine knew what she wanted to do with an entire day to herself.

She begged off from the expedition to the Prásino Shallows, with its extraordinary schools of fish. She excused herself from accompanying Nurse on a visit to the Singing Cave. The Cave was fascinating, and Sophronia – who lived there – equally so. She told stories more bizarre than any recounted by Father's fabulists. But all of the usual entertainments of the sea palled before those of the land.

As soon as the first sunlight began filtering through the water, Nerine set off for the shore.

Would Altairos be there? She'd not known of her freedom soon enough to warn him.

But he was there, dancing up and down the moment she emerged from the waves.

"Nerine! Nerine! Would you like to visit my father's palace? A palace on land?"

Would she? Yes, she *would*! The beach and the dunes were a marvelous playground, but she'd been wondering more and more what else there was to see and do ashore. There was a whole world inland to explore.

"Let's go!" she answered.

"We have to see Calla first and get you ready!" He seized her hand and drew her along, hurrying toward the trail to Calla's cottage.

Get her ready? What in the sea did he mean?

It was obvious once they'd arrived, and Altairos spilled their plans to his nurse.

Calla brought out Nerine's gown, told Nerine to lift her arms, and lowered the tube of gossamer cream fabric down over her head. When the hem reached Nerine's ankles, Calla turned the top of the tube down and secured the fold at each of Nerine's shoulders with plain bronze brooches. Then she gathered the waist – both the inner fall of fabric and the outer one draping from the shoulders – by wrapping a sash twice around Nerine's torso and tying it in a knot.

Nerine studied the result. It was strange to see gathered linen where she was used to bare skin. The gown brushed against her, very dry, almost rough, in comparison to insubstantial air or liquid water. She wished she could see herself in a mirror, but mirrors were luxuries and Calla did not have one. Nerine felt very elegant.

"There now," said Calla. "You look a proper Zakynthian maiden."

Altairos grinned, his eyes crinkling as they did when he was happy. "She's prettier than my mother."

"Of course, she is," said Calla. "She laughs. Your step-mother's a sober lady."

Altairos sighed. "She just stares blankly when my brothers make jests." He shook his head, then brightened. "At least she's too busy now with the new baby to bother with me. She used to give me guidance in courtly manners," he explained, seeing Nerine's puzzled look. "A more graceful bow, saying 'if it please your grace,' and kissing ladies' hands. Ugh!"

Nerine giggled. "My brother doesn't like that stuff either."

Calla tapped Altairos on the cheek. "For shame! After worrying that she might take you in dislike."

"She didn't have to like me so much!" Altairos blushed and shuffled his feet.

Nerine saw that Altairos was wearing sandals. "Will I need foot gear? To visit the castle?" She didn't have any.

"No, I walked in the town earlier."

How did that make any difference, she wondered.

"The streets can be dirty. But the castle floors are clean," said Calla.

"Then, am I ready? Can we go?" Nerine couldn't wait.

"One more thing." Calla pulled a sash from a basket – white to match Nerine's gown – and wrapped it around Nerine's brows, once, twice, and then knotted it behind her head.

Calla's face grew serious. "Even if you grow warm, you must not take this headband off." She patted Nerine's cheek. "The castle folk . . . do not love the people of the sea, and the dimples between your eyebrows would give you away, child."

Calla meant her spiracles.

"Is that . . . is that why you disliked me?" asked Nerine, feeling suddenly shy. "At the first?"

Calla patted her cheek again, then bent to kiss her hair. "I was worried that you might hurt Altairos."

"Altairos is my friend!" burst out Nerine. "My best friend."

"And Nerine is my best friend," said Altairos. "We'll always be gentle toward one another."

"Never you mind, child. Let the past be the past, and grab today's bright promise instead."

That made no sense to Nerine. Grown ups could be so obscure.

Altairos grabbed her hand. "Let's go!"

～

The path up the cliff was really steep. Nerine had to use different muscles than she did when running on the flat or even climbing the shifting sand of the dunes. And she had to hold the skirt of her gown up, so that she didn't step on it. As they climbed higher, the view out to sea grew ever wider. She saw the square white sail of a trading ship on the far horizon.

Just before the path reached the clifftop, it ran under the walls of the tower there. Nerine stared at the smooth, square blocks of white stone that loomed over them.

"Is this your father's guard tower?" she asked.

"No, it's a beacon tower to guide ships to the harbor."

Nerine wrinkled her brows, feeling the press of the unaccustomed headband, and wondering exactly what Altairos meant with his explanation. What was a beacon? And how did it help ships?

"My pappa has three fleets of warships to protect Zakynthos" – that was the name of the city-state ruled by Altairos' father – "and one trade fleet.

Great fires burn atop the beacon towers at night and in storms so that the mariners can find harbor. There's also a huge curved mirror of bronze to cast the light far out to sea."

Altairos sounded boastful, almost like Eilidh, but Nerine thought he might have reason. The beacons sounded impressive. She wished she could see one.

"I'll take you up sometime." Altairos knew her well.

Nerine smiled over her shoulder at him.

Then they reached the clifftop and rounded the corner of the beacon tower. Nerine's lips parted.

They stood at a high point of the island with a slope of scrub falling away from them to a ravine. A bridge supported by an arch of stone crossed the ravine. On the other side lay what must be the island king's palace. It was so different from anything Nerine had seen before that her eyes could scarcely make sense of what was before them. A vast jumble of connected white rectangles and squares of varying height with innumerable pillars and square windows. Small courtyards and stairways pierced the whole, which lay around one central oblong court. Walled gardens surrounded the enclave, and on its far side, she glimpsed the texture of smaller white buildings collected together.

Nerine shook her head.

Her father's reef palace was large, maybe even as large as this land palace if you could fold it up to make it compact, but her home was long and slender. And, except for the floors, it featured all the curves and irregularities of a structure built by nature. This land palace was . . . marvelous! *This* was what she'd hoped for in all her younger dreams of visiting ashore.

"We'll go in through the kitchen gardens," said Altairos. "That's closer, and nobody bothers you. If you go through the royal gate, the guards stop you and the verger records who you are scheduled to see. But the city gate is even worse." He grinned, then looked suddenly shy. "What do you think?"

"I love it!" exclaimed Nerine. "Thank you!"

Altairos bounced on his toes and laughed. "You haven't even seen inside. C'mon, let's go!"

He darted down the track on the slope, leading the way.

Nerine followed, taking it all in: the vivid greens and browns of the land with the white palace in their midst, the deep blue of the sky overhead, and the scallop of bluer sea just visible beyond the royal gate. She tripped more than once, since she wasn't watching her feet, but managed not to go sprawling. The second time she caught herself against Altairos' shoulder, he slowed and took her hand.

"I forget that you're a better swimmer than walker."

"I wasn't minding my steps," she confessed, then gestured. "I want to see everything, not miss anything."

As they got closer, Nerine could see people approaching the far right end of the palace – the royal gate – wearing gowns and robes more elaborate than the one Calla had made for her. The people working in the gardens wore much plainer garb, simple tunics like Altairos. She wondered if Altairos had to dress up for dinner the way she did.

Crossing the bridge, she craned her neck to stare upward. The palace seemed much taller than when she'd been looking down at it, with flights and flights of stairs climbing the slope and then pillars stacked atop pillars in the palace wall.

Climbing the steps felt strange. She'd thought it would be like the path up the cliff, but the level treads made the footing much easier and the low risers meant it wasn't as steep.

They entered the gardens through a low gate with square designs formed by its wooden braces. Inside, everything was very tidy, with straight walks – the gravel sharp under her feet – and rectangular beds of plantings.

Altairos paid no heed to the greenery, instead greeting the gardeners who pulled weeds or harvested herbs. But Nerine was curious to see the sources of their many beach picnics. There were those pungent green pods with the purple blush; okra, that's what it was called. And there, the narrow, bright red peppers that gave such zing to harissa sauce.

She sniffed, taking in the different smells – lemony, spicy, floral, and something else. What was that something else? It was the earth itself, she realized. Loamy and damp. Ah! *That* was the difference from Calla's cottage garden. They had more water here and people to carry it to the plants. The soil was moist rather than dusty dry.

They entered the palace through a small, open doorway and then traversed a narrow stone passage that turned left and then right, threading its way between workrooms and storage magazines. Nerine poked her head through one of the openings in the passage wall to see a walkway with square pits alongside it, each pit filled with a massive urn.

What in the sea?

Altairos noticed she wasn't following and turned back.

"I think those are the dried beans," he said. He seemed to be enjoying her wonderment. "Would you like to see?"

She nodded and followed him into the strange chamber. Really it was all strange to her.

Altairos knelt and hauled the stone lid off of the nearest urn. And, sure enough, there were the little round beans with a creamy yellow color. Nerine bent to touch – they were hard as pebbles. How long must the cook soak them to make them soft for eating?

Altairos shoved the lid back over the urn and led onward into the palace. It was almost like a maze intended to make intruders lose their way. After more turns than Nerine could keep track of, the character of the passage changed abruptly from cramped and plain to ornamented and broad. The walls were colored – red or yellow or brown from one corner to the next – and a wave pattern appeared at their base, a flower pattern at their top. Panels depicting scenes – dolphins splashing in the sea, ladies strolling a garden – graced larger expanses of wall. Polished wood outlined doorways.

Altairos gestured. "These are all sitting rooms and reception rooms and withdrawing rooms and the like. My brothers' wives use them." He shrugged. "Grown ups sure talk a lot."

Nerine had to agree with that. Her own parents' duties seemed to consist almost completely of talking. Although Father sometimes led hunting parties into the deeps.

"Are your brothers grown up?" she asked. She and Altairos spent their time racing and swimming and playing. *Not* talking. Or, at least not talking for the sake of talking. They talked about what they were doing. She knew he had brothers. But she didn't know anything about them.

"My oldest brother's oldest son is twelve. Like me." Altairos had recently passed the anniversary of his birth.

Nerine tried to imagine what it would be like if Tyr were grown up, and couldn't.

Around the next corner, stairs led up to the next level.

"My rooms are at the very top," explained Altairos. "I thought you might like to try my new *episkyros* table game."

She had no idea what *episkyros* was, but if Altairos thought it was fun, she likely would too.

Across from the top of the stairway lay another. And then another. They went up and up. Nerine's thighs started to ache. And then they reached the highest level.

A row of open square windows overlooked the great central court that she'd seen before from a distance. Small trees growing in urns created clumps of shade, and several oval basins of water with floating flowers and golden-scaled fish interrupted what would otherwise be a vast, hot expanse of stone. Several robed men – looking very grand and important – conversed beside one of the pools in which water actually spurted up into the air. Nerine could hear the water splashing. Two ladies walked together beneath a fabric canopy carried by servants.

"My rooms are here," said Altairos. He'd moved along the windowed hallway to a door that was solid on its lower half, but featured open louvers on the upper half.

Nerine trotted over to him. She was almost as eager to simply see where he lived as she was to try his new game.

～

Just inside the door lay a sitting room with many benches carved of dark wood and adjacent round tables. The walls were teal with frescoes of sea plants. How strange that Altairos might seem to sit beneath the waves even while he lived on land. Or maybe Calla had, before Altairos grew too old to need a nurse. Altairos didn't sit much! Nerine grinned and touched the puffy yellow cloth on the benches. It gave under her hand. Not sponges, but something land people used to make their furnishings soft.

Next to the sitting room was a dining chamber, with similar marine frescoes, teal walls, and yellow cushions. A rectangular table of the same dark wood occupied the center. Chairs with low backs clustered around it.

Behind these spaces were two more chambers with windows looking back toward the beacon tower and a sliver of sea just visible beyond the clifftop.

The walls of the room where Altairos slept were a rich cobalt blue with images of sky things: curling rays of a smiling sun reached from one corner, a sleepy crescent moon sailed from another, and fanciful creatures such as pegasi and gryphons soared between.

Altairos' sleep circle wasn't circular. It was a rectangular cushion supported by legs carved to resemble huge conch shells, and with a short latticed screen at the head, where a cylindrical pillow lay. Nerine's eyes felt very round. Land princes possessed much more ornate quarters than did sea princesses, evidently.

She glanced at her friend. He was looking at her, happy because she was happy.

The fourth room was the most interesting of all. Its pale blue walls featured frescoes of birds and ships. Below these images, shelves and chests held toys. Glass figurines shaped like warriors and noblemen. Whittled boats rigged with linen sails. Small bronze chariots drawn by ceramic horses. It seemed like a treasure room to Nerine.

Sitting on the floor, Altairos pulled out a circular tray with a post in the middle, and started setting wooden pawns on the dots painted on the tray, half of them red and half of them yellow. He handed Nerine a small paddle – twice the length of a finger, with a wide part at one end – and placed a blue glass ball in the tray.

"The goal is to hit the center post with the marble without knocking down your own pawns," he explained. "Like this." He shifted from sitting to kneeling and tapped the marble with his paddle. The glass ball shot across the tray, missed the central post, and knocked down two of the pawns – one of each color.

Nerine burst out laughing.

"Well, not like that!" Altairos laughed with her. "But you understand?"

"What happens if you knock down your own pawn?" she asked.

"Nothing. But the game ends when all the pawns of one color are down, and each player subtracts one from her score for each of the pawns that fell. You get one point for each time you hit the center post."

"Can I try?" asked Nerine.

"Of course! I want you to play it with me."

Nerine lined up her paddle and hit the marble where it lay.

Thock! It hit the post, bounced off, and knocked three pawns down, two yellow, one red.

"You're good!" said Altairos. "But now let me show you the rest of it. We don't take turns hitting, but fight one another to take a shot. Like this!" He picked up another paddle and dueled with himself. "And you're not allowed to knock over pawns with your paddle. If you do, the other player gets a free shot."

He handed Nerine another paddle. "We each have two," he explained.

And then they set to playing.

Nerine was more accurate than Altairos, but he was better at getting the marble away from her. He also knocked down more pawns with his paddle, which gave her a lot of free shots. They played three matches, and the score was close. But Nerine won all three.

Altairos didn't seem to care. His eyes blazed with excitement when he scored, but he seemed to enjoy the playing so much that the winning (or losing) wasn't as important.

When they put the game away, Nerine noticed a set of colorful blocks in a box on the same shelf.

"What are those?"

"Oh! You'll like them!" Altairos dumped the blocks onto the floor and started arranging them. There were several dozen. "See how this side is all oranges and yellows and reds? But this one is blues and greens? And this one has some of every color?"

Nerine nodded.

"First you turn them so the same color combination is up." He began turning them so a brown and green combination faced up. A few had a stripe of blue along one edge. Nerine joined him, noticing the smoothness of the blocks and the fine detail of the painted patterns.

"Then you fit them together."

Nerine couldn't quite see how he was deciding which blocks went next to each other, but she watched as he created a narrow shape surrounded by blue. "It looks like your island when we were standing by the beacon tower," she observed. It had some of the same textures: the scrub of the slope, the tangle of the wild cork trees, the smoother greens of gardens. Ah! And there were the white squares of the palace, with more buildings between it and an inlet of water filled with ships. "It *is* your island, isn't it!? With the sea around?"

Altairos looked pleased and nodded. "It's a map of Lapadoússa. This is where we are." He pointed at the white squares Nerine had identified as the palace. "And this" – he moved his forefinger in a circle around the palace, the smaller buildings, and the inlet of water – "is Zakynthos, my pappa's city."

"It looks . . . small." Nerine nibbled her lower lip. "It's so big, when you look out the window."

"It's not big compared to Libúa or Aegyptus. Or the Hellenic peninsula," he added. "But the island's seventeen stadia wide and almost seventy stadia long. It's big enough for us!"

Nerine didn't know what *stadia* were, so that didn't mean anything to her. She frowned.

"Don't you have maps under the sea?" asked Altairos. "How do you travel places?"

"Father has charts, but they don't look like this. In the sea . . . it doesn't really matter how far it is from Pelagie to Albora. What you need to know is how strong the current is and what direction it flows. And the phase of the moon."

"The moon?" Altairos sounded astonished.

"The tides are stronger at the full moon and the new moon," she explained.

"Oh! Of course! I knew that."

Nerine grinned at him. He probably did know, but sailing atop the water was different from swimming within it.

"How does parchment not dissolve underwater?"

"What?"

"Your father's charts," he said.

"Ah! The charts are pressed into thin sheets of copper."

"Huh. I wish I could visit your home!" Altairos straightened his back. "I bet it'd be fabulous!"

Nerine sighed. "But you can't breathe water, silly." And he wouldn't go unnoticed at home the way she – apparently – did here. But she felt a little sad for him. How would she have felt if she could *only* breathe water? That would be terrible!

Altairos turned his attention back to the map made of blocks. "If you were a bird and flew up really high, maybe as high as the moon, this is what Zakynthos would look like. It's small if you're far away and big when you're standing on it."

Yes, that made sense.

"Do the other block sides have other maps?" she wondered.

They did.

He showed her Aegyptus with its red and orange sands and the narrow strip of blue river and green banks. And sandal-shaped Oenotria with its central mountains. Then his stomach growled.

"Are you hungry? Shall we get some luncheon?" he asked.

She hadn't been, but the mention of food brought on appetite almost instantly. Her own stomach gurgled. "Can we?"

Altairos nodded. "I could order it brought to us, but . . . it'll be faster if I pester Cook." His eyes crinkled the way they did with his happiest grin. "And we'll get more treats!"

ᴍ

Out in the hall, a servant waited beside the door to Altairos' rooms. Her white gown looked a lot like the one Nerine wore, except it didn't have decorative embroidery along the hems. Was that why no one seemed to really notice Nerine's presence? They thought she was just another servant? This servant bowed. "How may I help you, my prince?"

"No need, Sahar. I'm going to pester Cook myself." And Altairos pattered toward the stairs.

Nerine trotted after him, but she noticed Sahar smiling and shaking her head indulgently. Nerine tried a tentative smile in Sahar's direction. Would Sahar react the way Calla had at first, turning somber and disapproving? No, Sahar nodded and smiled back. That was a relief.

Halfway down the stairs, Nerine heard a lovely humming sound, almost like singing but not quite. The music grew louder as she descended, and she stopped to listen when she reached the stretch of hallway between the bottom of the stairs and the top of the next flight.

"Altairos, what is it? Do land people sing without words?" Sea people sang both ways – with words and without – but Nerine felt as though there were still a lot she didn't know about land people.

"My mother plays the pandourion." He turned back from the top step to take Nerine's hand. "Come see!"

Nerine hung back. She wasn't sure she was ready to meet the Queen of Zakynthos.

"It's alright," Altairos reassured her. "We'll just peek; not go in."

Nerine allowed herself to be drawn forward to the nearest doorway.

Peering through it with Altairos, she saw another doorway aligned with the first. Beyond that second opening sat a plump, green-gowned woman, playing an instrument like none that Nerine had ever seen. Sea people played a variety of water pipes, but nothing stringed. The queen's pandourion had three strings that passed over a narrow, round-backed, oval base and then up a long skinny neck.

Her left hand moved up and down the neck, pressing the pandourion's strings, while her right hand plucked and strummed the strings where they passed over a circular opening in the base. The humming sounds thus emitted varied from low to high, but the melody was slow and calm. A cradle, suspended on silken ropes from a wooden frame, stood before the queen. The queen's face was tender.

"Does she have a new baby?" whispered Nerine.

"My sister," murmured Altairos. "Thank the blessings! Now she's too busy with the baby to plague me with lessons on etiquette."

Nerine stifled a giggle. "But she's not truly your mother, is she? Calla called her your step-mother. What happened to your birth mother?"

"I'm not sure."

Nerine's gaze flew to his face. He didn't look sad, just solemn, but what a strange answer to her question. How could he not know?

Altairos tugged on her hand. "Come away," he urged. "I'll explain, but not here."

Indeed, Nerine was no more eager to attract the queen's attention – or wake the baby – than was he. She took a last look through the doorway. The queen wore a green gauze cloth – that matched her shimmering gown – over her red hair, bound in place by a sash. Perhaps the headband wrapped around Nerine's brows was not so unusual after all. Most of the palace people she'd seen were bare headed, but they were servants.

Altairos went more slowly down the next flight of stairs, so Nerine was able to keep up, descending at his side rather than in his wake. Would he explain about his mother? Or did he not want to talk about it?

"When I was really little, I didn't know about mothers. I thought everyone had a nosokóma, like I did."

"Was it Calla?" Nerine wondered aloud.

Altairos grinned. "Yes, Calla. She loves me like a mother, I think."

Nerine nodded. She didn't *think* Calla loved Altairos like a mother; she *knew* it. That was why Calla had been mistrustful of Nerine, surely.

"So when did you learn about mothers?"

"I must have been four or five. I don't really remember, but I think I started asking questions when I realized that the servant's children had mothers only, and no nosokómi at all. I was confused and wanted to know why. But no one would answer me, and finally Calla told me to ask my father."

"What did he say?"

"He said that my mother had become very ill and had to go away."

"So she died?"

"That's what I'm not sure of. Maybe it's just because I was so little that I didn't understand death, but I thought Pappa really meant *away*, not *dead*. Except . . ." Altairos shook his head. "It doesn't make sense. She has to be dead, or he couldn't have married my step-mother. Not if my Mamma were alive, and just not here."

Nerine tried to imagine how it would feel if her mother went away, and Father married someone else. She was hungry, but her stomach felt even more hollow at the idea. Mother was not . . . easy to feel close to, but . . . Nerine was realizing that she loved her anyway.

But Nerine had known Mother all her life. Altairos had never known his mother. Could you miss someone you'd never met? Nerine suspected that you could.

"When I was older, I assumed she was dead. That 'going away' was just how you explained dying to a little boy."

"Did you ever ask again?"

Altairos stopped. They'd reached the ground floor, and there were more servants passing to and fro on their duties here. "I didn't," he answered. "Pappa . . . hadn't liked answering me. It pained him. I could see that, even though I was so young. And Calla had been uncomfortable, too."

The hallway they were following ended. Altairos turned left at the intersection, and then made a quick right, his hand still on Nerine's, gently guiding her.

"I wasn't upset when I asked about my Mamma. Or . . . I was, but not about her. I just didn't like being confused." He sounded like he was dredging at his memories in a way that he hadn't before.

He shot a quick sideways glance at Nerine. They'd never talked about serious things before. Was he wondering if she'd rather not?

She squeezed his hand. "I understand. Calla loved you, so how could you feel lack?"

He grinned. A relieved grin, not his happy, eye-crinkly one. "Yes. That's it exactly. So I didn't even wonder about it for the longest time. Calla loved me. Pappa visited my nursery every day, and I eventually realized that he loved me just as much. Just different, because he was a man, not a woman. And my brothers . . ." He broke off and laughed.

"Your brothers?" What was so funny?

"They're so much older than me, I can't think why they liked me so much. Included me so much."

"How do you mean?"

"My oldest brother, Dardanus, is thirty-five. He helps father rule Zakynthos now."

Nerine's lips parted. "Thirty-five!" She did some quick arithmetic. "He's twenty-three years older than you?" Land people were . . . really bizarre!

Altairos nodded and made another right turn. "The brother closest to me – Hilarion – is twenty-six now. But my brothers took me everywhere with them when I was little. I rode on Dardanus' shoulders when they raced in the pastures. Planos – he's next oldest to Hilarion – invented a leash for me, so they could take me aboard ship without worrying I might fall into the sea." He chuckled, then grew sober. "My brothers were fun. Really fun. And really kind to me." Had he not realized it until just now? Maybe not.

They passed out of the passageway into a small internal courtyard with a small fountain at its center. The sun was bright after the shadowy corridor, and a mist of water around the fountain glinted rainbows.

Ah! Nerine swayed toward the water, pulling Altairos with her. She'd not realized how dry her skin felt until this moment.

⁓

The moist air was refreshing, bedewing her face and arms, soothing her breathing passages. She closed her eyes and breathed in.

"Does it hurt you to be out of the sea for too long?" Altairos sounded worried. "Should we go back to the shore right away?"

Nerine dipped her left arm into the pool at the fountain's base. The water felt surprisingly cool and different than what she was used to. Heavy? Denser? She frowned and nibbled her lip. Oh, of course. It was fresh water, not salt. How peculiar! And Agnippe preferred it. Nerine shook her head.

"No, I'm fine. My oldest sister will go to the retinue of a goddess on Mount Olympus. She'll be away from the sea for years, and my parents would never send her if it would endanger her health. This just feels good, that's all."

"Your sister will be handmaiden to a goddess?"

Altairos was impressed, Nerine could tell. But it didn't seem extraordinary to her. "Mother was handmaiden to Hera when she was young. It's part of who we numeni are, cousins to the divine. Of course we serve them."

Altairos' eyes widened. "Land people don't. Can't. I've never heard that any mortal reached the top of Olympus by climbing, or came there unless a god brought him or her."

Nerine laughed. "Well, Eilidh won't be doing any climbing either. She's too dignified. Hera will send a chariot, of course."

"Huh." Altairos scrutinized Nerine's face. "Are you not mortal?"

"I . . . I'm not sure."

He looked just as surprised as she'd felt when he confessed to not knowing what became of his mother. "Do you have funeral observances when people die? Or memorial celebrations?"

She leaped on the one phrase she understood out of his questions. "We have a grand feast every winter in remembrance of grandfather."

"So he died. Which means you're mortal." Why did Altairos sound so relieved? Was immortality so scary?

"N-no. He didn't die. He just . . . went away." That sounded so silly. No wonder Altairos was concerned. "Mother said that his watery essence grew too strong, as it does sometimes among the sea people, and he became one with the waves."

"I bet he's dead," said Altairos. "Land people say 'he passed into the

West' to mean someone died. I bet sea people say 'he became one with the waves.'"

"Maybe," said Nerine. Her voice sounded uncertain in her ears. "But I think it has something to do with our magic. Eilidh and Tyr are starting to learn it, but I'm too young."

Altairos looked at her again, perhaps noticing her trembling lip and uncertain tone, because his next utterance was dramatically different. "I'm an idiot! I'm sorry, Nerine!" He hugged her. His arms felt very strong, and she was reminded of when he dragged her out of the surf – nearly three years ago – and saved her. "I'm an idiot and ignorant besides. Will you forgive me?"

She wasn't sure there was really anything to forgive, but she nodded anyway.

"Tell you what? You stay here and soak in the air of the fountain, while I go get food and bring it back."

She sank onto the wide coping around the fountain, enjoying the sensation of mist falling there. She liked the idea of waiting in the moisture.

"Are you alright?" Altairos was still worried.

He didn't need to be. She was fine, and feeling better by the moment.

She smiled and reassured him. "Just hungry! You go on and I'll wait."

He nodded and hurried away.

For a while, she pondered mortality and immortality. Had Altairos' birth mother died? Had her own grandfather died? Dolphins died. She'd mourned the loss of her favorite when she was only six. Dear Pheep! He'd always been gentler, less boisterous, than the other dolphins who came to the calling post. She missed him still. Although she'd learned to love Mai'ip, while still loving Pheep's memory.

At some point her thoughts drifted away from life and death to the welcome feel of the sun on her forearms, the press of warm stone against the backs of her thighs, and a commotion transpiring in one of the corridors opening onto the courtyard.

She heard hurrying steps, a murmur of respectful voices, and then one stronger voice booming out, loud and careless and male.

"No, no, Jasser. The left hinge is broken on that box, the right will go soon. Take it to Karim to repair and fetch another from storage."

Another murmur from the passage. A question?

And then that strong voice answering. "Yes, pack the rest of my gear now. I'll be on shipboard by evening."

Then the carefree speaker issued from the shadowy corridor, a bounce to his stride and a grin on his face as he tossed another instruction over his shoulder.

Nerine stared at him in surprise.

～

He had to be one of Altairos' older brothers. He had the same mane of curly hair, although his was red, not black. He had the same straight nose and the same direct gaze. But he was so tall. Taller even than Father. And he seemed to take up all the room in the small courtyard.

He almost missed Nerine, focused on his own business and aiming for the stairs.

Just as he set foot into the passage that Nerine and Altairos had emerged from earlier, his head jerked around and he spun on his heel.

"Hey, little lady, what's t'do?"

Nerine stood as he approached, not in respect – as he was undoubtedly a prince – but because she didn't think she could withstand his overwhelming vitality sitting.

"I'm – I'm Nerine," she stammered.

"To be sure you are, sweetheart. A pretty name for a pretty lass. Where are your attendants, sweet Nerine? You shouldn't be left to fend for yourself. That's not right." He grinned down at her, very like Altairos, except his grin produced a dimple in his tanned left cheek, instead of crinkles around his eyes.

"The cool mist of the fountain felt so good," she explained, "and Altairos said he would bring our meal back to me."

"Ha! So it's Altairos who is neglecting you. Little brother needs a lesson in etiquette, it seems! Doesn't he know to send a servant for the food? Or, if he insists on wheedling Cook himself" – the prince chuckled – "to summon a maid to attend you?"

"I am comfortable, sir, truly I am."

"Nay, sweet Nerine. Here's myself troubling your reverie, instead of leaving you in peace as I should be." His teeth flashed in another swift grin.

Nerine plucked up her courage. "I should think you'd have troubled me all the same, wondering who the stranger in your palace might be. But you'd have introduced yourself, perhaps."

He looked thunderstruck. "Ah, it's me who needs etiquette lessons then. Perhaps I'd best apply to my new mother, after all! Hilarion Zeronou Lamperieus at your service, Kyría Nerine."

She laughed outright, feeling more comfortable as she grew used to his vigorous style. "I shouldn't think you'd like such lessons, Prince Hilarion." She'd been right. He *was* Altairos' next brother. "Altairos sounded very glad to get out of them."

"Ha! The little shirker! So the style of Queen Briseis is not to his taste. I'm not surprised, but she does our Pappa proud, and therefore all of us as well." He bent from his great height to scrutinize Nerine's face. "And what is your style, Kyría Nerine? You've a familiar look to you, though I can't recall seeing you here before." He meant 'what was her full name?'

Standing very straight, she declared, "I'm Nerine Merenou Pelagieus," and bowed. Or attempted to bow. The problem was that she performed the bow of her sea palace, which involved sweeping the legs back at the same time as bending from the waist and sweeping the arms back. It was a beautiful bow, when floating in the sea. On land, it didn't work at all.

She fell flat on her face. Or would have, if Hilarion hadn't caught her.

He was so strong. Far stronger than Altairos. Of course he would be, a man grown, rather than a boy still growing. But Nerine felt almost as if she hadn't fallen at all, his hands were so quick and sure and steady, placing her back on her feet with no fuss.

A strange expression passed over his face, so fleeting she wondered if she'd imagined it. Then he was all concern. "Kríousa Nerine, are you hurt?"

Somehow she wasn't embarrassed. She should have been, but she wasn't. "Thank you!" she gasped. "I'm not hurt at all. Just . . ."

". . . flustered?" he finished for her.

She nodded.

"Let me look at you, child." He placed a forefinger beneath her chin and tipped her face up. "You've never visited Mégaro Zakynthos? You're sure?"

He meant this palace, his home. Altairos' home. She shook her head and his hand fell away from her.

"Well, then." He grinned that quick flashing grin of his. "I trust my little brother has made you appropriately welcome, Kríousa Nerine."

"Oh, yes!" she assured him. "We've been playing his new *episkyros* game. It's fun! And I *think* we'll go out to the gardens next and play cache-and-dash."

Hilarion laughed. "Clearly Altairos is doing all the honors with all the flourishes. Good."

"Altairos is my best friend," Nerine asserted. She wasn't sure why she felt the need to defend him. Neither Hilarion's words nor his tone indicated he was belittling Altairos, but . . .

The prince grew abruptly serious. "Of course, Kríousa. Altairos is . . . all kind of worthy. You do well to place your trust in him."

That felt better. So much better that Nerine's smile went from small and wavering to wide.

"Now," said Hilarion, "shall I attend you until Altairos returns from the kitchens, or shall I summon a maidservant to do so."

"Oh, you're readying for a sea journey, aren't you?" She remembered him talking of boxes and packing when he first entered the courtyard. "I shouldn't detain you!"

"Why, little lady, tarrying by your side would be pleasure. Be sure!"

She couldn't help giggling. Hilarion played at gallantry, rather than meaning it, and he *was* entertaining. But also overpowering. She found herself longing for solitude. Or for Altairos' less dramatic humor.

"No, no," she insisted. "Be on your travels. You shall tell me tales of them when you return."

He bowed. A land bow, with *one* leg back, *one* hand back, and then the slight bend at the waist. His quick grin flashed when he straightened. "Be sure I will," he said. Then he placed two fingers in his mouth and whistled sharply. A maidservant appeared in one of the doorways.

"Attend Kríousa Nerine until my brother returns anon."

And then he was gone.

～

The maidservant dipped a curtsey and asked a bit breathlessly – she must have hurried to Hilarion's whistle – "What does my lady require?"

Nerine reseated herself on the fountain coping, enjoying again the moisture-laden air near the splashing water. "Truly, I require nothing. Prince Hilarion is . . . overly attentive. You need not stay."

"Oh, miss – I mean, my lady – I daren't leave when the prince bids me stay."

"Would he be angry?" Nerine couldn't imagine Hilarion angry.

"Oh, no, miss. I mean, my lady. But he's such a fine man. Who could bear to disappoint him. Not me, miss. I mean, my lady."

Nerine blinked. "I don't mind if you call me 'miss.'"

"Oh, no, miss. I mean, my lady. Anyone can see you're high born, miss. I mean, my lady."

Nerine giggled. But could someone really tell Nerine was a princess just by looking? Was that why Hilarion had switched from calling her 'kyría' – lady – to 'kríousa' – sovereign lady?

She frowned. Why had Hilarion gotten that strange look on his face?

"Is something wrong, miss? I mean, my lady."

Nerine wondered what this servant might know. Not much, surely. But – "Have there been other visitors to the palace like me? With blond hair and hazel green eyes? And pale skin."

"Oh, no, miss. I mean, my lady. Just the one. Oh, and her attendants, miss. I mean, my lady."

"Do all –" she caught herself before she said 'land people' "– do all of the palace people have black hair or red hair?"

"Oh, no, miss. We have all colors, though blond do be more rare. The princess from Hellas were blond and her ladies too."

"She was the one, you spoke of?"

"Oh, yes, miss. I mean, milady. Kríousa Oraia were so friendly and kind."

Hmm. So it wasn't her blond hair – her greeny blond hair – that had caught Hilarion's attention.

She took a deep breath of the deliciously moist air. And then she heard Altairos calling her.

"Nerine! Nerine! Cook has collected such a luncheon for us!" He burst out of the corridor down which he'd disappeared earlier. Three manservants followed him: one with a small table, one with a wicker hamper, and one with a tray holding a silver carafe and two goblets.

Altairos plumped down beside Nerine. "I think it took longer than I realized. When Cook understood I had a guest, he brought out every delicacy he had on hand. Were you horribly bored?"

Nerine shook her head. "It's lovely here."

Altairos noticed the maidservant. "Oh! Jihene's been looking after you. Good."

"I met your brother Hilarion. He was really nice, but . . . he doesn't sit still much, does he?"

Altairos looked surprised. "Yes! That's him exactly. He never sits still. Hates to." He tipped his head sideways. "You notice a lot, Nerine."

He sounded approving, but Nerine felt uncomfortable. Like his older brother, Altairos could bring a lot of focus to his attention. She knew that, but she was used to him focusing on other things, not on her.

The maidservant interrupted Nerine's discomfort. "Prince Altairos, shall I stay? Do you or miss, I mean, my lady, need me?"

Altairos started. Had he forgotten she was present? "Thank you for attending my friend while I was gone, Jihene." He smiled. "But I'm back, and I suspect my lady mother needs you."

"Oh, yes, my prince. Thank you, and thank you, miss. I mean, my lady." Jihene bobbed a curtsy and hastened away.

The manservants had placed the table before Nerine and unpacked the hamper, then set the empty wicker box against the wall by the doorway when they went out.

"Nerine, you've never tasted pomegranate juice, have you? It's so sweet, you'll love it!" Altairos was pouring from the carafe as he spoke and serving from the various platters to fill her bowl and then his.

She raised the goblet to her nose, inhaling the rich berry scent of the juice and appreciating its deep magenta color. She sipped, and her eyes flew wide. The flavor was intense and as sweet as Altairos had said. He was watching her, enjoying her enjoyment.

"Good?" he asked.

She sipped again and swallowed. "Better than good. Amazing!"

The food was different than their picnic fare as well, and eaten with silver spoons. The dishes featured a variety of new sauces – cinnamon and sage and pistachio – and were delicate, too much so to survive rattling around in a basket for half the day before being eaten. There were pastries shaped like flowers, savory morsels topped with roe, and fluffy baked eggs.

"Your brother said he was embarking upon a sea voyage," said Nerine. Would Altairos miss him? He seemed fond of his brothers.

"Oh, he always is."

"Always? He doesn't stay home?"

Altairos laughed. "Pappa says he's the wild one. That the temple never would have worked for him."

Nerine couldn't help thinking of Xianthe, her own wild sibling. Nerine gave Xianthe a wide berth, but Altairos didn't seem worried by Hilarion. "Your father intended Hilarion for the priesthood?"

"No, Mamma did. That's what Calla says. But everyone knew it wouldn't do before he took his first step."

"Your father doesn't mind?"

"He says he has four sober sons and doesn't need another. And Hilarion is anything but sober."

Nerine had to agree, but couldn't quite imagine how Hilarion could be allowed to shirk his royal duties. Her own siblings were expected to prepare for important roles. Eilidh would attend Queen Hera on Mount Olympus. Tyr would guard the welfare of the Tyrrhenian Sea, just as Mother did the Ionian Sea. There were no plans as yet for Xianthe, but they would come in time.

"So Prince Hilarion just . . . roams?" It sounded lovely. Nerine wished that *she* could just roam.

"Yes, exactly. But he brings home surprising treasure sometimes."

"Gold?"

"Better than gold. Oh, once he did drag home a chest of antique coins from ancient Sumer." His tone was offhand, but his eyes glowed. Ancient coins sounded pretty interesting to Nerine, but Altairos had other brotherly feats to boast of. "We're at peace with the people of Selinunte, on Sikelia, you know" – no, Nerine didn't know – "all because of Hilarion. While knocking around Galatia, he made friends with this guy who could play any musical instrument. They were like brothers, and then it turned out he was the son of the archon of Selinunte."

Nerine was impressed. The sea people had known only peace for centuries, but the oldest legends told of a time when the kings of the Aegean fought the kings of the Adriatic and the waves ran red with blood. If Hilarion had brought peace to the land people of Zakynthos, he had done a mighty deed.

"And he's always doing things like that," continued Altairos. "Following his latest curiosity and then turning up something valuable, like the time he discovered a new design for ship anchors that hold better in rough water." Altairos grinned. "I don't think Pappa regrets the priesthood at all."

"What will you do? When you grow up?" she asked.

"I don't know. My oldest brother already helps father rule Zakynthos. And my next three brothers command the warfleets. Pappa says there's plenty of time before I need worry about it. What about you? Do your parents have plans for you? The way Pappa and Mamma had plans for Hilarion?"

Nerine laughed. "No. They're the same as your pappa, saying I have time and to spare. I'm glad, I think."

"Me, too." Altairos gulped the last of his pomegranate juice. "Let's go outside. Are you finished?"

She snagged a last morsel of pork topped with caper spread, finished her own juice, and nodded. "Let's go!"

⟳

The gardens of the palace were a wonderful place to play cache-and-dash. They named a large fountain with a sculpted swordfish as "home" and the chaser stood there, eyes closed, counting. But there were so many more places to hide – to "cache" oneself – than there were at the shore. Winding hedges, clustered shrubberies, even nooks in the pedestals of statuary. And it was easier to move from hiding spot to hiding spot and then dash for the fountain, hoping to get there before the chaser tagged you.

They played until the shadows lengthened in the late afternoon.

"This has been the best day ever," said Nerine as they sat on a bench overlooking the ravine toward the beacon tower.

"Let's do it again," suggested Altairos. "There's so much more to see. I can show you the weaving rooms and the throne room and the olive presses. We can walk through the city, down to the harbor. Do come again, Nerine!"

It all sounded interesting. Nerine loved the land. "My next day without lessons," she promised.

And then it was time to go home to the reef.

Just as her very first day ashore with Altairos had ended with family uproar, so did this one. Although everything was peaceful when she arrived home. The uproar came later at the intimate family dinner that Mother and Father had arranged, wanting to hear about their children's adventures during the day.

They gathered in the smallest dining parlor, an irregular chamber within rust-colored coral, with a round bronze table tucked into a nook, and a sea sponge-cushioned bench around one side. Mother and Father tied the bench sashes over their laps and then secured little Agnippe between them. Xianthe snagged the other spot next to Father, which meant Nerine had to settle for the one next to Mother. Which was all right, just not her first choice. Eilidh and Tyr took the places across from the bench, anchoring themselves with the usual toe loops in the floor.

Tyr dominated the conversation at first.

He'd gone to the deeps with the warriors, in search of a sea chariot lost in their great grandfather's time. The sea floor of the deeps was too far below the surface to be safe for sea folk, cold and dark and crushing with the pressure of the water. But a shoal lay toward the north, reachable by a long swim. And one of the couriers from the Ligurian Sea had sighted what looked like wreckage in that shoal.

Tyr and the warriors went to see if it might be the lost chariot, along with the treasure it had carried – the dowry for a princess. It seemed unlikely. The chariot had gone down in the deeps beyond the shoal, and the deeps rarely gave up prey. But currents sometimes do strange things.

"It *was* the long lost chariot!" Tyr reported excitedly. "We're going to go back for it with Leem and Phorn" – two of the strongest and friendliest of the palace dolphins – "and drag it home. I can't wait!"

"The *warriors* are going back. *You* will attend your tutor in the schoolroom," corrected Father.

"Please?" pleaded Tyr. "Father, nothing like this will turn up ever again! I want to be there!"

"Hmm." Was Father really considering it? Tyr was such a shirker, and Father knew it. But Father was indulgent, too.

"There wasn't any treasure though," admitted Tyr.

Once the servants brought the meal – an assortment of fish morsels and different sea vegetables, skewered to a framework that made the food take the form of a giant swordfish – Mother shushed Tyr to give Agnippe a chance to talk.

Her babble about the schools of mackerel and the way their herder made them swim in formations wasn't especially interesting, but Nurse came to collect her early for her sleep circle. Nerine supposed it was only fair Agnippe got to have her say, and father seemed genuinely interested. He didn't play favorites.

The uproar came after Agnippe was gone – it was good she was gone – when Eilidh was going on about choosing jewelry to take with her to Mount Olympus. Nerine couldn't believe Eilidh had spent her free day that way: how tedious! And listening to her was almost more boring than listening to Agnippe, who didn't know how to tell a story properly.

Although it was beginning to occur to Nerine that she was going to be in trouble when it was her own turn. What would she say, if she didn't want to tell about Altairos and her visit to his palace on land? And she didn't want to tell. She wasn't quite sure why, but she just knew that her friendship with a prince of Zakynthos wouldn't be received well.

If Mother and Father knew about it, they'd put a stop to it.

Nurse was comfortable with Nerine's freedom, but Mother and Father wouldn't be. They thought she stayed to the lagoon, and she didn't. When they found out –

She'd lose her land visits. She'd lose her friend. She'd lose a part of her life that . . . she *couldn't* lose, *mustn't* lose. If she couldn't go to the shore – if she couldn't see Altairos – she couldn't bear it. She just couldn't.

But if she didn't tell the truth, what *would* she say?

∼

While Eilidh droned on about how she couldn't decide which gemstone she thought the most beautiful, there came a sudden stir in the hall outside the dining parlor. Voices murmured. The water surged from vigorous stroking. And then the palace major-domo stood in the doorway, announcing a visitor.

"Neomar, herald bearing a message from His Most Imperial and Majestic Eminence The Emperor Poseidon, Your Majesties and Your Highnesses."

The major-domo bowed and the herald swept in.

The people of the Outer Sea tended to be slightly bigger and more pigmented than those of the Middle Sea. Neomar bulked large and muscular, with skin so darkly green as to appear almost black. He wore his silver hair in a short, clubbed braid. His breastplate and belt matched his hair.

His bow was perfunctory – less graceful by far than the major-domo's – but he spoke proper greetings before making his announcement.

"His Most Imperial and Majestic Eminence The Emperor Poseidon requires seven young and beautiful maidens to return his seraglio to its proper complement. He requests and requires each of his vassal kings to search his domain for suitable candidates for the honor. Any royal daughters of an age will receive special consideration. Send word when Your Majesty's choice is made, and the imperial palace will dispatch an entourage to accompany the chosen one or ones to the Outer Sea."

Before the disturbance to their family dinner – a rarity – Mother had relaxed so far as to lean against Father's shoulder and to clasp Nerine's hand, smiling gently while she listened to Eilidh's challenges with jewelry and other elements of her trousseau.

She'd straightened when the herald entered. The moment he uttered the words "seven young and beautiful," her hand nearly crushed Nerine's, its grip tightened so abruptly.

Nerine glanced up at her face.

Mother's eyes had narrowed, her lips straightened, and her nostrils and spiracles pinched in, whitened. She opened her mouth to speak, but Father touched her wrist and she remained silent. With difficulty.

Father spoke all the appropriate acknowledgements to the herald and then dismissed him to his rest.

Then Mother loosed her rant. "Oh! Insufferable! As though any maiden superlatively beautiful desires only the pleasure of her imperial and sovereign lord. As though *you* need only find one sufficiently lovely and choose her. As though *every* emperor and king should keep a harem to support his dignity and comfort. Oh!"

"Well, our imperial master has always kept one," said Father apologetically. "And he does restock rather regularly."

"How can you, Meren! It's disgusting!" Mother sounded angry with the whole world, not just with Father and with the Emperor of the Ocean.

"What's a sera- . . . a seraglio?" asked Eilidh.

Tyr looked curious, too.

Nerine didn't have any more idea of what the word meant than they did, but it must be something pretty awful to make Mother lose her cool.

"They'll need to know sometime," said Father, glancing inquiringly at Mother.

Mother's hand around Nerine's relaxed. "What would you tell them, then?" she demanded. "That the sovereign of the salt waters finds himself uncomfortable unless he is attended by one hundred sublime naiads at all times?"

"Something like that," answered Father.

Mother drew herself up, sitting taller than tall, and cast an irritated look at Father. Nerine didn't see how that was an answer, but Father took it as one, because he embarked on an explanation.

"Emperor Poseidon's seraglio is comprised of one hundred nymphs between the ages of sixteen and twenty-one. They do not attend him at all times, but merely during his intervals of leisure – not that he has many."

Well, thought Nerine, that didn't sound bad at all. *Mother* had a retinue of six ladies herself. Indeed, Queen Hera possessed a similar cortege, and Eilidh would become part of it in a few years. Nerine didn't see why a man would want all ladies in his entourage. Father had only men in his. And why one hundred? How would Poseidon ever find enough for them to do?

"You'll have to tell them more than that," criticized Mother. "Or else we'll have our own Xianthe running off to join up! Thank the blessings she's too young!"

Xianthe grinned at this.

Mother frowned.

"What your mother means," continued Father, "is that the ladies of the Emperor's seraglio have personal duties to Poseidon that many would find unpleasant were they performed for anyone save the Emperor."

"Like what?" asked Tyr.

Mother directed a glance of alarm toward Father.

Father's eyes twinkled. "Such as massaging his sore muscles or accompanying him to the surging closet."

"Eew!" burst out Eilidh. "Father, surely that's not true."

Mother recovered herself. "Certainly, it's true, Eilidh. Emperors – and some kings – possess far more dignity than more ordinary individuals and do nothing unaccompanied."

Tyr looked boggled by this information. Nerine *felt* boggled by it.

Surging closets were cleverly contrived chambers, small and private, that shaped a flow of water from a channel in the ceiling to a channel in the floor. It carried wastes away very neatly. Why would anyone want company there? But apparently Poseidon did. Nerine felt sorry for the maidens of the seraglio. At least there *were* one hundred. She hoped that surging closet duty got passed around. No wonder Mother was angry. Nerine felt a little angry herself.

"Are we a more casual royal household?" Nerine wondered aloud.

Father laughed. "We are. That's why your sister Eilidh has so many lessons in protocol. But Eilidh" – Eilidh's eyes widened in alarm – "you need not worry that Queen Hera requires company for her necessities. Her palace is every bit as grand as Poseidon's, but she guards her privacy more stringently than he."

Eilidh wrinkled her forehead. "*Are* there surging closets on Mount Olympus? How can there be? It's not under the sea."

"Hah!" shouted Xianthe. "*I* know the answer to that!"

"Do you?" said Father.

Mother stared down her nose.

"Yes!" insisted Xianthe. "Queen Hera has a water closet just like the one that the queen of ancient Kréte once had. Her maids would pour a whole pitcher of water into the basin, washing the wastes away through a pipe at the bottom."

Nerine wrinkled her nose. That didn't sound as nice as a surging closet, where the water ran continuously. And if only queens had closets such as Xianthe described, how did everyone else manage? It must be nasty.

Father smiled. "That is correct, Xianthe, although several other land queens have similar arrangements in the present day."

Xianthe looked smug.

"However," continued Father, "Poseidon's seraglio has other personal duties that you will learn about when you are older. Your mother feels that these duties are even less suitable" – Mother stiffened – "and, indeed, I see her point." Mother relaxed again, if merely lack of alarming rigidity could be considered relaxed.

"I can't imagine anything more personal than the surging closet," muttered Tyr.

"When you're older –" began Father.

Mother interrupted him. "Tyr. And all the rest of you. Listen to me carefully. Public speculation upon the personal habits of Our Most Imperial and Majestic Eminence The Emperor Poseidon would be most unbecoming and improper from you. Should you have more questions or concerns, you may *privately* ask your father or me. But you must not speak of this with anyone else, or among yourselves where you may be overheard. *Do you understand?*"

Nerine nodded urgently. Yes, she understood. Poseidon, when everything was said and done, had the power to do anything he pleased. Being her father's daughter and subject would not protect her, if Poseidon grew angry. And she already knew that Poseidon did grow angry.

"Is the Emperor not a good ruler?" questioned Tyr.

"Tyr." Mother's tone turned dangerous.

Indeed, questioning Poseidon's fitness as a ruler was surely more unwise than commenting on his personal habits.

"No, it's a good question," said Father. "Although, think, Tyr. What did you just do?"

"I, um, speculated about the Emperor?"

"Good boy."

"But you said we could ask you and Mother."

"I did. But be mindful of what you say and where, Tyr."

Tyr looked thoughtful. Nerine suspected that he did realize what Father was trying to teach: you needed to be prudent when talking about people more powerful than you. And Poseidon was more powerful than everyone except the Almighty Zeus. And maybe Hades, the Emperor of the Underworld.

"Our Sovereign Poseidon knows everything there is to know about the World Ocean. He makes no mistakes regarding the sea. And were the sea to be ill regulated, the land would not long survive. The wellbeing of all rests upon Our Emperor's decisions."

"But you criticized the overly strong currents through the Pillars of Herakles," protested Tyr. "That killed all those poor sailors."

"No, I didn't. When Poseidon sent the currents of the Outer Sea through the Pillars, he undoubtedly had good reason."

"But Poseidon did it because he was angry."

"No, not *because*. He is a wrathful lord, no question, but his wrath serves his purposes."

"But the poor sailors!" cried Tyr.

"Yes, the poor sailors," agreed Father. "Glad be I that I must not make such perilous choices."

"The Middle Sea has storms," said Tyr.

"It does, but they are visited from the sky, not from the waters," said Father. "My realm is benign, especially when compared to the wider waves under Poseidon's control. And I am grateful."

"Huh." Tyr's eyes acquired a speculative look. "Maybe that's why the Emperor needs special attendance. Like his seraglio." He shook his head. "Surging companions. Huh."

"Perhaps indeed." Father winked.

Mother looked disapproving.

"But what will you do about the Emperor's request?" asked Eilidh.

"Send a message, in about a month's time, that there are no suitable young ladies."

"Will that work?" Eilidh sounded astonished.

"Of course," Father answered easily. "The age range is quite narrow, and only perfection will do."

Eilidh's spiracles widened in her relief. "Thank the blessings! What if *I* had to go!"

Mother straightened. "*That* would never happen. *You* are promised to Queen Hera, and no daughter of ours will ever even visit Poseidon's imperial palace, rest assured."

Father nodded. "Indeed. Your mother and I are as one on that."

"What if one of us wanted to go?" asked Xianthe.

"We would not permit it," said Father gently.

Mother pressed the clicker at her waist. *Click!* "Time you retired, all of you." Her gaze swept from Xianthe across Eilidh and Tyr, and then around to Nerine. "Swim along."

Nerine collected a hug from Father on her way out. She loved how solid and safe he felt.

"So, what did you do with your day free of lessons?" he asked.

Oh, no!

She'd thought she'd escaped that dilemma entirely, saved by Poseidon's herald. But Father never played favorites. Indeed, she didn't think he *had* a favorite. He loved all five of his children, and everyone but Nerine had talked about their doings.

"I . . . I practiced walking on land," she gasped. Which was true, even though it wasn't her purpose in going ashore.

"Really?" said Father in an admiring tone. He set her away from him, but kept his hands on her shoulders. "You went to shallow water? How did you do?" He was genuinely curious, not judging.

"I didn't just go to shallow water." She'd passed through the shallows, yes, but not lingered. "I walked on land."

Father laughed. "Excellent! My little prodigy!" He pulled her in for another quick hug. "You must be tired then. To sleep with you!"

And that was that. She'd escaped after all, just not the way she'd hoped. But without an outright lie.

～

10 ~ Running Risks

SOME MOONS AFTER the visit of Poseidon's herald, Nerine and her dolphin friend Mai'ip swam toward shore in the afternoon. The sun shone down through the waves strongly, creating a dazzling ripple pattern on the sand below and turning the water brightest turquoise.

Mai'ip bent his dark, soulful eye upon her – that meant mischief, in him – gave a mighty lash of his tail fluke, and surged upward. He breached the sea's surface, clearing it entirely, and smacked down in a fizz of bubbles to circle Nerine, gloating.

Nerine laughed and kicked upward herself, not with her legs only, but using a whole body undulation with a lot more power. As she neared the point where water kissed air, she swept her arms down, flying out of a wave crest to mid-thigh before she fell back.

She never could clear the surface completely, but Mai'ip teased her enough that neither could she give up trying.

The dolphin veered away as they approached the shallows, and Nerine came to land alone. She waded ashore through the gentle surf of low tide. Myriad small shells flecked the wet sand, crunching under her footsteps. Mai'ip breached again from the deeper waters, and Nerine waved both her arms in acknowledgement.

The air hung hot and still. She dried almost instantaneously.

Just when she reached the garlands of seaweed left at the highwater mark, Altairos popped over the dunes and dashed down the slope to greet her, hair tousled and face flushed with excitement.

"Nerine! The tide's lower than it's ever been before! I could see it from the cliff top! Some of the rocks –" he gestured toward the tide pools where the cliffs drew near the water "– are completely dry!"

"So?" She kept her tone nonchalant, but she couldn't help grinning. She loved it when Altairos arrived in the grip of a new idea for fun.

He bounced up and down, and then – yelling, "C'mon!" over his shoulder – took off running.

She caught up with him before he'd gone too many strides and they raced side by side along the beach. "Where are we going? What are we doing?" she asked.

"I think we can get all the way around that big rock that shuts off the rest of the shore in this direction. Who knows what we'll find! There could be anything there, because the cliff is so steep and there's no beach. No one goes there. There could be pirate treasure! Or a secret cave! Or the bones of a sea serpent!"

Nerine quickened her footfalls. She doubted they'd find the skeleton of a sea serpent – Father's warriors would have said something, and surely they'd know. But there might be a cave. Or, even better, a cave *with* pirate treasure!

"What kinds of treasure do pirates have?" she wondered aloud.

"Hah!" shouted Altairos. "Magical toys from Phoiníke, frozen water from Thoúle, and unicorn horns from Indus!"

Some of that sounded as unlikely to Nerine as sea serpent bones, but surely there would be something amazing beyond that massive boulder – bigger than Calla's cottage – where no one had ever gone before.

They had to slow down when they reached the sunbaked rocks above the tide pools, picking their way around the uneven levels of the evaporated basins and over the roughness of encrusting barnacles. They paused a moment in a shallow skimming of residual water to cool their bare feet. The rocks were uncomfortably hot.

Only the narrowest margin lay exposed at the base of the massive barricading boulder. Occasionally the slap of a careless wave moistened the ledge. They went single file, Altairos first.

As he rounded the last bend of the meager pathway, Altairos came to a dead halt.

"Ooh!" he breathed.

～

Nerine tried to peek over Altairos' shoulder, couldn't – she didn't have the right angle – and poked him. "Hey! Let *me* see!" she demanded.

He stepped forward, and then she echoed his, "Ooh!"

Sheer red cliffs enclosed a diminutive inlet of clear turquoise water, about the size of a ballroom – spacious were it within a palace, but tiny as a scene in the great outdoors. Nerine and Altairos stood on one side of the inlet's opening to the sea. Across the small channel loomed more cliffs, but it was a feature at the back of the cove that riveted Nerine's gaze.

Carved into the rock were the steps and columns and sculpture-adorned friezes of a temple front, with balconies and column atop column going all the way up to the rugged and heavy overhang crowning the cliff. Between the lower columns, a shaded anteroom stretched back to the deeper black of a great doorway.

"Altairos!" breathed Nerine. "It's better than a cave!"

He shook his head in wonderment, apparently speechless.

A gull squawked, amidst the murmuring rush of the tide. The sun beat down on their heads, and the scent of hot rock blended with the clean salt odor of the sea. A curl of water slopped across Nerine's toes.

As she stared at the temple, a trickle of rubble released from the capital of an upper column, rattling down the facade until – *plink, plink, plink* – the stones fell into the water.

Only then did Nerine notice that time and weather had scoured every cranny and every knob of the temple. Jagged cracks crawled across the frieze. The pediment was missing large chunks. Several of the columns were mere stumps, and one of a pair – shaped to resemble beautiful women, caryatids they were called – leaned precariously out from the facade.

"I – I don't think we should explore it, do you?" said Nerine. She wished they *could* explore it. What might lie hidden inside? *Temple* treasure might be even more exciting than pirate treasure. But the whole thing looked like it might collapse at the mere brush of a fingertip, roaring down in an avalanche to the sea.

Altairos turned toward her, the same mix of elation and regret on his face that she felt in her heart.

"No, no," he said slowly, "I don't suppose we should." He grinned. "But I want to!"

Nerine studied the ruin, envisioning herself and Altairos swimming over to its steps. Even if they dodged the pebbles crumbling from the exterior, the interior was likely just as dangerous. No, they really couldn't explore it, but she hated to tear herself away. The tide might never fall this low again.

Altairos continued to look over her shoulder, out to sea. "Hey!" he exclaimed. "There's Mai'ip! He's coming in!"

She turned her head.

The dolphin surged toward them in the effortless and swooping glide of his kind. Then he dove toward the rocky, ripple-patterned floor of the inlet. Nerine followed him with her gaze, down and down through the pulsing sea to a litter of rubble. There, in water three times as deep as she was tall, lay a balustrade, there a column, and there a huge triangular piece of pediment.

What was Mai'ip doing? Had he visited this cove before?

A sharp crack sounded in the air.

"No!" gasped Altairos.

Nerine jerked her head up just as the leaning caryatid swung out and away from its mooring, falling headfirst past three balconies, and plunging into the waves with the low, hollow sound of massive bulk entering water. The stone statue plummeted to the inlet floor like a javelin hurled by a warrior – slowed not one wit by the depth, surely it should slow – hurtling to a stop against the colossal chunk of pediment.

And pinning Mai'ip just behind his dorsal fin.

～

Nerine screamed and leaped for the water.

She felt Altairos' hand grip her elbow as her feet left the rock ledge. They splashed in together, a tangle of arms and legs enfolded by the sea, like warm liquid light. Then Altairos was yanking her back to the surface and yelling, his face close to hers.

"Nerine, you can't! The other caryatid is poised to go! You can't! Come back!"

But she could only think of Mai'ip, trapped and unable to surface. Dolphins needed air like land dwellers. Mai'ip had no spiracles that would open, no gateway between lungs and gills that could swing from inhaling air to imbibing water. He would last longer than Altairos – perhaps the time it would take to knit half a handspan of ribband, no more – and then he would drown.

Nerine scrabbled at Altairos' clutching fingers, prying them off her arm.

"I must!" she shouted. "Let *go*!" She couldn't believe her best friend was thwarting her in this. How *could* he? She had to save Mai'ip.

"I won't let you!" Altairos shouted, hauling her back toward the ledge.

Fury ignited within her. She would never forgive him, never.

Desperate, she fought, splashing mightily, arms flailing, legs kicking, straining to see Mai'ip all the while. Was the dolphin moving? Had the falling caryatid stunned him? Was he alive? She'd lost Pheep. She *couldn't* lose Mai'ip.

Oh, blessings, help!

Nerine's foot connected solidly with Altairos' belly, and then she was free, diving for the sea floor as water flooded her spiracles and washed her gills, welcome and lifegiving. Heart pounding, she raced over a cracked fragment of balustrade, around the statue of a hippocampus, and under a pillar tilted against an undersea boulder, darting to where the leaning caryatid pinned Mai'ip to the massive chunk of pediment.

The dolphin lay alarmingly still, but his eyes were open and no stream of bubbles rushed from his blowhole.

Nerine darted to him and laid her trembling hand against his flank above one flipper. "Mai'ip? Mai'ip?"

He quivered, and she realized he was afraid.

How could those dark eyes, so soulful in mischief, look so terrified now?

"I'll save you," she declared. "I promise."

And then she tried to figure out how, patting him to see if he were really unhurt, noting how tightly the stone gripped him behind his dorsal fin, and peeking over the caryatid – which seemed about three times larger close up than it had while falling – to find that the flesh above Mai'ip's tail fluke was even more cruelly squeezed.

The caryatid would have to move, that was all, and Nerine would have to move it.

She wedged herself between the flat side of the pediment and the caryatid's hip, and pushed.

Oh, blessings! The massive thing didn't move at all.

She wriggled, getting her back more firmly set against the stone and bringing her feet up, so that she could shove with both arms and legs.

Still nothing.

Panic bloomed in her belly. She *had* to move this stone lady. *Had* to.

She tried again. And when it didn't work, she moved to the other side, where Mai'ip's tail fluke emerged from his prison. The angles looked worse, but she had to try. She braced her back against the caryatid's thigh this time, thrusting against the pediment with her feet and hands.

Oh, gods! She was going to fail. If only Altairos were down here with her, pushing the obdurate stone at her side. Together they would shift it.

But she was alone, and Mai'ip was going to die because of it.

She buried her face in her hands.

～

The sounds of more rubble falling came to Nerine's ears – *plonk, plonk, plonk.*

Then a hand touched her shoulder, and she looked up.

Altairos hovered in the water before her, his cheeks puffed to hold air in his lungs, and gesturing urgently to her. He would push from this side. She should return to Mai'ip's head, where the angles of caryatid and pediment were better, and push there. Together they would free the dolphin.

Oh, blessings! She'd thought all was lost.

She'd thought Mai'ip would drown in front of her, while she watched, helpless.

She'd thought she faced this all alone.

But Altairos was here, just as she'd so intensely and frantically longed for him to be. He would save Mai'ip, just as he'd saved her, on their first meeting. He would make everything all right.

She dug her shoulders into her side of the pediment. She positioned her hands and feet against the rounded hip of the caryatid. And she pushed with everything that was in her.

This time – with Altairos pushing on the other side – she felt a little give in the adamant stone.

Yes, yes, yes! It was going to move. It was going to move. It was going – oh, blessings! – it had moved! Just a finger width, or two, but it was enough.

In a flash, Mai'ip was gone, a full body length from his rock fetter and streaking toward the surface and air.

She'd done it! *They'd* done it! Mai'ip was safe!

As she rejoiced, the caryatid's hip – right where her feet thrust against the curving stone – broke away. The pressure of her shoulders against the pediment hurled her feet first in the fragment's wake. And the statue fell instantly to its previous tilted stance, all its weight pressing against the massive pediment.

Nerine flailed twice, before regaining control of her position in the water.

And then she saw that everything was worse than before.

Much worse.

Disastrously worse.

The caryatid now pinned a fold of Altairos' tunic between its weighty thigh and the pediment.

Nerine was at his side faster than Mai'ip had bolted for the surface, tugging at that fold of tunic, wrestling it, hauling on it, anything and everything to get it loose.

It was no good.

Altairos shook his head and gestured for her to push at the caryatid again from the other side, while he pushed from his. But that was no good either. The trapped fabric at the waist of his tunic meant his poor angle was even worse. And the missing chunk of caryatid hip meant hers was too.

Oh, blessings!

She could have counted to a thousand while Mai'ip was caught, and still saved him at a thousand and one, but Altairos had so much less time. And he'd already used most of it up freeing Mai'ip. Did he have even a count of thirty left? Twenty? Ten?

She darted back to his side.

If that tunic wouldn't pull free, she'd rip it free.

Altairos' cheeks were still puffed with air, but his eyes held a look of strain, and his hands – ripping at his tunic with hers – were frenzied.

Oh, gods! Oh, gods!

Of course a prince of Zakynthos would have clothing made of the finest stuffs, tight woven and beautiful and strong.

Without a knife or something sharp, they'd never tear that captive fold free.

～

Horrendous visions swarmed Nerine's imagination.

Altairos gasping and choking on water.

Altairos lying pale and lifeless in the caryatid's embrace.

Scuttling crabs nibbling at his dear face. His bones sliding out of his tunic.

Dear. Gods.

Sliding out of his tunic!

She would slide him out living, if she did nothing more in all her days to come.

She placed her hands over his, to still their violent clawing, and to get his attention. His eyes were very, very wide when he looked at her, and a few bubbles clung to his nostrils. Oh, blessings!

She lifted his arms overhead and began to pull on his legs.

He got it instantly, and then he was helping, tugging the tunic over his head and shoulders, while she yanked the hem to his waist – he wore loin briefs underneath – and hauled on his ankles.

A moment later he was free.

Go! Go! She gestured with her whole body. Why did he wait?

He looked dazed. Would she need to carry him up to the air herself?

As she reached for him, a sudden shadow fell upon her, upon him too. It was large and growing larger: the silhouette of a gowned maiden, standing straight to support a temple frieze on her head.

Oh, blessings! The second caryatid, falling to crush them both.

Altairos had said it was ready to tumble after its sister.

Nerine hung in midwater, with nothing to push against. Mere swimming, no matter how powerful, would never beat the hurtling speed of the plunging stone. And Altairos drifted equally bereft – bewildered and trapped between Nerine and the pediment.

So much she saw in an instant.

And then some brutal force seized her – like the fist of a Titan or a thunderbolt of Lord Zeus – battering her ribs, tangling her together with Altairos, and thrusting them abruptly from here to there.

The low, hollow *gaahlunk* of a great mass entering water sounded. The plunging caryatid flashed past her feet in a fizzing cloud of bubbles. And the dolphin – the source of the explosive power that had saved them all – finished carrying her and Altairos up to the surface of the sea.

Nerine was laughing when her head broke into the air.

She and Altairos had saved Mai'ip.

And then Mai'ip had rescued his rescuers.

Beside her, Altairos gulped and wheezed, his tanned face a strange blue tint, while the dolphin held him above the water.

Nerine choked her hysteria down. Altairos needed land and needed it immediately. Mai'ip had angled them out of the cliff-encircled inlet and away from shore. They would need to clear the rocks of the tide pools, before they came to land.

Mai'ip did most of it, supporting Altairos and bearing him up, while Nerine swam alongside. When they reached the shallows, Nerine took Altairos from the dolphin and got him onto the beach. His legs tottered, but he could walk.

"G-g-gods, Nerine, what happened?" he stuttered, teeth chattering.

She shook her head, pulled his arm over her shoulder, and steered him toward Calla's cottage.

The wind had picked up, and the day was cooler. A faint haze of cloud, far overhead, softened the sun.

Calla took one look at Altairos, when they reached her terrace, and bundled him into bed with an extra blanket wrapped around him. She heated water for a warm mint infusion – its pure, sharp scent pierced the air – and fed it to Altairos spoonful by spoonful. Only when the color in his face looked normal did she relax. Nerine, hovering at her side, felt her own tension blow out of her at last.

When Altairos pushed the extra blanket off and sat up to look around him, Calla gave vent to some of her worry. "What in Hades were you up to, agoraki mou, to half drown yourself? Or was it the naïáda who pulled you to the bottom of the sea?"

Nerine stiffened. She gotten so used to Calla's affection that she forgotten Calla's initial reaction to her: dislike, distrust, and a firm intent to see her gone from Calla's nursling. Had Calla forgotten that she'd come to love and trust and approve of Nerine?

Nerine shivered.

Altairos, answering his old nurse cheerfully, seemed not to notice Calla's relapse. "Mana mou, there's the most amazing ruin just around the headland! I wish you could see it! It's carved out of the cliff and goes up and up to the very top." His eyes glowed with his enthusiasm. "I can't believe no one knows it's there, so close!"

Calla shook her head. "I might have known you'd discover it eventually." She sniffed.

"You knew!" Altairos' jaw dropped.

Calla looked at him resignedly. "There's no keeping up with you, is there? If I'd told you of the old temple and forbidden you to visit it, you'd have sought it out the next day. But when I kept my mouth closed, you found the place anyway. I suppose Nerine had the saving of you rather than the drowning of you, did she not?" Calla glanced apologetically at her. "Does my foolish agoraki mou owe his breath to you?"

Nerine cleared her throat. "It – it was a little more complicated than that."

After Calla heard the full story – as best as Nerine could tell it – Calla said, "Humph! I can't decide if the pair of you are better together or apart. You get each other into and out of trouble so fast there's no knowing!" But kindness had returned to her face, and her mouth twitched upward as she left the room.

Nerine sat quietly, staring at the floor.

Then she looked up, surveying Altairos' face. His cheeks were a little flushed and his eyes alive. He looked altogether recovered from his ordeal.

"I'm sorry!" she burst out, at the very moment when the same words burst from him. Laughter bubbled up in her, and he laughed with her, their laughter dissolving into giggles of relief.

"I almost got all three of us killed," she said when they subsided. She could imagine it all too vividly. What if that second caryatid had fallen a moment earlier, while she and Altairos labored to free Mai'ip? She and Altairos and Mai'ip would all have been crushed.

"Nerine, don't," said Altairos, almost as though he knew what she were thinking. "I was right, but you were right, too. I didn't understand about dolphins."

She frowned at him, puzzled. "What?"

"I thought they were like fish," he explained. "That they could breathe underwater. Like you. I thought we had time. I thought we could figure out some clever way – with levers or something – to get Mai'ip free. I didn't know he needed help right away."

"Oh." She couldn't imagine how he'd played with Mai'ip for so many moons without noticing that Mai'ip breathed the air, but somehow he'd done it.

"So we were both right and both wrong?" she said.

Altairos nodded decisively. "It was dangerous, and it had to be done right away."

"I'll forgive you, if you'll forgive me?" she suggested. She suddenly remembered her kick to Altairos' belly and her private vow that she'd never forgive him for hindering her rescue of Mai'ip. She felt unsettled, as though she were a fishnet full of right and wrong all jumbled together. Would she ever sort herself out?

"It might have been better, if we hadn't fought about it first," said Altairos. He laughed again, a brighter sound than his – and her – helpless giggles a moment ago. "I think Calla would say, 'Cut another notch in your roster of close calls.' It's not like we really knew what we were doing."

Now *that* she could agree with wholeheartedly. *She* had decidedly *not* known what she was doing.

But she thought about the day's mishaps later that night, as she lay curled in her sleep circle in the dim glow of the laval brazier. Altairos had been such a friend through all their innocent fun and games on the beach and in the water. And a good guide in their first exploration of the land palace. She'd never questioned his judgement before. There'd been no call to. He'd saved her on their first meeting, and she'd trusted him ever since.

Today his judgement had been both right and wrong. Oddly, it made her trust him even more.

Except . . . she decided that further adventures should be inland, where Altairos knew all there was to know. The shore, where the sea caressed the land, was too chancy a place – neither sea nor land in itself – to trust any mortal to know all that needed knowing.

⁓

11 ~ Gifts of the Sea

HER VISITS ASHORE with Altairos were more varied from that time onward. Oh, they still *played* on the beach and in the surf. And they spent many intervals in Calla's cottage – Nerine helping Calla with the weaving and fine needlework, Altairos whittling – sometimes all three of them playing abacus, a counting game with pebbles, dice, and a tray painted with thin triangles.

But they also made the climb to Altairos' palace often.

The vertical looms in the palace weaving rooms fascinated Nerine. They were much more elaborate devices than the simple ground loom used by Calla, and the cloths woven on them were more complex. Indeed, the most complex created pictures with the threads, destined to adorn the walls of the island's temples – non-ruined ones, located in the city and in the countryside.

Even more strange were the workrooms where olives were transformed into the oil that gave many land foods their unusual flavor.

The newly picked olives were washed in great vats. Altairos said that oil pressed from the unwashed drupes tasted like soil, not nice at all.

Workers scooped the washed olives out of the vats with pierced buckets, the water draining away through the holes, and dumped the olives into a stone basin in the next room. There, an ox yoked to a wooden beam walked around and around the basin, causing two massive grindstones to roll and crush the olives into a paste.

The paste was spread across disks made of hemp fibers, the disks stacked six high and pressed by a lever weighed down with hanging boulders. The liquid thus extracted – a mix of oil and water – was allowed to sit until the oil floated to the top, to be skimmed off and stored in amphorae.

"They have to wash the stone basin and the grindstones and the hemp mats after each batch," said Altairos. "Or else the oil tastes bad in a different way. They're very careful. Our oil is the best!"

Nerine had to agree. The palace foods always tasted wonderful to her.

Nerine and Altairos eventually spread their explorations to the city, which lapped against the north wall of the palace and spread down the slope to a magnificent harbor. The city was a maze of twisting streets and stairways through modest whitewashed buildings, housing shops, storage rooms, workrooms, and – of course – the people living there.

Nerine loved the marketplace best of all, with its squares of canvas strung overhead to cast patches of shade and the vivid contents of the stalls: deep purple aubergines, bright red peppers, and dark green courgettes; aromatic sesame paste, fermented leeks, and ground cinnamon; greasy sheep fleeces and fine-spun goat yarns; and the lively sellers with their calling voices and alert eyes.

She would have visited every day, if she could. And since she couldn't, she begged Altairos to take her there often when she walked ashore.

At home, she learned lessons as usual, moving into more advanced mathematics, as well as learning the tongues of the land peoples living along the shores of the Middle Sea. The Aramaya, spoken in Persia, had difficult sounds uttered in the very back of the throat. The Metremenkemi of the delta people in Aegyptus was easier, with short syllables and lots of 'm' and 'n' sounds. While the Punic language of the citizens of Carthage, just to the west and very near, possessed trills, like her own language of the sea.

Most startling was the Ionic, used by the traders in any region near the salt water, but originating in Hellas, the peninsula between the Aegean Sea and the Ionian. Ionic proved to be *Ionikós*, the language Nerine had been speaking with Altairos for the last three, almost four, years.

She got very good at Ionic, very fast, and her tutor was pleased.

Eilidh and Tyr began to learn the mastery of their "water gifts," a phrase Nerine had heard often, but had only the haziest idea of what it meant or what was involved. She knew Tyr would need it in order to successfully sustain and protect the Tyrrhenian Sea when he was invested as its guardian.

All three of them continued to practice the transition from breathing water to breathing air. And since Nerine had confessed to practicing on her own, no one was surprised when she moved about confidently on land, without stumbles or falls.

Eventually Xianthe joined them. Her negative reaction to breathing air surpassed even Eilidh's. But she was braver, clinging to Father merely so as to keep herself above the water, while she coughed and gasped and turned blue in the face, because her gills were slow to settle, her lungs slow to open.

But she grew practiced at the transition rapidly, and once ashore, surpassed both Eilidh and Tyr rapidly with her ease of striding and sprinting.

Soon after Nerine passed the twelfth anniversary of her birth, Mother announced that she herself would initiate Xianthe, Nerine, *and* Agnippe into the wielding of their "water gifts."

~

"Illustrious Panagiotas" – he was the "water gift" teacher – "is all very well for Tyr and Eilidh, but Agnippe, especially, needs some unusual coaching." Mother lifted her lovely jaw, the better to look down her nose. "And it will be a treat for me to enjoy more time with my youngest daughters."

She'd sought them in the nursery, so Nurse nudged Agnippe, who was playing with her favorite doll, combing its long hair. "Heed your mother," she murmured, urging Agnippe to pay attention. It was unusual for Mother's decrees to include her youngest child, so Agnippe had reason to carry on with her own activity.

"Isn't Agnippe too little?" asked Nerine.

Xianthe was fourteen (and wearing belt and pectoral, just as her elder siblings did). It made sense that she and Nerine might be ready. But Agnippe was only eight.

Mother smiled graciously. She was always gracious, especially when she corrected someone. "Agnippe will benefit uniquely from her water gift, as you will see. Follow me, please."

She led them to a large, shadowy chamber on the reef face. Nerine had always assumed the space to be reserved for Father's warriors, a staging area where they prepared their weapons and their gear before embarking across the deeps. Apparently it served other purposes as well. She wondered if Eilidh and Tyr learned from Illustrious Galeno in this same spot.

Mother took her place in front of them, facing to one side so that her daughters confronted her flawless profile.

"Watch me," she instructed.

She closed her eyes, hanging peacefully in the water, rocked slightly from side to side, because the rooms on the reef face were more affected by the waves rolling in from the deeps than those on the lagoon side.

Mother raised her left hand, palm down and arm horizontal to the floor.

The water at her fingertips started to move, whitening with bubbles as it sped.

Nerine felt her eyes grow wide. Her mother was creating a current where none had flowed a moment ago.

Mother opened her eyes, and the gush of bubbles from her fingers grew furious, a powerful jet arcing through the calmer water of the vast, dim chamber. Then the spate lessened and died away.

Mother lowered her arm and turned to face them.

"What did you perceive?" she asked.

"Oh! I want to do that!" exclaimed Xianthe. "Me first! Me, me, me!"

"Tell me what you noticed, Xianthe."

"But, can I do it, too, Mother?" Xianthe persisted.

"In time."

Mother said no more, but Xianthe got the message and delivered what was wanted.

"I saw a disturbance in the water on the surface of your skin, and then it pushed away from your fingertips to move the water before it."

"Very good, Xianthe!" Mother sounded surprised. "That's precise and much more accurate than I would have expected."

Xianthe blushed. Nerine figured she must be more used to scolding than praise.

"What of you, Nerine? Agnippe? Did you see what Xianthe saw?"

Nerine shook her head. "It looked like you created motion in the water, but I couldn't see the beginning of it."

"Yes, that is more usual in a novice. And the finer perception is not necessary, although it's a promising sign."

Xianthe's cheeks flushed again.

"What of you, Agnippe?" Mother bent forward to encourage her youngest.

"How will this help me especially, Mamma? You said it would."

"Patience. You will understand soon enough. What did you see?"

"Just what Nerine saw." Agnippe bit her lip, regretful that she might not measure up.

Mother nodded. "The heart of the water gifts is water. And you, as daughters of the sea, bear a unique affinity for water. It is the womb from which you came, and it is the quietus to which you will return.

"You are so accustomed to water that you barely notice its caress on your skin, its embrace around your limbs, and its lifegiving flow through your spiracles and over your gills.

"Close your eyes and notice these sensations now. Give them your full attention and release yourself into them. Be one with the water."

Nerine had already closed her eyes and was following Mother's instructions as she spoke them.

The water was cooler in this reef face chamber than the water in the lagoon side rooms. Nerine let it rock her, swaying her body and lifting her limbs. She felt cradled and comforted, as though she rested in Father's embrace.

"Now focus on your hands," came Mother's voice. "Let your hands melt as though they were liquid, as though they were water, not flesh and bone."

Nerine's hands felt almost boneless. Had they become water? Were they the very stuff of the waves and the tides and the great body of Tethys herself?

Nerine cracked an eyelid open.

And screamed.

᷈

Her hands were still hands, her tapering fingers curving from gently cupped palms, the narrow backs extending from her slender wrists.

But they were translucent like the most diaphanous of jellyfish.

The moment she screamed and tensed, her hands regained their solidity. Not all at once, but in a swift progression from translucence to opacity to full density.

Nerine gasped as though her gills were failing to pull enough air from the water.

And then Mother was there, her arms around Nerine in an embrace, but her voice cool and serene as always. "Stop kicking and thrashing, Nerine. You're fine." Nothing perturbed Mother. Well, except maybe seraglios and harems.

Nerine's operculi spasmed in a weird hiccup, and then she gave a choked laugh.

"That's better." Mother stroked Nerine's hair. "Now let your spiracles do their work and the rest will follow in train."

Mother's calm was so strong – unshakeable – that Nerine could feel it spreading through her own body from the skin inward.

She became aware of her sisters close by and peering over Mother's shoulders.

"What happened?" they chorused, Xianthe startled and rude, Agnippe shy and scared.

"Your sister is one of the true daughters of Tethys. She achieves the form of water at the start of mastering her gift, rather than at the culmination of her mastery."

Agnippe's brow wrinkled. "What does that mean, Mamma?"

Mother laughed, a lovely rippling sound. "Nerine will show you."

"Oh, I can't!" If she had to do that again, she'd . . . she didn't know what she'd do, but the idea scared her silly.

"Of course you can," chided Mother. "Why ever not?"

"I . . . I . . . I –"

"What are you afraid of, Nerine?" Her voice was that strange combination of gentle and stern that only Mother could do.

"W-will I – will I just dissolve into the water?" Nerine's teeth were chattering. "L-like great grandfather. B-become one with the waves and go away forever?"

"Aah" – Mother drew the sound out like a sigh – "it is true that your great grandfather was a son of Okeanós. And it's also true that when we people of the sea grow weary in spirit, we give ourselves to the water to be borne on its currents and washed of our world weariness.

"But to be a daughter of Tethys or a son of Okeanós bestows greater control over the change rather than less."

Mother turned and moved, her arm still around Nerine's shoulders, but bringing Xianthe and Agnippe into her view.

"Your sister will have more choice over her transition than most. Just as great grandfather chose when he would leave flesh and bone behind."

Nerine felt reassured, but still confused. What *did* Mother mean?

"Did great grandfather die?" she asked.

Mother tilted her head. "What do you know of death?"

"Pheep" – her first dolphin friend, before Mai'ip – "died."

Mother nodded. "True. And we of the sea can die. Crushed by a tidal wave, eaten by the kraken, pierced by a spear. But that is not our usual fate."

"What is, then?" demanded Xianthe. She sounded angry. As usual.

"When a sea numen grows weary and jaded, the water draws her more and more, until she can no longer resist it. Her body grows translucent, as your hands did, Nerine. And then it loses its coherence, becoming one flow of water amid all the flows, washed from shore to shore, drawn deep under and then thrust to the surface."

"That sounds like death to me," grumbled Xianthe.

"But it isn't," countered Mother. "Your great grandfather did not lose his awareness. Merely his awareness has changed. More fluid, more patient, and welcoming the long days as blessings to receive and savor. In another millennium or two, your grandfather will be renewed and return to his form of flesh and bone, ready to live life with urgency and angst and exuberance again.

"He'll come back?" Agnippe's eyes were as big as scallops.

Nerine summoned her courage to give voice to what really scared her. "Will my whole body be like my hands were? Will I dissolve?"

"Ah, no wonder you were alarmed." Mother's left eyebrow twitched. "No. It will take years of practice before you can claim the water form for more than your hands. And even then, your natural state is as flesh and bone. When your concentration falters, it is to flesh and bone you return.

"Even when you grow very old" – she smiled seriously – "and the sea draws on you as a tide, *you* will have a choice in the matter. Unlike most."

That made sense. If Nerine were consulting logic only, she would be reassured. And she knew Mother would never urge her toward a danger such as her imagination had conjured. She trusted Mother.

But the idea of seeing her hands hover as ghosts in the water still scared her silly.

"Now." Mother slid her hand down Nerine's arm and gripped her hand. She met Nerine's terrified eyes very squarely. "I'm going to talk you through it again, and you are going to show your sisters exactly what we've been talking about."

Nerine couldn't imagine how she could relax at all, let alone how she could relax enough to achieve the boneless state she'd managed before.

But she closed her eyes obediently when Mother instructed her to do so. She took in Mother's prohibition on opening her eyes until permitted. And she listened to Mother's cool, flowing voice as though it were her only refuge in a storm.

When Agnippe gasped and Xianthe exclaimed, she ignored them and kept her eyes closed.

"Notice how warm your hands feel, Nerine," said Mother.

Ah, yes, they did feel warm. Much warmer than the water surrounding them.

"And notice the limit between the warmth that is you and the cool that surrounds you."

Yes, that was what she was noticing. That she still had edges separating her from everything else. There was a reassuring thought. She wasn't dissolving. She could guess what her hands must look like, but they were hands, not water. Or, if they were water, they were yet hers, not the sea's.

"Now see in your mind's eye your translucent hands."

She gotten there before Mother, but she held the vision in her awareness.

"And now slowly let your eyes open, knowing that your hands in front of you will match those you see in your mind's eye."

Nerine opened her eyes.

And there they were: translucent, ghostly hands connected to the ever increasing opacity that was her wrists and the solid density of her forearms.

"Excellent," cooed Mother. "Now curl your fingers closed."

Moving her translucent hands felt just like moving hands of flesh and bone, no different. But the instant she twitched her fingers, their translucency faded rapidly, quickly returning to the normal solid state.

Mother leaned in to kiss Nerine on the forehead. "Well done, daughter. You make me proud."

Nerine tried to smile, but her lips trembled. It had all been a little overwhelming. Thank the blessings that Mother had chosen to teach her. If it were Illustrious Galeno, Nerine would still be thrashing in hysteria.

"Now let's see what Xianthe and Agnippe can do."

It turned out they were each precocious in different ways.

～

Xianthe's hands stayed flesh and bone, but she could already make the water move in a current. Not so steady or so forceful as Mother's current.

But Mother said that power would come with practice. "You will be more adept in creating great tides and colossal waves than ever I am able," she pronounced, "which means that you will require exceptional control."

Xianthe actually looked enthusiastic about the necessity of practice. How odd! Xianthe never wanted to do what she was told.

Nerine kept her mouth shut. If she said anything at all . . . Xianthe might change her mind. And Nerine had a feeling that Xianthe not practicing would be a very bad thing for everyone, not least for Xianthe herself.

Agnippe's talent proved to be that small bubbles formed all over the surface of her skin, from head to toe.

"Perfect," murmured Mother.

"Am I?" asked Agnippe. "Really?"

"Truly."

Mother didn't play favorites either, Nerine realized, a little astonished at herself. How had she never noticed that before? Father's warmer style made it obvious in him. But Mother's cooler manner didn't mean her love was less. Or divided unfairly.

Huh.

Mother touched her forefinger to Agnippe's chin. "You love the fresh water that streams upward from the Sedes Fountain, do you not?"

Agnippe nodded.

"In time, your water gift will allow you to control the salinity of the water next to your skin. You will create fresh water around you always."

"That's why you said this would benefit Agnippe especially!" shouted Xianthe.

"That is why," agreed Mother.

That was the end of that day's lessons, but Mother gathered them again every few days for more teaching.

Nerine learned how to speed a current and how to slow one, how to strengthen the tide or to lessen it, how to warm water and how to cool it. She could summon sea creatures, proving especially adept with the swimming mammals. She didn't need to float beside the summoning post to call dolphins to her.

Xianthe was particularly good at moving masses of water powerfully, just as Mother had foretold. And Agnippe rapidly mastered control of the water's salinity. It was amazing how much less fussy she was. Nerine had never guessed that Agnippe's natural quality would be serenity. Had she just been physically uncomfortable before? Maybe so.

If Agnippe was serene and Xianthe passionate and powerful, what was Nerine?

She thought about it for a while.

She loved new things. And she loved Altairos' exuberance. But was *she* exuberant? She didn't think she was. She could be exuberant, when she first saw something new. But that was temporary, not a continuous quality. Maybe she was thoughtful, and liked new things because she wanted more and more to think about.

She would think about *herself* some more and see if she perceived patterns within her.

In her third lesson with Mother, Nerine figured out how to sustain the water form of her hands while moving them, but increasing the extent of it beyond her hands proved surprisingly difficult. Several months later, she'd succeeded only in persuading her wrists to join her hands in translucent bonelessness.

～

12 ~ Harbor Jaunt

JUST AFTER NERINE's thirteenth birth anniversary, Eilidh took her post in Queen Hera's entourage. Nerine felt a peculiar mix of sad and relieved to see her eldest sister depart. Eilidh's bossiness made Nerine feel safe even while it annoyed her.

Eilidh was tall and stately in her eighteen years. She still wore her hair in a clasp high on her head, with the wavy tresses flowing down behind her shoulders. Her pectoral and belt were platinum, like Mother's, but the gems were clear yellow topazes. Her legs looked very long and slender and beautifully curvaceous.

As Eilidh lingered to make her farewells, Nerine missed her already. Home would never be the same. But then, when Eilidh embraced Nerine and made condescending remarks – about finding a post for Nerine on Olympus, if only Nerine would apply herself more to her lessons on protocol and get almost as knowledgeable as Eilidh – Nerine couldn't wait to see her gone.

Of course, Eilidh would not wear her pectoral and belt once she went ashore.

The nymphs of Mount Helicon had fashioned her trousseau, which awaited her at Thérma, and Eilidh would don a gown that resembled the one Nerine wore during her land adventures with Altairos.

Nerine wore her own proper pectoral and belt now. Hers were a flexible mesh of tiny gold platelets adorned with pale green beryl. When viewed from the right angle, the green beryls gave the most lovely flash of warm gold.

She'd visited the shore the very next day after she'd received her grownup garb to show Altairos.

She hadn't given much thought to how he might react. She just knew that the change was new and exciting and that she wanted to share it with him.

When she emerged from the waves, water sliding down her flanks and the bright sun gleaming on her greeny-gold hair and striking brilliant flashes from her jewelry, Altairos was there waiting for her.

His eyes grew very wide and his jaw dropped. And then he was laughing, his eyes smiling along with his mouth.

He ran to meet her, putting his hands on her shoulders and holding her at a distance so that he could take in her glory.

"You're beautiful! Beautiful! Oh, Nerine!"

He pulled her in close and kissed her cheek.

"How come I never noticed before?" he asked.

She was laughing, too, strangely pleased by his admiration.

"Because yesterday I was a little kid, and today I'm not?" she guessed.

He shook his head and turned to sling an arm around her upper back, bringing her along with him, walking toward the dunes and Calla's cottage. "I don't know, but you look all new. I hope you're still you though. Are you, Nerine?" He seemed flustered.

"Of course, I'm still me. Don't be silly."

"Ah, that's my sensible Nerine. Phew! For a moment I thought you'd transformed into a goddess of the ocean or something."

She giggled. "Well, I am a numen of the sea. That's sort of the same."

"Huh!"

She sneaked a peak at his face. He looked startled.

"So you are." His voice was thoughtful. "So you are."

She tapped his collar bone and pulled away from him. "Race you!" And then she was running, hearing his feet beating on the sand behind her and his breath rushing.

She reached Calla's cottage first, but not by much. He was half a head taller than her now, and his longer legs partially made up for her quicker stride. It felt good to fall back to the competitive game of their first acquaintanceship. His perception of her as older – and beautiful? – was exciting, but also a little scary. Being a child again, however briefly, was a relief.

Calla was even more stunned by Nerine's begemmed appearance than Altairos had been, although not in a good way. She sat on the small bench before her loom, mouth opening and then closing hard, while her face took on that disapproving cast she'd shown on first meeting Nerine.

"Mana mou, *look* at her!" called Altairos from the doorway.

Then Calla recovered herself enough to give Nerine a warm smile and a hug.

"Well, mikroula, aren't you growing tall!" she approved. "You'll be a grown lady soon."

"Calla, are you still worried that I might hurt Altairos?" Nerine asked.

Calla's gaze flew to hers, and then she looked down. "No."

She was lying, Nerine was almost certain. But why? There was some mystery – that Calla and maybe a few others knew, and that Nerine didn't – and that mystery meant . . . something.

Altairos spoke before she could question Calla.

"Nerine, I've arranged passage for us on the *Lily of Aegyptus* as she sails out of harbor! Should you like it? We'll pass right under the Mermaid Beacon and get a glimpse of the harbor for the warfleets."

Oh! She'd thought she'd seen everything new that Altairos could offer her. What a delightful surprise to learn she hadn't. Except . . . a harbor cruise involved water, specifically a place where water and shore came together. Exactly the situation she'd vowed to avoid after their adventure of the temple ruins.

Don't be silly, Nerine, she told herself. They'd been too young to know better then. They were older now, and this would be different. Besides, it sounded like fun.

"I would like it," she assured him.

She retreated to the cottage's bedchamber to change into the gown and sandals necessary for landward adventures. Calla wrapped the long sashes around her: one for Nerine's waist, and the other for Nerine's head.

Calla paused for a moment after tying the knot at the back, that unusual worry in her face again. Then she brightened and leaned in to kiss Nerine on the forehead.

"You're a sweet child. Bless you, mikroula!"

But as she turned away, she muttered, "And you'll break his heart without ever meaning to."

What?

Then Altairos gripped Nerine's wrist, saying, "Let's hurry! The tide waits for no one, and I'd hate to miss our chance!"

~

They fell into their ordinary camaraderie as they walked up the steep cliff path, through the palace, and then along the twisting streets and stairways of the city, with its square whitewashed buildings, some with shallow domes, others with roof terraces and bright canvas awnings.

He told her about the latest amazing find brought home by Hilarion, and she told him of the latest ridiculous argument between Tyr and Eilidh as Eilidh prepared to depart.

But every now and then, when he thought Nerine wasn't looking, Altairos would give a subdued version of that admiring glance he'd succumbed to, when she'd emerged from the sea in pectoral and belt. It was just as exciting and unsettling as before, so Nerine pretended to ignore it.

As they descended to the harbor, the smell of the sea grew stronger, a brinier, fishier odor than was present on the open beach. The cries of gulls mingled with the calls of sailors and warehouse workers.

When they emerged from a side street onto the stone quay, the rumble of the two-wheeled carts used to load the ships, and the clanking of the amphorae being loaded, joined the noise and bustle, along with the slapping of gentle waves against the harbor walls.

Nerine had visited the quayside before, but never with the knowledge that she would embark on one of the many merchant ships tied up there. She followed Altairos as he led her along the cobblestones between the colonnade where the trade goods were stored and the smoother stone at the quay's edge, weaving amongst the cart men, the sailors on shore leave, and clumps of conferring merchants.

But her eyes were all for the harbor.

It was big – bigger than the entire land palace, she thought – and it had the shape of a squashed oval, with strangely straightened zigs and zags, as well as several long stone piers jutting out into the water. Altairos said that his great great grandfather had commissioned its creation, ordering the huge mortar blocks constructed on dry land and floated on caissons out to where the water was deep enough, and then sunk to build the walls where now dozens of ships tied up.

She wondered which one was the *Lily of Aegyptus*. They all shared a similar design, with a great curved keel beam reaching high at the stern, a lower straight beam rising at the prow, and a tall mast amidships. A square white sail was lashed to the yard at the top, so as not to catch the breeze.

Most bore painted designs at the bow, each one unique. Dolphins cavorted on one, while a storm petrel soared on another. Nerine caught a glimpse of a white-petaled flower surmounted by slender golden stamens.

She gripped Altairos' forearm. "Is that it? Is that the *Lily*?"

He looked where she was pointing. "Yes!"

She studied it more closely as they drew near.

Flat decking gave solid footing at the stern and the prow, but the ship was open to the bilge amidships and filled with amphorae, some with blocky necks and made of terracotta, others sinuous and formed of white clay, and a few of bronze. Three sailors – in their characteristic white tunics, thick leather belts, baggy drawstring pants, and wide-brimmed hats – were passing rope through the handles of the amphorae, securing each end to the ship's gunwales.

Two more men stood on the quay beside the *Lily's* stern. One looked to be an ordinary citizen of Zakynthos, although his clothing was finer than the common folk – his short blue tunic sporting extra fabric and draping folds, and his yellow cape featuring fine embroidery along its edges.

But Nerine had never seen anyone like the other man. His black hair shone as though oiled and clung to his head in ordered curls, while his black beard was almost a sculpture, neatly trimmed and ending in one perfect curl at the bottom. His tunic, falling just below his knees, was fashioned very straightly, with none of the normal draping folds, and its hue was a vivid scarlet with a pattern of black lines. A great fold of purple cloth hung from the front of his belt.

Altairos led Nerine right up to this very strange stranger.

"Ah, Prince Altairos, you arrive in good time." The intonation and rhythm of the stranger's speech was as strange as his dress. "And this young lady is your friend who has never sailed?"

Altairos drew Nerine forward. "Nerine, Captain Batnoam is master of the *Lily*. Captain Batnoam, the Kríousa" – Princess – "Nerine enjoys new things, and I hope to delight her with this short excursion."

The captain bowed, a peculiar courtesy that involved an abrupt bend at the waist accompanied by double circling motions with each arm. "Welcome to my *Lily*, Kríousa Nerine. Your wish is my command. I, too, shall hope to delight you."

Nerine nodded, already delighted to be meeting someone whose native land was clearly very far from Zakynthos. Before she had time to voice her delight, however, Captain Batnoam circled her waist with his two hands and lifted her across the gap between the ship's sternside and the quay.

She was too surprised to protest, and then additionally surprised by the peculiar feel of the deck under her feet. The *Lily* rocked, very gently, but she also slid about in the water, bumping against the quay at one moment, and then jerking against the ropes mooring her at another.

Altairos leaped across the gap unaided and put an arm around her shoulders to steady her. The ship's movement didn't seem to disconcert him or unbalance him.

She watched eagerly while the sailors continued to make the *Lily* ready to embark. They tucked a few more handfuls of straw into the small spaces between the amphorae, coiled ropes, and let the sail down by perhaps an arm span, no more.

The captain came aboard at the stern, joining Nerine and Altairos, while the yellow-caped Zakynthian man, with whom he'd been talking, leaped onto the bow decking. Two of the sailors unhitched the mooring ropes from the massive stone rings that held them, and shoved the ship away from the quay, each with a synchronized kick.

The sea breeze caught the small amount of sail showing. Captain Batnoam manned a great oar attached to the side of the stern. The Zakynthian man at the bow called back some direction, and the *Lily* glided into the open waters of the harbor.

～

Nerine's mouth was crowded with so many questions, she didn't ask any for a bit, taking in the changing vista of the many ships moored at the quays, and others gliding into and out of their berths. How did the captains control their vessels so precisely? Was it really as easy as it looked? Nerine suspected not. And *who* was Captain Batnoam? Where did he come from?

Altairos was watching Nerine as she watched everything, enjoying her enjoyment.

She turned to him abruptly.

"Is the captain from Carthage? He speaks and dresses so differently from Zakynthians!"

Altairos smiled. "He's a native of Phoiníke. All the best seamen are. They taught all the rest of us the maritime arts."

"Really?" Nerine didn't even know where Phoiníke *was*. Somewhere to the east?

Altairos nodded. "The design of ships safe for the Middle Sea came out of Phoiníke, along with the tricks for navigating tides and currents and weather."

"Is that why the *Lily* sailed so smoothly away from the quay? I would have thought it would be more complicated. But the sailors just untied the ropes and gave a shove with their feet."

Altairos chuckled. "Oh, they're good, no doubt. But the wind is in the right quarter. It often is. That's why Zakynthos is where it is. With the land sloping to the sea and the sheltered harbor – that's part of it. But the prevailing winds are from the northwest."

"What happens when the wind is in the wrong quarter. It is sometimes, isn't it? Are the ships stuck in port?"

"Nope. There's always kedging, but Zakynthos keeps a flotilla of longboats with stout oarsman. They'll tie a rope from the ship to two of the longboats and *tow* the ship out of harbor."

"What's kedging?" asked Nerine. She wanted to know everything! Sailing along the top of the water was so interesting. So different from swimming *under* it as the sea people did.

"They take an anchor in the ship's skiff, row out a hundred armspans, and drop the anchor. Then the sailors in the ship haul on the rope attached to the anchor, pulling the ship to it. Then they send the skiff out again." Altairos laughed at Nerine's horrified face. "It's hard work! That's why the flotilla of longboats for towing is so great."

All through her questions, she could hear the Zakynthian in the *Lily's* bow calling directions, and see Captain Batnoam adjusting his steering oar.

"Who is he?" She tilted her head toward the bow. "Why does the captain take his directions?"

"He's the pilot. He knows the currents and the channels and the shoals of this harbor. All captains – all wise ones," he corrected himself, "hire a local pilot to get the ship in and out of port. We'll return ashore with the pilot in his skiff once the *Lily* reaches the open sea."

Oh! Now the arrangements were making much more sense. Altairos was good at planning though. Nerine admired his efficiency privately.

The *Lily* was well out into the harbor now. Nerine could see a channel on the left connecting to what looked like a whole separate bay, with more elaborate quays and plainer buildings. The ships moored there seemed more sleek, fierce almost, with glaring eyes painted on their prows and sharp rams jutting forward between the eyes. One ship surged forward into the channel, banks of oars flashing.

"That's the harbor for Pappa's warfleets," said Altairos. Nerine could hear the pride in his voice.

The *Lily* slipped past the war harbor's channel, and her sailors unreefed a bit more sail. They picked up speed, and the shore – now a wide promenade flocked with townspeople visiting the whitewashed shops along it – scooted by more quickly.

Nerine could see a breakwater in the distance ahead, spanning much of the harbor mouth. She gestured toward it, but Altairos answered her question before she asked it.

"That protects the harbor from storm surges when the weather is bad."

The *Lily* was headed toward the far right. She rose and fell with the increasing waves. The angle of the shore was changing rapidly, and soon the famous Mermaid Beacon came into sight. It marked the gap between the breakwater and the right arm of the harbor shore.

The beacon tower seemed more a colossal statue than a building. It took the form of a mermaid sitting, her fish tail curving around the rock below her. Her arms rested in her lap, and a crown adorned her head, set atop long curling tresses that flowed over her shoulders.

"Look, Nerine! Look!" exclaimed Altairos excitedly.

She was looking. The mermaid was so beautiful. What an extravagant and wonderful thing to have in one's city!

"They light the fire within the circle of her crown at night and during stormy weather. There's a door to the inside stairs in the mermaid's back. You can't see it from here."

"Ah! I want to climb to her crown sometime! Could we, Altairos?"

"Of course. I'll arrange it soon!"

They never had visited the beacon tower overlooking the beach where they met. This one would be even better.

As the *Lily* neared the access to the open sea, the mermaid loomed taller and taller. Her crowned head seemed to touch the sky, and even the scaly curve of her fishtail bulked high above the top of the *Lily*'s mast.

The pilot's instructions came fast and urgent. The *Lily* entered the gap in the breakwater, and then she was through! The sailors bustled, unreefing yet more sail. The waves seemed suddenly much bigger, and the *Lily's* bow plunged and rose.

Nerine felt abruptly lightheaded. Her stomach churned, and her knees went weak.

"What's wrong with me?" she gasped.

⁓

Altairos looked worried. He guided her over to the gunwale so she could grab hold of it, instead of merely relying on him to support her.

"Calla doesn't like the sea," he answered. "But, oh, Nerine! I never dreamed that it could make *you* sick! You are *of* the sea!"

And then she *was* sick. Catastrophically and dreadfully sick. Hanging over the gunwale with sour bile filling her mouth and wishing she were dead.

Oh, it was awful. Her stomach felt as though she'd swallowed ten bowls of foul water, and her head swam, while her legs wobbled.

She burst into tears.

Altairos gripped her shoulders all through her throes, and then handed her a cup of fresh water – where he'd gotten it, she didn't know – to rinse her mouth. Next came a clean cloth to wipe her face.

She couldn't stop crying. Sea people sometimes contracted serious rashes or dangerous parasites. There was one nasty disease that made your skin bleed. But she'd never felt any distress in her innards. Never felt anything like *this*.

"Ssh, ssh," soothed Altairos. "You'll feel better once we go ashore again."

She slid down to sit on the deck, leaning against the gunwale at her back, and Altairos sank down with her, wrapping his arm around her shoulder.

"Oh, can we go ashore *now*?" she whimpered.

Altairos' face contracted in sympathy. "I wish we could, Nerine."

"We can't?" she wailed. "Oh! Oh, no!"

"We have to wait until the *Lily* doesn't need the pilot anymore," he explained helplessly. "Oh, Nerine, I'm so sorry!"

She tried to regain some self control, but it was hard. Her stomach kept turning somersaults, and her limbs felt so heavy, and it was all so unfamiliar and awful.

"I'm s-sorry I'm ruining everything," she sobbed.

"Ssh, ssh, it's not your fault. It's mine. I should have guessed. Or at least been more cautious."

She shook her head. It wasn't his fault. It was just . . . unlucky, perhaps.

Her stomach took a particularly energetic turning over.

"Oh, no!" she gasped.

Altairos heaved her to her feet just in time, and she leaned over the gunwale once again.

Her misery seemed to go on and on forever, and she squinched her eyes shut. Eventually she became aware of some additional commotion on the *Lily*.

"Nerine, they're launching the pilot's skiff."

Oh, thank the blessings!

"You needn't do anything. Captain Batnoam will lift you, and the pilot will receive you, while I steady the skiff. Just sit tight, alright?"

She thought she nodded, and then Altairos moved away from her for the first time since their voyage began. She huddled against the gunwale for a while, and then she felt strong arms lifting her up, holding her reclining. "I regret your indisposition, Kríousa," murmured Batnoam.

There was a moment of lightness, a sense of air beneath her, and then another set of arms – more wiry than the captain's – took her and lowered her.

"The boat's dry, Kyría, so I'll set you right down on the floorboards," said the pilot.

And then she was down. A moment later, Altairos had his arm around her shoulders, and the sailors cried farewell and thanks to the pilot. She heard the creak of oars. Then they were underway. And it was even worse than the *Lily*.

Her stomach had nothing left in it to cast out, but this small skiff tossed on the waves like a cork shaken in an amphora. She would have been amazed that it didn't dump them into the sea, but she was too nauseated and faint to feel anything but woe.

Although . . . what if she leapt overboard? Surely she'd feel better under the water, instead of lurching about on top of it in this boat. Except she was too weak to leap anywhere. And what would happen to the beautiful dress that Calla had made her? And how would Altairos feel about her abandoning him? And where was she? How would she find the way home from here?

She'd left Mai'ip – who might guide her – near the beach where she always came ashore.

Each stroke of the oars added a lurching movement to the pitching. Nerine curled tighter into a ball in the bottom of the skiff and endured.

The pitching slackened, and Altairos murmured that they'd entered the harbor.

The harbor hadn't bothered her on their way out, and it was much calmer than the open sea. But now that her stomach was upset, even the gentle surge was too much. Nerine couldn't help moaning. Would she never get to shore? How much longer would this go on?

And then it was over.

The skiff was tied up somewhere along the quay, and the pilot was lifting her onto solid stone. Altairos guided her to a shadowed bench. The stone felt cool and solid under her, blessedly solid. She wasn't moving. *Nothing* was moving. Thank you, thank you, yes. She'd never known that stillness could feel so good.

Her stomach was calming, her head stopped swimming, and the faintness passed off.

She opened her eyes and straightened.

Altairos' arm left her shoulder, and he took her hand.

"The pilot is fetching bearers and a palanquin. You won't have to walk, and then you can rest in my rooms at the palace." He paused. "I'm so sorry, Nerine! I meant for this to be fun for you!" His face looked so worried, she felt bad for him.

"I'm better," she reassured him. "And the bit before we left the harbor was marvelous! I still want to go up in the Mermaid Beacon."

He brightened. "You do! Really?"

"Of course. I want to see how they light the beacon. Do you think they might do that even if it's day and not stormy?"

"For *you*, they will! I'll see to it."

She couldn't help laughing. She felt so much better, and he sounded a bit self-important.

When the bearers – four of them – arrived with the palanquin, she eyed it askance. The idea of getting into any conveyance – that might move up and down like the sea, even if it were just the swaying of the men as they walked – did *not* appeal.

"Altairos . . . I really think I'd rather walk. If you don't mind."

"*Can* you?" He seemed surprised.

She stood, and the stone paving under her feet with her weight on them felt really good.

"Yes, I think I can. If we don't go too fast," she added prudently. She and Altairos had a tendency to scamper everywhere.

So he dismissed the bearers after handing them a few coins, and started up the slope with Nerine toward the palace. Her legs were a little wobbly still, but every moment on solid ground saw her strength returning to her.

Altairos lost some of the constraint that the failure of his pleasure outing had brought, and began teasing her about how her beauty persuaded even rough seamen to courtesy. His glances grew admiring again. So that was all right.

She still wasn't sure how she felt about his admiration, but she'd have been disappointed if the unpleasantness of her seasickness had killed it.

By the time they reached the top of the slope and the palace, Nerine felt fine and in no need of rest.

"I think I'd better go straight home," she told Altairos. "It's getting late."

"Are you sure?" he asked her.

She nodded. "I'm fine. Really. Maybe a little hungry." She laughed.

"I could get you a few morsels from the kitchens," he offered.

"Walk me to the beach?" she suggested instead.

"Of course!"

After they reached the sands, and just before she plunged into the waves, he forestalled her.

"Nerine, even though today didn't go well, will you still trust me for future excursions? I usually choose better than this." The words seemed a little hangdog, but Altairos wasn't drooping and his gaze was straight. He just wanted to know.

She hesitated. But Altairos knew what he was doing on land. It was only when the sea got involved that trouble came. She could trust him on land, and she would.

"Of course!" she answered, brushing his cheek with a kiss. "See you!"

Then she dove into the water to join Mai'ip, who awaited her there.

~

13 ~ Wild Xianthe

THE REEF PALACE was calm upon her return, unlike other days when she'd been away, but a sense of tension pervaded the water after Eilidh departed for Mount Olympus. Nerine would encounter her mother coming away from her father with her mouth pressed straight in anger. Or see her father amidst his warriors, embarking on a swim to the deeps with extra vigor in his kick. Once she entered a parlor to find both Mother and Father shouting at one another. They stopped the instant they saw Nerine.

What in the sea was going on?

If she were younger, she would have worried that they were growing estranged. But she was more observant now that she was in her teens. Father still circled Mother's waist with his arm, most tenderly. And Mother welcomed his caress. It must not be a problem between them, but an external problem they disagreed on how to solve.

But what could it be? Nerine wanted to know. Her vague unease, with nothing to pin it to, was uncomfortable.

She found out after a particularly tiring lesson with Mother. Nerine had held her hands and wrists in water form for the entire time while moving from one water gift to another – cooling water to heating water to moving the heated water and so on – with no rest break between.

She wanted a nap, and the nursery was noisy with Agnippe and Xianthe practicing a humorous dialog they planned to present as a surprise to their parents. So Nerine sought out her favorite family parlor, a two-lobed chamber with amber coral and lots of sponge cushions within restraining nets. She swam through the outer lobe to the inner, wriggled in amongst the largest clump of sponges, and was asleep in mere moments.

An indefinite time later, she awoke to voices in the outer lobe.

"Give her time, Ionia. She's full young yet," said Father.

"She's fifteen, Meren, and it's time she began preparing for *something!*" Mother was already exasperated.

Nerine was still stupid with sleep, but this relieved her muzzy worry that they were arguing about her. She'd be fourteen soon, yes. But it was Xianthe who was the fifteen-year-old in the family.

Nerine scrubbed her hand across her spiracles and tried to open her eyes, but they were still too heavy. She was half asleep yet.

"Did you know what you wanted when you were fifteen?" That was Father again.

"Really, Meren! You know the answer to that. I was already destined to protect the sea for which I am named. Had been since my birth." Mother's sense of humor was back beneath her chiding tone.

"And were you ready?" Father probed.

"Oh, ready!" – she was dismissive – "Undoubtedly not. But I wanted it. Knew it was right for me."

"Nerine doesn't know what she wants yet," said Father.

Nerine struggled to wake up enough to do something. If they were going to talk about her, she *really* didn't want to eavesdrop.

"I have every confidence in Nerine. She's already three times more disciplined than Xianthe. Not that that's saying anything. Xianthe has no discipline at all. *Which* is what we were discussing," reminded Mother.

"Have you anything to suggest? I am listening, my dear."

"My cousin Hester was very wild, too." Did Mother sound tentative?

"Not that again," came Father's weary answer.

"It did her good to be sent to your grandfather's court!" Goodness! Nerine had never heard Mother defensive.

"So much good that she ran away! Again!"

"It wasn't the same, Meren!"

"How was it not the same? She left. Without permission. And to her detriment. I'm not sending any daughter of mine off to a strange court where they won't care about her nearly as much as we do."

"It wasn't the same," Mother insisted. "She quieted down when she came here. Grew more controlled, less impulsive."

"Not that I ever noticed," said Father.

"You didn't know her in the Aegean, Meren. I can assure you that she was beyond impulsive and impetuous under the protection of her father, King Evander. Really, it wouldn't be fair to her memory to speak of her choices then, so I will not.

"But she did improve here. And she became my friend. My closest friend." Why did Mother sound so sad? "We went about everywhere together. And she *didn't* run away. She ran *to*. You know that it's so, Meren."

"Mmm." Was that Father's reluctant assent? "Nonetheless, I'm not sending Xianthe to the Aegean."

"But she's refused the position under Pyralis, managing the currents in the straits, and that's the offer she'd be most suited to. Could you imagine her guarding the golden apples in the garden of the Hesperides? Or tending Cerberus for Hades? I cannot."

"Naturally not. But there will be other offers, Ionia. No need to leap on the first few possibilities."

"But the best positions are offered to those who prepare for them. Xianthe isn't preparing for anything. Doesn't want to prepare. And she, especially, would benefit from a greater commitment."

"Undoubtedly, but you're putting the dolphin before the chariot, my dear."

"What do you mean?" Mother actually sounded surprised.

"When Xianthe is able to *make* a commitment, she'll be steadier – and happier. But imposing a commitment on her before she is able won't achieve anything at all."

"Hmm." Mother was thoughtful. "You're always so clear-sighted, Meren. I could almost resent it, if I didn't love you so much for that very quality."

Incoherent murmurs followed this exchange for a while. Nerine suspected they were kissing.

Then Mother spoke again. "I still worry, Meren. She goes from one prank to the next. Placing a moray eel in the warriors' spear rack was just the last one. What will she think of next? And she's so impassioned! So wild!"

"Oh, I know. I do share your worry." Father sounded resigned.

"Yes, you do."

"We'll figure it out, Ionia."

And then came the ripple of the water that indicated they were leaving the parlor.

Huh, thought Nerine. Things would likely be tense for a while then, because she didn't see Xianthe changing anytime soon. And Mother and Father sounded stymied in developing a solution.

∾

The next time she visited Altairos, the topic of how you decided what you might do in life came up between them, although in a more upbeat way than it had been discussed between Nerine's parents.

She and Altairos walked along the shore and talked, as they did more and more often now. The sky was the deeper blue characteristic of autumn, and the air was mild, not hot. The wet sand packed firmly under their steps, and every now and then a frill of sea foam curled over their feet, cool and refreshing.

Nerine sniffed the gentle sea breeze. The difference between the pure smell of the water and the briny smell of the air still charmed her.

"Pappa is too lenient with me," Altairos complained. "All he'll say is that he has four hardworking sons already and doesn't need another. But I want to work hard. I want to *do* something! Accomplish something. And I don't think I can count on being lucky the way Hilarion is."

"Have you no inclination of your own? Surely your father would not refuse you, if you went to him with an occupation that attracted you."

"That's the demon in the plot," he admitted. "I suggested that since Hilarion had been destined for the temple, but failed to go, I might take his place there." Altairos bit back a chuckle. "Pappa just laughed at me, and he was right to. I'm clutching at straws, and he knew it. Becoming a priest, when I've neither talent nor calling for it, would be as much a waste as doing nothing at all."

Nerine sighed. "It's so strange. Your father is paying no heed to your future, while my father and mother are angsting over Xianthe's enough to make the entire reef palace uncomfortable. If we could give half of their worry to your pappa, it might balance out about right."

Altairos laughed with less constraint, then sobered. "Oh, how I wish we could."

A wave curled onto the beach with a rush of surf, and a gull cried, lonely and piercing.

"How is Xianthe causing trouble now?" asked Altairos. "She always is, isn't she? Why are your parents more upset this time?"

Nerine explained, concluding, "So, it's not really Xianthe. Or it is, but it's nothing new from her. The newness is that Mother and Father are looking ahead, and they weren't before."

"Caught up with aiming Tyr and Eilidh," speculated Altairos, "since they were due to leave the reef much sooner."

"Yes, I think you're right. And now Eilidh is gone."

"To attend the queen of the gods," said Altairos in a wondering tone. "I still can't believe that your sister will speak with Hera face to face; that anyone can. The priests claim they speak with Poseidon in prayer and ritual, and that he answers them. But that's different."

Nerine didn't say anything. It still startled her that Altairos regarded the gods so abstractly, while for her they were neighbors. *Distant* neighbors, but part of her community.

"Have you heard from your sister? Did she arrive safely?"

"Oh, yes! She sent a message by one of Hermes' heralds, saying that Queen Hera had received her most graciously, that the Olympian court was very grand, and that she loved her new duties. She sent a special thanks to Mother for preparing her so well."

Nerine shook her head in amazement. Eilidh recognizing a debt was . . . not the Eilidh Nerine knew. Maybe her sister's place as handmaiden would be good for her, tame her pride instead of inflating it.

"And your parents are satisfied with Tyr's destiny," continued Altairos.

"He's like Mother," Nerine realized.

"No!" protested Altairos. "Your mother is haughty and reserved. And your brother is gregarious and tells jokes. What in the sea do you mean, Nerine?"

Nerine giggled and grabbed Altairos' hand. He gripped back and swung their arms together, but he didn't let go when he quieted the pendulum swing. She liked the feel of his palm: warm and dry and bigger than hers, but gentle.

"No, not like that," she attempted to explain about Tyr. "But Mother was destined to rule the Ionian Sea from birth, just as Tyr was given the Tyrrhenian Sea with his naming."

"How did they manage that? Without making a mistake?"

"The palace oracle did a divination. And he didn't make a mistake. Tyr's looked forward to it all his life, and he's more keen now than ever."

"Huh," grunted Altairos. "He'll be leaving soon, won't he?"

Nerine nodded.

Altairos tightened his clasp on her hand momentarily. "You'll like that, won't you, Nerine?"

"Yes, he's an awful tease." Even as she spoke the words, she had second thoughts. "Except . . . Altairos, if Mother and Father started worrying about Xianthe when Eilidh left, don't you think . . ."

"That they'll be thinking of you when Tyr departs?" Altairos nodded. "Probably. Is that a bad thing?"

"I don't know. Maybe not. They never seem worried about me."

He squeezed her hand again, then said, "We should turn back. We'll arrive at the harbor if we walk much farther."

Reluctantly, she released his hand and turned around. He put his arm around her waist as they started walking again. He was so casual about it that she almost didn't notice, but she liked the feel of his muscular forearm against her skin above her jeweled belt.

"My parents will ask me what my inclination is, just like I asked you," Nerine continued, following her thoughts. "And I won't have an answer."

"You should tell them that you love seeing new things and new places and new people. The way I do!" He sounded surprised. "They'll have ideas for occupations that require that!"

Nerine glanced up at Altairos excitedly. "You should tell your pappa that!"

Altairos grinned, and his eyes crinkled in that way she loved. "You're right, Nerine! You're absolutely right!" He pulled her close in a quick, sideways hug. "Thank you!"

Nerine was abruptly aware of the warmth of his flank against her and the strength in his body. They'd been the same height for so long, and then she'd been a little the taller for a while. But now that he would soon turn fifteen, he was half a head taller than she.

He released her waist to grab her hand again.

"I've got another poem," he announced.

That was another new thing. He'd started writing poetry some months ago, and Nerine loved hearing his poems, just because they were new and because his viewpoint was interestingly different from her own.

"I can't wait to hear it," she told him. "It's ready to recite, isn't it? What's it about?"

He started right in.

"The tumblers of Aegyptus came tumbling
They tumbled right into the court
With the blare of a horn and the flourish of drums
Flipping – hands feet, feet hands, hands feet
And then upright into a tower
The squattest on the bottom
The lightest at the top, her golden hair a pennant
And then they were down again
Turning cartwheels in a circle
Turning somersaults in the air
They bounce like balls
They fly like birds
The youngest looks like my friend."

Altairos bowed, grinning.

Nerine clapped her hands and skipped in place. "I can almost see them!" she exclaimed. "In my mind's eye. Thank you!"

Altairos leaned in and kissed her cheek. "Thank *you*, Nerine. A poet needs an audience, you know."

"Do you not share your poetry with your family?"

He shrugged. "It's just something I do for fun." He hesitated. "And for you."

"Other people would enjoy it," insisted Nerine. "It's not fair you keep it from them. Promise me you'll recite for your pappa. Or your brothers."

He wrinkled his nose.

As he resisted, she waxed enthusiastic. "You could be a bard, traveling from land to land, telling tales, singing songs, and reciting poetry!"

His resistance changed to laughter at that. "I'm a horrible singer," he confessed.

"Really?" She liked his speaking voice, especially now that he'd gotten through the stage where it cracked in the higher registers, and had settled to a deepish tenor.

He laughed some more. "Really really."

"Oh." She'd quite liked her idea for his future. Although . . . if he sailed from one shore to another, when would *she* see him?

"But I will ask Pappa about other things I might do that involve travel. That was a good notion of yours, Nerine. I bet he'll have ideas."

Well, it was his idea, but . . . Oh! If Altairos traveled, even for something else, he'd still be traveling.

Except . . . if her parents had some good ideas for her, then she'd be away a lot, too.

That might be just fine, she decided. They would see each other whenever they returned home at the same time. Which would probably be just as often as they could snatch time from lessons and other duties now.

They both were busier, now that they were older.

～

Nerine continued to learn the languages of the lands surrounding the Middle Sea and to practice the use of her water gifts. She'd progressed from arithmetic to algebra and geometry. She was memorizing the contours of the sea bed and learning the geology that had formed it. And she was drilling in the protocols of the different courts of the gods and their vassals.

Apparently her parents wanted her to be prepared for any and every position that might be offered her. (And no wonder they worried about Xianthe, who was absent without leave from the schoolroom more and more.)

Altairos' studies were just as rigorous. In addition to languages, algebra, and geometry, he was tackling the philosophies, oratory, and the protocols of the courts of Aegyptus, Phoiníke, Hellas, Oenotria, Iberia, and more.

They didn't meet often. But when they did, it was so satisfying. Nerine loved talking over the things they were learning. Some of it overlapped, which was fun. And some of it didn't, which was even better. And Altairos continued to share his poetry with her alone.

She did find a moment to ask Father and Mother about vocations and travel.

Her parents had just returned from a few days' visit to the Sea of Kréte and were lingering by the summoning post, thanking the dolphins who had propelled their chariot so unflaggingly.

The summoning post was a tall column of bronze, ornamented – appropriately enough – with bas relief sculptures of dolphins and porpoises. It stood in a sheltered ravine, with the lagoon face of the palace on one side and a bluff on the other, riddled with hollows in which many of Father's subjects dwelled. Drifting sea plants in green and purple fringed the bluff, along with colorful anemones and algae.

Mother had just trailed her hand along Leem's departing flank, when Nerine arrived.

The dolphin sounded her high-pitched call of farewell.

Nerine had been hoping to catch both Mother and Father before they entered the palace and were claimed by the demands awaiting. But she hadn't known whether they'd be in a rush to take up the reins of their responsibilities, or more in a mood to prolong their holiday.

It seemed the latter.

Mother saw her first and opened her arms. "Nerine!"

Nerine allowed the hug. Mother wasn't usually so demonstrative.

"Hey! Here's my good little girl, come to welcome us home." Father's hug was strong and enveloping as always. After he'd snugged her in close, he held her away to look at her. "Except you're not so little any more. Another daktylos or two in height and you'll be a woman grown."

There was a perfect lead-in, if ever she'd been given one.

"Father, Mother" – it was important to include Mother in this; Father would decide nothing about his children without her – "I've been thinking about when I'm grown." She felt dizzy, putting her wishes to the test.

Father chuckled. "What did I tell you, Ionia. She's our little prodigy, in everything." He turned back to Nerine. "Good. Very good. You're a little early, but that's a virtue in this, not a flaw."

Mother provided Nerine's next lead. "What have you been thinking, darling?"

"About what I like to do. Or *would* like to do," she added hastily. Her parents still knew nothing of her excursions on land. "And I know about myself, but I don't know what positions feature what I like. I thought you might know."

Father smiled and Mother nodded.

"What do you like, Nerine?" asked Father. He sounded interested.

"I like *new* things!" she answered, her enthusiasm overcoming her nerves. "I like meeting new people and seeing new places and discovering new ideas." She bobbed a little in the water, causing bubbles to rush away from her skin and up. They tickled.

"Goodness!" Mother looked surprised. "How in the sea would you know, Nerine? You've never been anywhere."

Yes, Nerine had figured that would be an issue.

"Part of why I enjoy my lessons is because I'm always learning something new. And my tutor is teaching me all about the different courts of the gods now, and I'm fascinated. I'm longing to travel to all of them, to participate in their different cultures, and to meet all the different personalities."

Would that convince them? She *couldn't* come out with her secret at this point. They'd see her as disobedient and deceitful, reversing all their previous good opinion of her. She couldn't bear it. She liked being "the good one." And she'd die before she betrayed Nurse's generous (and unspecific) permission.

Mother was nodding again. "Really, that does make sense. Good thinking, Nerine. But keep thinking, darling. You're young to fasten on any one interest yet."

Nerine stifled the protest she wanted to make. She might be young, but she'd experienced her penchant for adventure when she was a very little girl. And acted on it when she was eight, meeting Altairos for the very first time that wonderful afternoon. Her love of new sights and new experiences was not a new thing.

But her parents could not know that. And she wasn't about to enlighten them.

"I will keep thinking, but is there a position for a sea *numen* that includes travel? I've never heard of any." Nerine's gills felt starved of air. What if they said there weren't any such positions?

Was Father looking dismayed? She could see that Mother disapproved. Why was liking to travel something to disapprove of?

"Well . . ." Father hesitated and then continued. "His Fleet and Clever Eminence The Prince Hermes presides over his company of messengers, but such a position would not be suitable for you, sweetheart."

"Certainly not!" sniffed Mother.

"Why not?" It sounded perfect to Nerine. She'd be given winged sandals and fly from Mount Olympus to the great city of Athens or her rival Sparta. She'd see *everything*!

Father glanced uneasily at Mother. "The heralds are sent into danger. Sometimes they light on the battlefield amidst swinging swords, sometimes they travel to the courts of the Norse gods in the far north, braving the monsters of Niflheim and Jotunheim en route."

Oh. That didn't sound good.

"Is Prince Hermes the only god with messengers? I know Poseidon has them, but of course I wouldn't want to be . . ." She hardly knew how to finish. Poseidon was respected. Of course. But Mother and Father had always been quite clear on the necessity of keeping some distance from the passionate Emperor of the World Sea.

Mother nodded. It seemed she understood what Nerine meant without Nerine saying more. "Indeed, each of our three Eminent Emperors possesses heralds to proclaim their desires: Almighty Zeus, whose heralds are managed by the Prince Hermes; Hades; and" – Mother swept her eyelids down – "Poseidon."

Father continued where Mother left off. "But the heralds face danger just as certainly as the messengers." Father paused. "They're all big, brawny warriors with great skill at arms."

Oh. Nerine was not big and brawny. And she had no skill at arms whatsoever. Surely there was some other option. She looked up pleadingly at Father's face.

"Isn't there something . . . ?"

Father stroked her cheek. "Sweetheart, don't be so sad. This is just your first idea. Your second will be even better. And your third, better again. Don't take this to heart." He hugged her again, plainly perturbed by her disappointment.

Mother weighed in less sympathetically. "Really, Nerine, you don't know that you'd like traveling – which can be very uncomfortable, let me tell you – or meeting new people. Enjoying learning and new ideas isn't the same thing at all. Don't sulk, dear. It's most unbecoming."

Nerine wasn't sulking, but it was hard to bear up under the crash of her dreams. She'd been afraid her parents might not have any answers. But her fear derived more from how important this was to her than from a real doubt of her parents. They knew so much more than she, they knew the world better, and they were resourceful. She hadn't seriously expected them to be at a loss.

"Let's go in, Meren, and take first touch at the catastrophes undoubtedly awaiting us." Mother hooked one arm through Father's and the other around

Nerine, drawing her toward the palace. "I wonder who will be first? Your chancellor or my senior lady? Or perhaps little Agnippe will come greet us, too." Mother flicked Nerine's nose, trying to lighten her mood.

Nerine forced a smile, but slipped away as soon as Lord Spiro and Lady Philena engaged her parents' attention.

She sought the inner chamber of the double-lobed parlor where she'd overheard her parents arguing about Xianthe. It was more private than her sleeping nook off the nursery, and she wanted to be alone to think.

But once she was tucked into one of the sponge-filled nets, her eyes resting on the soothing amber of the rough coral walls, she didn't have any thoughts to contemplate. She just felt numb. It was very uncomfortable. What was the use of thinking when you *couldn't* think?

She'd asked her parents the question that was most important to her being, and they'd simply dismissed it, telling her she was young.

That was worse than uncomfortable. It was awful.

She'd thought she could trust Mother and Father completely, right down to the sea's deepest bedrock and beyond. She thought they'd take her concern seriously. She'd thought they'd have answers and ideas. She'd thought she'd go away from the discussion of her question filled with possibilities.

Instead she had nothing. No, worse than nothing, because she'd lost her boundless reliance on Mother's and Father's support. Now she knew that while they often had her back, they didn't – and wouldn't – always have it. Sometimes – even when it was critical – they wouldn't. They hadn't this time.

She bit her lip, suppressing tears.

Her next idea was to confide in Nurse. She still remembered the conversation with Nurse – about this very same topic, come to think of it – in which Nurse was so reassuring. But Nerine had been younger then. Much younger. And Nurse hadn't so much given her new ideas as pointed out how wise Mother and Father were.

Nurse wasn't an idea person. She might reassure Nerine. In fact, she *would* reassure Nerine. But there wouldn't be any real substance to her reassurance. That had worked when Nerine was eight. If Nurse were to urge her to rely on Mother and Father now – hah! – Nerine would just say something bitter and unbecoming. And draw down scolding.

No, no consulting Nurse.

So in the end, Nerine simply resumed her normal activities. Which was thoroughly unsatisfactory.

～

Nerine took guidance in courtly protocol from Mother in the mornings or else practiced her water gifts. She learned lessons in the schoolroom from her tutor in the afternoons. She dined with Mother and Father – and their retinues and her own siblings – in the evenings. And she participated in other scheduled events, such as her first visit to the deeps, which was scary and mysterious, descending so far that the water grew dim and then dark, and they actually caught a glimpse of the kraken's massive tentacles as it swam through the murk some distance below them.

She discovered that pursuing one's daily responsibilities, no matter how mundane or trivial, actually did have some benefit.

Her numbness wore off, and she started enjoying her studies again. Quarreling with Xianthe could strike sparks from her when Xianthe said exactly the right mean thing. While interacting with Agnippe was now fun. Agnippe had a quiet sense of humor. She'd say something innocuous, and Nerine would only realize her sister had made a joke three sentences later. It was intriguing. And Agnippe was never mean with her humor.

As Nerine's engagement with life returned, so did her optimism. And she discovered that she had a few ideas of her own about what position she might fill when she was older.

What if she became the shepherd for the thermohaline current through the Middle Sea? The Middle Sea lost more water by evaporation than it received from rain and from rivers flowing into it. Which meant that water from the Outer Sea always flowed in through the Pillars of Herakles, a mighty flood that moved ever eastward, sinking all the while, until it reached the farthest shore of the Levantine Sea, where it doubled under itself and flowed back into the west, exiting through the Pillars of Herakles along the seabed.

She would see every depth and every shallow of the Middle Sea, every vassal sea within it, every shore, if she were guardian of the thermohaline current.

Or maybe she *could* become one of Hermes messengers. Perhaps he could create a cohort amongst them especially for women, who would go where a woman would be more welcome than a man. To the bedside of a goddess in childbirth. To a wounded hero being tended after his greatest fight. To summon a unicorn into the Elysian Fields.

Or maybe, just maybe, Father was right. And her third idea, or her fifth or her tenth, would be perfect. After all, *she* – not her parents – had found her very first adventure in life. *She* had chosen to go ashore alone. She'd survived her imprudence. And she'd discovered a whole world to explore.

She began to trust herself and her own ideas. *She* would solve this, even if Mother and Father could not.

Nonetheless, when Mai'ip was pronounced by Kriy, the matron of his pod, as ready to learn the ways of harness – both for drawing a chariot and for pulling a warrior on a tow line – Nerine felt a furious exasperation. Everyone seemed to have more choices than she did!

Boys could become messengers of Hermes and travel all over the world. Or they might become heralds for one of the great courts and go equally far. Even her brother Tyr – destined for neither the post of messenger nor that of herald – would have more freedom than Nerine would, once he took up the guardianship of the Tyrrhenian, because his duties would require that he coordinate with the neighboring seas.

And Mai'ip would be doing exactly what Nerine longed to do: visiting every shore and every basin of the Middle Sea, and all the islands within it as well.

It wasn't that she grudged Mai'ip his good fortune. She just wished she could share it.

Her jealousy ebbed when Mai'ip came to enjoy a last swim with her. They danced in spirals and leaped among the waves together. Mai'ip even gave her a rushing ride as she gripped his dorsal fin – just like Pheep, long ago when she was little – and she found herself laughing with the joy of it and her happiness for Mai'ip's happiness.

Mai'ip was even more exuberant than usual, eager for his changing fortunes. It showed in his every move, and Nerine could only wish her dolphin friend well.

She did wish him well, but she would miss his company. They'd been good comrades as he swam with her in the lagoon or out of it. But he was growing up, and so was she.

ᵔ

Soon after the fourteenth anniversary of Nerine's birth, Tyr departed for the Tyrrhenian Sea.

His departure featured none of the fanfare that went with Eilidh's when she took up her post on Mount Olympus. Tyr simply announced one evening over dinner that he was ready and that he intended to travel in the morning.

Apparently he'd been coordinating with Father in choosing warriors to accompany him, and selecting a retinue, as well as supervising the packing of necessary tools and supplies.

Mother seemed not the least surprised, but Nerine was.

Nerine crawled out of her sleeping circle early to bid him farewell, but his actual leave taking was as undramatic as the way he'd spoken of his plans the night before.

When had Tyr become so adult? Had Nerine just not noticed? Or had he grown up in the night? He looked a lot like Father, of medium height, a little less muscled, but strong. His hair was the same curly bronze as Father's, but shorter and a little lighter. His face had the same humorous eyes and a mouth ready to smile, just younger, and with the aquiline nose from Mother.

He shook hands with Father and kissed Mother's cheek, then punched Nerine's shoulder. Xianthe, also present, got a wink. And Agnippe, a hug.

Then he climbed into one of the seven chariots harnessed to dolphin quartets, and they were off.

Nerine found she didn't miss him at all. At least, not right away.

When they were all still children, Tyr had played mostly with Eilidh, his closest age mate. Nerine had teased him for treats and attention, which she received from him sporadically, well mixed with taunting. As they'd grown older, their ways had lain apart. The four years between them meant he'd moved into complex studies far ahead of her, and then into adult concerns as well. Eilidh had continued to be his companion in the adventure of growing up.

But when Tyr returned for visits home, he was different. He wanted to connect with all of his family, his three younger sisters as well as Mother and Father.

And he had such interesting stories to tell.

The Tyrrhenian Sea had been neglected for nearly a century, its wellbeing attended to as an afterthought by the ruler of the Middle Sea – great grandfather, when he found he had no heir suitable for the Tyrrhenian;

then grandfather, who experienced a similar lack; and recently, Father, while he nurtured Tyr for the role.

So there was everything to do, when Tyr arrived at his demesne.

He and his men discovered a species of spider crab living in great numbers offshore from Hesperia. The carapaces of the crabs measured a full cubit in width, while their legs spanned eight cubits.

Nerine tried to imagine a crab that stood taller than Father and shivered.

"Are they dangerous? Were you scared?" she asked.

Tyr just laughed.

The crabs were timid, evidently, and their molted exoskeletons were perfect for weaving shelter spheres in which Tyr and his retinue and warriors could live.

"The old palace, if there ever was one, is completely gone," explained Tyr. "So we fashioned globes woven of crab chitin and tied them together along with the right number of floats, attached the whole shebang to the anchors we brought with us, and that's my palace. It works well. And we can add to it whenever we need to."

It sounded primitive to Nerine, but Tyr was happy. And Father just nodded. They'd probably evolved the whole plan together, in the year before Tyr departed to take up his responsibilities.

Tyr visited frequently, once every few months, and his accounts of his doings seemed designed to entertain. He reserved dry, technical discussions for private conferences with Father or with Mother, and saved the amusing events for family dinners or swims with his sisters.

Nerine came to anticipate his visits and eventually, if he were delayed in returning, or had to postpone, she missed him.

It felt odd to miss him not at all when he first departed, and then to miss him a lot after he'd been living in the Tyrrhenian for a year.

∽

Right after Tyr left, Nerine caught up with Altairos again. They'd failed to meet for several moons. She'd arrive on the beach, and he would not. So she'd visit Calla instead, which was nice, but not quite so satisfying as talking with Altairos.

It had been the same with him, she gathered.

He'd come to the shore and, not finding Nerine, spend an interval in Calla's cottage, which he would probably do regardless. For he'd never thrown off his old nurse. If anything, his affection for her had grown. Nerine suspected that Calla had come to occupy the place in his affections that his birth mother would have, had she still lived.

It was a cool day, but very bright, when she emerged from the sea to find Altairos waiting for her just out of reach of the strong surf.

The waves were bigger and broke more violently than they had on that long ago day when she first came ashore. Nerine negotiated the transition from sea to land, from water to air, effortlessly. Her arms and legs – her whole body, too – were strong, and her sense of timing instinctive.

She felt very alive as she powered forward, surging from swimming to striding, leaving the pounding surf behind her as she splashed through the sea foam onto the packed, moist sand.

Altairos was bursting with excitement. She could see it before he spoke.

But when he opened his lips, he didn't spill his news. Instead he said, "You're so beautiful, Nerine. Do you know how beautiful you are?"

She kissed his cheek and laughed. "Not really. Am I so overwhelming?"

Altairos laughed, too. "Yes! To me you are," he admitted.

His admission pleased her. But just as his admiration for her after she'd donned pectoral and belt had perturbed her, so did this. She chose to turn it off lightly.

"Well, thanks! I think. But that's not what you wanted to tell me, is it? What's your news?"

"Let's get out of the wind first," he answered. "You're shivering."

It didn't bother her. She was accustomed to a feeling of chill as the sea breeze dried her. Neither her metal belt and pectoral, nor her hair, held the water, so she dried quickly. But today was cooler than usual, and the breeze was stronger, so she was happy to follow Altairos to a hollow in the sands on the leeward side of the dunes. He guided her to a driftwood log. When they sat, side by side, she was completely out of the wind. The still air felt warm.

Nerine turned to him and gripped his hands. "What's happened? You look ecstatic!"

"I asked Pappa last night, Nerine," he answered. "I told him I wanted to be *doing* something. Or preparing to be doing it. That he might be satisfied to have four ambitious sons, but that I was a fifth one, whether he wanted me or not."

"How did he respond?" She already knew that he must have responded well. Altairos would not be so elated if he hadn't.

"He laughed and started spouting ideas. He had a lot of ideas, Nerine. I never dreamed there were so many things in the world I might put my shoulder to."

Nerine felt a flash of jealousy amidst her happiness for him. Why did the King of Zakynthos have dozens of ideas for his son, while the King of the Middle Sea had none for his daughter? It didn't seem fair.

"Tell me!" she urged Altairos.

He laughed, perhaps echoing his memory of his father laughing. "I can't even remember them all. But I could be a courier, carrying sensitive messages from Pappa to our fleet admirals and to our ally kings. I could be master of one of the trade fleets, guiding it from port to port. I could organize the spending of the gifts we send to our vassal cities when they are in need. I could hunt for deposits of tin, which is rare, and then keep the site secret until Pappa sent miners along with warships to protect them."

Altairos shook his head in wonder. "You were so right, Nerine. I should have asked him sooner."

"Well, you did ask him a while ago. But you didn't tell him how you felt about it then. Did you?"

Altairos looked thoughtful. Then he grinned. "Right! I do believe you've taught me something."

That felt really good: Altairos admiring her ideas, in addition to admiring her beauty.

What did I teach you?" she asked.

"That being a little open about how I feel – with people I trust, at least – might be . . . wise." He looked more thoughtful yet.

She thought about what he'd said. Was she honest about how she felt? Should she be? These were a new questions. She wasn't so sure she was teaching Altairos anything. Maybe he was teaching her. If she wanted to learn. Did she?

The idea of being fully honest with her own parents – about her regular visits ashore, about her friendship with Altairos – was unwelcome. *Very* unwelcome.

Altairos continued with his own line of thought. "Even with people I don't trust, sharing how I feel – strategically – might work very well. Especially for what I want to do!"

Huh? There was a startling idea. Nerine wasn't so sure about sharing her complete feelings with people she did trust. Now Altairos thought he should share his feelings with people he *didn't* trust? What in the sea?

She grabbed onto the one thing that made sense. "What do you want to do?" she asked. Had he already decided? Out a list of possibilities so long that he couldn't remember them all?

"I shall become my father's Royal Envoy." He sounded solemn. Then he grinned again. "But I've a lot of preparing to do!"

"What does an envoy do?" Sea people had heralds and messengers to communicate between the many royal courts under the overarching jurisdiction of Almighty Zeus on Olympus. Which sounded a lot like the couriers Altairos had mentioned. But Nerine didn't think her father had ever spoken of envoys, not as an official position.

"My father cannot go to talk with the King of Phoiníke or the Pharaoh of Aegyptus or the Archon of Athens, because he must remain here, ruling all that is under him. So he sends his envoys to the courts of the powerful in order to make agreements with them. Some of his envoys reside in those courts for years, but his most important and influential envoys travel from court to court. I aim to be one of those!" Altairos sounded both proud and grateful at once, and a little overcome.

Nerine abruptly perceived two great truths – separate, but related.

⁓

The first truth felt like a sea quake followed by a tidal wave. Her world shifted with it.

The order of her mother's and father's milieu – that of the sea people and the gods – was stable and unified. Almighty Zeus ruled over all, with his brother Hades serving as Zeus' regent in the realm of the dead, and his brother Poseidon serving as his regent over the waters.

But the people of the land lived in a fragmented array, with agreements that must be re-made or adjusted or broken as their needs and wishes shifted over time. It could be scary or it could be wonderful, but it was always changing.

No wonder Nerine loved the land!

The gods lived in beauty and power, and sometimes they quarreled, but their world was static.

Only the mortals dwelling ashore transformed themselves and their surroundings utterly.

Nerine's knees felt weak. It was good she was sitting. The driftwood log felt very hard under her.

Her second realization was equally shattering, although much narrower in scope. She felt like she'd been through a second sea quake and a second tidal wave.

Altairos would be *excellent* as his father's envoy, and she loved him as much as she loved the land.

She loved his laugh. She loved his initiative. She loved his intelligence. She loved his care of her. She loved everything about him. And it was all too much, too intense, too overwhelming.

Feeling like she was choking, she shoved her love back down where it had lain before: hidden, even from her; a bedrock in her being that she rested against, while remaining unaware of it.

She would be a child – at least a little longer – innocent of the love a woman might feel for a man, or a girl on the verge of womanhood for a boy crossing into manhood. She dug her toes into the sand, cool and silky in the patch of shade cast by the driftwood log.

Drawing in a deep, but quiet, breath and wondering how much of her inner confusion showed, she exclaimed in a way so natural that it amazed her, "Oh! You'll be perfect as a royal envoy!"

Altairos blinked. "I will?" he asked.

"Of course." Now she was calmer, regaining her balance in the normal conversation they enjoyed. "Just think, Altairos, you made friends with me, a *numen* of the sea who spoke a language in which – at the time – you understood not one word. And you were just a little kid then. Imagine me as one of those foreign courts you will visit. You were brilliant!"

He blinked again. "Huh."

Nerine laughed. She was amazed all over again at how natural her laughter sounded. She felt like she was a different Nerine altogether. And yet she was the same Nerine, in spite of it all. "I know you're excited. I can hear how excited you are. But does it feel right, too? It feels right for you to me. Does it feel right to you?"

Altairos gathered her into a hug, kissed her forehead, and released her. "You're amazing. You always know the right question to ask."

Nerine took another deep breath, having to find her balance. Again.

She managed it, and managed to meet his eyes naturally.

Altairos touched her hand. "It does feel right," he told her. "Really right. As though I've been moving toward this all my life without knowing it."

"You almost have," she said. "You speak the language of the sea as though you were born there, and I bet you'll soon be equally at home with the tongues you're learning with your tutor."

"I am good with languages," he agreed. "You are, too, Nerine. You sound like a native of Zakynthos when you speak *Ionikós*. And I bet you're *already* as adroit with the languages you are studying under *your* tutor."

She blushed and nodded. She never really noticed anymore which language she spoke with Altairos. They switched back and forth, depending on which one was more suited to what they were discussing.

They talked some more about what Altairos would be learning and practicing to prepare for his newly chosen employment. Nerine expected they would spend the rest of the afternoon sharing their thoughts about it. It was big. But Altairos eventually turned the conversation to her concerns.

"Have you asked your mother and father about possibilities for *you*, Nerine?"

Nerine sighed. "I did, but it didn't go as well as your question to your pappa did."

A shadow of concern crossed his face. "How so? What happened?"

She told him about the conversation with her parents, concluding with her new realization about her world. "Because things are so stable between the divine courts and because we use our gifts" – she meant her water gifts and the other gifts that the different *numeni* possessed – "where land dwellers use inventions and cleverness, there just aren't as many things to do."

"That's . . . discouraging," he ventured.

"Yes, it is," she agreed. "But I'm refusing to be daunted. It's *my* life, damn the blessings! And I'm determined to figure out what's right for me, even if it takes a while."

"Good for you, Nerine! And I'll help. If I can. I . . . don't know your sea as well as you know my land, but I'll suggest things from my world and you can see if there is a counterpart in yours."

She was almost fully recovered from her earlier revelations, with her new awareness of Altairos tamped down where it felt safer, and only her comfort in his friendship allowed to float free. His promise to help her discover her vocation completed her return to her familiar self and her familiar reliance on him.

She'd felt hopeful in her own commitment to discern or create a position that would be right for her. With his decision to help her, she went from hopeful to optimistic. When Altairos planned and did things, things happened.

Of course, she would be the one *doing* in this. But still, having him on her side felt really good.

It was too late in the day to go visit with Calla, but Nerine suspected she knew how Calla would feel about this change in Altairos' fortunes. She'd be so proud she was almost bursting, and she'd want to hear all about the conversation between Altairos and his pappa, all about his plans going forward, and all about how the new focus affected his studies.

Nerine wanted to watch Calla in the flow of her pride in her nursling. If Calla loved Altairos so much – and she did – then perhaps Nerine's love for Altairos wasn't so extraordinary. But Nerine wasn't going to think about that. She was going to go home to her own lessons, and then she was going to return to the shore, and everything was going to be the same as it ever was. Nothing would change.

And maybe because she wanted it so much, that was how the next couple of years proceeded.

～

Nerine's days were full of learning fascinating things, punctuated by satisfying talks with Altairos about their mutually changing view of the worlds they inhabited. Calla was just as proud of Altairos as Nerine had thought she would be, although Calla's pride didn't dim Nerine's affection the way she'd hoped it would.

She discovered that she could both enjoy her interaction with Altairos and not think about it, if she were careful to fasten on some new and interesting bit of trivia, that he'd shared with her, the instant that she started to think about how much she liked him. It was very helpful that her curiosity could distract her so effectively.

Tyr's visits home continued to be a joy, and Nerine grew ever closer to Agnippe, which surprised her.

Agnippe had been such a crybaby when she was little, that even when she stopped – after her water gift helped her be more comfortable in the sea – Nerine tended to think her youngest sister someone to avoid. Even after she'd enjoyed a few eye-opening discussions with her. Xianthe's increasing tendency to throw temper tantrums pushed Nerine to reconsider.

For Xianthe went from being a mouthy girl who *could* argue about anything to being one who *would* argue about everything.

Whether it was Father reminding her to "serve all you like, but eat all you serve" at the dinner table or Nurse telling her that it was time to turn in to her sleeping circle, Xianthe argued about it all and ended most of her arguments with a tantrum. And her tantrums usually involved her water gift, which meant that powerful jets of current disrupted the peace of home along with Xianthe's yells.

The sleeping dispute turned into a maelstrom of sand, shells, and neglected nursery toys that whirled around the space and blasted into the sleeping nooks.

Nurse summoned Father, and Father summoned Mother, and the three of them combined their water gifts to cancel Xianthe's wild spate. Then Mother issued stern remonstrance that Xianthe sullenly ignored, Father spoke loving forgiveness that Xianthe glared at, and Nurse merely ushered her to the sleeping circle in a guest chamber down the hall, which worked, oddly enough.

Nerine and Agnippe had vacated the nursery with Xianthe's first explosion, although they could hear it all from the shelter of Nerine's favorite parlor, the double-lobed one with the amber coral surfaces.

Tucked into the sponge nets of the inner lobe, which muffled the tumult a little, they stared at one another in consternation.

"Why is she *like* this?" gasped Nerine.

"I think – I think they're handling her wrong," said Agnippe.

"Huh?" Nerine hadn't expected an answer. She'd been complaining.

"Mother and Father," explained Agnippe.

Nerine studied her sister. At twelve, Agnippe was small for her age. She looked more like she was ten. Her hair was cut short – to give her better access to the water embracing her skin, to control its salinity – and it curled in smoother spirals than did the long tresses of her sisters and their mother, and possessed a brighter golden hue lacking their greenish highlights. She looked like a water pixie, but without the mischief. Her eyes were observant and seemed to hold more wisdom than was right for her age.

For the first time Nerine appreciated that Agnippe at twelve was really a different person than Agnippe at four or Agnippe at eight. Agnippe at twelve might be a valuable friend.

"What do you mean?" asked Nerine.

Agnippe opened her lips, closed them, and then tried again. Her thoughts might be mature, but her ability to express them was not. Or at least not yet.

"Well, Xianthe loves Mother and Father so much," she finally managed.

Nerine wrinkled her brows. That made no sense. "She's extra naughty because she loves them so much? Agnippe . . . ?"

"Xianthe needs Father to be stern and less understanding, and Mother to be softer and warmer and more loving. She'd feel safer that way. It's because she doesn't feel safe that she gets so wild." Agnippe scrubbed her hands through her short curls. "She feels like Father doesn't see how out of control she is, and like Mother . . . doesn't really love her. Which isn't true. Either of those. But . . ."

Nerine felt like her eyes must be as big as clam shells, so astonished was she at Agnippe's insight.

The sound of shattering traveled from the nursery, along with a wordless shriek from Xianthe.

"Have you told Mother and Father this?" Nerine demanded. She couldn't imagine Mother listening, but Father would. And she herself could see that what Agnippe saw was true. If Father could be more insistent that Xianthe behave, and Mother more affectionate, both verbally and physically . . . although it might be too late at this point, Xianthe was so far along in her wildness.

Agnippe shook her head disconsolately. "It wouldn't help."

"You think they needed to change sooner?" asked Nerine. She couldn't believe she was asking Agnippe. Agnippe! But Nerine had never had any ideas about how Father should do fathering or how Mother should do mothering. She liked the way they were just fine.

"No, if they changed it would help, but I don't think they can change," answered Agnippe. "Can you imagine Father being unyielding? He understands what Xianthe feels so well that he can't help but be sympathetic. And Mother . . ." Agnippe trailed off.

Nerine knew why she did. Mother was . . . Mother. She could show a sense of humor unexpectedly, which gave her more flexibility than you might guess. But she couldn't change her innate stateliness. Xianthe would never get what she needed from Mother. Nor could she stop needing it. Which was sad.

But surely Father could change. He was the truly flexible one.

The mutter of his voice rumbled through the water, understanding and compassionate as always. But not what Xianthe needed at that moment.

Nerine's brows wrinkled again. Father couldn't change, she realized. Not that, anyway. Which was an odd thought. Maybe Father wasn't as flexible as she'd always thought him.

"What's going to happen?" she blurted, feeling embarrassed to be seeking comfort from her youngest sister.

"Xianthe'll get worse," Agnippe predicted.

"Oh, no!" groaned Nerine. "It's already bad enough now."

When the pandemonium finally subsided, and after Nurse escorted Xianthe to an undisturbed sleep circle, she came to check on Nerine and Agnippe.

"Are you alright, lovies?" she inquired, smoothing Agnippe's floating curls.

"Mmm," murmured Agnippe. "I'm comfy here."

"Well, tuck more than your toes into that net, or you'll drift once you sleep."

Agnippe obediently scrunched farther into the net holding her feet, and blinked drowsily. The sponges in this parlor were softer than any others in the palace, maybe because they were older.

Nerine was already well tucked in, but she reached out her hand to stop Nurse from departing.

"What's wrong, lovey?"

"Do you think Mother is right, Nurse? That Xianthe would be happier living with Uncle Evander and Aunt Sophelia in the Aegean?"

Nurse drew in a large gulp of water through her spiracles. Did she not like criticizing Mother? Maybe Nerine should not have asked that question.

"I've never met your aunt and uncle, sweeting. It would depend on what they were like. Your sister . . . would not be easy, even were she well matched with her caretakers."

Nurse shook her head. "Go to sleep, lovey. The morning will be better."

Nerine smiled and cuddled down amongst her batch of sponges. Maybe she would sleep here always. Ask Mother and Father if this parlor could be entered in the palace rolls as truly hers.

The morning was better, but Xianthe grew steadily worse as the month passed. Instead of throwing two tantrums every *déka*-day, she threw three or four. Then she was tantruming every day, then twice a day. Where did she drum up the energy for it? Finally, Nerine spent a night in Calla's cottage, just to have some peace. And home was so disrupted that Mother and Father never noticed that their middle daughter was absent.

⁓

14 ~ Sister's Promise

WHEN NERINE ARRIVED HOME the next afternoon – she'd lingered with Calla – she discovered Mother sobbing in Father's arms in the great front hall, unheeding of the bustle going on around her.

Warriors swam across the pearlescent space, between its irregularly knobbled columns, and out the lagoon side gate, while others swam in, returning from their errand, whatever it was. Bunches of servants trailed through from the central passageway carrying bundles.

Mother – who rarely lost her cool, let alone ever indulging in a storm of emotion, even in private – ignored it all, seemingly oblivious to her audience.

Nerine checked abruptly, right in the center of the lagoon side opening, forcing an armsman to dodge around her, while a maidservant tangled an arm and her bundle in Nerine's flowing hair.

Nerine paid no attention to the effect her sudden stop had on the traffic.

What had happened? What *could* have happened to make Mother break down like this? Had someone *died*? It had to be something really bad.

Nerine clutched her hands to her stomach, scared to find out, scared not to find out, scared that her mother might not stop crying. She *needed* Mother to stop crying. To be calm and capable, the way Mother always was. To make the world safe, the way she always had. Except that Nerine had not realized it until exactly this moment.

"Meren, oh, Meren!" sobbed Mother, grinding her forehead into Father's shoulder. "It's just like Hester, only worse. My poor little girl! Oh!"

Little girl? Was it Agnippe? Nerine wouldn't call Agnippe little any more, but she could see that Mother might. What had happened to Agnippe? Nerine's stomach felt even colder than it had a moment ago.

Father wasn't saying anything, and his face looked nearly expressionless. Which was almost as scary as Mother crying. A twinkle of humor always lurked somewhere in Father's face – in the quirk at the corner of his lips, within the light in his eyes, in the tilt of one eyebrow. How could *Father* look grim? He held Mother firmly with one arm, stroking her hair soothingly with the other hand.

"She'll get lost!" choked Mother. "Or a storm will blow up! Oh! Will he *rape* her?"

What?!

Nerine gulped, swallowing back down nausea. She knew what rape was. Mother and Father had had that conversation with her when she was Agnippe's age. Oh, not about rape, but about sexuality, how it worked, and how it birthed a flood of strong emotions. The rape conversation had come later, not all that long ago, really. But, *rape*? And sweet Agnippe?

Nerine swallowed again, hard. Her stomach felt hot, now. Hot and roiling. A lot like when she'd gotten sick on the boat with Altairos.

"No, no," soothed Father. "He's masterful, no question. Overbearing. Overwhelming. But he's not a villain. Ionia, you know this yourself. He might seduce, but he wouldn't simply *take*."

Nerine's stomach settled so fast, she felt almost hollow. And cold again. *Not* rape. Thank the blessings!

Mother didn't seem to share Nerine's relief. She sobbed even more bitterly.

Who were they talking about anyway? Surely not Agnippe. And who was "he"? Nerine nibbled at her lower lip.

"But Meren, that's exactly what *will* happen! He'll seduce her, and then at the last minute she'll realize that she doesn't want it, and it will be too late! He won't *intend* rape, but it will *be* rape. Oh! No! My darling! Oh!"

It couldn't be Agnippe, decided Nerine. The only one it could be was Xianthe. Although . . . *little*? Really? At seventeen? Parents were strange. And who did they think was either raping or not raping Xianthe?

"Poseidon is wiser than that, love," said Father. "I can't deny that his tastes are . . . wide ranging." Father swallowed. "From sophisticated, requiring experienced partners, to . . ." Father was choosing his words carefully, and – apparently – having difficulty. "He does enjoy introducing naïve young women to . . ." Father faltered yet again, then spat, "But he's *good* at it. *Damn* him! He won't make the kind of mistake you fear." Father's unfamiliar grim look was back again.

Poseidon! Great and lesser blessings!

Nerine knew abruptly what had happened.

Poseidon's herald had been through just a month ago, and had promised to visit again on his return from the Levantine Sea, on his way back to Poseidon's court. Xianthe must have gone with him.

Mother gave herself over entirely to crying. Father pressed his cheek to the top of Mother's head, a look of anguish on his face.

Someone touched Nerine's elbow.

She looked around to see Nurse, also with tears in her eyes, but calmer than Mother.

"Come away, lovey. Come," she urged.

Nerine realized she still floated smack in the middle of the lagoon side gate. The warriors and servants had simply aimed for the gaps to each side of her, or above and below her, but she was very much in the way.

She allowed Nurse to draw her toward one of the columns, but she resisted leaving the front hall. She wanted – no, she *needed* to see, *hoped* she would see – Mother and Father regaining their balance, making a plan. Making a *good* plan.

"Where's Agnippe?" she murmured. She hadn't actually heard her parents mention which daughter they were mourning. It had to be Xianthe, she told herself. *Had* to be. But what if it weren't?

"She's in the nursery, sweet," answered Nurse. "She doesn't yet know . . . what has happened."

Nerine almost melted with relief.

"Nurse, what did happen? Is it Xianthe?"

Nurse nodded, her eyes reddening yet more. "She's run away, just as Ionia always feared. Just as she hoped to prevent by sending her to your aunt and uncle." Nurse shook her head. "Oh, your poor mother. After losing Hester, and now this!"

"Xianthe ran away!" Nerine hadn't guessed that part of it. Although . . . what precisely had she imagined? Mother and Father would never have given their consent for any daughter of theirs – or anyone else's – to join Poseidon's harem. That was the last thing they'd allow.

"And Cousin Hester also ran away?" Nerine didn't know much about Cousin Hester. Just that she'd been Mother's very great friend, and that Mother still missed her. And that Cousin Hester wasn't really their cousin. Or she might have been, but the relation was so remote as to be almost nonexistent. Second cousin of a second cousin, or some such thing. "Was Cousin Hester wild like Xianthe?" wondered Nerine.

"Oh, no, not like Xianthe," answered Nurse, the question steadying her. Distracting her from her present woe? "Hester was . . . just unusual. Very artistic, and saying outrageous things." Nurse sighed, compressing her operculi and expelling water from her gills. "People didn't understand her. She liked new ideas and new experiences too much."

Nerine wondered if Hester had been like Nerine herself was. Had Hester ever discovered the land the way Nerine had?

"Come to the nursery," urged Nurse again. "You can't help here."

But Mother was lifting her head and repinning her hair, which had become disheveled during her upset. Father relaxed his embrace to give her freedom to move.

"The sooner I depart, Ionia, the better."

Father was going somewhere? How could he? Mother needed him. *Nerine* needed him.

"Oh, Meren! Can you catch them?" gasped Mother.

Father didn't smile, precisely, but his face softened and took on a rueful expression. "They've got half a day's start on us, but I'm not giving up my daughter without a fight."

"Thank the blessings!" exclaimed Mother. "Go, Meren! Go!"

Oh! Nerine hadn't realized that Father could chase after Xianthe and the herald. Or – not so much not realized as just hadn't gotten to that thought yet. Everything was so . . . fraught. Had Mother not realized either?

Father drew Mother back into his arms, kissed her lovingly, and then set her from him to stroke vigorously toward the lagoon.

Nerine felt forlorn. It was good that Father was hurrying to rescue Xianthe. Of course. But . . . did he not even *see* Nerine?

Father checked abruptly, almost in the very spot where Nerine had checked, except facing the opposite direction. He reversed himself and glided over to the column where she now floated. His face was very tender. He took her hands, kissed the back of each, murmured, "Be good to your mother," and then dove for the lagoon gate, six of his warriors following.

Nerine felt warm again – no longer chilled, but not hot as when she feared for Agnippe.

Nurse moved toward the passageway that led back through the reef palace, pulling Nerine with her more insistently. "I must comfort your sister, and I'm *not* leaving you here alone."

Well, Nerine wouldn't be alone, but she knew what Nurse meant. Mother had already withdrawn, and the remaining warriors and servants – still in a bit of bustle – had other responsibilities. Nerine came along without resistance this time.

∽

They found Agnippe weeping in her sleeping circle, her face buried in her hands. The instant she saw them, she launched herself at Nurse, wailing.

Nurse scooped her in and held Agnippe as though she were a baby. "You know then, lovey?"

"I heard the maid who found the note," sobbed Agnippe. "Oh, poor Mother! How will she ever bear it?"

Nerine started to withdraw. Agnippe needed Nurse, not her sister.

Agnippe snagged Nerine's wrist. "Please. Don't go. I'd like you to stay. If you don't mind."

Nerine's hand turned to clasp Agnippe's. She felt like she ought to say something, but the words wouldn't come. Waves of fear, terror, then fear had passed through her. Washed her clean of any feeling at all. She was emptied out.

"Your mother will bear up just fine, sweeting," insisted Nurse. "Never you fret."

Agnippe kept a hold of Nerine's hand. Nerine squeezed it, and felt Agnippe's returning pressure.

"Father?" asked Agnippe.

"He's gone after your sister," said Nurse, her voice firming. "He'll catch her, too, the naughty lass. Oh! How could she give your mother such a fright?"

Agnippe's answering giggle was so subdued as to barely qualify as such.

Nerine's numbness was waning. It was reassuring to see Nurse recovering her usual tone.

"Why *did* she run away?" Nerine burst out. Could being in a different place really solve your problems?

Agnippe lifted her head from Nurse's shoulder, shedding her downturned expression. "She was suffocating here. She almost had to do something drastic."

Huh. Yes, Nerine could see it. She had her own outlet: Altairos and the shore. Which meant that being in a different place could help. It helped her. But Xianthe didn't have a different place. So she'd sought one.

Nerine blinked. How strange that she and Xianthe were alike in something.

But why was home so suffocating? Mother and Father weren't really restrictive or rigid. Father was so understanding. And he and Mother allowed their children a lot of freedom. But Nerine needed the shore. The freedom of the sea wasn't enough.

Agnippe wriggled in Nurse's embrace, and Nurse let her go.

Agnippe looked around at her sleeping circle, surveying the aqua of the coral and the lavender of her sponges. She frowned. "Nerine, can we go to your parlor? All of this" – she waved a hand to encompass her nook and the nursery beyond it – "just makes me think of Xianthe, and I *don't want to!*"

That was true. Nerine felt the same way. "Let's!" she agreed. It was nice of Agnippe to recognize the parlor as hers. It still wasn't. Not officially. But it *felt* like hers.

In the amber outer lobe of the parlor, well lit by glass globes enclosing glowing comb jellies, Nerine occupied herself with an algebra lesson assigned a few days ago. She didn't want to think about . . . much of anything right now, but she needed something to occupy her mind. Evidently Agnippe felt the same. Nerine wasn't sure what her sister was working on, but she remained focused on the copper sheet on her lap desk and the words she inscribed with her stylus.

Nurse stayed with them for a while, single-needle knitting something with a strand of white chitin.

It was soothing to float together without talking, soaking in the others' presence, but occupied with your own task.

Eventually Nurse folded her knitting neatly and thrust it into her work bag.

"I'll be in the nursery, lovies, if you need me," she said, pausing to be sure they'd be all right without her.

Agnippe waved without looking up.

Nerine nodded, then went back to her algebra.

Later, Nurse brought Mother to them.

Mother had regained her poise. On the surface she looked exactly as she always did: green-golden hair pinned elegantly to her head, cool confidence in her gray eyes, and controlled grace in her limbs. She wore a particularly refined belt and pectoral, white gold with pearlescent abalone inlay.

Why did Nerine sense that, underneath Mother's composed appearance, she was . . . fragile?

Mother settled herself in a sitting bowl and gestured for Nerine and Agnippe to join her. Nurse tilted her head to one side, nodded, and then swam out.

Agnippe curled up against Mother's right flank, while Nerine kept just a little distance between herself and Mother on the left.

"Did Xianthe confide in either of you?" Mother asked, not accusatory, but genuinely curious.

"She wouldn't," answered Agnippe.

Nerine just shook her head no.

"Hmm." Mother sounded pensive. "How are you feeling?"

"Xianthe scared me," proffered Agnippe. "I didn't wish her gone, but I did want her to . . . stop. Stop yelling. Stop slamming water about. Just . . . stop."

Nerine still didn't know how she felt. And she didn't want to talk about it with Mother. Now, if Altairos were here . . . she wished he *were* here. She could talk about it with him. In fact . . . if Altairos were sitting by her side, she'd know how she felt. Which would be a relief. She didn't like this nothing feeling.

"Nerine?" asked Mother.

"I just feel . . . blank," Nerine managed.

Mother stroked her hand. Her fingers were cool and firm. "I don't blame you," said Mother. "I feel a little blank myself."

Nerine didn't like that. It felt like Mother were appropriating Nerine's feelings. Nerine wanted to have her feelings to herself. It wasn't fair of Mother to take them. But she didn't say any of that. Father would have understood. Mother wouldn't. Couldn't.

"This is the note your sister left." Mother rummaged in the small mesh reticule hanging by a strand from her shoulder. She drew out a square sheet of copper and held it so they both could see.

I must go. I can't explain it. I'm sorry. But I'm going with Neomar to Poseidon's court, there to take a berth in the Emperor's harem. I know you will think this is awful, but it isn't. Don't grieve for me. Please! That's part of why I have to go. All my love, Xianthe

Something clicked into place in Nerine's thoughts. *That* was why home was so confining. Why Xianthe left in the way she did. Why Nerine had to go to the shore. Why Nerine kept her shore visits secret.

Mother and Father gave their children freedom to try things, freedom to roam the reef, freedom to think new thoughts. But undergirding that freedom was their view of how the world was and how to operate within it. And they expected that after all the experimenting they allowed their children, their children would eventually adopt their viewpoint.

That expectation – except it was stronger than an expectation – that *belief* was stultifying. To Nerine at least. And – evidently – to Xianthe as well.

Eilidh – Eilidh had simply adopted Mother's world view as her own, with nary a protest, almost as though she didn't notice herself doing so.

Tyr didn't notice that Mother and Father had a world view. Which was why Tyr seemed so free. He had built his own world view without worrying about anyone else's. He selected a few opinions from Mother, a whole bunch from Father, and forged the rest all on his own.

But Nerine couldn't be fully herself when she swam within Mother's and Father's sphere. She was always Nerine-in-relation-to-Mother or Nerine-in-relation-to-Father. She couldn't be Nerine-as-Nerine at home in the reef. And if she ever told Mother or Father about her visits ashore, then the land would become Mother's and Father's, and she wouldn't be able to be Nerine there either.

It wasn't even their fault, Nerine realized abruptly. Father especially would say that he wanted Nerine to be her own person, and he would mean it, heart and soul.

It was *Nerine* who found their presence to be so overpowering. Who couldn't separate herself fully from them unless she traveled where they did not.

And Xianthe must have felt the same way. Which was why she raged. It was her only way of getting free. Maybe Poseidon's harem *would* be a better place for her. Just as Altairos' shore was a freer place for Nerine.

"Does this make any sense to either of you?" Mother asked, gesturing with Xianthe's note.

"It feels right to me," answered Agnippe. "It feels very Xianthe. But I can't explain it."

"Mmm." Mother tucked the copper square away in her reticule. "*That* I agree with, and I'd rather I didn't. I wish I *could* explain it."

Nerine held her tongue. She could explain it. She could. But she wasn't going to. It would become just one more thing in which she couldn't hold her own against Mother. And she already mostly didn't hold her own against Mother. Giving yet more water to her would be giving what Nerine couldn't afford to cede.

Mother hugged Agnippe and patted Nerine's hand. "Do you have any questions, darlings? Any concerns or confusions? I want to listen, to help you, with anything you feel uneasy about."

"I think I need to sleep," volunteered Agnippe. "It's all been a lot."

Mother kissed Agnippe's forehead, just above the spiracles. "No dinner, darling?"

"I'm not hungry," answered Agnippe.

"Very well." Mother turned to Nerine. "What do you need, darling? Tell me."

"I think I need sleep, too," said Nerine. She didn't. Not yet. But she did need solitude. Needed Mother to let her be.

Mother nodded. "Come to me any time. Even in the night. I'm here."

Then she kissed Nerine and left the parlor.

∼

Over the next few days, messages from Father arrived, reporting his progress.

The herald Neomar had not stopped at Tyr's annex in the Tyrrhenian, which wasn't surprising. There were no women living there as yet. Tyr sent word along with Father's message, promising to remain alert for tidings of Neomar's whereabouts and urging all at home to trust Xianthe's ability to take care of herself. Apparently Tyr wasn't too worried about their sister, which was oddly reassuring. Nerine suspected that Tyr may have known Xianthe better than anyone else. Had she confided in her brother? Maybe, just maybe, she had.

Duke Anstice of the Ligurian Sea sent two of his nieces with Poseidon's herald. The Duke of the Gulf of Gallicus – who shared Father's opinion of harems – spoke of the five maidens accompanying Poseidon's herald. The two from the Levantine were redheads, while the three from the Ligurian comprised two brunettes and one blonde.

That cleared up one mystery.

How had Xianthe persuaded the herald to take her with him? She was too young to go on her own initiative. Neomar would have needed her parents' explicit consent, and he would not have foregone it.

Xianthe must have stowed away in one of the chariots and only revealed herself when she could pretend to be one of Duke Anstice's nieces. *After* they left the Ligurian Sea.

The King of the Balearic Sea, who sent a daughter to Poseidon, said that Father was a full day behind the herald.

Difficult sea currents slowed Father still more in the passage around the curve of Iberia, and the King of the Alboran Sea reported Poseidon's herald to be a full three days gone.

Father came home.

Nerine didn't see him arrive. Didn't see him, in fact, until after he'd conferred with Mother in privacy and emerged from their suite to greet his daughters, warmly hugging each.

He guided them to the garden outside the nursery to say his piece.

The day was sunny, and the water like liquid light. The scarlet of the fire coral and the yellow of the anemones were particularly vivid, and the green of the sea lettuce greener than ever. The spicy sweet scent of the sea grapes ebbed and flowed. The garden felt like a remnant of childhood, wrapping Nerine in her youth, when the competence of her parents felt safe and reassuring instead of confining. She leaned into Father's side, while Agnippe crept onto his lap.

"You'll be wondering why I returned without Xianthe," he said.

"Why did you, Father?" asked Agnippe. "Nurse said you would never give up."

"Two reasons, sweetheart. The first is that one doesn't approach the Emperor of the World Sea without his bidding. Diving into Poseidon's court without his leave would only have led to my immediate ejection. I will request an audience with him, which he will no doubt grant. But one doesn't ignore the protocol of the great courts to one's advantage. Storming Poseidon's palace would not have extracted Xianthe, which is what I wish to do."

"Will she come back with you when you meet Lord Poseidon?"

Agnippe sounded so young, much younger than usual. Had their childhood garden affected her the same way it had Nerine?

"That will depend on Lord Poseidon's will. And on Xianthe's."

"Mmm." Agnippe nestled closer to Father.

"What was your second reason, Father?" asked Nerine.

"It was something your brother said. That Xianthe's tantrums didn't stem from her weakness, but from her strength. That she was a woman grown, even though we didn't recognize it. Or, indeed, that she didn't either. That we should respect her choice, even though we disagreed with it."

Father patted Agnippe's shoulder. "I won't lie to you. I hate leaving Xianthe to the consequences of *this* choice. But – I suspect that my retrieval of her would do even more damage to her. So, I'll beg her to come home, when I see her, but I will not force her." He shook his head, then smiled. "And how are my two little fishies doing here at home? Your mother reports that she and you are regaining your equilibrium. Are you?"

"Can we just not talk about it, Father?" pleaded Agnippe. "I just want to be happy you are home and be . . . happy."

Nerine scrutinized her sister. This was the first time Agnippe had ever asked to not talk about anything. What was that about?

But Father let her get away with it, turning his gaze to Nerine instead.

"Father, am I awful for being glad that Xianthe is gone?" She hadn't known she was going to say that before it fell out of her mouth. She hunched her shoulders, worrying how Father might react.

He laughed.

"I can't be glad with you, of course, although I feel oddly hopeful for your sister's future. But, no, you aren't awful. Xianthe had turned home into a battleground where nobody could be comfortable. And you and she . . . had the least in common of all of your siblings, did you not?"

Father's arm had come around her, feeling steady and safe. She might find Father's strength confining, more and more often, but this moment wasn't one of them. She felt relieved, glad of his understanding.

"Xianthe never really liked me as a friend," Nerine explained.

"No," Father agreed, his voice gentle.

"But she didn't love me as a sister either." It felt good to say it. "I *tried* to love her as a sister. And sometimes I think I did. But not often." That did sound rather awful. But somehow Father's listening made it not awful. It just was . . . true.

Father kissed the crown of her head.

"Truth is always freeing," he said. "Always be true, Nerine."

He sounded proud of her.

"I've got to get back to my ministers, fishies. I left them without even a parting instruction, let alone preparation for transferring work in progress. I suspect I've got one unholy mess awaiting me." He chuckled. "But come to me at any time, should you need me. Your mother and I are here. And this has been a difficult thing. Needing support is no shame."

Agnippe bobbed up from his lap to kiss his cheek.

He chuckled again and swam toward the garden's dike. "Coming in with me?"

Nerine shook her head. She wanted to soak up the bright light flooding down through the water a little longer, enjoy feeling like a child a little more, and smell the spicy sweet sea grapes until the brightness dimmed.

"I'm staying with Nerine," declared Agnippe.

Father nodded and swam off.

Nerine floated with Agnippe, enfolded in peace, not talking. The garden was so beautiful, the water so clear, the light . . . almost holy. Were the Isles of the Blessed – the destination of mortal heroes – like this?

Agnippe's hand brushed Nerine's wrist.

"Nerine?" Agnippe's voice was drowsy.

"Hmm?" Nerine wasn't ready to let go of her silence yet. She wanted to listen to the swirl of the water, its gentle slap against the upper reef, and the distant tinking sound from the artisans' court.

"Promise you won't run off like Xianthe when home gets too small for you."

"Huh?" Nerine abruptly righted herself from the semi-reclining position she'd adopted.

"You could, you know," said Agnippe, a slight smile on her face.

"I could, but I wouldn't. Agnippe – !" Nerine couldn't believe she was hearing this.

"Two years ago, you would have followed Father inside," continued Agnippe.

That was true. Two years ago, she would have asked Father to stay outside, so that she could sort out how she felt with his help. And he would have stayed. And she would have felt comfortable and at peace with herself when he went to shoulder his responsibilities.

But now she was sixteen, not fourteen, and she needed to be away from him to sort herself out.

"I *love* Father. And Mother," she added.

"So did Xianthe," said Agnippe.

"But I'm not anything like Xianthe," Nerine protested.

Agnippe let herself drift upright. "I know you're not, but . . ."

"And I love home. I love it here." Which was true, and also not true. She loved it here as long as she could also go ashore.

"Nerine, if you went, then I'd be the only daughter left. I can't – I can't – oh, Nerine, please promise!" Agnippe sounded almost agonized, her tone at strange variance with her face, which remained calm.

Nerine wondered if Agnippe felt the same pressure she did from Mother and Father, to live up to their expectations, to fulfill all one's potential, to be or become . . . great.

"I won't run away," she promised. It was an easy promise. She couldn't envision ever wanting to. She might not always do what Mother and Father wanted her to. In fact, she could sense a clash coming. But her way was not Xianthe's way. She wouldn't tantrum or fling herself into the unknown in a huff. She wasn't quite sure how she would do it. But . . . now that the idea had come to her, she almost looked forward to it. She would throw off her duty to her parents and claim her independence. It would feel good. It would feel great! Except . . .

She could see Father, looking crushed and bewildered and sad. And Mother looking furious, but with that hidden fragility underneath. That hurt her.

Blessings, but this business of growing up was a pain.

She didn't want to hurt Mother and Father, but how else was she to stop being a little girl? Go from being just a daughter to being fully Nerine?

"Promise and *mean* it," insisted Agnippe.

Had Nerine sounded like she didn't mean it? Very well, she would try again.

She swirled her left foot to move her nearer to Agnippe, and took both Agnippe's hands in her own. She gazed seriously into her sister's eyes. "I, Nerine Merenou Pelagieus, do solemnly give my word and my breath that I will never run away from home." She squeezed Agnippe's hands. "Do you believe me now?"

Agnippe's eyes looked a little red. Had this meant so much to her? "*Thank* you," she breathed, flexing her operculi to pull more water through her gills. And then she buried her head in Nerine's shoulder.

Nerine's arms closed around her. Agnippe was precious, and Nerine never wanted to hurt her. She'd come a long way since she was eight, and Agnippe was four, and Nerine just wanted Agnippe to *stop whining*. Agnippe *had* stopped whining, and she was lovely to have as a sister.

∾

They settled down to a palace without Xianthe fairly quickly.

Mother and Father took the longest. Most of the time, they seemed their normal selves, but every now and then some topic arising in conversation would remind them of their missing daughter. Father would get that no-expression, grim look on his face. Then he'd sound sad. And then he'd push his melancholy aside.

Mother's nostrils and spiracles would pinch in, white, as though she were angry, but with a look of vulnerability under her anger. Then she'd toss her head and smile graciously.

But eventually both parents ceased to be so reactive. At least, overtly. Likely they still grieved in private.

Nerine quite liked Xianthe's absence. Not only was the peace in the palace welcome, the absence of small, barbed remarks from Xianthe was equally soothing. Nerine hadn't realized how many times in a day Xianthe had jabbed at her verbally. She almost wondered if her sense of restriction at home was due to Xianthe's frequent hostility, rather than ever-present parental expectations.

The next time Nerine visited the shore, Altairos wasn't there, so she walked to Calla's cottage. She'd already told Calla all about Xianthe's tantrums. Which was why Calla had offered her sanctuary that one night – the night before Xianthe ran away, as it chanced.

Nerine wanted to fill her in on the latest episode.

The island's summer had reached its peak, with the afternoons too hot for pleasure unless one were swimming. But the early mornings remained lovely – clear and cool and very, very bright.

They sat on the ledge built out from the exterior wall on Calla's terrace. Cushions covered the mosaics now, which were a lot more comfortable. Dappled shade from the bougainvillea covering the arbor above them eased the brightness of the sunlight.

Calla poured a chilled mint infusion from an amphora into two drinking bowls. Nerine took a sip. *Mmm.* She'd loved the sweet fruit drinks of the land when she was younger, but the utter freshness of unsweetened mint made this infusion her favorite now.

"And how are you, mikroula?" asked Calla, a comfortable tone in her voice. Nerine loved that tone. Just hearing it made her sure that everything – even the worst of troubles – would be well in the end. Her own Nurse had a similar tone, but Nerine could always hear a tinge of worry under it. Calla could worry, but she didn't make a habit of it.

"I'm well," said Nerine. She glanced at Calla, wondering how she would take Nerine's news. "Xianthe ran away. Two *déka*-days ago."

Calla shook her head slightly, smiling. "Ah, she was always going to run away, that one. She wasn't big enough to hold herself; how could any place then be big enough?"

"You knew?" Nerine was surprised. "Why did you not warn me? I could have warned Mother and Father."

Calla looked skeptical. "Could you?"

Hmm. Calla had a point. She couldn't have said, "Calla says Xianthe will run. Beware." And any other words would have merely sounded as though she harbored fears needing reassurance.

Calla nodded, obviously following Nerine's line of thinking from the expression on her face.

"Nothing would have stopped Xianthe, would it?" Nerine wasn't so much asking as concluding.

"No, mikroula, nothing. How are you managing?"

Nerine felt herself blushing. "I like it."

Calla nodded again. "Of course you do." She knew why without Nerine having to explain. "And your parents?"

Nerine sighed. "She ran away to join Poseidon's harem. Mother hates that. And Father . . . is deeply worried."

Calla's forehead wrinkled. Nerine suspected that she was like Altairos in still finding it astonishing that the gods worshipped in the temples of the land were merely neighbors – distant neighbors, but neighbors all the same – to the people of the sea.

"A father would worry," agreed Calla. "But your sister's a tough girl. I suspect she needs a spell of living with – hmm, not enemies, but – folks whose first concern is not her well-being. Although your mother is right. The harem of the Lord of the Oceans isn't the right place for her."

"Tyr thinks she'll come to no harm," Nerine volunteered.

"Does he not?" Calla tilted her head. "That's interesting. Very interesting." She patted Nerine's hand. "Likely he's right then. Your brother isn't a thoughtful sort, but he always perceives the obvious. I think you needn't worry for your sister then. Hear me?"

Nerine decided she wouldn't worry from that moment. Calla was as shrewd as she could hold together. If she thought Xianthe was safe, Nerine would believe her. She only wished she could pass along her belief to Mother and Father. For herself . . . not fearing for Xianthe meant she also needn't feel guilty about enjoying Xianthe's absence. Home felt more comfortable than ever.

When Nerine finally caught up with Altairos, he had news. *Big* news.

～

Nerine learned Altairos' news when she came ashore early one evening.

Father's ministers had been honored earlier in the day at a formal noontide feast, celebrating their excellent management during the ten days when Father had been absent, after departing so abruptly. Both Nerine and Agnippe attended. The merry mood of the gathering was pleasant enough that Nerine hadn't minded when it lasted for three full courses of food. Conveniently, the feast meant that supper would be small, casual, and very late. She told Nurse that she might make do with the morsels the palace cook arranged in the guardsmen's anteroom for the night, and not to worry.

Then she slipped away.

On the beach, the shadow of the cliffs had crept out across the dunes. Only the strip of sand along the sea remained in sunlight. The waves were mild in the slack tide, and the breaking surf seemed more a murmuring rush than a crash. The air stood still and cooling. The sky overhead shone a very deep blue.

Nerine paused with her ankles in the sea foam, reveling in the chill as the water evaporated from her skin, and then welcoming the warmth of the sun once she was dry.

She didn't see Altairos, waiting in the shade, but then she didn't expect to. She'd come ashore just to feel the sand under her feet and the air around her like a gossamer cape. The evening wasn't their time to visit with one another.

She stepped away from the water at the same time as Altairos stepped out of the cliff's shadow.

He looked serious, and older, but glad.

"Nerine," he said, walking closer and holding out both his hands to her.

She placed her hands in his. He drew her in and kissed her cheek very tenderly.

"You're more beautiful every time I see you," he murmured, almost to himself.

She smiled and kissed his cheek in return. His admiration had grown more comfortable over the last few years, to become just part of him, part of who he was. And she loved who he was. She always had. She always would. It was part of being Nerine.

He led her to her left, toward a spot where the cliffs were lower and the sunlit sands wider. His silken cloth of golden yellow lay there, with a stone at each corner to prevent it from blowing away in an errant breeze.

They sat facing the sea. The waves had that metallic blue that they acquired later in the day, adorned with a lace of foam. The sky grew lighter at the horizon, making a sharp line between air and water.

Altairos stayed silent for a while. Nerine savored his presence: so different from any of her family. Agnippe was quiet, so quiet she was almost dense with it. Mother was more diffuse, but cool, so cool that it defined her. Father was warm and comfortably weighty, like a quilt wrapped around one on a cool evening on land. This evening would be cool were she not bathed in sunlight.

Altairos was comforting, like Father, but buoyant. As though he were the warm breeze from a scented garden, carrying laughter on its tendrils. Nerine loved Altairos best of all.

Abruptly, he turned toward her, eagerly. "Nerine, my tutor has declared me ready to learn by observing and doing. Reading scrolls and practicing oratory and devising clever arguments in the schoolroom has gotten me as far as I can go. Pappa will send me with Lord Calix to seek allies against the pirates of the Middle Sea and to make plans for their defeat!"

Lord Calix was King Zeron's most able envoy. Being appointed to him said something about Altairos' progress and his skills.

"I'm glad for you," said Nerine. And she was. She'd expected to feel elation when he eventually passed from studying diplomacy to practicing it, but somehow this was too important for fizzy delight. She felt deep and glad and . . . golden. Almost as though she were a great bell that had come to rest after being struck, still humming with a low vibration.

"I'll keep records of all the most fascinating people and places I see. Should you like that, Nerine?"

"Yes, I *would*! Thank you!" Reading over his notes, with him by her side to answer all her questions, would be almost like going herself. He would make those far lands come alive in her mind's eye. She would see the pharaoh in exotic Aegyptus. She would hear the wild conch blowers in rich Phoiníke. She would smell the spices in the bazaars of Persia. It would be glorious!

"I will be gone nearly two years. We plan to visit every king with a navy to secure a treaty. And then to sail again to secure the coordination between the fleets. I'll miss you, Nerine."

She would miss him too, but she didn't want to think about that right now.

"Are the pirates so dangerous?" she wanted to know. Should she be scared for him?

"Pappa's warships guard our merchant fleet and our harbor, so Zakynthos is untroubled. The same for Aegyptus and Chios, Athens and Rhodes. But many of the smaller polises cannot provide such protection to their merchants. And too many shipments of tin – from Tyrrhenia, particularly – have failed to arrive."

That caught her attention. She wondered if her brother, whose sea bordered this land with the tin mines, might act against the pirates. It seemed a shame that King Zeron was reaching out to the land people only. Imagine if

Tyr were to conjure a great wave to smash the pirate ships. Or Duke Anstice in the Ligurian Sea. Sea people might be the best allies of all.

"Will you sail with the warfleet?" she asked. "When battle is joined?"

He nodded. "Likely I will. The foreign fleets will need translators."

She shivered, despite the warmth of the sun. "Your Pappa would risk you in battle?"

Altairos laughed. "He risks my brothers – the admirals of our three warfleets – whenever there is conflict at sea. But our *triereis* and *tetrereis* are among the strongest warships in the Middle Sea, and our marine warriors, the stoutest. And each fleet possesses at least one *penteres*. I shouldn't worry, Nerine."

She looked at him, assessing his words. Did he really mean them? Or was he merely reassuring her, because he didn't *want* her to worry?

No, his face was relaxed, and his eyes met hers without strain. He wasn't worried and he didn't think there was any need for her to be either.

She puffed out a sigh of relief. "This is – this is – really *incredible*! You've – you've *arrived*!"

Now she was feeling some of the elation she'd expected to feel. Maybe the surprise of his announcement had overwhelmed it before.

He grinned – the grin with the crinkling eyes that she loved.

"Well, not *arrived*, Nerine. But *started*. That for sure."

"Are you excited?" she demanded.

"Yes, I can hardly wait! We embark in a *déka*-day. And four days after that we'll moor in the harbor of Carthage!" He beamed.

"And then you'll meet with –" she paused a moment, digging in her memories for knowledge of the great city; Carthage didn't have a king . . . or a queen "– the two Suffets, the Judges," she pronounced triumphantly.

Altairos grinned again, clearly recognizing that she'd had to fish for the right term.

"Then we'll sail for Trípolis, and then for Cyrene," he exulted.

They talked for a time about what they knew of these exotic ports and talked even longer about what they didn't know, piling question atop of question.

The cliff's shadow crept out across the sand and then across the sea.

Altairos pulled the back corners of the silken cloth out from under their rocks and draped it over Nerine's shoulders. She leaned against him comfortably.

The sky darkened to a deep, deep turquoise and the first stars appeared, shining like diamonds.

Their conversation wound down. Altairos kissed Nerine's hair just above her ear.

"I'll miss you," he said, his voice light, but with a wistful note.

She would miss him, too, but she didn't want to admit it. "Remember everything," she told him, "so you can share it all when you get back."

"You remember too!" he said.

"I won't be going anywhere," she pointed out.

He snorted. "Nerine, you'll be changing every day for two years. Of course I'm going to want to hear all about it."

She felt foolish, but she also felt . . . loved.

"I'll remember," she promised.

He walked her to the edge of the sea. The last whisper of a wave slid over the sand to curl around her ankles. His hand circled her arm, just above the elbow. His palm felt warm and supportive. He gazed into her face, his own softening from a laugh, to a look of deep affection.

He bent nearer.

Nerine closed her eyes.

His breath caressed her, soft and gentle, like the touch of a rose petal against her cheek. Then his lips met hers, firm and silky smooth. Something leapt within her and she leaned into his kiss. This was right, so right, but it lasted only a moment.

When his lips retreated, she opened her eyes.

His smile was so tender it melted her heart.

She smiled back at him, feeling shy.

His eyes held more than tenderness, and she felt as though the expectant silence of Gaia herself, in the hour before the goddess birthed the hills and the sea, infused the evening all around them. Why was she suddenly breathless?

A strange disquiet swayed her.

She turned and dove into the sea. The waters of her origins embraced her. The flutter within her calmed. His kiss had been brief, chaste. But as she swam home through the gathering dusk, she could still feel his lips on hers – warm and inviting, urging her like the tide toward depths unexplored.

She skipped supper and fell into sleep.

～

15 ~ First Bitter Loss

SOON AFTER ALTAIROS DEPARTED, the muses of Mount Helicon offered Agnippe the guardianship of their sacred spring.

Mother was thrilled, because it was a considerable honor. Agnippe would receive respect equal to that of her sister Eilidh. Father also was pleased, because Agnippe liked the position. And Nurse was exceedingly happy, because the fresh water of the spring would not irritate Agnippe's skin the way salt water did.

Agnippe herself was over the moon with delight and a little overwhelmed.

"Nerine, do you realize . . . the inspiration for Euterpe's songs, for Clio's dances – for all the culture of the Hellene world – flows from the springs of Mount Helicon. And it will all flow from me!" Agnippe sounded stunned. "My care for the waters must be flawless."

Nerine squeezed her sister's shoulders. "You'll have some preparing to do to be ready."

Agnippe nodded vigorously, her eyes wide.

"But, Agnippe, you *are* careful. I should think you're the perfect choice. Really."

"I hope so!" Agnippe quivered. "Do you think I can justify their trust in me?"

"They wouldn't have chosen you else," Nerine assured her.

Agnippe's lessons took an abrupt shift. Not only did she concentrate on the dynamics of water within more closed systems and the ecology of freshwater plants and fishes, but she also delved into esoteric metrical rhythms and obscure rhyming schemes, as well as archaic musical conventions.

Nerine discovered that she and Agnippe could now enjoy fascinating discussions about their studies, since Nerine's focus on languages meant she looked at culture from a practical, feet-in-the-water angle, while Agnippe approached it from an artistic, creative one.

Nerine had expected to miss Altairos dreadfully, and she *did* miss him. But not dreadfully. Her growing friendship with her sister and their ongoing discussion of all they were learning filled the gap left by Altairos in many ways.

Instead of comparing notes with Altairos, she compared them with Agnippe. Instead of seeking time ashore to get out from under Mother and Father, she sought time with her sister. It answered very well. She did still visit Calla. Dear Calla, who was so comfortable and steady and shrewd. But whose hair had changed from silver-gray to silver-white, and whose skin grew soft with age.

Nerine felt very content.

And, yet, she did miss Altairos. Not for anything he could do for her, but just because no one around her could *be* him. She missed his laugh. She missed his energetic approach to life. She missed his liking to take action. She missed the way his eyes crinkled when he grinned. She missed *him*.

But still, life was good. And the feeling that she was developing an ability to hang onto herself, even in Mother's presence, was more than good. That sense of herself – where other left off and where Nerine began – was what she had needed so desperately, what had propelled her secretly to the shore for the last eight years.

Maybe she had just needed to grow up. Maybe it was just the middle part of growing up that was hard. Maybe she'd reached an easier stretch at last.

She entertained that comforting belief for several *déka*-days.

And then she went ashore again.

It was a dry, cool day with wisps of cloud scudding across the deep blue of the sky, which meant rain was coming, perhaps tomorrow. But Nerine wanted company and conversation, not communion with the beauties of nature.

The instant the dry air sucked all the moisture from her skin and hair, she headed for Calla's cottage.

Agnippe's growing excitement about her new vocation emphasized Nerine's own lack of vocation. Her parents hadn't been much help with that. But Calla – sensible and perceptive Calla – might have some useful ideas.

Nerine hurried her steps when the cottage came in sight. It looked dustier, somehow, maybe because the garden had few blooms and the matte green leaves and stems dominated. Even the bougainvillea vine on the arbor lacked its usual bright pink flowers.

A feather of unease stirred in Nerine's belly. Her fast walk became a trot, and she skipped the shallow steps up to the terrace altogether, leaping from pale earth to stone flagging in one bound. The shock of landing that traveled up from her bare feet barely registered.

Just inside the door from the terrace, Calla lay on the floor.

～

Nerine fell to her knees in alarm. "Calla! Calla!" she called.

Calla stirred, but her eyes stayed closed. Her face looked haggard and sunken, and her white hair straggled out of its usually tidy pinned arrangement on her head. A sour smell rose from her body.

Nerine tried to lift her.

Calla moaned, very faintly. Was Nerine hurting her? She dithered a moment, then bent to speak urgently in Calla's ear. "Calla, it's Nerine. I'm going to get help. You'll feel better very soon, when the *physiatrós* comes to you."

She ran all the way to the palace.

The servants were swift to summon the *physiatrós* and swift to accompany Nerine back to Calla's cottage. Nerine was thankful for the many visits she'd made to Altairos' home over the years. She was not strange to its denizens, although their eyes widened to see her in the belt and pectoral of the sea, rather than the gown of the land dwellers. She hadn't paused to change.

The maidservants brought a smooth linen cloth to spread over the sheepskin that made Calla's bed soft. Three strong men lifted her. Gently, carefully, and still she moaned.

Nerine sponged Calla's face and noticed the entire right side lay slack compared to the left side, in which the eyelid tightened in pain, and the lips crimped.

The *physiatrós*, when he came, brought no good news.

"She suffers a hemorrhage of the brain," he pronounced after examining Calla, even successfully prompting her to lift her left arm and her left leg. He shook his head – "I am sorry" – and prescribed trepanning as a treatment.

When Nerine saw what that meant and the dreadful tool that would be used – like a small spear with a cross piece and strings to spin it – she tried to stop him, but the servants held her, unfazed by her wild struggles. And when the blood trickled from the small hole in Calla's skull, she did seem to grow easier, calmer.

Nerine refused to leave, even after sundown arrived. She didn't care what might be happening in her home under the sea. Calla needed her, and she would not go.

She offered her small sips of wine. She sponged her hands. And she sang to her.

In the night, in the dim flickering light cast by the oil lamps, Calla roused from the stupor that had claimed her. Her left eye said she knew Nerine, and the left side of her lips moved as she tried to form words.

"N –" she said. "N –"

"Yes, I'm Nerine," prompted Nerine.

Calla shook her head ever so slightly. "A –" she tried again.

"Altairos?" guessed Nerine.

Calla nodded, the motion small, but definite.

"He's in Aegyptus, learning all the subtleties of diplomacy from Lord Callix."

Calla's lips twisted and her forehead wrinkled, unhappy with Nerine's obtuseness.

"You remember that and wish I wouldn't state the obvious," said Nerine.

Calla nodded.

"I'll try to be smarter," Nerine apologized.

The ghost of a smile lifted the left side of Calla's mouth, and her left hand pressed Nerine's.

"You want to tell me something about Altairos," Nerine said.

Calla nodded.

"Is it about his new profession?"

No.

"Is it about his future?"

No.

"His past?"

Yes.

Nerine felt a beat of surprise within. She knew Altairos so well. How could there be a secret in his past?

She tried various suggestions for Calla to say yes or no to. Something that had happened? Something he owned? A place he had visited? Someone he knew? Male or female?

Calla got very tired, and Nerine had to urge her to rest. But she wondered about the female in Altairos' past. She'd been only eight, and he only nine, when they'd first met, so she thought Calla must be referring to an aunt or an unknown sister. Or maybe Altairos' mother. But she wasn't sure. And she really didn't need to know. She could always ask Altairos when he returned.

But Calla struggled mightily to communicate. Because it was important to Calla, Nerine wanted her to succeed. Nerine pressed her teeth into her upper lip. She felt so helpless!

∽

In the morning, Altairos' brothers – three of them, including Hilarion, who happened to be home – visited the cottage. Calla had been their nurse too, and Nerine could see that they loved her. The eldest, with his stern face and spade beard, merely sat and stroked Calla's hand. A tear slipped from his eye as he turned away. The brother with a scar across his cheek thanked Calla for all her care of him when he was small.

Hilarion told her jokes, and Calla's lips twitched in appreciation.

Each of the brothers bowed to Nerine and spoke to her, both on arrival and before departure, which surprised her. She'd met Hilarion only the once and never met the others. They seemed to recognize her as Altairos' friend. Perhaps he had spoken of her to them.

In the afternoon, the king himself came.

Nerine had wandered outside onto the terrace, while the servants changed Calla's linens. Dark gray clouds hid the sky, and the air felt heavy, almost moist – the precursor to a storm. She plucked a few leaves from the sage growing near the steps and crushed them between her fingertips. The dusty, earthy scent of the herb seemed to seep into her bones, shoring her up. She was very tired.

The sound of many footsteps made her look up.

The king and his small retinue were just emerging from the gully beyond the garden. His draping robes were very grand, cobalt blue with gold embroidery at the hems. Two guardsmen flanked him, while a few courtiers trailed behind him.

Nerine shrank toward the cottage wall as he strode through the garden and up the terrace steps. Would he approach her? She felt suddenly unready to meet Altairos' pappa. What would he think of her? Would he forbid Altairos the friendship when his son returned?

There on the terrace, although the king's gaze had never intersected hers, he stopped and turned to face her. His retinue clustered close about him, their faces impassive. But his face was alive and suddenly gentle.

"Who are you, child?" His voice was very deep, but as gentle as his face. He looked a lot like his oldest son – with that black spade beard and short black hair – but much less stern. And older, of course. He had all his presence, though, and more.

Feeling breathless, she managed a land-style bow – one leg back and one arm back, not both – and answered, "I'm Nerine, your majesty."

"Ah, Altairos' young friend." He sounded pleased. "I didn't realize you were one of the *numeni*, Kyría Nerine, but I am most happy to make your acquaintance." The light in his face dimmed. "Even amidst these unhappy circumstances."

She bowed again, tongue-tied. The king seemed genial and approachable. He probably *was* approachable, if you were a member of his court. Or his family. Just like Father felt ordinary and comfortable to her and her sisters and brother. But even Father could be august when the occasion required. And Altairos' pappa seemed as cloaked in majesty as he was by his robes.

"Will you wait for me, child, while I attend Kyría Calla's bedside? Don't run away." He smiled, perhaps guessing that she *wanted* to run away. She wouldn't. Calla still needed her. But she wanted to.

"I shall wait, your majesty," she assured him.

"Good!"

And then he was gone, entering the cottage with his courtiers in his wake.

Nerine drew in a long breath. Goodness! Father was the only king she'd known. Was this how his subjects felt when he gave them audience? Altairos' pappa was impressive. But he'd seemed pleased that she was *numeni*, rather than otherwise. The servants – seeing the dimples of her closed spiracles for the first time – had directed some disapproving looks her way. If they hadn't already known her, hadn't been preoccupied with Calla's distress, she almost thought they might have ejected her from Calla's presence.

Thank the blessings that their king didn't share their disapproval.

∾

When the king emerged from the cottage, he sent his courtiers into the garden, obliged Nerine to seat herself on the cushioned wall bench, and seated himself beside her. A servant offered them a cool lemon mint infusion. Nerine drank thirstily and realized she was hungry. She'd taken nothing for herself during the long vigil over Calla, neither food, nor drink, nor rest.

The king spoke. "Were Altairos here, he would give you his thanks. In his absence, I must offer mine. Kyría Calla is . . . very dear to us all. We have urged her to accept apartments in the palace many times, but she prefers her cottage." The corner of his lips twisted.

Nerine gathered herself from her mental disarray. "Was . . . was she your nurse, too, when you were . . ." She couldn't quite finish. Mentioning that the king had once been a child or a baby seemed rude somehow.

"She was, dear lady. As much a mother to me as she has been to Altairos. We both lost our mothers young."

"I love her, too," confessed Nerine. "But the *physiatrós* said . . ." She faltered again. "Oh, your majesty, is it really true? That she will not recover?" She swallowed down the sob that threatened to break through.

The king's face grew somber. "Only the fates may see all ends, child, but the *physiatrós* is a wise man. I cannot doubt his pronouncement." He sighed. "I wish I might."

The threatening sob escaped her, and she covered her face with her hands. Oh! Oh! She had known, and yet she'd hoped. Hoped Calla would wake another day, and another, and return to her stalwart, cheerful self.

The king touched the backs of Nerine's hands. "Have you broken your fast, child? Have you rested?"

That steadied her. She wiped the tears from her face and took a deep breath.

"No, your majesty. I . . . I took no thought for myself. I thought . . ."

He smiled at her tenderly. "Your mother and father do not know that you've come to land, do they?"

Oh! Her eyes flew to his. How did he know?

He continued, "And lacking their care, you have forgotten to care for yourself."

That was true. Or almost true. Without Nurse and the routines of home, she'd paid no heed to her need for . . . anything. She blushed, feeling foolish. She stood nearer womanhood than childhood. She should have managed better.

"Will you go home, child? Or will you guest in my palace on the hill?"

That pierced her embarrassment. "Oh, please don't make me leave Calla! She keeps trying to tell me something. Something really important. I cannot leave her!"

He gave her a bemused glance. "Very well. I shall not constrain you, but this is what I will do. One of the kitchen maids shall be sent with meals. And you shall both eat and rest. Is it agreed?" His tone pressed her to consent.

She nodded. What he asked was only sensible.

He looked as though he wished to broach another topic, but only tightened his lips and took his departure. She had some idea as to why. Her own father was equally beset, with many urgencies competing for his time and attention. This king had undoubtedly left several counselors urging his swift return, when he decided to visit Calla.

The approaching storm broke before the kitchen servant arrived with food.

Nerine took shelter inside, closing the western shutters against the wind, then standing by one of the eastern windows, staring out at the violent rain pounding the dunes and the sea beyond, the individual drops of water leaping up from the nearer clay of the garden, so fierce was their fall.

The first crack of lightning startled Calla, and she cried out.

Nerine hurried to her side to soothe her.

Calla's left hand seemed to search something amidst the bedding – something she could not find. She quieted when Nerine stroked her cheek.

"N –, n –," Calla muttered, but Nerine could hardly hear her for the roar of the rain, the gusting wind, and the crashing thunder.

"Ssh, ssh," Nerine hushed her, "we'll try again when the storm is past."

It did pass, just before sunset, and the dinner from the palace arrived via several servants.

Nerine coaxed a few spoonfuls of chilled mutton broth between Calla's lips, and Calla was able to swallow, although not easily. When she fell into a light doze, Nerine carried her own meal out to the terrace. No one had brought the bench cushions in, and they were soaked, so she sat on the steps – already dry – to eat.

The air was very, very clear and cool; the now-cloudless sky, a blue so deep it seemed an ocean turned upside down; and the world so still, Nerine wondered if time had stopped.

A melon salad, cold and sweet, awoke her appetite. She ate heartily of the grilled lamb on skewers, the cheese-stuffed olives, salted eggs, and honeyed figs. A few sips of the sharp white wine made her feel dizzy, so she left her cup mostly full.

Three stars shone in the sky as she re-entered the cottage.

Calla still slept, and the servants busied themselves with clearing up after their meal.

Nerine sat at Calla's bedside, watching her as the last light of evening faded and the oil lamps were lit. The left side of Calla's face looked fretful, as though she dreamed unquiet dreams, the eyelid fluttering and the corner of the mouth twitching. The right side of her face looked dead, the mouth sagging, the cheek slack, and the eye sunken.

She awoke with a gasp and a start. Nerine touched her shoulder, brushed the strands of hair back from her face, and murmured, "I'm here, Calla. I'm here and I'll help."

She urged another spoonful of broth, but Calla refused it.

"N –, n –," she tried again, her left eye fixed on Nerine's face.

"Is it Altairos' mamma?" Nerine guessed.

The left side of Calla's lips smiled, and the rest of her left side relaxed.

Nerine relaxed, too. She'd figured out who. That felt like the hardest part. Now that she knew who, surely she could guess the what.

"Is it something she said?"

No.

"Is it something she did? Or failed to do?"

No.

"Is it how she died?"

No.

"Something that happened to her?"

No.

Calla grew more frustrated as her attempts to communicate bore no fruit. And Nerine grew frustrated with herself, that she hadn't sufficient imagination to make better guesses. If Calla had been able to say even one word, anything to prompt Nerine, they might have made better headway. The real problem was that Nerine knew so little of Altairos' mamma. He'd been so young when she died, and he'd said very little about her. She didn't have much to go on.

Calla tried harder to speak. A red flush mottled the skin of her left cheek, and perspiration broke out on her brow. Her breathing roughened, and then her flushed cheek whitened.

Nerine clutched her hand, suddenly frightened.

"Please rest!" she exclaimed. "We'll try again after you've rested."

But there would be no trying again for Calla.

She did rest, and resting she dozed.

Her breathing grew more ragged. Nerine gripped her hand more tightly, as though she could pull her from death's jaws by her clasp, and drew in deep breath after deep breath, willing her own lungs to breathe for Calla.

Then Calla breathed no more.

Nerine stared at her, eyes wide, waiting, waiting . . . surely there would be another breath.

Please. Please.

There wasn't.

She burst into wracking sobs and buried her face in the folds of cloth on Calla's still chest.

"Calla! Oh, Calla! Oh!"

One of the servants touched Nerine's hair, his face kinder, apparently softened from his previous disapproval by her grief. "Kyría, I shall go to the palace and tell them."

Nerine nodded, snuffling. "Yes. Thanks."

She stayed until Calla was carried out of her cottage by six stout bearers, bearing her up the cliff path.

～

Swimming home through the night dark waters, Nerine almost didn't care what might await her. Would Mother be furious? Would Father berate her, spurred by Mother's anxiety? Would Nurse be frantic? Would Nerine's long-held secret come out at last?

It didn't matter.

She felt numb with Calla's loss.

Nurse *was* frantic. But none of the other possibilities came to pass.

Neomar, herald to Poseidon, had arrived at the reef palace the same day of Nerine's departure, summoning King Meren to the court of the Lord of the Outer Sea. Father left immediately, taking the proffered seat in Neomar's chariot.

Mother, too, was absent.

Father had been on the verge of traveling to the Calypso Deep in the Ionian Sea with a group of warriors. There were indications that a kraken of unusual size had taken refuge there, following a fight with four warships of Athens, and Mother wanted the matter looked into. The Ionian Sea was under her guardianship.

Neomar's summons pre-empted all else, but Mother was not one to leave responsibilities unattended. *She* went to the Calypso Deep.

Nerine entered by the nursery door, as usual.

Nurse jittered there, swirling a foot or a hand, as though she would race off somewhere, but then thinking better of it and swirling the opposite limb to stay herself. Agitated, but unable to form a firm intention of what to do.

The instant she set eyes on Nerine, she burst into furious scolding. "How could you? Oh, how *could* you! I trusted you –"

Then she really saw Nerine, saw her face, and stopped. "Oh, sweeting! What has happened?"

Nerine shook her head dully.

"Oh, lovey." Nurse swam close to embrace her. "There, now. There, now, everything will be alright."

Nerine couldn't find it in herself to respond. To say anything. Even to hug Nurse back. She just wanted to be alone.

Nurse was guiding her to her old sleeping niche, murmuring endearments, hooking the net over her. "There now, just you have a good sleep out, and you'll feel better when you wake."

She swam away, very steady and sure now that she had a nursling to comfort. Nurse knew what to do with children under her care. Or thought she did, anyway. But Nerine was not a child any more. Not yet an adult, but beyond the confines of childhood.

She waited until Nurse was gone. Then she wearily unhooked the sleeping net and retreated to the double-lobed chamber she'd made her own.

The light globes had extinguished sometime during her two nights' absence, and she sat in the dark. Not thinking. Not feeling. Too tired for anything, even sleep.

Oh, Calla. Dear Calla.

Nerine had never lost anyone but her dolphin friend Pheep. And this was not the same. Not the same at all.

She wanted Calla back, desperately. And kept bumping up against her knowledge that Calla was never coming back. Not ever again.

She longed for her. And knew she would not be coming. And longed for her again. As though Calla's death were a rough seashell in the waves, scratching Nerine's heart as a breaker rolled in. Scratching Nerine's heart again, as the undertow dragged it out.

Bearing a light globe in cupped hands, Agnippe found her there.

Nerine didn't look up, but she knew who approached. Agnippe brought her own unique aura with her, and . . . a sister would know. Nerine knew.

Agnippe said nothing. Nor did she clutch at Nerine the way Nurse had.

Instead, she placed her light globe in an empty bracket in the outer lobe of the chamber, and swam into the inner lobe to rest silently at Nerine's side.

A sense of comfort stole into Nerine's awareness.

Agnippe's quiet peace radiated out from her, enfolding Nerine more gently that even caring words or loving embraces might. Nerine clasped her sister's hand. Agnippe returned the pressure of her fingers only enough to acknowledge Nerine's gesture.

Nerine's tense tiredness gave way to a soft weariness. She tucked her feet into one of the nets securing a bunch of sponges and drifted into sleep.

When she awoke, all the light globes in the outer lobe had been replenished. The fringes of their warm glow brought the darkness of the inner lobe to a cozy dimness.

But she was alone, which was a relief.

Aside from a strange hollowness, her feelings remained . . . not numb, but absent. She didn't want to talk about anything at all. And Nurse and Agnippe would be sure to have questions.

But when Nerine joined them in the nursery, they didn't.

Nurse brought a comforting warm fish broth in the traditional enclosed globes, as well as kelp-wrapped crab dumplings, and talked about the petty thievery that had broken out in the palace pantries.

Agnippe explained why Mother and Father were both absent and chattered about how pleasant it had been to enjoy informal living for a couple of days.

Nerine could only be grateful. Their lack of probing was just what she needed. And the ordinary routine soothed her. Only after a few days of this careful treatment did Nerine wonder about it. Nurse never left well enough alone. Why wasn't she poking and scolding? Why was Agnippe holding herself gently aloof?

Well, Agnippe was . . . Agnippe. Perceptive, intuitive, and naturally kind. Of course she would sense what Nerine needed.

And Nurse . . . Agnippe had undoubtedly told Nurse to let Nerine be.

～

16 ~ Nerine's Secret

FATHER RETURNED BEFORE Mother. With . . . not bad news, but not truly good news either.

Lord Poseidon had received him most warmly, even generously. But Xianthe refused to emerge from the harem, even with reassurance that Father would not drag her home, that he merely wished to speak with her. To hear that she was happy and well from her own lips.

"Xianthe is her name, eh?" had said Lord Poseidon.

"Don't you know?" asked Father, startled.

"She's a reclusive one, your blond daughter. Always out in the garden when I'm with the ladies in the boudoir. Or in napping when I lounge outside in the garden. Why did you send her?"

Father explained that he *hadn't* sent her.

Lord Poseidon chuckled. "All the same these lovely young women, too hot to handle."

Father agreed that Xianthe was strong-willed and quick-tempered.

Lord Poseidon grew serious for moment, evidently unusual for him. Or so Father said.

"You'll be worried for her, then. Here. In my menage."

Father knew not what to reply. He was worried, but wished not even to imply criticism of his liege lord.

Lord Poseidon nodded. "I shall be as an uncle to her," he concluded, and then turned the conversation to matters affecting the Middle Sea and the neighboring Euxine Sea.

With that, Father had to be content.

Floating in his private cabinet – a soft brown chamber within the royal suite, furnished with sand-hued sponges and numerous small mother-of-pearl cupboards – he gathered Agnippe and Nerine close and kissed their foreheads.

"Do you not trust Lord Poseidon?" asked Agnippe.

"I do, and I don't." Father shook his head.

Agnippe looked curious.

"Lord Poseidon would never deliberately break his word. But . . . speaking of the orca calling the squid's ink black. Lord Poseidon is . . . tempestuous. What he would never do while calm, he might stray into when impassioned." Father smiled wryly. "I'm glad that your sister is keeping her distance."

Agnippe frowned. "It's strangely unlike her," she mused.

Nerine had to agree with that. When had Xianthe ever failed to close for a fight? Or a treat? Or merely to stir trouble?

Father chuckled. "I suspect she's finding the grandeur and the sheer size of Poseidon's court overwhelming. His palace is far larger than ours, you know. Out of her element, your sister may be discovering sides to her personality that even she never guessed she had."

By the time Mother returned, Nerine felt almost normal.

Nurse had always been a creature of the moment, capable of dealing with the trivial occurrences of the moment, less capable of tackling larger problems. With the flow of time distancing her from Nerine's unexplained absence – and unexplained distress – Nurse simply let them go. Or maybe she'd learned that too much intrusion into a child's life did no one any good.

Whatever Nurse's thoughts, she hadn't shared them with the king and the queen.

Which meant that Mother and Father accepted Nurse's assurances that all was well, and treated Nerine as usual. Only Agnippe knew that there was something to know. But Agnippe never pried. She would wait until Nerine wanted to tell her secret. And if Nerine never wanted to tell, Agnippe would never ask.

Mother had her own exciting saga to relate, although she reserved it for the splendor of a formal dinner, amongst their highest lords and ladies, in the hall of fuchsia coral with the great mother-of-pearl table.

One of King Evander's grandsons – who sounded even more wild than Xianthe – had run away from home several years ago and never been seen since. Leukonos, his name was.

What was it about wild sea people? wondered Nerine. Mother's friend Hester, her own sister Xianthe, and now a distant cousin. Would there always be someone going off the deep end every few years?

Evidently Leukonos literally went off the deep end, settling at the bottom of the Calypso Deep and using his water gift – a strong affinity with the creatures of the deeps – to chivvy the frill sharks, the giant isopod crabs, and the kraken.

"Really, it was too bad of him!" Mother exclaimed. "The kraken gets restive all on his own, without additional stirring up. In the ordinary way of things, I safeguard the ships of mortals *from* the dangers of the sea. But this time I secured the peace *for* a danger of the sea." She tossed her head.

"And in so doing," interjected Father, "you secured safe passage for the mortals. What measures did you take for your own safety, Ionia?"

Nerine suspected that Father regretted *he* had not been the one traveling to the Calypso Deep.

"Really, Meren, safety from the kraken was a simple matter. All I need do is sing, and he lies down like a manatee. And you know that frill sharks and isopods pose no real threat to we of the sea."

Father stifled a smile.

Nerine exchanged glances with Agnippe, who nodded. Yes, Father was jealous, all right, but laughing at himself for his jealousy and not wanting to offend Mother by laughing aloud. She wouldn't understand.

"No," said Mother, "Leukonos himself posed the biggest problem."

Father grew abruptly serious. "If he threatened you, Ionia –!"

Mother laughed, in a haughty, looking-down-her-nose way. "Goodness, no! He wouldn't dare. No. The problem was figuring out what to *do* with him. Evander and Leukonos have never got on well together. I had to find a spot for him, or he'd just find more trouble."

Mother glanced around the table, her triumphant eyes inviting each of them to guess what she'd come up with.

None of the lords and ladies ventured a guess, however. They knew Mother nearly as well as Father, Agnippe, and Nerine did.

Mother lifted her chin proudly. "I sent him to Tethys!"

"Great and little blessings!" exclaimed Father. "You didn't!"

"Think about it, Meren. What Leukonos needed was a firm, but gentle hand. The only problem being that anyone with strength enough isn't sufficiently mild, and anyone mild enough hasn't the strength of will."

"Ardashir," suggested Father. "Or Torvald."

Mother sniffed. "The King of the Hyrcanian Sea is merely rigid, not tough, while the Duke of Balder's Sea is simply a youth disguised in an old man's body."

"But, Tethys?" objected Father.

Mother's eyes glinted. "Confess, you've never visited the court of the Mother of All Waters since you were six. Am I right?"

Father blushed. "She was . . . suffocating," he insisted.

"Precisely. Leukonos could do with a little suffocation." Mother tilted her head to one side. "Come, Meren, you know I'm right. There's no one with the Mother's power. Even Lord Poseidon, dominant as he is, cannot manifest the pinpoint potency of Tethys."

"I'll concede to your judgment, my love, which is impeccable, but I cannot say I'd want to switch places with Leukonos."

Mother laughed again, this time more freely and with a warmer note. "Naturally not, love. Tethys poses more challenge for a man than for a woman."

"However did you get the Lady Mother to agree?" asked Father.

"That's an entirely other story," answered Mother. "Perhaps for another time."

But if she told the tale of Tethys, it must have been to Father in private. Nerine was curious, not because she wondered how Mother might persuade a goddess – honestly, Mother could probably persuade *anyone* – but because Tethys was so mysterious. How could she be more powerful than Lord Poseidon and yet so reclusive? Why did Poseidon rule the oceans, and not Tethys? What was she *like*?

Perhaps Nerine would travel to the sanctuary of Tethys and find out one day.

One day.

But first she must return to the shore.

Could she bear it? Would she break down in tears the moment she emerged from the sea to the lonely sands where no friends awaited her? She had to know. The shore had been her refuge.

⁓

She headed for the beach during the slack tide, the waves rolling in long, gentle curls – Altairos would call them combers – too mellow to drag on her legs as she waded through the water.

The day was gray, uncharacteristically overcast, and the air cool with the softest of breezes. The wet sand felt very firm under her feet. The cliffs and dunes appeared somber without the sun. And the sea sighed, rather than crashed. And yet . . . despite the mournful mood of the strand, beneath her sadness, there was something . . . anchoring?

She walked along the water's edge for a bit, testing herself. Would her inner strength ebb away, leaving her weak and weeping? Here where she and Altairos were wont to stroll? Would she miss him too much?

No. She missed him. She missed him a lot. But she could bear it.

I feel whole, she realized. It was a good feeling.

What of the greater challenge? She would see Altairos again, but she would not see Calla. How would she feel en route to Calla's cottage? Could she walk it and not fall to her knees in tears?

She turned inland through the dunes.

A gull screeched. The loose sand slid silkily through her toes. Her calf muscles worked as she climbed the shifting slope.

And then she was on the narrow path to the cottage. The scent of sage rose about her as she brushed against the plants edging the way.

Her grief strengthened.

Oh, Calla, dear Calla. When Nerine had realized that Calla's last breath *was* the last, she felt as though a piece of her heart were ripped away with it. A scab now covered the wound, but it remained raw underneath.

She descended into the shallow gully, strode out of it, and there was Calla's cottage, looking just as it always had: a squarish mass of white stucco with a bite out of it for the terrace, the green vine of the still-unblooming bougainvillea draping the arbor.

A pang went through her. Calla would not be meeting her at the terrace door with her warm greeting. Or showing her a new embroidery stitch. Or scolding Altairos when he teased Nerine a little too rudely.

Nerine's eyes stung.

She drew in a deep breath and entered through the gate, tramped through the garden, stepped up onto the terrace. The stone flagging felt warm under her feet, as though the overcast had hidden the sun only recently.

Fighting a sob, she opened the terrace door and went in.

The rooms were very tidy, very clean. Unlived in. The palace servants must have been through. And yet they had taken nothing away. Surely the furnishings should not remain in an untenanted dwelling.

In the front room, Calla's last weaving lay on the loom, unfinished. It was a fine piece – as fine as anything woven on the vertical looms of the land palace – silk, with an undulating pattern composed of greens and blues that reminded Nerine of water moving through the sea meadow, where the manatees grazed.

Abruptly Nerine knew what she wanted to do. She would complete this beautiful cloth. As a tribute to Calla. As pledge that Nerine would always remember Altairos' *nosokóma* and her generosity to a little sea child with no claim on her. As a memorial to the love that had grown between them.

Her suppressed sob escaped when she knelt before the loom, but still she fought against the next one.

Her knee brushed against a roll of papyrus just under the edge of the loom's frame. She frowned and drew it out, unrolling it.

The alphabet used by the land people was a little different from that of the sea people. She and Altairos had compared them. And learned one another's. But she was not as fluent in his as in her own.

She traced the lines with her forefinger, shaping the sounds with her lips.

Kyría Nerine, child, I have not ordered dear Calla's cottage cleared as yet. Perhaps you regard it as a second home, a place to meet your playfellow, my son, and shelter on days when the sun burns too brightly, too hotly. If this is so, I should wish you to continue here in comfort. Send me word, if the notion pleases you, and I shall instruct a maidservant to keep the cottage in comfortable condition for you. I beg to remain yours in gratitude, Zeron Damonou Lamperieus

It was an informal letter. Nerine knew the style of a formal missive. The language of this one was . . . intimate. And yet, it was formal, with the king's seal pressed into the parchment, creating the raised emblem of a lit torch.

He must mean his offer of the cottage to be binding – thus, his seal. But his only prior communication with her had been that of friend to friend – thus, his cordial wording.

She knelt there a moment.

How kind of him! How very kind. She would have felt bereft indeed, had she found the cottage swept bare. Where would her fortitude have been then? As it was . . . he had foreseen her need.

She scrambled up to fetch one of the wax tablets and the stylus Calla had used to plan out the more complex cloths before she tied the warp threads to her loom.

Pressing through the wax coating on the thin slab of wood felt very like pressing letters into sheets of copper as Nerine did under the sea. But she didn't have much practice forming the land letters. She would keep her note as short as it could be and still convey her appreciation.

Basileus Zeron, I had not thought so far ahead, but I should very much like to visit Calla's cottage and think of her while there. I shall be weaving the cloth that she and I warped to the loom together, and I should be very honored if you would accept the finished length of silk when it is done. I remain your grateful and faithful neighbor, Nerine Merenou Pelagieus

There. It was done. She would leave it atop the warp threads of the loom when she left the cottage today, and trust that the servant who delivered the king's roll of papyrus might also convey her tablet and its message.

But where would she keep the papyrus? She could not bring it under the sea, for the water would destroy it swiftly. She looked around the room. Calla had owned no writing desk; she'd possessed no need for one.

There was a chest of weaving supplies. A shelf. The loom itself. A cushioned bench.

What about the bedchamber?

Calla's narrow bed – empty now, but so recently the place of Calla's last breath – oppressed Nerine's heart.

Momentarily, she had the odd sensation that Calla awaited her at the loom, having sent Nerine to bring a ribband or a mantle in order to match its color.

Was it like that? Except that Calla roamed the Fields of Asphodel, entrusting Nerine with the finishing of her work on earth? Altairos might believe that. Nerine was not so sure. And if Calla did roam the Fields of Asphodel, was she lonely for the friends who could not come with her? Nerine hated to think of Calla lonely and sad. But she *would* finish Calla's work.

Several chests sat along one wall of the bedchamber. One with bedding, another with Calla's folded linen gowns. And one with various sundries and the ribband shawl Nerine had made for Calla. Ah! Another pang in Nerine's breast. Calla had loved that shawl. And now she would wear it no more.

Swallowing another wayward sob, Nerine tucked the king's papyrus missive in amongst the ribbands and returned to the front room to weave.

As she got into the rhythm of it – passing the shuttle through the shed, beating the weft tight, lifting the heddle rod up to its jacks, passing the shuttle through again – she could imagine Calla sitting beside her, praising the smoothness of her weave, or offering tips for negotiating tricky bits of the pattern.

I am Calla's hands, thought Nerine, dreamily. *Her memory lives in this cloth.*

She wove a double handspan of the silk, comforted by memory. Squares of light appeared on the floor beside the loom as the sky's overcast passed away and the sun shone through the windows. Slowly, the squares of light traveled and slanted into diamond shapes.

When Nerine realized that she must stop, she knew a stab of worry. Would her sense of connection with Calla break the moment she stood and walked away from the loom?

She stood.

She walked away.

And realized that Calla's memory lived not within the cloth of her weaving – or not only within those woven strands – but within Nerine. Not Calla herself. How Nerine *wished* that Calla lived. But Calla's memory. And memory . . . was worth a lot.

Hanging onto her memories, Nerine walked through the golden evening light to the waters' edge, and dove in.

∼

Arriving home, Nerine found Agnippe in the verdant nursery garden.

Her sister had paused amidst a game of catch-cradle, the relaxed strands lying tangled around her fingers in her lap, as she gazed into space. What was she thinking of, with her face serenely aglow? She didn't see Nerine, until Nerine swam over the low dike bounding the garden, and even then Agnippe's expression changed little, her lips curving into a gentle smile.

"Where do you go?" she asked, her reverie unbroken, her voice abstracted. "When you swim away from the palace for the day?"

"I go ashore," answered Nerine, not meaning to answer, "to visit my friends there and to see wonders not possible under the sea."

"You always seem so much more yourself," said Agnippe, "when you return. Like you've retrieved something precious that cannot breathe for long in the reef."

Nerine stared at her sister in astonishment. How could Agnippe know this, when Nerine herself had not. Not with such precision. And yet . . . Agnippe was right. Nerine felt free on the land. And she brought her freedom with her when she returned to the water, but it slipped away in drips and drabs until there was none left.

"I lost a friend," she told Agnippe. "Two *déka*-days ago."

A shadow crossed Agnippe's face. "I know. I grieved for you."

Nerine opened her arms, and Agnippe swam into them. Nerine clung to her, resting her brow against her sister's hair.

Their embrace loosened, and they hung in the sunlit waters together, silent, Nerine honoring Calla's passing, Agnippe honoring Nerine's loss.

"How old were you?" asked Agnippe. "The first time you went ashore?"

"I was eight. And it was scary. And wonderful. And I wish . . ."

"You wish?"

"I wish I could do it all over again. Find something so new and different that I was scared. Something so wonderful that I felt . . . reborn."

"That's why you want to travel the world." Agnippe looked surprised at her own acumen. "Seeking out new and different places, new and different people. Being scared and amazed with each journey."

"Yes," answered Nerine. "Yes." The way Agnippe put it sounded so exactly right. As though Nerine's heart had come home with her words. As though her destiny were inevitable. How could her thoughts and emotions feel almost like weight, certain and sure, while her outer life was in such disarray? Calla gone forever, Altairos away for at least a year more, and no vocation calling her toward her future. Somehow, she must make a way for her inner certainty to find its match in the world around her.

"Who did you lose?" Agnippe asked softly.

And Nerine found herself telling Agnippe all about Calla. How she'd disapproved of Nerine at first, how she'd softened, and how she'd come to treat Nerine as another nursling to guide as their acquaintance lengthened.

The waters had dimmed into dusk when she fell silent again.

"Calla was special," said Agnippe.

"Calla was special," Nerine echoed her.

They went into the nursery together. Just before Nurse entered, Agnippe smiled and said, "I shan't share your secret."

Nerine hugged her, a quick squeeze. "I know." She hadn't been worried; truly, she'd taken it for granted that she could trust her sister's silence. Agnippe would never betray a trust. It was just who she was.

In the days following this conversation with Agnippe, Nerine felt a lasting connection between her land self and her water self for the first time. She found herself missing Agnippe while she knelt before the loom in Calla's cottage. And she found herself missing Calla and Altairos at home in the evenings after dinner.

She took up *nålbinding* – single-needle knitting, which she'd previously done only ashore – and fashioned ribbands of chitin-strand for her sister, an elegant snood for Mother's hair, and a belt pocket for Father to carry his water flute while traveling.

Just as she could almost hear Calla's voice when she knelt at her loom, so could she see Calla's fingers on the yarn, demonstrating different stitches.

She felt peaceful, as though she were the coral reef itself, alive with sea creatures in all its crannies, pulled by the tides, buffeted by the waves, but anchored in the bedrock of the ocean floor.

Father's comforting presence became something to cherish and enjoy, rather than an invading force to be resisted. Likewise Mother's dominating aspect. She was who she was. Father was who he was. And Nerine could still be Nerine. Nerine who admired Mother. Nerine who adored Father. Nerine who found a close friend in her sister. Nerine who mourned Calla. Nerine who missed Altairos. All those Nerines, as well as simply Nerine herself at heart.

This was what she'd been seeking.

～

The *déka*-days turned into moons. The moons turned into a year. And then another year.

Soon after Nerine passed the eighteenth anniversary of her birth, Agnippe turned fourteen, the age at which the muses were willing to accept her as guardian of their sacred spring. And Agnippe was going. The saltwater had never been her natural milieu. She'd learned to compensate through the use of her water gift, but the fresh water called to her. She was ready.

Mother wrote lists of the clothes that Agnippe would need for her trousseau. Agnippe made outlines summarizing the world of culture and creation. And a fizz of excitement pervaded the reef.

The servants were proud of the youngest royal daughter, who was always so gentle in her speech to them. Mother's ladies were happy, because Mother was happy. Father commented that he almost couldn't believe that his fussy little daughter had grown into such a poised and elegant young woman. And Nurse was elated that Agnippe would at last go to a milieu she found soothing: fresh water.

Nerine partook of these sentiments, too. At first.

The déka-days of preparation felt a lot like the time before Eilidh went to Queen Hera. Except that Nerine liked Agnippe a *lot* more than she liked Eilidh.

It was fun teasing Agnippe each time she discovered another item that belonged on her outline. Fun helping her consider the gowns Mother proposed for her trousseau. Fun imagining the interesting letters that Agnippe would write home once she was ensconced on Mount Helicon.

The night before Agnippe's departure, Nerine confronted the other side of Agnippe's ascension to her sacred spring: Agnippe would be gone.

Nerine's heart felt hollow.

She retreated to her double-lobed parlor, its outer sphere of amber coral enclosing her like the outer chamber of a nautilus shell.

"Oh, blessings," she whispered. How would she manage without Agnippe? Letters wouldn't be the same at all.

No Agnippe in the evenings when Nerine worked on her *nålbindning*. No Agnippe in the afternoons when they took a break from lessons and compared notes. No Agnippe with whom to exchange amused glances when Nurse treated them as though they were three years old. No Agnippe to talk things over with after Mother had been particularly overbearing. No Agnippe. For years and years. Forever, really. Because Agnippe would never live in the reef palace again.

Nerine's eyes prickled and grew hot, while tears slipped out of them into the sea. Salt tears and salt sea, indistinguishable.

She covered her face with her hands, and her shoulders shook.

My sister, oh, my sister. She couldn't bear it.

A soft hand touched her forearm.

"Nerine?"

Nerine looked up to see her sister hovering beside her.

"Oh, Agnippe!" she wailed.

Agnippe's arms closed around her. "Ssh, ssh," she murmured. "Shall you miss me so much?"

A chuckle bubbled out of Nerine amidst her tears. Which felt very odd – laughing and crying at the same moment.

"Of course I'll miss you that much, you parrotfish! How could I not?"

"I'll miss you too." Agnippe sounded wistful.

Nerine squeezed Agnippe's shoulders, finding that her own tears had fled along with her mournful mood. She would have home, unlike her sister, who was leaving everything she knew. Besides, Nerine was the elder. She should be comforting Agnippe, not the other way round.

Except . . .

The truth was that she envied Agnippe. If only *she* were the one traveling somewhere new and strange, she'd not mind leaving home one bit. Whereas Agnippe did mind. Oh, Nerine knew she wanted to go, was eager to go. But unlike Nerine, Agnippe really would miss home.

Nerine nibbled at her lip. She'd been crying not only for herself without Agnippe, but for herself *at home* without Agnippe.

Pull yourself together, she told herself. *Tonight shouldn't be about you.*

"I'm sorry," she said aloud.

"For what?" asked Agnippe.

"I wanted to support you, and instead the first thing I do is elicit support from you." She shrugged. "And that feels wrong to me."

"We can support each other," offered Agnippe, sounding tentative. Was she afraid her words would just make Nerine feel yet more foolish? They did, but Nerine wasn't going to admit it.

"Yes. We can," Nerine agreed. "What do *you* need? Tell me."

"Nothing, really," answered Agnippe. "Except . . ." She didn't continue.

"Except what?" prompted Nerine.

"I'd just like to spend the evening with you. In the usual fashion. With you knitting and me thinking. And both of us saying whatever thoughts come to mind."

"We can do that. If Mother and Father don't mind." Some evenings all four of them floated together. Not most, because Mother and Father were often too busy, their duties from the day bleeding into the night. But surely they would want to spend Agnippe's last evening at home with her. Wouldn't they?

"The chariot master just discovered that one of the tether rings on my chariot is broken. Father is coordinating both its repair and the assessments of the three older chariots I might use." Agnippe giggled. "He's convinced there might be an accident at sea, somewhere between here and Thérma."

Ah! So Father was avoiding his anxiety over parting by indulging in anxiety about safety.

"And Mother?" asked Nerine.

"Found three links missing from the belt she'd planned to wear tomorrow to bid me farewell. So she's putting together a whole fresh ensemble."

Nerine chuckled this time. Mother had found her refuge in concern for propriety and dignity. Of course. She disengaged from Agnippe and gave a soft flick of her foot, drifting toward the parlor wall where a leash held her *nålbindning* bag. "Do you mind? About Mother and Father?" she asked Agnippe.

"No, I'd just as soon not have them fussing at me," confessed Agnippe. "And you know they would. Mother would say, 'Agnippe, are you sure you wouldn't prefer a deeper shade for that aqua gown? It's not too late.' And Father would ask me, 'Do you truly feel ready, Agnippe? You need not go now. Next year would be just fine. The muses will understand.'"

Nerine laughed. "You're right, of course."

"And if they really needed – and wanted – to fuss, I'd let them. But I *am* ready. And I think they would be ready, too, if they'd let themselves. But they won't, because feeling ready feels a little too much like not loving me. Which is silly." Agnippe shook her head, smiling fondly.

"How do you come to be so wise?" Nerine asked, almost involuntarily. "You deal with Mother and Father so gracefully. So much more gracefully than I do." Although she'd done a lot better over the past year or so. But Agnippe had always been able to keep her balance with Mother and Father. While Nerine still had to work at it.

"You still want to make them happy," answered Agnippe slowly. And then she looked shocked, as though her words were an accusation.

"Don't you?" asked Nerine, puzzled.

"Well, I do. But . . ."

"But?"

Agnippe bit her lip. "I want them to *be* happy. But that's not the same thing, is it? I mean, they mostly *are* happy. Whether I make them so or not."

"You mean you let them make their own happiness," murmured Nerine.

"Yes! That's it, Nerine. Thank you!"

"Thank me? Why?"

"Because you put words to it. I'd been trying to, and couldn't." Agnippe pushed the mass of her hair – more tightly curled than Nerine's – back from her face.

Nerine pulled the pale pink ribband she was knitting out of her bag and disentangled the strand that formed the working circle from the smooth sheen of the completed tail. She looped the loose end around and under the working thread, then through the loop she'd made, and pulled it tight.

"You've been thinking about this for a while," she stated.

Agnippe nodded. "I hoped I'd sort it out before I went. I wanted to know why Mother and Father bothered Xianthe so much. And you." She looked at Nerine, then glanced away. "And why they don't bother me and Tyr and Eilidh. Well, I know why they don't bother Eilidh, of course."

Nerine sniffed. "Because she rarely thinks about anyone but Eilidh."

Agnippe giggled. "Well, yes."

"Why does Tyr remain unruffled?" Nerine asked.

"Because he enjoys the world around him so much that he can't conceive that anyone else might not. And if they're having fun – which of *course* they must be – then there's no need for him to worry. So he doesn't. That, and he's so focused on what he's doing or wants to do."

Nerine nodded. That made sense. It made a lot of sense. And it made Tyr a restful companion, especially once he'd grown up and reserved his high spirits for enjoyment rather than playing pranks. She suppressed a chuckle, remembering some of his old pranks.

Agnippe continued, "But Xianthe cared a lot about pleasing Mother and Father, maybe because her temper tantrums meant they were often *displeased* with her. Mother was convinced for the longest time that Xianthe just wasn't trying hard enough. And Father was sure that if only he and Mother did a better job of it, Xianthe would be happy. And if she were happy, then she wouldn't tantrum."

Nerine's hands stilled for a moment. "But they were both wrong, weren't they?" she said.

"Yes, Xianthe is just one of those people who is bothered by things." Agnippe sounded sad.

Nerine made the obvious connection. "And by the time Mother realized that Xianthe *was* trying. Trying really *hard* . . ."

"It was too late," finished Agnippe. "Xianthe had learned the habit of trying harder and harder. Which just wound her up more."

"And by the time Father realized that the thing Xianthe needed most," continued Nerine, "was calm parents, Xianthe had learned his trick of thinking that if she did better at being a daughter, everything would be alright." Nerine nibbled at her lip again. "Poor Xianthe. She kept trying harder, without really knowing how."

Agnippe nodded. "And feeling disappointed each time she tantrumed and more disappointed with Mother's and Father's every disappointment."

Nerine resumed her knitting. Over and around and through, then pull the thread snug.

"Am I like Xianthe?" she asked.

"You are a little," answered Agnippe.

Nerine winced. "I suppose I am. Except Xianthe was trying to stop disappointing Mother and Father, while I . . ."

"Know that they are pleased with you," continued Agnippe, "and want them to continue to be pleased."

Nerine sighed. "I've gotten better at it. Not working to please them, I mean."

"Have you?"

"Yes. I have." Nerine was certain of that. "But I have to remind myself. It still doesn't come naturally, and, oh, I wish it did. Knitting helps. How do *you* do it, Agnippe?"

Agnippe looked self-conscious.

"I don't really know. It's almost like there is this place inside me where no one can come. It's always there. And it keeps me . . . anchored somehow. At least, it has ever since I learned how to make fresh water and how to keep a flow of it next to my skin." She laughed, still self-conscious. "Sometimes I'm a bit lonely. But mostly, I feel . . ."

"Free?" suggested Nerine.

Agnippe brightened. "Yes, that's it exactly! I feel free. The way your shore makes you feel."

"I'm worried that even my shore – and my knitting – won't keep me free once you're gone, Agnippe," Nerine confessed. Would that make Agnippe feel guilty? She glanced at her sister. But Agnippe looked curious, not guilty.

"How is it that I do that for you? I mean, why does it work that way?" asked Agnippe.

Why *did* it work that way? That was a good question.

"Some of it is just that you're someone else for Mother and Father to focus on," said Nerine.

"Mmm?" Agnippe's tone had a mischievous quality to it. Did she know the answer? Or was she merely enjoying the discussion? This was the sort of topic she loved, after all.

"But I guess . . ." continued Nerine, probing her own heart as she guessed, "it's because I can sense that inner place of yours when I'm near you, and it anchors me, too. Huh."

"You need your own inner place," said Agnippe.

"But I don't know how to create it! If I knew . . . I'd have it already." She looked Agnippe straight in the face, steadily, hoping she might see some clue there. Agnippe looked calm, almost serene.

"I trust you, Nerine. You can do this."

Agnippe's assurance felt very, very good. If Agnippe believed that Nerine could fashion her own inner lagoon, then maybe Nerine could believe it, too. She had to. Without Agnippe at home, belief was all she would have to cling to when the maternal and paternal tides surged too high.

"Thanks, 'Nippe," she said.

Agnippe kissed Nerine's cheek.

∽

Then Mother and Father swam in. Apparently they did want to spend some of the evening with their departing youngest daughter. But neither one fussed. Father told jokes. Mother told stories from when she left the Aegean Sea to come to the Isles of Pelagie, and of the cute things Agnippe did when she was a baby.

It was very pleasant, and Nerine wondered if she'd been unnecessarily worried about her ability to maintain her equilibrium in Agnippe's absence.

The next morning, in the remise court beside the summoning pole, she and Agnippe enjoyed a laugh when they set eyes on the chariot chosen to bear her away to Thérma. It was an unwieldy thing of bronzed chitin, shaped to resemble a great bluefin tuna. Agnippe would undoubtedly be comfortable with all the extra room provided by the old-fashioned conveyance. And it had been refurbished with soft new sponges, the disintegrating hardened ones pulled out.

But she'd be several days longer on her journey. The new chariots were sleeker, more streamlined. What in the sea would the nymphs of Helicon think when Agnippe drew up in this antiquated thing?

They were still laughing when Mother and Father entered the court.

Four dolphins were harnessed, Agnippe's luggage was loaded, and the warriors accompanying her – together with the dolphins who would pull them via towing harness – congregated.

It all seemed to move too fast.

Mother kissed Agnippe's cheek, Father hugged her, and Nerine both kissed and hugged her sister.

The next moment Agnippe had entered the chariot, and the whole entourage was swimming away. They passed around the curve of the reef and were gone.

Nerine had a blank feeling of anti-climax and then a horrible feeling that nothing would ever be right again. She glanced at Mother and Father. They were chatting comfortably, seemingly unmoved by Agnippe's departure. Should she go to them? Would they comfort her? Or merely not understand her discomfort?

As she turned away, she thought she saw Father start toward her, but she didn't wait. She was going to the one source of comfort that had never failed her. The shore.

On the shore, she would feel the gritty, wet sand between her toes as the surf dashed her ankles. On the shore, dune grasses would tickle the backs of her knees. The gulls would cry, sharp and lonely. The sun would dazzle her vision. And she would remember Altairos so vividly, it would be as if he walked by her side.

~

17 ~ Practicing Hope

SHE CAME ASHORE amidst a heavy, surging tide, the breakers rough, the undertow strong.

She stumbled and nearly fell, would have fallen had she been only eight years old like the first time.

With that memory before her, it did almost seem that Altairos was with her. His steady arms around her, his laughing voice speaking to her, his eyes crinkling in the way that they did.

She came ashore smiling, the water dripping off her gilded by clear morning sun, the surf thundering behind her.

She felt new, as though she *were* only eight years old, as though she would meet Altairos for the first time, as though she were embarked on the adventure of her life.

She walked along the water's edge, enjoying the sense of visiting her past. At any moment, a nine-year-old boy would run down the cliff path. Or she'd see him spreading a silken yellow cloth on the dunes. Or he would dash up to greet her.

Her exalted mood lasted until she turned to walk back toward the tide pools.

She was alone.

There would be no Altairos of any age coming to greet her. Nor Calla in her cottage. Nor Agnippe awaiting her in the reef under the sea. The three people who made Nerine feel most like Nerine were gone, one of them forever.

She stood still, looking out to sea. The waves stretched away to the horizon, where a thin white line of sky marked where air and water touched. She wished she could travel to that horizon and then to the fresh horizon that would be visible from that vantage.

She turned to stare up at the bluffs behind her. They seemed to shut her in, walls of rock to cage her on this beach. She'd not climbed them once since Calla's death.

Abruptly she made a decision.

Calla's last weaving was long since finished, removed from the loom and folded to rest in a chest. Nerine would take it out today, wrap it in linen to protect the fine silk, and carry it to the king. She'd promised it to him. She intended it for him yet. Why had she never delivered it?

In the cottage, she dithered. Should she don the gown of a land dweller? Or wear merely her own belt and pectoral, the garb of the sea people? If she wore a gown, should she also wrap a sash round her brow, hiding her spiracles?

The palace people knew what she was now. They'd not liked it much. She remembered their frowns, that night of Calla's death. But the king had not cared.

I go to the king, she decided. *Not to his servants. I will go as myself, in the garb of my people.* Agnippe would approve.

That thought drove a pang of loss through her. Agnippe was gone.

No, that wasn't true. Agnippe was traveling.

Imagining Agnippe reclining on the sponges in that monstrous old-fashioned chariot made her grin. She felt better, much better, as she prepared Calla's weaving for its short journey up the bluffs to King Zeron's palace.

Facing King Zeron's guards at the ceremonial east entrance, she knew some doubt in her choice of garb. The guards were more than disapproving; they looked downright hostile. But they passed her along quickly from one official to another, which they would likely not have done, if she'd looked an ordinary maiden.

Following a chamberlain through the narrow, twisting corridor that led from the east gate to the central court, she felt more qualms. Would she be ushered into the throne room, there to confront the king under the interested eyes of a crowd of courtiers?

All her contacts with the royal family of Zakynthos had been informal thus far. She'd imagined meeting King Zeron in a private study or a pleasant salon. Should she turn back? Try another day, entering the palace through the gardens as she always had with Altairos?

The chamberlain stopped before a modest wooden door, with a latticework in its upper half to let the breeze pass through.

Oh, blessings! She'd arrived.

The chamberlain knocked softly, opened the door, and announced her: "Kríousa Nerine Merenou Pelagieus to see His Majesty King Zeron Damonou Lamperieus!"

She walked in, holding her breath.

⁓

Inside was a study. A comfortable study with red walls, a fresco of playing monkeys on one, and shelves stacked with scrolls. The king stood behind a tall writing desk, but moved out from behind it the instant Nerine was announced.

He nodded dismissal to the chamberlain, and once this dignitary had departed, greeted Nerine warmly. "I will not say, 'child,' for you have grown into womanhood in the many moons since last we met, but you are most welcome." He smiled, and his eyes reminded her a little of Altairos' – black and alive. "Will you sit?" he urged her and gestured to one of several backless chairs placed against the wall.

She sat, her bundle in her lap, wondering what to say.

King Zeron had such a presence. She'd forgotten that in her hurry to redeem her lapsed promise.

"Would you wish refreshment?" he asked, seating himself in the chair beside hers.

No, she really didn't want to be sidetracked by matters of hospitality. Why had she come here today? Because she hoped to find some sense of anchorage in Altairos' pappa?

She wrestled her unease into submission and spoke.

"No, I thank Your Majesty. I came to give you this." She lifted her bundle and pulled back the corners of the linen covering, revealing the shimmer of the silk and its flowing patterns of blue and green and aqua. "It has been long finished." She looked up at him shyly. "I'm not sure why I delayed bringing it to you."

He reached out a reverent finger to touch the silk. "Calla's last weaving?"

She nodded.

"Perhaps you would like it for a keepsake, child." He had said he would not call her "child," but no doubt she seemed very young to his many years. He was not old – his black hair and robust figure spoke nothing of age, although he had to be in his fifth decade, surely – but a weight of experience hung about him.

"I should like you to have it, Your Majesty. Truly. That was not what delayed me. It was . . ."

"What is it, child?"

"Altairos always accompanied me here. I was not sure . . . the servants looked at me so severely, that night when Calla died. I was not sure they would admit me. But *you* do not mind, do you?"

The king's face softened. "No, I call your people friends, though I see you but rarely."

Her gaze clung to his. "Why do we not meet more often? My father sends and receives messages to all the kings of the sea, and you send ambassadors to all the kings of the land. Why do the people of the sea and the people of the land remain so separate?"

He looked sad. "Ah, but we of the land are mortal and cannot breathe beneath the waves, while you of the sea partake of the divine and long for your waves eventually."

She couldn't see how that was an explanation. Not truly. Yes, the people of land and sea were different, but so were any two individuals. How should mere difference stand in the way of friendship?

"You are friends with my son," said King Zeron, perhaps reading her confusion in her face. "Do you not sense that in time your different natures will demand that you part?"

"Will they?" She sensed nothing of the sort. Never had. What did King Zeron know that she did not?

"I would caution you, Kríousa Nerine, to be friends, but no more than that. There will come a time when even my young son Altairos will show strands of white in his dark hair, and the gates of Hades will claim him. How bitter might this be for you, should you love him too well?"

Nerine felt again the pain that had come with Calla's death, as though a piece of her heart were ripped away. To feel that with Altairos' death. *Oh, blessings no!* Why had she come here? Today of all days, when she needed comfort? The land king heaped yet more grief upon her.

Were she not sitting, she would dart away, flee from him.

Were he not so impressive, she would leap to her feet and flee.

Were he not so kind, she would look daggers at him and flee.

"What have I said, child?" His hand reached out to touch her chin, to lift her face.

"My sister departed for the mountain of the muses this morning," she burst out. "I will not see her at home again. And Altairos is not here to comfort my sorrow." Tears slid down her cheeks.

The king's face changed, growing more fatherly, less kingly. He took both her hands in his. "You will find your own place in time. Is that not it?" he asked, his voice kind. "Were you following your calling, you would grieve, but you would also rejoice. Is it not so?"

Oh! He did understand! Just as Altairos would have.

She was impressed all over again with Altairos' pappa. He did not have the years of her confidences that Altairos possessed. And yet he'd discerned the heart of her sorrow very quickly, and despite her own incoherence.

"I will prescribe for your trouble, child, if you will listen. Do you wish it?" He sounded even kinder, even gentler than before. How could so mighty a king make her see his humanity even as his discarded majesty hovered around him like a cloak? Why did she feel his advice would be good, while her own father – who loved her so much – could not advise her on the most essential thing?

She nodded.

"Trust is your challenge, Kríousa Nerine," he said seriously.

Trust! She didn't know what he meant, but trust was what she lacked at home. She trusted that her father loved her, that he would do everything in his power for her, that he always had her best interests at heart. But she didn't trust him to say, "*This* you must do. This is not something that I or anyone else can do for you. *You* must do it, find it, solve it." And that lack of trust . . . undermined all her other trust in him.

King Zeron continued, "Some lucky souls possess a simple vocation: to wake with the dawn, to enjoy their meals, to work in their cottages and gardens. The act of living fulfills them. They are blessed, indeed. Calla was one such. Do you agree?"

Nerine still didn't know where he was leading her, but the very unfamiliarity of his thoughts reassured her. He knew something her father did not know, and his knowledge would comfort her. She had been right to come.

"Yes, Calla was content, deeply content," she agreed.

King Zeron went on. "Others born to this world are not so easily satisfied and do not find their sources of satisfaction quickly. My youngest son was one such. But as he grew, his inclinations and skills manifested, and we – he and I – perceived his way. Do you agree?" he questioned her again.

Her feeling of calm had grown, and her tears had stopped. She looked King Zeron in the face, drawing yet further strength from the wisdom she saw there. "Yes," she answered.

"There are yet others who do not find or make their life's calling until later, Kríousa Nerine. And some who never find it. I think you fear you may be one of the latter, doomed to drift, always longing for your anchor, your safe harbor, your rightness. Am I right, child?"

Oh, he was right. He had named her fear, and named it without fear. Why did he feel so confident? Had her father named her fear, he would have felt fear. Was that the difference? Instead she felt certain that King Zeron had an answer, and a good one.

"You are right, sire," she whispered.

"No, I am not your king, Kríousa Nerine," he corrected her. "Merely your confessor. In this."

"You are right, Your Majesty."

An almost merry look flickered in his eyes. "Then listen to me now. There is a danger in your fear, but the danger is not that you never find your life's calling. The danger is that in your fear you miss it, or cease to look, and give up hope. Do you hear me, Nerine?" His voice strengthened. "When you find your right doing, your right being, your right way, you will look back and know that you wasted too much of your life in fear. Unless you cultivate your trust."

Her eyes widened. She almost had it, almost understood what he wished her to understand. Almost, but not quite. She clung now to his words as strongly as her eyes had clung to his face earlier. If she could just take this in . . . then what? She didn't know what, but she knew this was supremely important.

"*You* will cultivate trust, Kríousa Nerine. You *will* do it, because I know you can. And when you find the wonder that is yours, you will not look back with regret. Instead, you will know – and feel – that all your struggles merely add to the richness you have discovered. You will not regret the lost years." His voice softened. "You will celebrate them, child. You will rejoice."

He fell silent, smiling.

She felt overwhelmed, as though he'd given her a gift of incalculable worth, but which she could not identify as yet. She suspected she would not receive another interview like this one, however, and focused enough to ask him the only question that occurred to her.

"Was it so with you, Your Majesty?"

"Ah!" he sighed. "No wonder my son loves you so. Yes, Nerine, it has been thusly for me."

"Did you not know your calling, even though you were born a prince?"

"I did not." He laughed. "I was a younger son."

"But you know your calling now?" She felt overly inquisitive asking, but she needed to know. She *thought* he was speaking from experience, but she needed to be sure. This was too important.

"Holding the reins to my people's world and holding them steady gives me much joy as I see the prosperity that results. I was meant to do this," he replied.

Nerine felt all the tension go out of her. She'd gotten an answer. She still didn't entirely understand it, but she knew she now possessed what she needed.

King Zeron lifted a hand. "Ah! Ah! Nerine."

She frowned. "What is it?"

"This moment is a joyous one, no?"

She nodded. Indeed it was! She didn't understand his note of caution.

"The moment of knowing is important, but do not mistake it for the doing. In this moment of revelation you feel that all will be well, do you not?"

She nodded again. All *would* be well with her.

"The knowledge points the way," he explained, "but you must follow the knowing with choices and actions and perseverance over time. That part is hard. Old habits – both of thought and of doing – will sway you.

"It is in those moments of forgetting, of falling into old ways, that your challenge – and your opportunity – will come."

He took hold of her hands again. "Look at me, Kríousa Nerine. When you feel lonely and adrift, certain that your life has little purpose, that is when you must practice trust. Trust in yourself, trust in your future. It is in your exertion at such moments that you will become the woman you want to be. Will you attempt it, child?" His eyes were very steady and his face very kind, but there was a challenge behind his empathy.

She felt stirred by him; ready to work, even when the work was hard; determined to succeed, if only to respect his effort in helping her.

"I will!" she answered. Her voice sounded very clear in her ears. "I will do it."

"Excellent!" He stood and walked to the door. "Bide a moment, child." Then he called through the lattice, "Éla!" and instructed the servant waiting in the hall.

❧

He returned to her, saying, "Shall we admire Calla's weaving in its entirety?"

She liked the idea. It had been nearly a year since she'd seen the full length of the cloth. It was more tapestry than robing, the pattern so large that it repeated only twice, and then in mirror image. Sea urchins, sand, and shells were depicted at each end, while streamers of sea grasses drifted up from the sands to hide swift darting silver fish, soaring blue fish, and lurking black fish.

King Zeron secured two corners of the cloth atop the scroll shelves, and the shimmering fabric hung down from them, gleaming and so delicate that it rippled in the slight movement of air.

Nerine stood to admire it, the king beside her.

"I had thought to fashion a robe of it, but it is too beautiful for that," he said. "I shall hang it in this room, on the wall beside the door, that I may see it from my desk as I work." He glanced down at her. "Am I right, Nerine, to do thusly?"

She felt honored. She had woven but the last third of the fabric, but though she knew where Calla's work left off and hers began, she could *see* no mark of it in the silk. She wondered if the king loved it because Calla had made it or because it was beautiful. And maybe – a little – because his son's close friend, a nymph of the sea that embraced his island kingdom, had completed it. Perhaps all three.

He must have read her thoughts on her face, because he touched her arm and said, "You have given my house a treasure. Thank you, child."

Two servants entered then, one bearing a tray with food and drink, the other carrying a small box carved in filigree of polished olive wood. They set their burdens on a side table and served both Nerine and their king.

Nerine discovered she was hungry after all.

The lemon drink stung her tongue – more tart than she'd ever tasted – but she liked it, and it woke her appetite. The small pastries with a pungently sweet filling – dried cherries from Scandia in the far north – formed a delicious contrast to the citrus, while the savory prawns on skewers satisfied her hunger.

"Better?" asked the king when she'd finished.

She felt much better. Comfortable in mind and spirit, comfortable in body. How much of her upset had been due to Agnippe's departure occurring before she broke her fast?

No, that wasn't fair. The question of what post Nerine might occupy – doing what? – had been troubling her for as long as she was old enough to wonder about it. Had she thought about it when she was little? Just eight, perhaps? She rather believed she had. A snippet of a memory of asking Nurse tickled the edge of her thoughts.

King Zeron asked the servants to bring him the small, filigree box and then dismissed them.

"So, Kríousa Nerine," he said, "you have made me a promise. Do you still hold by it?"

Could he doubt her? She didn't doubt herself. Should she? "I do," she answered strongly.

"Tell me the substance of your promise," he commanded her.

She opened her mouth to reply, then shut it. What exactly had she promised? She'd passed through a storm of feeling and come to rest in the safe harbor of King Zeron's presence. She felt as though something important had resolved within her. But what was the work ahead of her?

"I will work to hold trust in myself and my future," she said slowly. "Why . . . that's hope," she realized. "I will cultivate hope, even when all feels hopeless." She felt her heart rise within her. "I will *practice* the virtue of hope!" Her smile flashed out to him.

"Very good, Kríousa Nerine." He opened the box in his hands, took something out, shut the box, and set it aside. "I should like to give you something to remind you of your promise. Will you accept this from me?"

It was a dainty armlet of woven gold links, with three beryls in the shape of small teardrops dangling from it.

"Oh!" It was lovely! "Thank you, Your Majesty!"

He opened the clasp and fastened it around her wrist. "Will it help you to remember, child?"

She nodded, certain that it would.

She bade him farewell soon after, escorted to the bluffs by a young man who seemed to be some sort of secretary – and much nicer than either the guards or the chamberlain. Perhaps he was another friend of the sea people.

Nerine stayed on the beach all that afternoon, admiring the way the green beryls on her armlet flashed gold in the sun, when she reached down to pick up a shell from the rushing surf or dabbled her fingers in a rocky tide pool.

She felt anchored and at peace with herself, despite Agnippe's departure, despite Altairos' absence and Calla's more profound absence.

"I can do this," she murmured, and returned home in time to join Mother, Father, and Tyr – who'd arrived in the late morning – for an intimate family dinner in one of the smaller parlors.

∽

Tyr had big news.

"Mother, Father." He paused to gather their attention. " Rinara – the daughter of the Duke of the Gulf of Gallicus – has accepted my offer of marriage, and I would like to bring her to stay here with you for a time."

So *that's* why Tyr had not visited for some while. He'd been traveling to Gallicus instead of Pelagie, when he could afford to leave the Tyrrhenian for a few days.

Mother's face lit up. "Oh, Rinara is the dearest girl!" she exclaimed.

"You know her then?" asked Tyr, surprised.

"Of course I do! Don't you remember guesting with Duke Arius when you were just six? Rinara was three and the two of you played together charmingly. The Duchess" – one of Mother's dearest friends – "has written me of Rinara's growing beauty and intelligence through all the years, but she never breathed a word about this!"

Mother turned to Father. "Meren, we must give a party, perhaps a grand ball."

Father nodded and smiled.

"But tell me about her, Tyr," continued Mother. "How will she manage in your rough quarters?"

It turned out that for all Rinara's beauty, she was a bit of a tomboy.

Upon hearing of her accompanying the Duke's warriors on an expedition to deal with a stray great white shark before the beast killed someone, Nerine had to admit that Rinara would likely feel quite at home in the Tyrrhenian Sea. Clearly she thrived on discomfort and danger, not that Tyr's home was exactly dangerous. But still.

The next several *déka*-days were so unusual that Nerine had little need to practice hope as she'd promised King Zeron.

Tyr was eager to bring his Rinara to Pelagie immediately, so Nerine dove into the preparations for her visit along with all of Mother's ladies. There were the rooms to be readied, the social schedule to plan, and the betrothal gifts to decide upon, as well as innumerable small details.

And then Rinara arrived.

She was an athletic maiden with long chestnut hair that she wore in multiple long braids, and she was very friendly, almost merry in her demeanor.

Nerine liked her very much. She was effervescent, and yet reined in her energy to suit the occasion. Nerine realized that even though Father possessed a strong sense of humor, at heart he was serious, even a bit pessimistic. Altairos was more lively than Father, and his serious vein more optimistic. But Rinara was the first person she'd met with a truly bubbling personality.

Rinara was *fun*.

And she made all the events planned in her honor a joy for everyone attending them.

When she finally departed for the Gulf of Gallicus, where the wedding would be held in a year's time, the reef palace felt very quiet.

Nerine had thought she would welcome it. She'd barely had a moment to herself ever since Tyr brought his news. Shouldn't she be exhausted by the social whirl and ready for quiet? But Rinara's vitality had supported Nerine through it all, and now . . . she was one more person to miss.

The return to the ordinary – practicing the languages of the lands around the Middle Sea, learning about the architectural wonders of Aegyptus (her latest interest), and visiting Calla's cottage to weave – was tolerable. For a while. But not welcome.

Mother was exceptionally busy restoring the balance of the Ionian Sea, after the disturbance there caused by Leukonos, and often gone for a moon at a time. Father began helping Tyr upgrade the amenities in the Tyrrhenian Sea and was away with equal frequency. Nurse, while still a companion for Nerine, had requested permission to receive the twins born to Lady Philena into the royal nursery, which was a good thing. All the royal nurslings had grown up, and Nurse was not ready to retire.

But Nerine grew very lonely.

Knitting *nålbindning* ribbands in the evening, sitting alone, was lonely. Pouring over the complex grammar of Celtiberian was interesting – fascinating, actually – but lonely. Working the equations that allowed the denizens of Aegyptus to build their fantastic pyramids was frustrating. And lonely. Wandering the beach without Altairos and weaving alone in Calla's cottage was lonely.

She could have befriended an older daughter of one of Mother's ladies-in-waiting. As a princess, she could command anyone's attendance. But it hardly seemed fair. Young Ellyra was perfectly happy playing with her own friends, and Nerine did not want Ellyra for herself. Wanting to just have company, any company, wasn't a good reason to disrupt someone else's life.

Although she didn't merely want company.

She longed for Agnippe, for Tyr, for Rinara, for Calla, for Altairos. Ellyra could not substitute for any of them, and Nerine refused to burden her with the trying.

And . . . being honest with herself, even the presence of Mother and Father, or Nurse, would have been irritating, not comforting.

～

Nerine began spending most of her days ashore, wandering the beach in the mornings, setting up Calla's loom in the afternoons, with a fabric even more complex than the last one from Calla's imagination. It would be a rendition of one bright corner in the gardens of Altairos' land palace, with large leaved plants, vivid flowers, jewel-like insects, fluttering birds, and a plashing fountain.

She grew happy again at the loom, utterly absorbed in the intricacies of her tapestry and feeling Calla's presence once more.

She grew extravagantly unhappy while she roamed the sands by the water, the desolation in her heart increasing as she mourned absent friends.

Then, one day, the armlet above her wrist caught her attention, its green beryls flashing gold in the sun on the beach. She'd grown so accustomed to its presence during all that time when she'd not needed its reminder that she'd forgotten it was supposed to *be* a reminder.

King Zeron had intended her to be hopeful about her future. He had spoken of the futility of nursing despair, and cautioned her that present despair would undermine her future satisfaction, when she finally came to inhabit her life more fully.

As he spoke, she'd been thinking of her lack of vocation. Her unfulfilled wish to travel. But didn't his advice apply to more than that? If she despaired in her loneliness, would it undermine her times of companionship in the future?

She rather thought it might.

What if she welcomed her loneliness instead of fighting it? Was that even possible?

She didn't know, but she decided to try it.

That afternoon, instead of repairing to the cottage to weave, she remained on the beach, walking through the curling foam of the slack tide and contemplating the emptiness in her heart.

How could you not fight the pain of loneliness? She wished it were gone. She wished she felt differently. She wished Agnippe or Altairos or Rinara were walking by her side. She wanted the now to be a different now.

So . . . what if she decided that this now was a good now? What if she decided that being here, on these sands, with this cool water circling her ankles, and this warm air pillowing her shoulders, was a good thing. That her solitude was welcome. That she was complete exactly the way she was, alone and glorying in the beauty of this stretch of coastland.

For just an instant, she felt it.

Felt whole in and of herself. Felt the loveliness of the great blue sky canopying her, and the perfection of this shore. Felt no need for anything else.

She almost held her breath.

The moment felt that fragile. As though a breath could shatter it.

And then she was laughing and plunging in a shallow dive to swim across the top of the waves as land people did, thrilled by the surge of her muscles, the buoyancy of the water, and the knowledge that she possessed everything she had ever needed within her awareness of this moment now. And *this* moment now. And *this* one too.

Every moment held the potential for wonder, so long as she accepted that it did.

Her contentment lasted when she came ashore again and walked to Calla's cottage.

It lasted as she weaved.

And it lasted as she swam home.

When she awoke in the night, it was gone.

Howling loneliness swept through her heart and she wept, this time not only for her loved ones, but for the departure of her serenity. Oh, but she wanted it back as badly as she wanted Agnippe and Altairos to return.

By morning she was wept out, and her desolation felt flat and dead, rather than living and monstrous.

She swam again to the shore and practiced acceptance just as she had the day before, but it didn't work. She felt lonely and sad and disappointed. And tired.

At Calla's loom, she realized that she'd *not* practiced exactly as she had the day before. She'd grabbed for acceptance, in the expectation that it would bring the exaltation that had followed it the first time. Whereas the first time, she'd held no expectation of what might transpire.

I must be willing to feel terrible, she realized.

And with that thought, acceptance arrived and her pain fled. Once again she felt complete and fulfilled, there at the loom, passing the shuttle through the shed, beating the weft tight, lifting the heddle rod up to its jacks, and passing the shuttle through again.

This is what *practicing* hope means, she decided. It's not about feeling good in spite of terrible circumstances. It's about being willing to feel bad. Fully willing. And the paradox is that full willingness opens a door to . . . serenity. How very strange that was!

She marveled at it. And continued to practice.

She discovered that it was possible to feel wretched and serene at the same time, which was very odd indeed. But wretched and serene together was much better than wretched only.

She wondered if anyone in her family had ever done this, practiced in this way, felt this way. She worried that she was passing into a freedom from her corporeal form the way her grandfather had, and that when she next used her water gift, not only her hands would become one with the waves, but her arms and shoulders too. Would she become water entirely, as grandfather had, and drift on the currents for millennia?

Gritting her teeth, she practiced hopefulness on this new worry and found she could be both fearful and serene together, which made her laugh. How was it even possible? But it was, for a little instant of time before the serenity washed away the fear.

On her way home she used her water gift to create a current that would propel her without the need to swim. It was fun, but her hands and forearms took their water form as usual, not the rest of her. Apparently her fear was without substance.

～

18 ~ Consummation

A DÉKA-DAY LATER, Father returned home. Tyr's abode was ready for his bride. Then Mother came home as well. The net of life in the Ionian Sea was restored. And Nurse took a nursery maid under her fin, which meant she had more time and attention for Nerine.

Nerine was even more irritated by their presence than she'd considered she might be during her early loneliness.

Mother started planning a visit to both her land-dwelling daughters, imagining that Nerine would accompany her. The mere thought of sharing a chariot with Mother for days and days made Nerine want to wring Mother's neck. Mother's haughtiness – the same as ever – seemed more unbearable after its absence. Her attempts to interest Nerine in a trousseau for the journey felt interfering. And her questions about Nerine's studies seemed condescending. Never had mother and daughter accorded so poorly.

And Nerine found that while she could practice acceptance – hopefulness – in solitude, she could not do so in company. That was the unkindest blow of all. Apparently her temporary abandonment by all her kin had been more a gift than she'd realized. She would never have discovered the potential for joy in every moment, if she'd been teased by unwanted companions.

She felt that she should be able to practice hope under any conditions, and was frustrated that she could not.

When the chief of Poseidon's heralds – Neomar had advanced to that exalted position – brought word that the norns of the north sought a handmaiden to live with them and learn their ways, Nerine was tempted to accept the offer on the spot.

She held her tongue, only because Mother and Father found so much to say about it, after Neomar retired to the chambers offered for his rest and refreshment.

They lingered by the summoning post, the setting sun slanting through the lagoon waters, and the glimpse of the deeps glowing very blue in the distance, between two upthrusting masses of the reef.

"Darling," began Mother, "don't reject this post out of hand. I think it might be just the thing for you."

Father chuckled. "She'd travel farther than any other nymph of the Middle Sea has done." He turned to Nerine, amusement in his eyes. "You'd like that, sweetheart, wouldn't you?"

Mother interrupted before Nerine could answer. "Meren, don't be silly. She's outgrown that foolish dream. But Nerine" – and she, too, turned to her daughter – "just think of all that *nålbindning* knitting you do. It's true that the weaving of the fates is rather different than knitting, and I shouldn't think the norns do knit, but textile work is much the same, surely?"

Nerine would have laughed, if she hadn't been so irritated.

Apparently Mother and Father had been worrying lately about Nerine's vocation as much as ever Nerine herself had. Why could they not have raised the subject with her? Why mightn't they all have discussed it sensibly together? Instead of treating Nerine as a child who required them to shape her life for her?

Why couldn't they recognize – as King Zeron had recognized – that this was something *Nerine* must do. His trust of her as capable, even if it were merely her ability to wrestle with her vocation unsuccessfully, had felt so freeing. So strengthening. She'd felt like she could do anything.

"And it's a position of honor," continued Mother. "Just as the culture of our world flows through Agnippe's hands, so the very fate of the world would flow through yours." Mother had the grace to look daunted by the idea.

As well she should.

Nerine deciding who should live and who should die? Except it wouldn't be Nerine. The Weaver, the Patterner, and the Shuttle-catcher would do that, and Nerine would merely assist.

Mother was correct that being the fates' handmaiden was an honor, not that Nerine cared for that. And unbeknownst to Mother, Nerine was far better prepared than anyone in the sea could guess. All those years under Calla's instruction meant her fingers were deft, and her eye for the warp and the weft, well-trained. The norns wouldn't find her backward.

But did she *want* to do this? Was *this* her vocation?

Finally her mother left an opening into which Nerine could speak.

"I won't reject it out of hand, Mother, I promise. I will think about it." And she would. It was worth thinking about. The journey north would be . . . thrilling. Learning the ways of the northerners and dwelling among them would be fascinating. Caring for the tapestry of the world – the fruit of the norns' weaving – would surely bring some measure of satisfaction. Wouldn't it?

She would think.

And she did think.

Falling asleep at night in the refuge of her double-lobed parlor, she would imagine herself crossing the tall mountain peaks that rose between Hellas and Scandia, and she longed to make that incredible journey.

Walking the beach and failing to practice hope, she could see herself winding a skein of yarn onto the shuttle of fate and passing it to the Weaver with a shudder of dread.

Weaving at Calla's loom, she contemplated never seeing Altairos again and *knew* she could not do it.

Like a racer on the land, sprinting around a racing oval, her thoughts made the circuit through the possibilities over and over. She could find no certainty that outlasted each change in her activity and venue. She could no more decide to accept the norns' offer – or reject it – than she could identify a calling that would permit her to travel while pursuing her vocation.

Both Mother and Father continued to point out the benefits of being handmaiden to the fates, but they did not press her for her decision. They recognized – and told her so – that it wasn't a decision to be made quickly or carelessly. But Nerine could see that they wanted her to accept.

Only Nurse seemed to really be seeing Nerine during this interval of confusion.

Nurse looked at Nerine and brought her globes of spring water or offered to brush her hair. But she said little, and fussed . . . not at all. Which was completely uncharacteristic of Nurse. Did she sense the vigorous tides of feeling within her nursling? Sense that she could not help at all, and thus knew that staying out of the conflict would be best? Nerine had little attention to spare for Nurse, but Nurse's forbearance reminded her a little of King Zeron's trust.

This was for Nerine to decide, because Nerine alone would bear the strongest consequences of her decision.

One sunny afternoon, she went to the tide pools, hoping to reclaim some of the wonder she'd felt when Altairos showed them to her for the first time. The surf dashed vigorously against the outer rock, white foam spraying into the breeze and spattering cool drops on Nerine's face. But the tide was low, so only a thin skimming of clear water flowed into the tide pools with each wave. The tentacles of orange sea urchins and aqua sea anemones undulated along the bottom of one basin. A red and white striped starfish lay amongst them like lost pirate treasure, and a black spiny crab crawled across a pink sponge.

Sitting in the shallower water at the edge, Nerine reached out her arm to place her hand in the crab's way. It climbed over her fingers, its scuttling legs pricking her skin.

Nerine smiled. This bright pocket between sea and shore was like a jewel box, but better because life brimmed within it. She and Altairos had spent whole days dabbling here and running races between crabs, or transferring the small fish caught in a drying pool to another with more depth.

She felt the tension draining out of her.

Maybe she'd needed to spend some time away from deciding the future of her life. Maybe the answer lay in enjoying the present.

She gave herself to the present, noticing the coolness of the sea spray and the warmth of the tide pools, hearing the roar of the surf and the sharp cries of the gulls, tasting the salt on her lips, and feeling at peace, for the first time since Mother and Father had returned to the reef.

The rhythm of the waves felt like Mother Ocean's heartbeat, anchoring Nerine within contentment, while the great blue freedom of the sky reminded her that this moment now offered every freedom she cared to claim.

As she sat in reverie, a shadow – the silhouette of a young man – fell across the tidal pool before her.

~

She turned, squinting against the sun, to see Altairos grinning down at her.

Jumping to her feet, heart beating with joy, she had just an instant – to note how sun-bronzed he was, to see that his chin sported a short neat black beard, that his shoulders were broader than ever, but that his eyes crinkled just the same – and then she flung herself into his open arms.

"Nerine, Nerine," he murmured, hugging her close.

And then he was kissing her. Her cheeks, her eyes, her ear.

And then her lips.

His lips felt satiny soft, but firm and urgent. His entire body, pressed against her, felt firm and urgent. She felt like she'd come home, and like she was embarked on a whole new adventure, strange and exciting.

She murmured a protest when he drew back.

"I almost think you're glad to see me," he teased. And then he bent to her lips again, slower, sweeter, lovingly. She wanted him never to stop.

When a larger wave slapped the backs of her calves, he drew back again, laughing gently.

"The tide has turned," he said, and guided her toward the sands, his arm around her waist. "Will you marry me, Nerine?"

Her heart, wild with joy and love, felt as though it leapt from her body.

Oh! Oh! Oh! This was what she'd wanted, what she'd been waiting for without knowing it, why she'd been unable to decide her future. She wanted a future with Altairos. Adventuring with him, traveling with him, being with him.

She stood still, gazing into his happy, crinkling eyes, feeling wonder beam out of her own.

He moved to stand in front of her, taking her hands in his. "Will you, Nerine?" His voice was so tender, her beating heart melted and she could not speak. Wordless, she nodded.

He raised her hands to his lips, kissed the back of each, and then leaned in to kiss her brow, just over her spiracles, dimpled closed. His lips moved against her skin, and he whispered, "I love you, Nerine. I love you more than my heart can hold."

And then she found her voice. "I love you, too. I've always loved you. I always will."

She clung to him a moment, and then stepped back so that she could see his face. "Why did I not know? Before?"

He shook his head, and kissed her lips again.

They wandered along the water's edge after that, holding hands, pausing to embrace, and strolling onward again. She felt very full, and still, and content. Altairos loved her, and she loved him. All her life, she had been moving toward this moment. And this moment would anchor all the rest of her life. King Zeron had been right. This moment was richer because of her hope.

"What are you thinking, sweet Nerine?" asked Altairos.

"I'm thinking about how amazing you are," she answered. "And how happy we will be."

He smiled and kissed her. "Good."

"Do you remember dragging me out of the surf? The day we met?" she asked.

His laughter was a shout. "How could I forget? Of course, I remember." He swung her hand in his, forward and back. "Do you remember? What were the first words I spoke to you?"

"I will save you," she answered slowly. How strange. She hadn't known his language then, but his language was hers now. Or would be. And, *I palírria ínai pou érkhetai*, he'd shouted. *The tide is coming in.* Just as now, he'd said: The tide has turned.

Her tide had indeed turned, from confusion to sense, from sorrow to joy, from emptiness to fulfillment.

"Nerine?" he probed. Had her thoughts shown on her face? Probably.

"Life without you has been like those tumbling breakers," she answered. "I think you've saved me again."

"Tell me," he said.

She didn't want to. She wanted to dwell in her present happiness a while longer. So she told him about practicing hope instead. And about how she couldn't do it when she wasn't alone.

"Practice it now," he urged. "Can you when *I* am present?"

She laughed. "I'm too happy now, silly."

He grew suddenly serious and hugged her close. "Are you, Nerine? Are you?" he murmured into her hair.

Only when the beach was entirely in shadow, with just the wet sand along the water still lit by the setting sun, did she realize that the afternoon was gone, and that she must go home.

"Come to me in the morning," Altairos beseeched her.

"Of course," she answered.

She kissed his cheek, and then turned to dive into the waves.

～

Swimming through the dimming water, she thought of him, sun-limned as he had been when she turned to see him.

At dinner – a large gathering with all Mother's and Father's retinues included – she ate little and remembered the feel of Altairos' lips on hers.

Knitting, with Nurse in attendance, she heard Altairos' voice saying he loved her.

Tucked into her sleeping net, she dreamed of being with him always.

And in the morning, he met her on the shore as she emerged from the sea, glistening in the clear light, and they spent the day in lovers' bliss.

Only after several days passed did either of them bend their thoughts to practical matters.

Seated side by side, on a driftwood log on the flank of a dune – similar to that first one ten years ago, but not the same; that one had long since been carried away by storm waves – their thighs touched.

"When shall we be married, Nerine?" Altairos dropped a kiss on her hair. "Can it be soon?"

Nerine scooched a little away from him, so that she could see his face, a tiny shiver of dismay running through her. "Altairos . . . how will we *do* this? Land people and sea people *don't* wed. Do they?"

He didn't know the answer. She could see that he didn't.

"I'll ask Pappa. He'll know how we can manage it."

"You haven't told him, have you? That we're betrothed."

A shadow of confusion showed in his eyes. "Have you told anyone?" he countered. "In your reef?"

She sighed. "No."

"What's wrong with us, Nerine? We should be shouting our happiness from the roof tops. Or" – he took her hand and grinned – "reef tops." Then he grew sober. "I wanted to. But I didn't. Why?"

"Land people and sea people don't marry," she repeated.

"But why shouldn't they?" he argued. "We're perfect together. We've been perfect together for ten years, we just didn't know it until now. We can't be the only ones."

Nerine frowned. There was something . . . she knew something. Except she didn't know it. Some part of her dreaming mind knew it, but her waking mind couldn't parse it.

"The servants in your palace hate me, now that they know I'm *numeni*. Only your pappa accepts me as I am. And maybe your brothers?"

He shook his head. "I don't know. I haven't mentioned you to them since I've come home."

Home.

The land palace was his home. Would it be hers when they married?

She tried to imagine herself living there, but all she could see in her mind's eye were the glares of the manservants and the spite on the faces of the maids. Would the warm expression on King Zeron's face change to disapproval, when he regarded her as his son's wife, rather than his son's friend?

Hadn't he once cautioned her against being more than Altairos' friend?

The shiver of dismay within her strengthened enough to move her shoulders in a shudder.

"Nerine!" Altairos let her hand go, so that he might encircle her with his arm and draw her close.

"Altairos, it isn't going to work." Her voice was tight.

"Of course, it will work. We'll make it work." His voice was so calm and sure, she almost believed him. But she couldn't quite, no matter how much she wanted to.

"Altairos, where will I live? After we're husband and wife?"

He looked surprised. "With me, of course. Nerine, you know I cannot live below the water in your reef!"

She couldn't help laughing. Just being with him made her feel good. She poked his stomach, the muscles firm beneath his tunic. "Silly! Of course I know that!"

She leaned her head on his shoulder, not wanting to follow her thoughts to their logical end. That end . . . wanted avoiding. But she couldn't avoid it.

"When you're traveling as an ambassador, where will I live?" she asked, already knowing the answer.

"You'll come with me, of course." His arm around her shoulders tightened, and he took her other hand with his. "Oh, Nerine, you'll love it! I'll show you the great pyramids in Aegyptus and the Artemision in Ephesus –" Uncertainty laced his voice as he broke off, seeing the trouble in her face.

"But, Altairos, I can't!" Had he forgotten how ill she'd been aboard the *Lily of Aegyptus*?

"Oh." All the gladness ran out of him and he slumped. "Oh, Nerine!" Pain threaded the words, and he turned to rest his brow against hers. "What will we do?" he whispered.

"I don't know," she gulped, fighting tears. "But I can't live on a ship, Altairos, I just can't!" Her own memory of how sick she'd been remained all too vivid.

Altairos straightened and took both her hands. "Nerine, even people who get very sick on the sea acclimate after a few days."

"Land people." Somehow she knew that many things pertaining to land people would not pertain to sea people. And Altairos had been desperately wrong before about sea dwellers.

She remembered his misconception about how dolphins breathed. She remembered his surprise at her own seasickness. She remembered her decision to trust him on the truths of the land, but not to rely on him regarding the blending of land and sea. Marriage between a numen and a mortal would be the blending of sea and land with a vengeance.

"Couldn't you try it?" he begged. "Maybe sea people are just the same in this. We're the same in so many ways."

"And if I didn't acclimate? What then, Altairos? Would you put me ashore in Carthage? Or Trípolis?"

"I'd instruct the captain to turn back."

She just looked at him. They wouldn't be sailing on a pleasure cruise. He had to know that turning back from a mission of diplomacy wasn't an option. And that leaving her alone in the harbor of a strange port would be just as dangerous as déka-day upon déka-day of illness, down into debility, eventually death, if it went on long enough.

And even if their first journey were a pleasure cruise, from which they could turn back, what then?

She going to live amidst those who hated her in the land palace, while he sailed away from her? Seeing one another once every two years? She'd end by withdrawing to the reef palace, and it would be as though they were not married at all.

Her belly felt very cold, despite the warm sun shining on her skin.

Altairos' grip on her hands tightened. "Nerine, we have to figure this out."

She didn't see how they could.

"Nerine, would you renounce me?" His face and voice were shocked.

"No! No!" she choked, and wrested her hands from his to throw her arms around him.

His arms closed on her, drawing her close, and he rained kisses on her face, mumbling, "I'll never let you go! Never!"

His lips met hers, and the kiss grew passionate. He lifted her onto his legs to bring her closer still, and she felt a strange charge of excitement rush through her. His hands roamed her body, gentle touches on her breast, her thigh. How could such gentleness leave such tumult in its wake? She twined her hands in his hair and clung closer.

His caresses stopped, and he set her away from him, despite her inarticulate protest.

His bronzed skin was flushed and his black eyes, very dark. She wondered if the dark of her own eyes had overtaken the green. He brought his breathing under control. "Nerine, this is the converse of husband and wife. We must wait."

Sudden recognition chimed within her. So *this* was what those lessons on the intimate joining of man and woman had meant. Somehow the bare facts conveyed by her tutor, and repeated by Mother at intervals, were so very different from experiencing them.

Altairos was right, of course. They must wait. But she didn't want to wait. His lips drew her even as she sat staring at him. She wanted to move close, to touch, to caress, to feel his lips on hers.

With a groan, he pulled her to him again, kissing her and kissing her, until her lips parted and his tongue entered her eager mouth, teasing and questing. She shifted to straddle him, wanting more. The warmth that shot through her startled her. Ah!

His arms tightened, but it wasn't enough.

She broke the kiss, gasped, "Loose my belt!"

His eyes were wild, and he was breathing as hard as she. "Gods, Nerine!"

He loosed her pectoral instead. His hands on her bare breasts were blessing, and then he bent his head to kiss them, and his lips were more than blessing. Ah! Ah!

She pulled her hands from his neck to release the hooks at each side of her belt and drag it out from beneath her. The feel of him against her nakedness was like nothing she had ever felt before.

His lips returned to hers, but his hands – oh! His hands roamed once more, behind her and before her, and into her most intimate terrain. Warmth turned to heat turned to piercing sweetness, and then she was cresting a wave within herself, mounting and mounting, then breaking in white fire, like magnificent surf against black rock, exploding into the sky.

She stiffened, transfixed until it passed, the wave swept out to the ocean once more.

She opened her eyes.

"*Blessings*, Altairos! What *was* that?"

His eyes were very, very dark; intent. He kissed her tenderly. "That," he said, "is a husband's gift to his wife."

Her racing heart was quieting to match the languorous feeling in her limbs.

"And the wife's gift to her husband –?" Surely he should receive something equally magnificent.

He smiled, almost unwillingly. "Must wait until we *are* husband and wife."

"I could caress you with my hands," she suggested.

"Oh, gods, Nerine! If I were naked, I'd never be able to hold back."

She could hear the truth of that. She doubted she could either.

He bent to retrieve her pectoral from where it had fallen in the sand, shaking it gently and fastening it around her neck, around her back.

"If I were clothed?" she offered.

"Gods, Nerine!" Could his eyes grow any darker. "No! Your belt would loosen under my fingers like a tangled fishing net addressed by its fisherman. No!"

He fished her belt from beneath the gray log, and she stood reluctantly. He stayed seated to clasp the hooks and pressed a kiss to her belly after.

"Do you not want . . . the wife's gift?" she asked. She knew he did.

But he seemed to be recovering himself.

He stood, tall on the slope above her, and kissed the top of her head. "Walk with me," he said.

~

Beside her, he was still tall, but her head reached above his chin instead of just to his chest. They strolled together across the flank of the dune, toward

Calla's cottage. They'd not entered it since his return, preferring in unspoken accord to roam the sands the way they had when children.

In the weaving room, her tapestry of birds and butterflies, amidst broad leaves and splashing fountain, rested unfinished on the loom.

Altairos stepped toward it, a look of wonder in his eyes. "Yours?" he asked.

She nodded. "I finished Calla's. The one of fishes and sea grasses," she explained. He'd seen that one started before he left. She stepped up beside him, and his hand sought hers.

"Did she pass peacefully?" he asked, a slight catch in his voice.

She sensed that wasn't his real question.

"She spoke of you often, before the hemorrhage struck her down." Her voice caught as his had. "She said she would always love you, even when she roamed the Fields of Asphodel." Nerine swallowed. Painfully. "I miss her. Dreadfully." Her eyes stung.

"I always thought she would be here when I returned," said Altairos. "When Pappa told me –" He shook his head.

Nerine threaded her arm around his waist. "You were as a son to her. More even than your brothers, because they had your mother, while you did not."

"I just wish I'd been here –!"

"Ssh, ssh," she hushed him. "She was never alone, through those last few days."

"You stayed with her?" He glanced down at her.

"I stayed with her."

He sighed. "Do you think – that your presence carried a little bit of mine within it?"

"I think *she* felt that way."

Nerine felt his lips on her hair.

"Thank you for being here, Nerine."

It felt odd that her mere presence could mean so much. But Altairos' presence meant that much to her. And his mother's *absence* must have meant as much to Altairos.

"What was your mother's name, Altairos? You've never told me."

"Hester," he answered, his attention elsewhere, probably still with Calla.

"Really?" She thought about it. That was strange. Sea people and land people had a few names in common – Maris, Ianthe, Clio – but mostly their names were different. How odd that Mother's dear friend and Altairos' mother had the same name.

Altairos bent to examine the tapestry on the loom more closely. "You've captured the lines of color on the breast of the bluethroat so perfectly!"

"Mmm." She tugged on Altairos' elbow. "Let's sit outside."

He looked up at her, surprise on his face. "What's wrong, Nerine?"

She didn't know, but that uneasy feeling, the same uneasiness that had surfaced when Altairos had said, "We're perfect together," shivered in her belly now.

"It's too cool in here." She would feel better in the sun – the warm, warm sun – its rays baking the shivers out of her.

He looked concerned, as well he should. It wasn't overly cool in the cottage, with the warm air borne in through the window openings on the soft breeze. He guided her onto the terrace and to the steps descending to the garden, their broad treads full in the sunlight. The scent of sage hovered around them.

She sat, and he sat beside her. The stone steps were still cool from the night, but the air was warm.

"Better, Nerine?"

She nodded, but she wasn't better. Wasn't better at all. A chill seemed to rise from deep within her, raising goosebumps on her arms.

"Altairos, what was your mother's full name?"

He frowned. "Hester Evandrou Lamperieus. Why?"

"Oh, blessings, no," she whispered.

"Nerine!" His voice sharpened with alarm. Was her face white? She felt like it might be. Mother's friend had been Hester Evandrou.

"Before she married?" she asked.

His face went abruptly still. "Oh gods, oh gods, no!"

"Altairos?" She knew what he would say.

He said it, slowly, as though it would be a different name, if only he waited long enough to pronounce it. "Aegaiou."

Mother's friend. A *numen* of the sea. Nerine buried her face in her hands. After a heartbeat, she straightened, desperate to see Altairos' face.

It was agonized. "She was one of the *numeni*, wasn't she?" he asked. "And it didn't work. Her marriage to my pappa."

Nerine straightened to whisper, "No, it didn't work. She was Mother's dear friend."

Altairos turned and seized her hands. "Nerine, what happened?"

Nerine could barely make herself speak. Her voice came out low and soft. "The sea longing came upon Hester while she dwelled on the land. It grew stronger, until she could not withstand it. She entered the sea, and her water form took her. She became one with the waves, to travel on the currents forever." A sob shook Nerine's chest, and a tear fell from her eye.

Altairos' finger touched Nerine's cheek, traced the tear's track. His face was stricken.

They stared at one another for a long moment.

Then Altairos gathered her in his arms, and they clung to one another in silence.

What more was there to say? Like Nerine, Mother's friend had run away to the land. Like Nerine, she'd fallen in love with an island prince. And then she'd left him and their sons, drawn inexorably back to the sea, leaving King Zeron so bereft that all his people hated the *numeni* still, nearly two decades after.

Nerine stirred, extricating herself from Altairos' arms.

"I won't do that to you, love. I'll leave now, before I hurt you so badly." She wasn't sure she'd be strong enough. How could she? They'd had only five days as happy lovers. How could she bear to give him up?

"Nerine!" Altairos was fierce. "It's too late for that. You'll tear the heart out of my body, if you leave now. Don't go!"

She felt the same. But she knew – *knew* – that it could get worse. That it *would* get worse. Leaving now would break his heart. Leaving later would rend his soul. And leaving later still would kill him. She *had* to leave *now*.

She stood and stepped away.

"Nerine! We'll talk about it! We'll figure something out! Please!"

Oh, blessings! The agonized tone in his voice was shredding her heart even as she listened. She must make an end quickly, or she'd never tear herself away. Her best friend. Her childhood friend. Her lover. Her husband-not-to-be. How could she renounce him?

"I release you from your betrothal oath," she pronounced, trying to still the wobble in her voice.

"Nerine!" He screamed it, on his feet now.

"Do you release me from mine?" Her voice was steadier, her belly cold, instead of quivering.

"No!"

"Then I release myself." It sounded so final. "Goodbye, Altairos."

"Nerine! Don't go!" He leapt toward her, and she leapt away.

Once started, she ran, the hard earth jolting up through her heels.

Through the garden and into the gully. Out of the gully and through the dunes. Across the shifting sands of the beach and onto the firm wetness bathed by the surf.

She expected to hear the pounding of his footsteps behind her. She *wanted* to hear the pounding of his footsteps behind her. Desperately wanted. But he did not follow her. Did not try to stop her. Was not there, at the edge of her vision, as she dove into the waves.

He could have caught her, if he'd tried. His legs were longer now.

Her heart was breaking.

～

19 ~ Nadir

SHE SWAM OUT to sea. Swam and swam. First atop the water like a land dweller, and then just below it like the *numeni* she was. The surface waters were warm, so warm, like her salt tears. Would they wash away her grief? Could they?

She swam, hoping for absolution – would Altairos ever forgive her? – hoping for a cessation of her pain. But the pain went on and on, just as the waves went on forever.

If she swam to the horizon, could she outswim her loss? If she swam to Poseidon's palace, could she outswim her very nature as *numeni*? If she swam to the edge of the Outer Sea, where the waves poured over a precipice into the abyss, could she outswim her memories of Altairos' last cry of her name? "Nerine!" he'd screamed, as though she'd indeed torn the heart right out of his body. Oh, blessings!

Eventually she surfaced to look behind her. The isle of Lapadoússa was very small, a smudge of grayish green on the horizon, where the vast blue sky met the equally vast blue sea.

Nerine sighed.

If she kept swimming, she might not make it back. Mai'ip did not glide beside her to guide her way. The island would grow smaller and smaller and pass from sight. When she turned to return, if her line were anything but straight, or even if it were, she might miss Lapadoússa altogether, ending far out in the Ionian Sea. Or the Sea of Kréte beyond it. Or would she have perished before she got that far?

She turned back.

It was merely early afternoon when she entered the reef palace.

She snuck into her mother's dressing chamber to consult the polished bronze mirror there.

Was her hair ragged from her tearing it? Were there links missing from her belt and pectoral? Was her face ravaged and her eyes red? She felt as though her person must bear witness to the devastation she'd passed through.

But she looked quite as usual.

The curling mass of her green blond hair waved around her. The belt around her hips and between her legs gleamed softly gold, with its green beryls flashing gold when she moved slightly in the water. Her pectoral clung neatly to the curves of her modest breasts. Her face was slightly pale perhaps, and her eyes a little wide, but nothing obvious.

She could pass for normal, if only she could keep her voice steady.

Her mother entered the chamber just as Nerine turned to go.

Mother's face lit. "Darling! Have you decided?"

This would be easy, then. "Yes. I've decided to accept the position with the norns," she announced.

"Darling! Oh, I'm so happy! I knew you would see that this is just the position for you." She swam forward to gently embrace her daughter. "Should you like a pectoral of white gold and diamonds for your departure? Or, no! Red gold and amber beryl would become you more. Darling –?"

Nerine interrupted her. "Mother, I should like to tell Father of my decision, and I would like to depart immediately. Tomorrow." Did her voice break on that "tomorrow"? She thought not. She hoped not.

"Oh, darling! Of course it's painful. I understand."

For a miracle, she *did* understand. Or thought she did. Nerine was leaving home for the first time ever. Short and quick for her departure would be better than a prolonged leavetaking. What a convenient misunderstanding!

Mother sent messengers ahead to Thérma with orders for Nerine's trousseau. She must have been planning it the whole time Nerine dithered. She overruled Father's desire to hang onto his last daughter for as long as possible, and overruled his native caution which preferred to move slowly and deliberately. She summoned the warriors back from their sweep of the deeps, so that Nerine would have the necessary escort.

Nerine did indeed leave the very next morning.

As Father handed her into her chariot – a sleek and modern vessel shaped like a teardrop – he halted her before the door.

"I wish you would tell me, sweetheart. I have more resources than you may realize, and I'd put them all toward solving your trouble."

Dear Father. Of course he had guessed that she was troubled, that there was more behind her abrupt departure than mere decisiveness. But, oh Father, she thought, you cannot heal this trouble. Only time – and distance – might do that.

She hoped.

～

Crossing Európi

20 ~ Black Despair

NERINE FELT NUMB, frozen like the ice that covered the sea in the farthest north. Or petrified like the Greek heroes turned to stone by Medusa's gaze.

She'd bade farewell forever to the man she loved most in all the land and sea. And she'd relinquished any hope of puzzling out a life possessing contentment or satisfaction. This journey – one of a kind and not to be repeated – was nothing but defeat. Comprehensive defeat.

She wondered that she could move. Surely her limbs were bound like a dolphin caught by strangler kelp.

But she could move.

She could shift from sitting to reclining on the comfortable sponges that cushioned the interior of her chariot. She could retrieve the traveling peg game from the net of sundries near at hand, set the game up, stare at it blankly, and put it away again. She could pull her *nalbindning* from that same stash, knit a stitch or two, and then forget that she was knitting. She could eat the crunchy morsels of sea celery provided for her, without tasting their mild sweetness or enjoying their crispness.

Of course she could move. It was her heart that felt cold and numb and devoid of life.

How could it still pump blood through her body, beating steadily, steadily, in spite of her desolation? Yet beat it did.

But a heart did more than sustain life. A heart felt delight and good cheer and hope. But not hers.

When her outriders – each warrior towed by a dolphin – performed acrobatic tricks to entertain both her and themselves, she managed to nod and clap. A princess had obligations to her retinue, and Mother had trained Nerine well. She could simulate pleasure.

They passed into the Ionian Sea and ventured across the Calypso Deep. The water was darker, bluer, and possessed a sense of the unfathomable abyss lurking below. Where was the wonder and the awe that differences once awoke in her breast?

The sea slipped past her chariot in a hushed murmur, a lullaby to soothe an unquiet child. Why could she not be soothed?

The ambience of the sea changed again when she left the wide reaches of the Middle Sea to enter the Aegean. The waters were clearer and more aqua in hue. Her chariot plunged through schools of fish, and the shallow sea bottom sported corals, urchins, and algae in even more abundance than home. From dawn to dusk, the underwater world shone bright and beckoning.

Where was her fascination? Her interest?

The night time was harder.

At the end of each day's travel, her escort would find a calm cove in which to moor the chariot. They'd tend the dolphins and loose them for the evening. The warriors would go spear fishing or crab hunting, and prepare a simple meal. Therius, the captain of the cohort, might play his water flute. Or Heiro, who came from the Levantine Sea, would tell tales of his birthplace. When darkness arrived, they'd tether themselves to an outcropping of rock or coral to sleep.

Nerine, bedding down in her chariot was physically more comfortable, but she couldn't sleep. The warriors, on the dolphin tows all day, were weary. While she had lolled at her ease from sunup to sundown with only bitter thoughts for occupation.

The warriors slept.

Nerine fell through the ice numbing her emotions to the black despair waiting beneath, like the gelid waters that waited beneath the northern ice, with a cold so brutal it came as a blow, and a liquid darkness so deep, it mirrored the moment when life extinguished.

Nerine lay and grieved.

What had she done?

What had she *done*?

She found herself second guessing all her choices.

Should she have stayed to discuss everything with Altairos? Maybe they would have devised an unexpected solution. Maybe there was an answer she couldn't see, present, but hidden, that only wanted searching to be found.

If she'd taken her parents into her confidence, they might have known exactly how to make things right. Except . . . when had they ever resolved an impossible situation before?

Never.

If she and Altairos had consulted King Zeron, he might have developed an answer. If anyone could, he would be the one. But he was also the one most wounded by the departure of his *numeni* queen. And he'd outright warned her against feeling more than friendship with Altairos. He would never have wanted his son to marry a *numen* of the sea. Nerine could imagine his kindly smile changing to the downturn of disappointment or the straight line of disapproval. How could she betray his trust after he'd helped and supported her in her time of need?

She couldn't.

And if she'd delayed – discussed with Altairos, confided in Mother and Father, consulted with King Zeron – and still found no happy resolution, tearing herself away would have been impossible. The happiness between herself and Altairos would have devolved into more arguments like the one they'd started – don't go, I must go – only more bitter and dragging on for as long as they could stand it. This way she had mostly happy memories. Except the happy memories hurt most of all, and they flowed inevitably to the agony in Altairos' voice as he begged her not to leave.

She had done that to him. It hurt. It hurt almost more than the missing of him hurt. And she tossed and turned in the night, wishing they need not stop to rest the dolphins, who saw just as well in the dark as they did in the daylight.

She had wanted to run away from herself, and she could not. So she'd run away from her life instead.

And it hadn't helped at all.

～

The next stage of her journey to the norns passed as a series of vivid vignettes, piercing the darkness of her despair, their warmth capturing her attention for a short time, but powerless to dispel her anguish.

When she came ashore at Thérma, the sweet sounds of panpipes, backed by the beat of drums and the murmur of strings, greeted her. Nymphs danced across the dappled grass from a festal table, laden with tureens of berries and carafes of wine.

"Welcome! Welcome!" they called.

The merry crowd fed her, as first one bowed to proffer a blackberry and then another twirled by with a strawberry. Nerine was drawn into the dance and passed from one laughing maiden to the next, each one white-frocked and curly-tressed and prancing.

Borne to Mount Olympus aback a pegasus, Nerine discovered her sister Eilidh, kinder and more caring than ever before.

One evening, she attended an opulent feast at which nine of the most august Olympians were present, reclining on their magnificent divans. Queen Hera occupied a low dais, sitting – not reclining – on her couch of scented applewood.

Hera's gown of gold-embroidered garnet silk complemented her statuesque beauty, but it was her immense presence – like the majesty that hung around King Zeron, but far, far greater – that made Nerine's knees tremble as she executed a land person's bow.

Hera nodded her acknowledgement and then addressed the cupbearer offering her cherries. Her voice was low and sweet.

Eilidh settled her sister before returning to her queen's side. She played the lyre at the goddess' request. She delivered a succulent apricot from Hera to Lord Zeus. She circulated amongst Hera's guests, even returning to Nerine for an interval to converse about the special bond between the pegasi and the muses.

Eilidh performed her duties flawlessly, but that was not what riveted Nerine's attention. It was Eilidh's demeanor. At home in the reef palace, Eilidh's haughtiness had annoyed Nerine nearly every day, seeming conceited and pretentious.

On Mount Olympus – with the greater gods looking on, each of whom bore the astounding majesty that mantled Hera, a few sustaining even weightier potency – Eilidh's pride looked very different.

It wasn't pride, Nerine realized.

It had transmuted into self-respect.

And not all of Hera's handmaidens possessed enough. One blushed furiously whenever Hera's attention fell on her. Another giggled too often. Yet another angled for the divine attention, hoping to curry favor.

Eilidh's demeanor was perfect, conveying reverence for the glorious beings she served, while yet reserving recognition for her own worth.

And that was why Eilidh could now greet her once-disdained sister with genuine warmth. Eilidh lived in circumstances which both fed and demanded dignity, and thus no longer needed to exercise her talents inappropriately.

Eilidh truly had found home.

Agnippe proved equally suited to her post as guardian of the sacred spring of the muses.

Carried to Mount Helicon by a pegasus, Nerine stood with crab apple trees and climbing roses at her back, staring at the water rushing from a cleft in a low bluff to fill the rush-encircled pool.

Agnippe rose from its depths amidst the rushes – slender and girlish, not yet entered into full womanhood – water streaming from her pale skin. She wore a belt and pectoral fashioned from small plates of nacre, and the sun lit rainbows in their gleaming surfaces. Her tightly curled blonde hair had grown to hang past her shoulders. She was luminously beautiful, like her spring.

She leapt from the water to wrap Nerine in glad arms.

"Nerine! Nerine! Oh, Nerine!"

Nerine burst into tears. Seeing Agnippe after so long, feeling Agnippe's embrace – it overwhelmed her.

"I've missed you," gasped Nerine. "I've missed you so much."

Agnippe laughed tearily. "I've got your gown wet. I'm sorry."

They talked, of course. And Agnippe was wise as always, producing insights that should have helped Nerine – *would* have helped Nerine a year ago – but couldn't lighten her misery now.

Agnippe's duties included more than the care of her spring, with its waters, the darting fishes, and its underwater caves – stretching back under the cliff, in twisting passages and varied chambers. She served as a muse to the muses.

These patrons of knowledge as expressed through the arts were just as impressive as the divinities of Olympus, but in a very different way. All of them exuded glory – a nimbus of exaltation and brightness that quickened the pulse and flushed the cheek. Nerine felt more overborne by it than she had by the potency cloaking the greater gods. If Hera were a spring tide – massive and inexorable – then the muses were a fountain bursting from the earth in joy and abandon.

As the afternoon blended into the golden light of a summer evening, they sang roundels under Euterpe's mellow guidance and then engaged in impromptu comedic drama with rosy Thalia. Terpsichore led them to a meadow to dance. Polyhymnia called for an interval of meditation before a hymn.

Nerine's sister participated in everything, consulted by all, radiant. Might this arpeggio be better if extended another beat? Would that rhyme be more effective if moved to the middle of the line rather than falling at the end?

Agnippe filled her post on Helicon just as surely, just as joyously, as Eilidh occupied hers on Olympus.

Nerine *wanted* to be glad for her. For her and for Eilidh.

She *was* glad, but she couldn't feel it. Once she bade her sisters farewell, Nerine's despair returned like the night.

~

By the time the arrangements were complete for Nerine to set off across Európi, her despair had given way to a sort of barren hollowness, emptied of life like the shades of mortals who drifted through the shadows of Hades. If someone could have shouted her name down into the canyon of her soul, it would have echoed – *Nerine . . . Nerine . . . Nerine* – and then faded away to nothing.

She almost wished for her anguish back again. Its very pain had anchored her to herself, connected her still to Altairos.

Why had she ever decided to travel north? Agreed to take the post with the norns? Running away from her life in the Middle Sea had proved futile. But she'd run. And here she was, accepting a cohort of Lord Hermes' elite guards for protection on her journey – the Poniró Peltastés, as well as a muse's handmaiden for her companion, and a strange costume for riding on horseback.

She turned the garments in her hands, examining them. The riding outfit was very different from the draping gowns with their elaborate folds that Nerine had always worn on land.

Close-fitting tunic and breeches were fashioned from knubby fabric, with a strange crisscrossing pattern of cream and white – "plaid" said her new handmaiden companion. The brown leather boots possessed tall tops to protect her calves. And a marvelous cloak – woven of two shades of green and cream and forming a vast square of fabric with fringes along two edges – would shelter her in inclement weather.

Apparently the Keltoi of Európi wore such cloaks and tunics and trews, and the plaid patterns were peculiar to their clans.

She supposed the costume made sense. During her brief flights by pegasus, the bunching of her gown between her legs and the steed's flank had been irritating. The tunic and trews would work better for full days on horseback.

Although . . . the sleeves of the tunic were too narrow to permit the wearing of King Zeron's bracelet.

She looked at its gold links and green beryls, glimmering on her wrist. She'd kept the king's trust by leaving his son, but she was failing in the promise he'd asked of her. Practicing hope was beyond her in the dreariness that dragged at her.

She would pack this reminder of her failure.

A glimmer of curiosity about the Keltic textiles tugged at her. She rubbed a fold of the tunic between her fingers, noting its texture and its weighty drape. A mixture of linen and silk in the threads, and something else. Ah, she had it: wool. The trews were fashioned of the same blend, but the cloak was pure wool and a little itchy.

She let the garments fall to a divan, her interest ebbing once her curiosity was assuaged. Life seemed a lackluster affair altogether, but the demands of basic civility required that she fight the depression of her spirits.

So Nerine pushed against her own lethargy to engage with Galena, her handmaiden companion, released temporarily from a post beside the muse of history, to travel with Nerine across Európi.

Galena was a tall brunette, possessed of a cool demeanor and a dispassionate way of speaking. Her reserve attracted Nerine, rather than the reverse, reminding her of Mother, whom Nerine found herself missing. Who would have guessed that she would miss Mother? But Mother's assured confidence and calm reserve would have been comforting, just now.

Galena proved effusive about the customs of the peoples who lived beyond the confines of the Hellenic peninsula. She turned all questions about herself aside, but waxed eloquent on the social castes of the Keltoi and the extensive web of trade maintained by them. She grew indignant – her voice acquiring a tinge of warmth – that many Hellenes dubbed the Keltoi barbarians, and she promised to teach Nerine the Lepontic tongue spoken by the tribes.

In her turn, Galena quizzed Nerine on the ways of the sea people, the architecture of the reef palace, underwater eating utensils, and much more. She brushed aside mentions of more personal things – such as Nerine's satisfaction in Eilidh's and Agnippe's comfort in their posts – which was disconcerting, but also a relief.

Galena's attention to the outer world and its fascinations pulled Nerine's focus there too.

Perhaps the long trek from the edge of the Aegean to the coast of Balder's Sea would capture more of the appreciation it deserved from her. Perhaps Európi – seen through Galena's scholarly eyes – would banish the horrible grayness that dragged at Nerine's mood.

Nerine hoped so.

～

Nerine arrived with Galena in the city of Karasoúli – northeast of Olympus – via a morning's flight by pegasus. Amidst the white marble of an open, arcade-wrapped square, the magnificence of her escort guards, the Poniró Peltastés, awaited her.

The score – no, not quite a score – of men made a brave sight in the sunlight at the square's center. Each warrior wore an unusual sort of blazingly white armor. More than a mere breastplate, such as her father and his warriors preferred, it seemed to wrap all the way around the torso. Broad straps trimmed with bright scarlet borders came over the shoulders and fastened at the ribs, while a series of flaps along the bottom – also trimmed with scarlet – covered the thighs. A red sword belt held the scabbard with its blade.

Was this the linen *linothorax* armor she'd heard mentioned once or twice on Olympus? It must be, she decided.

Their head gear was equally bizarre, a white conical cap with a red stripe around the base and a rounded peak that folded forward. She knew the term for this, too: it was a Phrygian helmet, originally worn by the allies of Troy in Anatolé.

Cresent-shaped shields strapped to their backs completed the *peltastés'* accouterments. And their horses gleamed golden brown.

An older warrior, with gray showing in his hair and deep lines around his eyes, stepped forward to introduce himself as the *peltastés'* captain, Bartholomai Chaonieus. His demeanor was stern, but he greeted them cordially and pledged himself to conduct Nerine safely to the norns in Scandia.

"I shall welcome your requests during our journey," he declared, "but I commend Jason as my best recourse for your detailed comfort." He gestured toward a formal young warrior, who reminded Nerine of her brother Tyr on his best behavior.

The captain nodded and turned back to his men.

Jason stepped forward with his hand on the headstall of a mild, dark-eyed mare. Her golden brown hide shone richly compared to the white of the pegasi of Olympus, but the majestic presence of the winged horses was lacking.

Nerine looked anxiously at the red felted cloth strapped firmly around the horse's barrel and even more nervously at the knotted reins resting on the neck. This mount, she suspected, would not simply carry her from Karasoúli to their night's resting place without input from the rider. And Nerine had not the faintest idea of how to give the necessary guidance. But Jason was holding out his hands for her foot. She placed it as expected and was boosted onto the back of her horse.

It felt much the same as being boosted onto the back of a pegasus, which was reassuring. But this steed was not so broad, as well as being a little bonier along the spine, which was traced by a stripe of a darker hue. Nerine was grateful for the padding provided by the thickly felted cloth.

"Have you ridden before, Kríousa?" asked Jason.

Nerine made another quick decision. "Please call me Nerine. We'll be traveling together far too long for formality."

Jason's stiffness fled when he smiled, and he looked very young indeed, perhaps younger than Tyr. "I'm Jason, of course."

Good. He seemed comfortable with a casual style.

"Do you know your way around a horse, Nerine?"

"I don't," she confessed. "Not at all. I don't think being carried by the pegasi of Olympus counts, do you?"

He laughed, looking younger still, not only younger than Tyr, but younger than Nerine herself. "No, probably not."

She noticed that Galena was mounted now, and that Galena seemed to know exactly what she was doing, gripping her horse with her thighs while letting her lower legs dangle, and taking the knotted reins in her hands. Nerine looked back at Jason, hopeful that he might have a few useful tips.

"Efyenés is a gentle sort. She'll follow the horse in front of her until you get the hang of it."

Nerine wanted something a little more specific than that.

Jason continued: "Touch the right rein to her right neck when you want her to turn left, and touch the left rein to her left neck when you want her to go right."

Oh, blessings! Exactly backward. Nerine hoped that there wouldn't be too many more backward instructions or she'd never keep them straight.

"Touch her sides with your lower legs when you want her to speed up." He smiled. "But she'll mostly be walking. Trotting is hard on the rider. Too jolting. And a canter tires the horse."

Jason seemed to be the only *peltastís* still on the ground. All the others were mounted and milling around the square. Most possessed a pair of leather bags strapped behind the riding cloth, and Nerine wondered what had happened to her belongings. Then she spotted the mounds of baggage carried by three pack horses and felt reassured.

She looked back toward Jason to see him vaulting onto his horse straight from the ground. Blessings! Did the boy have dolphin's flukes for legs to be able to do that?

The cavalcade was moving out.

She found Galena in front of her, while Jason went behind her. Her own mount – Efyenés, she dredged from her memory with effort – did indeed seem content to simply follow along. Maybe this wouldn't be as hard as she thought it would.

She had to concentrate on gripping with her thighs. She didn't feel that sense of stability that had characterized the pegasi. Maybe the pegasi had special air gifts just as the sea people had water gifts? At any rate, if Efyenés were to swerve suddenly, Nerine would definitely fall off. Nerine hoped Efyenés would *not* do any sudden swerving!

By the time she felt secure enough to pay attention to anything but staying on her horse, they were outside the city, riding on a dirt road along the river. The Bardários. Its brown water roiled as the current flowed around rocks in midstream or over fallen trees.

She'd never seen water so opaque. Would her journey across Európi be one new thing after another? She rather thought it might: strange rivers, strange mountains, strange people, strange customs, and more.

The next new thing was less welcome.

The muscles in her thighs began to tremble with fatigue. Then her sitting bones grew sore. And eventually a stinging pain afflicted the inside of her right knee.

When they stopped to let the horses drink from a trough served by a wayside well, Nerine scrambled down eagerly. And landed on her rear, even though Efyenés was considerably closer to the ground than a pegasus. Nerine's trembling legs simply folded.

The jolt of landing swallowed Nerine's embarrassment.

Jason rushed up, looking alarmed. "Are you alright, Nerine?" he asked.

Galena strolled over sedately. "I expect she's got some sore spots. Haven't you, Nerine?"

"I think I'm sore everywhere," admitted Nerine. She was exaggerating, but not much. Her arms were tired from holding in one position for so long. Same with her shoulders. An incipient headache didn't count, she decided. But everything from her waist down . . . ouch!

It was striking how physical discomfort acted as a much better distraction from unhappiness than anything else since she'd left home. There could be no retreating into dreary depression when her knees burned, her thighs burned in a different way, and her backside throbbed.

"Any blisters?" asked Galena.

"My knee, I think," said Nerine.

Jason winced. "I'll get a wrap for it," he volunteered. "You'll need something to manage the rest of the afternoon's ride."

Nerine echoed his wince at the thought of getting back on her horse.

And, indeed, her first moments back on the riding cloth were bad. Especially her sitting bones. But the pads of cloth Jason had tied around her knees – both knees, so as to prevent the unblistered one from blistering –

helped. And after the sun had slipped farther down the sky, she found her sitting bones too numb to hurt.

The breeze picked up, bringing the resinous scent of the pines on the heights to her nose, along with the wet, oozy smell of the river water. She'd not realized she'd grown hot – with no quick dip in a clear sea to cool her off – and the moving air felt good. But she wished her various body parts didn't shove their aches and pains so insistently into her awareness .

～

21 ~ Friendship's Solace

WHEN THE CAVALCADE stopped for the night at a small inn in the early evening, Nerine never wanted to see another horse again.

She stayed aback Efyenés until Jason arrived to help her down. She knew exactly what would happen if she tried it on her own. His hands were strong and careful as he eased her to the ground. She would have fallen without his support.

"Shall I carry you, Kríousa?" he asked anxiously.

"Nerine," she corrected, lifting her chin. She would *not* be a jellyfish. She *refused* to be! "And, no. If you'll give me your arm, I can walk."

Perhaps that was overstating it. Her legs felt like seaweed, and the numbness in her sitting bones was wearing off to become the deep ache of a bad bruise. She hobbled, leaning heavily on Jason.

Galena directed an evaluating glance at Nerine. Was there mockery – very slight – beneath Galena's composure? Surely Nerine was doing her an injustice.

"I packed a liniment salve, because I knew you'd be sore," Galena said.

Noticing Galena's limber stride, Nerine stifled her resentment to muster gratitude that her companion possessed a remedy she was willing to share.

Very little else penetrated Nerine's awareness. She was tired. She hurt all over. The bed provided for her was soft and smelled clean. Galena's salve helped. And then Nerine was asleep, never mind that she'd not eaten since the strip of dried lamb given her, when they first watered the horses. She was too exhausted to be hungry.

She was less sore in the morning, but more stiff. And the instant her sitting bones touched Efyenés' back, it felt as though she'd sat bare-skinned on fire coral. Pride alone kept her from leaping off.

Her stiffness dissipated as her muscles warmed, but her body aches grew worse. Only Galena's liniment made it possible for her to go on, day after day. And she barely noticed where the road took her.

As it chanced, the valley of the Bardários featured little variety. The water continued a turbid brown. Sometimes it broke into white foam where a rapid descent sped the current. Always it flowed between forested ridges, interrupted by the occasional bluff. The modest inns were similar to Calla's cottage back home, except with more rooms in them. And the people possessed the Hellene culture familiar to Nerine.

Nerine soon realized that the Poniro Peltastés' directed very little of their attention to her, even while she rode in their midst, the sole reason for their excursion into the north. They focused outward, assessing their surroundings for potential threats and ensuring that the necessities of travel were performed – dealing with innkeepers, caring for the horses, and so on. Captain Bartholomai checked on Nerine, but left her largely to Jason and Galena. His concentration was all for his men.

She appreciated that their vigilance lessened the need for *her* to be vigilant. Vigilance wasn't possible when everything throbbed.

Nerine's first impression of her handmaiden companion as more interested in the study of cultures than in anything or anyone else seemed accurate. Galena was cool outwardly, and also cool at heart; in comparison to Nerine's mother who (Nerine now understood) was cool outwardly, but passionate at heart. Mother's concealed warmth and Galena's thorough coolness might produce a similar effect, but were in fact utterly dissimilar.

Nerine still found Galena's resemblance to Mother appealing, and she wondered if she might finally understand her family, if she just met enough strangers to compare them to.

Despite Galena's nonchalance, the handmaiden proffered up her liniment salve regularly. And it was Galena who thought to braid Nerine's hair with ribbands and then tie it up on Nerine's head, giving some relief from the heat otherwise trapped on her neck and back.

Jason's help came to the fore on the road. He wrapped the pads around Nerine's knees for as long as she needed them. He pinned an extra thick square of felting to Nerine's riding cloth to cushion her seat. He made sure Nerine drank enough in the heat of the afternoons. And he took a warm interest in how Nerine felt.

Eight days later, Nerine had acquired the toughening her body needed. It amazed her how different the demands of riding were from swimming. But, thank all the blessings, she could now ride without discomfort.

With the blur of physical pain behind her, it seemed she'd put her desolation behind her as well. At least, she could pretend that she had. The Middle Sea seemed a long, long ways away. If she fastened her attention firmly on what was right in front of her, maybe she could be . . . not happy, but engaged in the here and now, no longer lost in the past.

Soon after her emergence from past and pain, they traveled through a spectacular gorge on the western flank of a mountain named – in translation – the Black Ridge, and then traversed its lower slopes around to a river with an entirely different character.

⁓

The Moirios curved and looped like an eel as it crossed the land, and its water was clear – unlike the cloudy Bardários – but black in hue. In the sunlight, it reflected the cloud-scudded sky better than the finest bronze mirror. In the shade, it shone like polished jet.

The road they followed had narrowed to a track – requiring them to ride in single file. It threaded through the woodland flanking the Moirios, only emerging on the riverbank at intervals. Jason explained that the banks were treacherous, prone to crumbling in places were the current had undercut them.

The shade of the woods was pleasant, especially in the warm afternoon. The leaves rustled, a bird sang, and somewhere a brook bubbled as it flowed toward the river. The muscles of Efyenés' back moved comfortably under Nerine's seat.

Galena had been tutoring Nerine in phrases of greeting in the Keltic tongue, but as she gave examples of how to address a poet versus a druid versus a goddess, Nerine's questions persuaded her onto a personal tangent.

"The goddess of the hunt and the chase – Artemis herself – had come to my family's valley to see what sport our realm might offer her. I hadn't been told of her visit. I was just a little slip of a girl, and I didn't know." Galena laughed.

Nerine almost held her breath. She'd been trying to get Galena to open up ever since she met her. Unsuccessfully.

"I wasn't speaking Lepontic then," Galena continued in her reminiscent tone, "but I mangled my salutation to one of the greater Olympians just as badly in my own tongue." Galena paused. "It didn't matter. Artemis has a kindness for the nymphs of the glens and the mountains, even obscure ones like myself. She spoke with me most gently."

So Galena was an alseid or an oread. Nerine had wondered. She made an encouraging sound, hoping Galena would go on. Would she? Or would she break back for more instruction, as she always had before?

Efyenés snorted. Leather creaked. The horses' walking steps met the peaty earth of the track with muffled thumps. In the distance, children called to one another.

Nerine wished they could go two-by-two, so that she could see Galena's face. She risked a glance over her shoulder. Galena was smiling dreamily, her eyes far away. How unlike her!

Galena's next words held wonder in them. "I'd never known before that the world could be so big and strange, until Artemis showed me" – another pause, and then her voice turned waspish – "that I needn't smother forever in the gossip and giggling, in the herding and hoarding, in the feasting and fooling."

The shouts of the calling children grew louder.

Galena's tone softened again. "Artemis did not forget me. When I left childhood behind, she procured a post with the muse of history for me."

Nerine really wanted to hear more about this. Evidently Galena, too, had had her struggles with vocation. Perhaps they could compare experiences, learn from one another.

"Did you know you wanted to study history before you went to Clio?" asked Nerine. "Or did you discover your love of scholarly pursuits only after you arrived at Mount Helicon?" She took another quick peak back. Galena looked startled, as though she'd just awakened from sleep, and struggled between the dangerous allure of dreaming versus the safe comfort of the waking world.

As Nerine turned her gaze forward, Efyenés stepped out of the woods and into the sun. A patchwork of small fields filled the broad clearing: meadows on the outskirts with a few oxen or goats and, farther along, fenced plots of wheat or barley or rye. A cluster of wooden cabins huddled around a steep-roofed hall raised on a mound.

Nerine's eyes widened. This was a hamlet of the Keltoi! The first one of her journey.

In the distance, men worked the fields. Nearby, two small boys with gleaming blond hair and pale skin chased one another through a meadow, laughing and shouting. They wore tunics and trews of a brown and beige plaid.

Galena urged her mount up beside Nerine's, and stated in her customary tutorial mode, "The Keltoi build their homes four-square from stacked logs, and roof them with layer upon layer of bundled twigs, from the eaves to the peak. The chieftain's is the largest and stands on a hill. The floors inside are of beaten earth, but their furnishings show artistry and craftsmanship, often adorned with gilt and spiraling designs."

Nerine suppressed a sigh and allowed Galena to direct her attention away from Galena herself. The Keltic hamlet and its inhabitants *were* utterly exotic, but Nerine had enjoyed Galena's brief excursion into the personal. She hoped they could resume their conversation later.

After their horses climbed the mound surmounted by the chieftain's hall, Captain Bartholomai held a friendly exchange with a Keltic spokesman. The Poniró Peltastés dismounted. Nerine followed their lead. She still needed a leg up to mount, but she could dismount unaided.

The Keltic chieftain emerged from his fastness amidst a crowd, the anchor point of those surrounding him, drawing them with him toward Nerine.

His hair was white and pulled sharply back from his weathered face into a long horsetail. Stranger than that were his mustachios, grown so long that each flowed from his upper lip to frame his chin and then down across his chest to be secured in the belt at his waist.

Despite the warmth of the day, he wore his woolen cape – woven in a crisp black and white plaid. His face shone with good will.

Nerine gathered her courage to try out one of the greetings that Galena had just been teaching her. She received an enthusiastic response. Klanos oni Oletu seized both her hands, drew her toward him just close enough that he could kiss both her cheeks, and burst into a flow of language that meant absolutely nothing to her. Clearly her modest attempt had delighted him.

She repeated her salutation, since she had no other words in his tongue.

He spread his arms wide, palms to the sky, and pronounced what could only be a blessing, so solemn was his tone. Then he spread his cloak in the shade cast by his hall, urged Nerine and Galena to sit upon the plaid, and settled himself beside them.

The tribespeople and the Poniró Peltastés sat nearby on the grass, while below – on the slope of the mound – three men took their station in a line. They, too, were draped in black and white plaid cloaks. Each carried a peculiar instrument, comprised of a leather sack, held under the arm, with three carved tubes protruding from it. One tube slanted back against the shoulder; another went up to the lips; and the other was held between the hands, fingers placed over a row of holes in it.

The trio puffed their cheeks to inflate the bags, and then the most glorious music burst onto the bright air: vivid and martial and stirring, as though the Keltoi celebrated the legendary victory of the Olympians over the Titans.

Nerine listened, enraptured.

～

As the shadows lengthened, the pipers brought their paean to a triumphal finish. The tribesmen and women turned to the chores needing attention before the night came down. Klanos oni Oletu spoke quietly with Captain Bartholomai.

Galena drew Nerine aside.

When they stood some distance away from everyone, she murmured, "Did you understand that Klanos oni Oletu granted you signal dignity in his greeting?"

Nerine was still lost in the magnificence of the music. She dragged her attention back to her companion. "He blessed me. Something about holding me up to Ingeld's light?"

"Ingeld is the Keltic god of sunshine and fair weather," explained Galena.

Nerine nodded. The chieftain's manner had been extravagant enough to alarm her. The Keltoi seemed an altogether more demonstrative people than she'd expected, than even Galena's words could have prepared her for.

Galena laid her hand on Nerine's arm and leaned closer, urgency in her voice. "Nerine, he named you a daughter of his house and bade you call upon him at will, should you ever require his aid. That is an honor rarely granted. Nay, it's an honor *never* granted. You should be proud!"

Nerine didn't feel proud, just confused. Really, she'd done very little, merely attempting a salutation in her host's own language. But she had to agree that her first attempt had proven successful – disconcertingly so. She'd better ask Galena to teach her more words and phrases.

Soon. This very evening.

Perhaps a different greeting on her part would evoke a calmer response from her host at the next Keltic hamlet. She hoped so.

She also hoped that Galena might be induced to speak more of her childhood amongst the nymphs of the mountains and how she came to love history so much. But Nerine couldn't be direct. She'd learned that Galena always brushed even sympathetic questions aside. Nerine would try to edge the conversation around from vocabulary practice.

So Nerine recited Lepontic phrases such as: 'May the morning sun shine brightly upon you, noble warrior,' and 'Soft winds bear you up, mighty prince,' and many other variations.

They went inside the chieftain's hall when the dusk deepened, continuing the lessons by firelight, while the Keltoi served a lavish supper to honor their guests. Nerine asked the Keltic words for the goblets and platters and tureens, as well as the roast boar, stewed rabbit, and fruit pickle. Galena answered readily, often inviting the Keltic matrons to join in Nerine's education, but the handmaiden was not beguiled into further reminiscence.

Much later, during a brief visit under the stars in the soft summer night, Galena provided an opening for Nerine's pent questions.

Nerine began carefully. "I've always longed to travel, and I didn't fit in very well with my family at home, because they could not see a life of journeying for me. From something you said, just before we arrived here, I wondered if you also held interests that your mother and father could not approve."

Galena laughed, but it was careless, mocking laughter, not heartfelt as had accompanied her memory of Artemis. "I've wanted to apologize all this evening, Kríousa," she said. "I can't think why I imposed upon you so. My personal struggles and exploits can be of no more interest to you than yours would be to me. Come! Let us spend our time and attention more profitably! The matrons are gathering to sing the nocturne. I understand it is very beautiful."

With that, Galena led the way inside again.

Nerine followed, discomfitted, feeling thrown back on herself. She *had* felt interest in Galena's experiences. Did Galena truly believe the personal to possess little worth?

～

In the morning, Nerine awoke with a splitting headache.

The Keltoi urged their guests to linger and enjoy another day of revels, but Captain Bartholomai got his cohort up and out promptly. The shore of the Sea of Balder was yet moons away, even with only enough rest to keep the horses fit. Delay for mere merrymaking wasn't prudent.

Nerine had previously found the shady track paralleling the Moirios pleasant after the hot, sun-drenched road along the Bardarios, but the cooling canopy of leaves brought her no relief this morning. With each step Efyenés took, Nerine's head pounded. Apparently the refreshing and bitter brew served by the Keltoi with their meals had unpleasant consequences to those unaccustomed to it. In future, Nerine would insist her portion be mixed with water. In the meantime, she softened the erect posture demanded by proper riding, letting her back sway in the hope that it would ease her headache.

It didn't.

She looked yearningly at the river, each time a glimpse of it offered through the trees. The other flaw of the Bardarios had been its turbid water and rapids, which forbade bathing. The Moirios looked so inviting. Nerine wrinkled her nose at the grime that had settled in the creases on the insides of her elbows and wished for a bath.

She felt sticky all over. And none too fragrant.

Her head continued to throb.

The next time the trail emerged from the trees on the riverbank, Nerine sat back on Efyenés and exerted a gentle pressure on her reins. Efyenés stopped moving and stood still, just as Nerine had intended her to. She was getting the hang of riding.

The black water of the Moirios shone utterly placid and smooth, as though it were barely flowing between its forested banks.

"Jason," Nerine called to him, riding ahead of her. "I'm dirty and grubby after more than a *déka*-day without either a bath or a swim. And my head aches. *Please,* might we pause for an interval here that I may enter the

Moirios?" She hated how pitiful she sounded, but she longed with everything that was in her for the touch of water on her skin. She was a sea *numen* after all. Perhaps it was not so strange that she longed for the water.

She expected an argument. Captain Bartholomai had kept them to a steady pace. But when Jason relayed Nerine's desire, the Poniró Peltastés dismounted and began tending to their horses.

Nerine didn't hesitate.

Off came her boots and *nålbindning* stockings. Off came her trews. Off came her tunic. And the instant she was naked, she stepped into the Moirios.

It was shallow at this spot on the bank, and its cool water around her ankles felt like liquid light. A layer of partially decomposed leaves underfoot was an odd mixture of prickly and squishy.

Nerine waded further out until the water reached her waist. She had a sense of the world opening out as the trees behind her receded, and the length of the river upstream and downstream stretched to either side.

The water was *glorious*.

She curved into a shallow dive, dipping all of her under the surface and feeling her spiracles opening to let the water flow through them. The water had a flat edge to it – no doubt the tannins that Galena said gave the water its black hue – but Nerine felt clean and refreshed already. The stabbing in her head ebbed and vanished, while the dirt on her skin turned to mud and then washed away.

She dove deep and touched the silty bottom of the river at its midpoint. She spun in flips, forward and backward. She glided as a sea *numen* was meant to. Oh, but she'd missed her water. She'd not realized how much. This was good. Beyond good. She *needed* her water. Even when it was fresh, not salt.

When she came ashore again, her head felt heavy from the mass of hair still tied atop it in ribbands, but her headache was gone. She pressed the water out of the piled hair. It did not relinquish the moisture so quickly as it did when loose. But she didn't want to take the time to undo it and then redo all the braids.

Her swim had been brief, and she was eager to get going again. Surely Captain Bartholomai must share that wish.

She did pull on the spare set of trews and tunic that Galena had put out for her.

When Jason prepared to give Nerine a leg up onto Efyenés, Nerine saw that he was blushing. She frowned.

"What is it, Jason?" she asked.

He blushed redder, but didn't answer.

"The Poniró Peltastés rarely see naked maidens," came Galena's cool voice. Nerine could hear hidden mirth underneath it.

Nerine studied Jason's red face. "Is that it? That I swam bare?"

"No, Kríousa. I mean, yes, Kríousa. I mean –"

Nerine hadn't thought it possible for Jason to grow any redder, but he did.

"I apologize for embarrassing you," she said. And then she thought a bit. Was her behavior something she needed to change? No, she decided. Certainly she would not strip bare in a Keltoi chieftain's house. Or anywhere amidst mortal land dwellers. But the Poniró Peltastés were kin to the Olympians and the *numeni*. Their frequent travel at Lord Hermes' request meant they'd accustomed themselves to the ways of mortals. But they were not mortals, and she would not treat them so.

"But this is the way of the *numeni*," she concluded.

Jason, still red-faced, nodded and tossed her onto Efyenés' back.

⁓

The rhythm of travel along the Moirios was similar to that they'd followed along the Bardários. The summer sun rose early and was well up by the time they took the trail. Captain Bartholomai was aiming for steady progress rather than swift.

They followed the track that paralleled the river, but paused around the noontide as soon as they found a scrap of meadow – with the horses in mind. Usually this grass was near a Keltoi hamlet and its fields, for the natural state of this land was forest.

The Poniró Peltastés removed the bridles and the leather sandals strapped to the horses hoofs, allowing them to graze and roam bare hoofed on the softer ground. Their riders ate provisions procured from their latest host. And Nerine bathed in the river, if it was nearby and sufficiently screened from the Keltoi settlement. Galena often joined her, although she stayed nearer the bank than Nerine. More rarely, the Poniró Peltastés took to the water after the two ladies were done.

The afternoon ride was longer than the morning's, but curtailed well before the late sundown in the next Keltoi hamlet. Each hamlet seemed to possess its own chieftain, who provided exuberant hospitality.

Picking up bits and pieces of the language, Nerine grew more adept, not only at communicating with her hosts, but in seeking some portion of solitude while the sun was yet above the horizon.

She'd follow her escort to the fenced meadow where they tended the horses, and watch how they cleaned the tack, curried and combed hides, and fed handfuls of grain to augment the hay provided by their Keltoi hosts. The horse sandals, in particular, fascinated her. They were thick, tough soles of leather with zigzag-shaped bronze rivets studding the lower surface. Leather thongs passed through bronze rings on the edge of the sandal and were wrapped around the toe and coronet to secure the sandal to the hoof.

Jason explained that horses were meant to walk on grasslands or even desert sand, but not rocky ground. "The paved roads of the Hellene cities, or even the packed earthen tracks like these, liberally provided with loose stones and tough roots, would tear the horses' hooves down to nothing without protection." He shook his head and concluded solemnly, "A horse with broken hooves is a dead horse."

Nerine came to know the *peltastés* better – putting faces and names together. Learning which men were talkative and which, more taciturn. But her real intent in tagging along to the meadow was neither lessons in horse care nor getting in the way of her escort.

While the *peltastés* groomed their steeds, she quickly settled to the contents of her writing satchel. She'd been too despairing on Mount Olympus to even consider keeping a record of her experiences. And she'd been too saddlesore riding beside the Bardários to notice the interesting details, let alone write notes about them. At the time, inhaling the fumes of Galena's liniment salve, she'd told herself that there was nothing terribly interesting about the Paíones of the region, that they were just like the Hellenes who were familiar to her. But now she wondered what she'd missed.

She'd heard the Paíones mined their salt from the ground rather than evaporating sea water. Did it taste different? She'd not paid enough attention to notice. What a shame.

And some of the metalsmiths worked with iron instead of bronze. She'd heard the Poniró Peltastés speculating about horse sandals formed of iron instead of bronze-studded leather. Could Nerine have watched an iron smith at work, if she'd asked?

She vowed she wouldn't miss anything now. Nor would she forget what she saw through lack of making a record.

So she perched on a convenient rock or fallen tree at the edge of the meadow, with her portable writing board on her knees, dipping her reed stylus into a dish of ink and inscribing notes on a roll of papyrus.

Altairos had promised to log all the experiences of his travels, and she had curtailed his chance to ever share them with her. Now she began a similar history that she would never share with him. The symmetry of it seemed to balance . . . something.

Nerine took a twisted sort of comfort in that.

She couldn't resist describing the horse sandals, even drawing a sketch of what they looked like, while castigating herself for not focusing on the strange customs of the Keltoi. Then it occurred to her that the details of traveling by horse through Európi were just as unusual to someone whose mode of travel was a triaconter sailing the Middle Sea. Anything different from the isle of Lapadoússa was fair game for her stylus.

With that realization, she let herself go.

She recorded all her new Keltic words, of course, along with drawings of the Keltoi's log houses and the extravagant reaction of the first Keltoi chieftain to her mangled salutation. Which hadn't been repeated. The other chieftain hosts had been appreciative of her growing fluency, but not moved to declare her a daughter. Thank the blessings! That would have been too much!

But she also described the Poniró Peltastés in their now-growing-smudged white *linothorax* armor and funny Phrygian helmets. She wrote about Jason, who when he was relaxed reminded her of Tyr, but was nothing like Tyr when he stepped up on his dignity and grew stern.

Once she'd scribed a word picture of Jason, it seemed only fair to pass on to Galena. She was sure Altairos would be interested in Nerine's insight about how Galena was entirely unlike Nerine's mother, but contrived to appear very similar on first acquaintance. And Nerine herself found Galena quite interesting. She served as a lady's maid to Nerine, tutored Nerine in the tongue of the Keltoi, and entertained Nerine with stories about Keltic culture. She fulfilled all the duties of her position as Nerine's companion, and yet held herself aloof.

When they arrived at a Keltic hamlet each evening, Galena ascertained whether Nerine needed anything. If not – which was usual – Galena left Nerine to her solitary note-taking, and mixed with their hosts, often joining the Keltic women in their chores. She explained that the best way to learn about another culture was to participate in it.

The contrast between Galena's thorough, but detached attentiveness to Nerine and Galena's true passion – history and history in the making – boggled Nerine, although it didn't offend her. She found herself studying Galena as much as she studied the Keltoi and the forest around them. She couldn't imagine her own behavior being so divorced from her thoughts and feelings.

Over the twenty-five days that they traveled along the Moirios, the character of Nerine's notes changed.

They started out as haphazard descriptions of everything that caught her attention. And almost everything did catch her attention. Traveling was just as fascinating as she'd always thought it would be when she was younger. And travel through Európi was extraordinary.

After a déka-day, her records grew less spontaneous. First came the recounting of the events of their travel. Next followed orderly sections on Keltic language, Keltic clothing, Keltic food, and Keltic customs. And last were observations about the Poniró Peltastés and Nerine's closer companions, Jason and Galena.

Then her writings took on a more personal tone, as though she were not merely making a record of everything that might interest Altairos, but were writing a letter to her dearest friend. He was still her dearest friend.

Part of why Galena's detachment didn't bother Nerine was that Nerine couldn't imagine ever being as close to anyone as she'd been to Altairos. Having lost her best friend, she didn't want to set another in his place.

But she was lonely.

Galena was attentive, of course. And Jason was sweet. The peltastés were friendly. Their Keltic hosts were genial and welcoming. But there was no special person to share a joke with. No one whose eye Nerine could catch when a Keltic baby lifted his tunic to pee in the hearth fire and no one even noticed, because that was what Keltic babies did! No one to tell Nerine that she was loved. No one for Nerine to tell she loved him. No one.

So Nerine wrote all those things into her letter. How much she missed Altairos. How much she loved him. How sad she was that so many things – his sea mother's abandonment of his pappa, Xianthe's swimming away from home with never a goodbye, Nerine's own vile seasickness – made it impossible for them to marry. How much he would have enjoyed making this journey into Európi with her.

And while she wrote, she didn't feel so lonely. It was almost as though Altairos sat beside her, nodding and smiling and wrapping his arm around her waist in a sideways embrace.

The echo of his agonized last words – *Nerine! Don't go!* – began to fade. In her mind, she returned to the long years of their friendship, when she'd loved Altairos without knowing it. When he'd loved her, but not spoken of it.

Their brief time as lovers and betrothed, ceased to exist.

As husband and wife, Altairos and Nerine could *not* exist. *Did* not exist.

But as friends, they might live forever. Even if they never saw one another again. As Altairos' friend, Nerine did not feel so despairing. Surely they would meet again! One day she would make the long trip back to Pelagie to see her brother and her parents. And while she was there, she would go ashore, as she always had, and Altairos would be waiting on the beach, as he always had. They would pursue another adventure together and laugh. They would part, as they always had, and come together again. As they always had.

So – in the early evenings – Nerine wrote to her friend and found solace in it.

And at all other times she enjoyed her journey, eagerly gathering gems of experience and feeling to share with her absent friend.

∼

The lower reaches of the Moirios were much wider than the upper, its waters yet black and polished, but slower moving than ever. Nerine doubted that even her father could throw his spear from the west bank, where they rode, to the east bank. It had to be close to a full stadion across. The Moirios was *big*! The biggest river she'd ever seen.

The track they followed turned away from the Moirios and did not return to it.

They had to water the horses at the noontide from a tributary creek, feeding several handfuls of grain as well, because there were no grassy meadows to be found.

As evening approached, they emerged from the forest onto a strip of narrow wetland along the mighty Danouvios, and Nerine was forced to revise her estimate of large rivers. This stretch of the Danouvios was relatively straight and wide, oh, so wide.

Its water shifted and shimmered, a silvery blue broken into countless facets by the action of breeze and current. The rushes of the wetlands – glowing green in the golden light – edged it like ribbands. Nerine imagined a goddess wrapping that blue and green around her divine head like a crown, the might of the river blending with her own potency.

Some of the Keltoi spoke of the river as Danu, the deity of the inland waters. Nerine could see why. Only a goddess could wear this river as her crown. How wide was it? It must be four times as broad as the Moirios.

Blessings! More than four of Altairos' stadia. How in the sea would they get across it?

They rode along the wetlands for quite some time. Nerine saw strange birds on stilt-like legs fishing in the shallow water, while the rhythmic chattering of frogs mixed with the rustling of the breeze-blown rushes. An eggy smell rose from the mud.

The trail bent away from the river. With the sun so low in the sky, it was dim under the trees. The birds were trilling their twilight lullaby. Somewhere, a dove cooed.

It was dusk when they arrived at the outlying fields of a large Keltic village. The sky glimmered pale gray, but shadows filled the lower reaches of earth.

The Keltoi welcomed the travelers in, warmly, as befit the greeting of friends.

～

22 ~ Wolf of the Danouvios

IN THE MORNING, Nerine saw immediately how they would cross the great river.

The village sat a fair distance back from the bank on higher ground, but a few huts with fishing tackle perched next to a wooden quay built out over the water. Dozens upon dozens of boats were drawn up to the quay.

They were utterly different from the sea-going vessels that plied the harbor of Lapadoússa. These were riverine craft, long and narrow and shallow, with flat bottoms and squared-off prows and sterns.

Nerine walked over to examine them more closely, and a Keltic fisherman seized the opportunity to boast about his particular boat. Three very wide and very thick boards – as thick as the width of Nerine's palm – formed the flat bottom of the vessel, curving gently up toward the prow and stern. The sides were straight, but angled outward, and a variety of braces and seats connected one side to the other.

At the fisherman's enthusiastic invitation, Nerine sat on one of the plank seats. The boat slid about on the surface of the river, in that greasy way that boats had, but she didn't feel sick. Perhaps crossing the Danouvios would be like sailing in the harbor of Lapadoússa: exciting and fun, not scary and nauseating. She crossed her middle finger over her third finger for luck.

The boat's seats would accommodate two passengers each quite comfortably, and there were – what? – nine of them. Which meant the Poniró Peltastés and Galena and Nerine could all fit in one of them. But what about the horses?

Efyenés was a calm and sagacious creature, but would she stand still enough to not capsize one of these shallow river craft? And where would she put her hooves? The boat bottom was flat, not angled, but it was studded with blocky protuberances that seemed part of how the boards were tied together.

If Efyenés shifted a leg to keep her balance when the boat rocked, she'd hit one of those blocks, lose her balance altogether, and fall. Likely overboard, submerging the boat as she went.

Were they going to leave the horses behind and go forward on foot?

Nerine didn't think so. No mention of such a change had been made.

These further questions also were destined for a speedy answer.

When it was time to set off, the Poniró Peltastés bundled all the riding cloths, headstalls, and horse sandals into two of the boats, as well as the bags carried by the three packhorses. Half of the warriors along with a complement of Keltic paddlers cast off in one boat, while Captain Bartholomai rode bareback on his own Sophé into the water.

The rest of the horses – all twenty-one of them – clustered on the river bank. Behind them, Keltic men brandished long leather straps which they cracked in the air while uttering loud cries.

"Hiyah! Hiyah!"

Crack! Crack! Crack!

The horses rapidly followed their leader into the river. It was shallow near the banks, the water coming to just above the horses' fetlocks. As they moved out, the river deepened slowly, rising to their knees, then their bellies.

Jason helped Nerine and Galena into a second boat. Then the rest of the Poniró Peltastés and another complement of Keltic paddlers piled in, and they were off.

The river was beautiful, sparkling in the clear morning sunshine. But all Nerine's attention remained riveted on the horses. Were they really going to walk all the way across the broad, broad Danouvios?

When Sophé was chest deep, Captain Bartholomai climbed from her back into the lead boat, patting his horse's neck and murmuring, "Good girl!"

And then Sophé was swimming! Nerine could see the water swirling around her churning legs as the mare followed her rider's boat toward the middle of the river. The rest of the horses followed Sophé, and Nerine's boat followed them, staying upstream of the herd to give them room.

The breeze was stronger mid-river, and the waves more noticeable, but Nerine's stomach remained calm. It *was* like the harbor of Lapadoússa, maybe even a bit less choppy. Nerine would be all right.

But the horses? Would the horses be all right?

"It's like a gallop for them," came Jason's voice, reassuring her. "They'll have to rest when we reach the other side. There's a hamlet not far from the river."

Nerine sighed her relief. The horses were moving steadily, their heads and noses well clear of the water. She was probably silly to be worried.

Efyenés was lagging, the last of the herd, even a bit behind the second boat –
Nerine's boat – but swimming well and not distressed. In fact, Nerine would
guess that the mare enjoyed water. Her eyes had an alert, perky look in them,
and her legs, a comfortable rhythm.

Her golden brown hide – dun, in proper horse parlance – was darker
with the wet, and the deep brown stripe along her backbone had turned black.

A sharp whistle and sudden shouting from the Keltoi broke out on the
bank behind them.

"Ulkos! Dieu kosio! Ulkos oni Danu!"

What? Nerine didn't have enough fluency in their language – or enough
vocabulary – to understand their words, but there was urgency in their
voices. Something about the goddess?

One deep voice roared above the clamor of the others. "Pull! Pull! Pull!"

That was clear enough. And the Keltic paddlers had quickened their stroke.

Nerine looked at Efyenés in alarm – the mare was fine, although farther
behind the boat than before – then glanced at Jason, her seat mate. "What is
it? What's wrong?"

Jason was staring upriver, his face pale. "A floater. A big one."

Nerine still didn't understand, but her gaze followed Jason's.

At first she couldn't make it out, amidst the glitter of the shifting water
and the long vista of river upstream. Then a dark twiggy shape, much closer
than the far horizon, caught her attention. She followed the twigs, back to a
branch, back to a semi-submerged –

Oh, blessings!

– a massive tree trunk, replete with too much of its leafy canopy, a vast
sprawl of entangling branches attached to a natural battering ram, propelled
by the force of a big river's current.

This was the kraken of the Danouvios. *Ulkos*, the Keltoi had shouted.
Wolf, wasn't it? A ravening wolf of a beast to trap and sink a boat.

The paddlers dug in with their paddles like a sea bird flapping its wings
to escape the gaping maw of a leaping shark.

The lead boat was clear of the danger.

The main clump of horses were clear.

Her own boat – her boat – was clear! They were safe!

Then Efyenés' ringing neigh of alarm smote her ears. Lagging Efyenés,
just a hint too slow.

No! Ah, *no!*

The snatching twigs and leaves of the floating fallen tree tangled in the mare's mane. Her eyes rolled, wide and terrified, and then the Wolf of Danu dragged her down.

Nerine didn't even think. She leapt to her feet, stepped up onto her plank seat, and dove overboard into the river.

The water was cool – and possessed a surging push to it – but all downstream, unlike the back-and-forth rocking of the sea. As it flooded Nerine's spiracles, she could taste its complex flavor, mellower than the blackwater of the Moirios.

She kicked out strongly, feeling the drag of her tunic and trews and, especially, her boots. There was no time to disrobe. Efyenés had moments – just moments – in which her rider might save her.

Nerine kicked and stroked, searching, searching. The water of the Danouvios was not turbid and cloudy – thank the blessings! – but neither was it cleanly translucent like the Moirios. It was as though Nerine peered through many gauze veils, her vision clear nearby, but rapidly closed down by an aqua opacity.

Where? Where?

There!

A thrashing hoof churned the water into fizzing white bubbles, and Nerine plunged toward it.

There was Efyenés' chest and neck and wild-eyed head.

Nerine swirled around to the mare's other side to get at the mane. Oh, blessings! It was tangled hopelessly in an array of grasping small branches. Why hadn't Nerine grabbed a knife before jumping into the water? She needed something to cut Efyenés' mane. Desperately needed – or could she break the branches?

Dodging Efyenés kicking legs, she bent the branches back. They were pliant and flexible, too waterlogged to break.

Think Nerine, she told herself fiercely. You're a sea *numen*. This is your realm. No other passenger in those Keltic boats could dream of being here, attempting this. She dodged another series of swipes from Efyenés' hooves.

And then she had it! Of course! How could she be so foolish? Her water gift!

Before she'd finished castigating herself, her hands were melting into the liquid surrounding her. Water and wood had tangled Efyenés' mane. Water and Nerine could untangle it as swiftly as the cut of any knife.

An undulating swirl of water here, a tickle of a spiral there, a flowing combing of the current all over, and the mare was free, her churning legs propelling her to the surface – which had never been far, just out of reach – and away toward safety.

Nerine went limp with relief.

And then Efyenés' hind hoof struck Nerine's left thigh a mighty blow.

Pain like a tidal wave swamped her, and her vision went black.

～

Faintly, someone was calling her name. "Nerine! Nerine!"

But she couldn't breathe. She couldn't *breathe*!

The fight for breath was everything. Her spiracles gaped, but no water flowed through them. Her operculi flexed, striving to pump water over her gills, but there was no water. She was dry, too dry. She would die of her dryness.

Oh!

Abruptly she realized she lay on the ground in the air, not on the riverbed in the water. With realization, her systems switched over smoothly. Her spiracles closed, her operculi settled, her gills folded, and the miraculous gateway in her throat opened to allow air to rush into her lungs.

She could *breathe*! Thank the blessings!

Her eyes flew open. Jason was hovering over her – his tunic soaking wet, but his *linothorax* absent – still shouting her name. His eyes were nearly as wild as Efyenés' had been.

"I'm alright," she gasped.

He stared at her, then buried his face in his fists. His shoulders heaved, once, twice. Then he lowered his hands and gripped her shoulders. "If you ever. Do. That. Again!" The last word was a shout. Then he finished more moderately, "I'll never forgive you."

Nerine frowned, feeling puzzled. "Is Efyenés alright?"

Jason nodded, calmer.

"Then . . ." Nerine nibbled her lip. "I was the only one who could save her. Surely."

Jason rolled his eyes. "Nerine. She's a lovely horse, but she's a *horse*. You – you're the reason why I'm here, in the middle of Európi. Why we're all here. To escort you safely to the cottage of the norns. *Please* don't endanger yourself."

Had she endangered herself?

She became aware of Galena and Captain Bartholomai and a few of the other *peltastés* clustered around her, all looking worried – even Galena, for a change.

She thought about what she'd done, leaping into the river, approaching a terrified horse, risking her own entrapment by that mighty fallen tree. Yes, she could see that it had been dangerous, but she was the one person in all the company who didn't risk drowning. Well, until they pulled her out of the water unconscious. A sea *numen's* default was breathing water. If she'd fainted while on land, she'd no doubt carry on breathing air. If she fainted on land and then fell into water, she'd switch to breathing water, even unconscious. Pulling her unconscious out of the water . . . *that* had been dangerous.

But the rest of it?

The tree?

No. There might have been trouble there, yes, but a sea *numen* was well accustomed to avoiding being smashed into the reef when the surf was heavy. Or eluding the clutching streamers of certain kinds of seaweed. The tree might have entangled her. In which case, she'd have untangled herself the same way she untangled Efyenés. The tree had *not* been truly perilous.

What about Efyenés?

Yes, she had to admit that Efyenés was dangerous. What if she'd smashed Nerine's head instead of Nerine's thigh? Then Nerine might be dead.

Her thigh began to throb with this thought.

She met the eyes of the group surrounding her, Jason's last of all. "I'm sorry. I didn't understand how dangerous Efyenés might be. I don't know enough about horses." And she didn't. She recognized that now. But she knew plenty about the rest of it. "But the tree and the water really were not dangerous to me. Truly."

"Can you stand?" asked Captain Bartholomai quietly.

The ache in her thigh deepened, and it throbbed more angrily.

"I'm not sure. Will you help me up?"

Galena – her brief anxiety apparently gone – and Jason raised Nerine to sitting. Nerine could see the horses being rubbed dry nearby. A *peltastís* was already loading one of the pack animals. The few morning clouds had vanished on the breeze, and the sky was deeply blue. Her thigh gave an extra fierce twinge, and she winced.

Captain Bartholomai gestured for Galena to give up her place to him. She did, and then the two men lifted Nerine to her feet. Her left leg nearly buckled under her.

"Hold me!" she gasped.

They held her, and she did not fall. Her thigh felt like it had been shattered into more pieces than she could count.

"Is my leg broken?" she asked.

The captain answered, "No. Badly bruised."

"Good," she breathed, and stood there panting from the pain. "I think . . . I *think* I can ride. If you can get me up on Efyenés."

"You need dry clothes first," interrupted Galena. "And Jason does too."

As it turned out, she didn't need to ride. Two of the *peltastés* rode the short distance to the inland village and brought back a dozen Keltoi with a litter.

Lying on the litter in dry clothes, Nerine fainted again. Being undressed, and then dressed again, had been too much stress on her injured leg.

She waded back to consciousness on a divan in one of the large halls typical of Keltic royalty. The roof beams looked subtly different to her – lighter in hue? more plainly carved? – she couldn't figure it out and didn't try to.

She lay under her woolen cloak, warm, but unpleasantly scratchy, because she was naked. A dozen Keltic matrons surrounded her. The oldest, a crone with a wrinkled face, had just lifted a corner of her cloak to lay a moist poultice of large green leaves on Nerine's leg.

As the poultice made contact with Nerine's bare skin, a burning sensation passed through the flesh of her thigh. Not strong enough to hurt, but definitely strong enough to startle. As the heat subsided, she felt a tide in the opposite direction, pain flowing out. Out of the flesh, out through her skin, passing away into the poultice.

"Drink," said the crone, as a matron offered her a birch bark cup of liquid. It was dark and bitter, very bitter, but Nerine drank it all.

Then they left her, all except the youngest, really a maiden, not a matron, who sat beside her and sang Keltic lullabies.

The swollen feeling in Nerine's thigh ebbed, and she fell asleep.

～

During the first few days of her recovery, Nerine kept to her divan, waited on by the Keltic matrons and visited by Galena. From Galena, she learned how she had drifted near the surface of the Danouvios, unconscious, one of the ribbands in her hair undone and trailing.

At the sight of that ribband, Jason threw off his *linothorax* armor and his helm, and dove into the river to retrieve her.

"The *linothorax* is nearly a thumb-width thick, you know," said Galena seriously. "The weight of the water it would absorb could easily drag a man to the bottom."

No, Nerine hadn't known that, but neither had she expected anyone to fish her out of the water.

"You were drowning, Nerine." Galena laid her palm on the back of Nerine's hand. "I did not think a *numen* of the sea *could* drown."

Nerine sniffed, an involuntary puff of air gushing out of her. "Not in the water, no. But I can drown in the air. I *was* drowning, when Jason pulled me onto the bank. There was no water flowing through my spiracles from which my gills could pull the breath of life. I was not awake to awaken my lungs."

Faint horror entered Galena's eyes, tarnishing her usual poise. Nerine was intrigued to see that something could do so. She'd wondered if Galena were entirely impervious.

"But . . . we might have killed you!" Galena's voice echoed the feeling in her face, barely present, but present nonetheless.

"It would have been better to let me wake underwater, once Jason brought me to shore," Nerine explained.

Galena nodded. "I think . . . I'll let the Poniró Peltastés know that," she said, standing to go. "Although I trust" – she looked back over her shoulder – "that we will not need that knowledge in future." Her cool poise had returned.

Nerine sighed.

Soon after that conversation, she ventured to stand and then to limp outside.

Once she was walking, she healed rapidly. The deep purple bruise extending from her hip to just above her knee turned ugly greens and yellows, and any pressure on it stronger than the weight of her clothing hurt. But she had taken no permanent damage from Efyenés' hoof.

Wandering around the chieftain's hall, and then down the hill to its hamlet of lesser dwellings, she noticed that the Keltoi north of the Danouvios possessed some marked differences from their kin south of the Danouvios.

Oh, they wore the same plaid tunics and skirts or trews, but they favored the warmer hues – red and amber – over the cooler blues and greens. Their buildings were shaped the same – four-square walls with a steeped pitched roof – but the roofs were thatched with reeds and grasses rather than bundles of twigs. And the walls, instead of stacked logs, were formed of great square timbers, filled in with woven withies, and plastered over with a yellow-tinted daub.

The differences intrigued Nerine. Were they due to cultural differences? Or was there another explanation?

But one gruesome distinction made Nerine shiver.

The jewelry, furnishings, and tools of the northern Keltoi featured the usual spiral and scrolling designs of the southern, but in amongst the geometric and vining shapes were renditions of skulls and bleeding heads severed from their bodies.

Who would want to drink ale from a goblet fashioned to resemble a skull? Or sit on a backless chair with armrests upheld by posts like severed heads? Ugh!

Before Nerine worked up the courage to ask – she wasn't sure she wanted to know – they were traveling again. The bruise on her leg was fading and hurt only if she bumped it against something. Walking still jarred the injury, but the gentle gait of Efyenés troubled it not at all. And the horses had enjoyed a nice, long rest.

Their route lay along the Danouvios for three days and then the track turned north, leading past a series of Keltic villages, so close together that the land seemed a variegated patchwork of flax fields, sheep meadows, and forest glades. Around the noontide of the second day after they left the great, glinting, silver-blue of the Danouvios behind, they found themselves following the eastern bank of the Pathissus.

The Pathissus was a modest river, although Nerine grinned at how her idea of "modest" had changed. Like the Moirios near its mouth, the Pathissus was a good stadion wide, maybe even wider, but it looked friendly and approachable compared to the mighty Danouvios.

Its water was very clear, with a greenish hue to it. Willows overhung its banks, their dangling fronds dipping in the slow current. It was interesting how the woodlands had changed all along their journey.

Conifers had prevailed along the muddy Bardários. Oak and beech joined the mix beside the blackwater Moirios. But the course of the Pathissus seemed a greener valley altogether, with its willows and poplars and ash trees. Nerine fancied it an arboreal ocean, with currents of rustling leaves that welcomed her as did the waves of her own Middle Sea. It felt restful, peaceful, and possessed of a living presence that made her feel accompanied by a friend.

This was fortunate, as the Pathissus was also a long river. They traveled beside it for forty-one days, and Nerine's traveling companions were pleasant, but not friends of the heart.

As Nerine became proficient in Lepontic, Galena's tutoring grew perfunctory. The Keltoi right before Galena were too fascinating, and that was where her focus lay. Not that she neglected Nerine; that was not Galena's way. But all her conversation involved the latest fascinating detail that she'd learned. It was more monologue than real conversation, thought Nerine, dreamily listening to the whistling chitter of a warbler, clinging to a reed above the river.

Jason's liking for Nerine was genuine, and he was a nice youth. He really was a lot like a younger Tyr, if only he didn't revert to such sternness whenever he grew overly conscious of his duties and responsibilities.

But she had the river and a feeling for the soul of the river. She wondered if a river *numen* swam in its limpid current, and if she would ever meet her. The *numen* was shy, if she existed. Nerine could sense that much.

And she had her ever expanding letter to Altairos.

Between the two – the spirit of the Pathissus and the memory of Altairos – she was content.

～

23 ~ Passion of Lugh

As THEY TRAVELED NORTH along the Pathissus, on the eighty-second day of their journey across Európi, they approached a Keltic settlement of an altogether different scale from the small hamlets and villages they'd passed by – or stayed the night in – along the tributaries of the Danouvios.

When they broke from the trees, the fields and grazing meadows of Sican-oni-Cean stretched several stadia ahead to a steep hill, girdled by thatched Keltic houses past easy counting, and topped by a great hall with golden pillars flanking its portal.

The Keltic leaders thought of themselves as princes.

Nerine had realized that early on, but been unable to shake her inner view of them as tribal chieftains. It was true that they were far more civilized than the Hellenes gave them credit for, possessing fine clothing, beautiful jewelry, and courteous manners. But any Hellene city could hold ten Keltic hamlets in its confines, while a Hellene king dwelled in a marble palace with elegant carpets on its polished floors, not in a rude timber hall with an earthen floor.

However that might be, the Keltic leaders were princes to their people, and the ruler of Sican-oni-Cean was High Prince over all the clans north of the Danouvios. And the extent of his domain supported his status.

The road from the river bank through his wheat fields was paved with thick, squared timbers, while the winding way up the hill to his hall featured shallow granite steps, interspersed with more of the wooden roadway. Nerine, by now accustomed to the dull thud of horse sandals on earth, noticed the sharper echo of sandal against wood and stone.

When they reached the terrace before the prince's doors, Nerine saw that the flanking golden pillars were etched to depict falcons – falcons soaring, falcons diving toward prey, and falcons perched upon a ring of golden skulls at each pillar's base.

Ugh! She never had asked about the northern fascination with severed heads and skulls.

Two door wardens – garbed in brilliant red plaids – greeted the Poniró Peltastés. They conveyed the welcome of their prince and guided the *peltastés* to a series of side chambers where they would stay. The prince's hall was far larger than those of his chieftains, possessing room enough for more than just the main gathering space. And its floors were polished oak, not beaten earth.

Servants brought Nerine and Galena a basin of water in which to wash face and hands, and then offered them slices of ripe plums along with a creamy cheese.

Nerine was ready to relax into this hospitality, of greater comfort than any available since she'd left Mount Olympus, but their host had other plans for them. After she and Galena had washed and eaten, one of the door wardens came to them.

"Cean-oni." He bowed to Nerine, his scarlet plaids swinging with his movement.

She remembered that 'cean' was the Lepontic word for prince and that 'oni' meant 'of' or 'of the.' Which meant that 'cean-oni' was 'of a prince' or 'princess.' She'd learned enough of the Keltic tongue to understand a lot, even though her ability to speak it was rudimentary.

"Our tribe celebrates the death and rebirth of our god Lugh, and my lord Ulkos Ard-cean" – Ulkos High-prince – "invites you to join in our revelries. Will you come?"

He'd been speaking to Nerine, but Galena rushed into speech. "We should like it of all things. Please convey our gratitude and acceptance to your prince."

Nerine repressed a smile. Even cool Galena could not contain her enthusiasm. Offer a historian the chance to observe firsthand (and record) the rites of the Keltoi? It was like offering a child honeyed figs!

Nerine added her acceptance to Galena's. "Will you guide us to the proper place? Or send a servant who is free to do so?"

The warden bowed again. "I will guide you, cean-oni."

It turned out that the festival of Lugh began with athletic contests – foot races, spear throwing, wrestling, and so on. And the tribe of the high prince had a special field of scythed grass, several stadia beyond their cottage-girded hill, where the contests took place.

Once on the other side of the prince's hill, Nerine could see yet more hills, the foothills of the Karpathian mountains, she realized. She'd come a long ways in her travels.

Nerine and Galena joined the throng encircling the festival field, just as a wrestling match concluded. A well-muscled man with his red hair in half a dozen long braids flipped his opponent over his hip, pounded him to the ground, and then dove atop him to pin the man.

The crowd roared. "Ard-cean! Ard-cean! Ard-cean!"

Nerine smiled. So the high prince was participating in the competitions. Somehow she was not surprised. The Keltoi were a physical people and much given to testing one another's mettle. A high prince would have to prove himself often to his tribal subjects. She studied the red-headed man, who bore a majestic presence similar to that of Altairos' pappa.

He had given a hand up to his downed foe, clapped him on the shoulder, and raised their gripped hands overhead.

"Oni Kuos!" the crowd yelled, acknowledging the defeated combatant.

The prince nodded and smiled, pleased with the peoples' response to his generosity. He clapped his foe on the shoulder again, then disengaged to thread his way toward his door warden – and Nerine and Galena, standing beside that warden.

The prince nodded to his warden and then focused on Nerine.

"Cean-oni Pelagieus!" His voice was a strong baritone, and he was clearly familiar with Hellene customs, since he'd named her 'Princess of Pelagie' rather than some other variant of her title. "This is a fortuitous happening, that you should come to us verily upon the Lunasad – the celebration of he whom your honor guard serves! Praise him with great praise!" Without raising his hands to the sky, he turned both palms upward at his sides, making an abbreviated version of the Keltic gesture of honor. "I bid you welcome, cean-oni, and inquire if this circumstance and our response to it please you."

Nerine firmly contained her frown of puzzlement. This prince would not understand that it was directed not at him, but at her own confusion. The *peltastés* served Lord Hermes and none other, but she would ask Galena about that presently.

"I am very pleased and delighted that you invite me to participate. Your kind generosity gives me gladness." She wondered if she'd judged him correctly, that he liked to have his generosity appreciated.

The prince's face lit. "Ah! You address the petitions of your heart to the divine Lugh yourself! I see it and bid you welcome as a daughter! This is well, indeed."

Then, like the very first Keltic chieftain Nerine had met along the Moirios, Ulkos Ard-cean seized both her hands and drew her just close enough that he could kiss each of her cheeks in turn. Only this time, unlike the other time, she could understand her adoptive father tolerably well, and the high prince possessed rather more gravitas than the chieftain. Blessings! but these Keltoi were impulsive!

"I accept your welcome as a father, Ard-cean, and I offer my thanks," she replied, most properly according to Keltic custom.

"Ah! Ah!" exclaimed the prince. And then, again like that chieftain before him, he spread his arms wide, palms to the sky, eyes to the sky, and pronounced a blessing. "May the Divine Lugh bear her ever in his heart!" He returned his gaze to Nerine. "Is it well, my daughter?"

Nerine nodded and replied according to custom again. "It is well, my father."

Ard-cean turned back to his door warden. "Why are the honor guard of the Divine Lugh yet absent?"

A tremor passed across the warden's face. He was a stately man, older than his prince. Nerine would not have believed he might quake before authority had she not seen that tremor.

The warden mastered himself to answer steadily, "My prince, you did not order it so."

"Ah, ha, ha!" Even Ard-cean's laughter was powerful. "Ha, ha! So I did not. Carry my invitation to them, good Maesil."

Maesil bowed and turned to stride away.

Ard-cean said, "Cean-oni, speak your desires to any of my people here and they shall be honored to attend your wishes! I must go!"

The athletic contests continued throughout the afternoon, and the prince participated in most of them. He did not win all of them, which Nerine found interesting, but he did win many. And always he was magnanimous to his defeated opponents, genial to those who bested him, and cloaked by the majesty that seemed part of him.

Apparently the Keltoi did not require that their high prince be completely victorious on the field, so long as he was victorious often. And – she suspected – dominated them with his personality.

The last contest – one in which the men competed to see who could lift the largest boulder – took place as the sun set, its golden rays casting long shadows across the shorn grasses. But the celebrants did not repair to the prince's great hall to feast as Nerine had expected.

Instead, huge round drums were brought forth and beaten in a slow rhythm, while threesomes joined hands to leap down the length of the field. Sometimes a man with a woman at each side. Sometimes a woman, with a man to each side. At the bottom of the field, the partner on the right crossed to prance under the upraised arms of the other two. Then the partner on the left did likewise. And then the trio leapt off the field, making room for the next threesome.

It was a very simple dance, but its very simplicity, combined with the drum beat, made it exciting.

Boom, boom, boom, beat the drums as the golden evening light faded to gray dusk, and torches were lit. Trio after trio leaped down the field. The sky darkened and the moon rose.

Nerine discovered Jason at her elbow. "Shall we try it?" she suggested to Jason and Galena.

Jason's eyebrows flew up in startlement, but Galena was eager. "Yes, yes! Let's!" she agreed.

Moments later Nerine stood at the top of the field on Jason's right hand, with Galena on Jason's left.

Boom, boom, boom, sounded the drums. And they were off and leaping, their legs kicking straight before them, their hands held high.

Boom, boom, boom.

Nerine felt as though her heart had leapt out of her body to sound for all to hear. Or the earth itself were beating, sending a rush of exaltation through the breast of every mortal and immortal living. Or perhaps the sky was the source of this divine heart rhythm, lifting Nerine up into the heavens where the planets themselves sang and the comets thundered.

Boom, boom, boom.

And now Nerine was passing under Jason's and Galena's linked hands. It was intricate and beautiful. It was magical and otherworldly.

310 ~ J.M. Ney-Grimm

And then they were leaping off the field, laughing and joyous.

Ah! She wished she could do it all over again.

A moment later, the prince was at her side with his door warden, and she did do it all over again, but as the centerpiece. At the bottom of the field, with two powerful men twining about her, she felt like a goddess being worshipped, the crown of her head touching the stars and her booted feet rooted on the depths of the earth.

Then the revelers ate, but not indoors.

All through the dancing, Nerine had been smelling the savory aromas of roasted meats.

The prince's cooks had wrought a meal over outdoor braziers, and serving boys now brought platters of the prince's bounty to each cluster of celebrants to eat of, while seated on the shorn grasses.

The festivities did not end there.

Next came a drama in which the goddess Danu prepared the lands of the river Danouvios for agriculture and then died of her exhaustion from the task. Her son Lugh fought with the demons of blight and famine to preserve his mother's legacy, but he was captured by them and imprisoned.

The young man playing Lugh's role reminded Nerine of Altairos. Not so much in his looks, for his curly hair was white blond, but in the way he laughed as he fought. Although he called mocking jests to his captors, and there was a bitterness to his humor that Altairos did not share.

Or did he? In the aftermath of Nerine's repudiation of him?

Nerine shook her head. That was behind her, and better forgotten.

She remembered to ask Galena why Ard-cean had named the Poniró Peltastés as Lugh's honor guard.

Galena looked surprised. "But Lugh is the Keltic name for our own Lord Hermes!" she explained.

Nerine felt surprised that she had not guessed it. Of course! That was why their passage through the lands of the Keltoi had been so smooth, so welcomed. The Poniró Peltastés were not merely kin to divinity, they were kin to a specific divinity much beloved by the Keltoi. Even the chieftain's – and Ard-cean's – claiming of Nerine as daughter made more sense now. What ruler would not seize a chance to claim a princess connected to their Divine Lugh as a relation? It was an excellent way to shore up their own authority.

Nerine shook her head in bemusement at her own slowness. Well, well. Perhaps the fact that she'd initially spoken nothing of the Keltic tongue explained why she'd not figured it out on her own.

～

An interval of respite came after the drama.

Nerine strolled on the shorn grass with her companions, enjoying the velvet gentleness of the warm night and the soft murmurs of the quieted crowd. Wood smoke and mown hay scented the air. The short grass underfoot had stiff stems that resisted momentarily before succumbing to each footstep. Nerine felt contained in a bubble all her own – secluded – and yet part of this celebration of Lugh and at one with the Keltoi who celebrated him.

Was it the ale she'd drunk? She'd mixed it well with water.

Or was it the uniqueness of this experience? The sea people held parties, but never festivals. The gods were their kin and their neighbors, respected, honored, but not worshipped. Perhaps that was it. Nerine did not worship, even now, but she waded in a sea of worship: the Keltoi adoring their god. And their adoration carried her, transported her.

"Do you feel it?" she asked Galena.

Galena nodded. "Oh, yes." Her serious voice held an undertone hinting that she too inhabited an altered state.

Jason guided them both toward a procession forming along one side of the field. The mood of the crowd was changing, from quiet satisfaction to nervous anticipation. Nerine felt the tension growing, entering her own body to produce wonder mixed with fear.

What was it? What would happen next?

She craned her neck, looking to her right, down the long line of waiting Keltoi.

Ah! There was a second part to the drama.

The demons of blight and famine – there were more of them now – carried a cage of tied branches in which Lugh capered, shouting insults and threats at his captors. They proceeded along the line formed by their audience, the demons grimacing, Lugh exhorting the demons to beware.

As the cage passed before Nerine, she saw Lugh's eyes crinkling, just as Altairos' eyes did when he laughed. A pang of longing and sadness and abrupt terror shot through her.

The young man was not Altairos, but she feared for him.

What would happen to him? Oh, what? This was merely an entertainment. Wasn't it?

When the demons and the cage and its prisoner reached the head of the line, four torch bearers joined them, and they moved into the darkness. The procession followed them, torch bearers at intervals just close enough that Nerine could see where to set her feet. She gripped Galena's hand on one side of her and Jason's arm on the other.

She wished she could leave the procession, return to her room in the great hall, and sleep, avoiding what came next.

But she could not have departed for sovereignty over all the waters of the seas, had Lord Poseidon offered it to her. She bore a part in this drama now, and she could not fail to play it, to follow it all the way to its end, no matter how horrific.

The procession curved, circling around until its head touched its tail, forming an oval. The torch bearers stepped into the center, and their light shone on a deep shaft cut into the earth. How far down did it reach? To the ice at the earth's heart? To the hell that awaited traitors and felons?

Nerine shivered.

The demons set down their cage at one end of the oval formed by the Keltoi. Two of them opened its door and drew Lugh forth. He was fighting in earnest now, not acting in a play. Two more demons seized his legs, and the four of them dragged him toward the pit.

They passed by Nerine. Lugh's eyes were wild – like Efyenés in the Danouvios – and he kicked at the demons gripping his legs.

Nerine jolted forward. She would plead for him. She would blast the demons with a jet of water. She would *save* him.

Jason and Galena jerked her back.

"No!" hissed Galena.

Nerine remembered her place in all this: a guest, invited to participate merely. She must not interfere. Her heart congealed within her, frozen, chilling her body and her limbs. Ah, blessings! How could she stand and do *nothing* when – when what? She did not know what, but it was awful, awful. That much she knew.

The demons reached the brink of the pit. They lowered Lugh to the ground and pinned him there by force.

Then Ard-cean stepped forth from the crowd.

How had Nerine missed him?

Yet there he stood, exuding a potency more robust, and more shocking, than before. He'd exchanged his garments – the plaids of the Keltoi, his as finely made as Nerine's – for the pectoral and belt of the sea people. They gleamed gold in the torchlight, with sparking gems shooting forth fire. He brandished a silver sword.

No, not silver. This was the iron of which Nerine had heard. The iron that the Paíones were learning to work.

The sword gleamed, polished to shine as bright as watered silk, and its edge was honed to the sharpness of broken sea glass.

Nerine pulled against her companions again. And again they restrained her.

Jason leaned close. "Don't look," he whispered.

She turned her head to stare at Galena. Galena, whose face remained cool and composed, whose arm had relaxed again after holding Nerine in place.

Nerine heard the swish of a blade swung fast through the air.

Galena's face remained calm.

Nerine heard the meaty thunk of a sword cleaving flesh, the crack of severed bone.

Galena's face remained unchanged.

A body tumbled into the pit. Nerine heard the thump of it hitting the bottom, not so far down after all.

And the crowd roared.

Nerine shuddered and looked down at the ground, shadowy and crossed by the flickering light of the torches. She felt sick and cold and angry. How dared Ard-cean claim her as daughter? How dared these Keltoi claim themselves as a civilized people? The Hellenes were right! To kill a man merely to add excitement to a barbarian festival. She was disgusted.

The crowd yelled again.

The king answered them from somewhere far to Nerine's left. Had he moved so swiftly?

"Imbibe the strength of his soul!" shouted Ard-cean.

"Yes!" roared the Keltoi.

"Feel the center of life itself!" bellowed the prince. He was drawing closer.

Nerine shut her eyes and tried to shut her ears. Looking at the ground was not enough. She wanted to not be here. To not be herself, the person who had surrendered to exaltation just such a short time ago. To be back in the Middle Sea, where life was cherished, not death.

"Let the god in!" intoned the prince. He was right beside her.

"The powers of the other world are yours!" Ard-cean stood right before her.

Jason and Galena jerked Nerine's hands in front of her, hers held in theirs, and warm liquid dripped on her skin.

She looked up and nearly fainted.

Lugh's agonized face met her horrified gaze, his hair gripped in the prince's fist, his severed neck bleeding on Nerine's fingers and wrists. Here was a severed head with a vengeance. Now Nerine knew the significance of its representation in the art of the Keltoi. And she did not want to.

Then the prince passed on, extolling the bounty released from Lugh's head and sharing it with his tribe.

Nerine swayed. Only Galena's grip on her right hand, and Jason's on her left arm, kept her upright. Blessings! When would this be over? When could she retreat? Into sleep, if nowhere else.

But there was more. The procession followed their head-bearing prince along a stony path up a hill where Lugh's head was planted as though it were a rose bush, and then a net spread over it and staked down.

And then Lugh himself sprang into their midst from the darkness, whole and entire, laughing.

What?

He danced among them, touching a hand here, a shoulder there, kissing a pretty girl, and then embracing a grandmother. He was alive and strong, joy shining in his eyes, which crinkled. Just like Altairos' eyes.

～

Nerine tossed and turned on her divan for what remained of the night.

Had she imagined Lugh's death? His severed head dripping on her hands?

Or did the Keltoi use some trick? A bronze sculpture enameled to resemble life – or, rather, death – with berry juice poured through it?

She had *seen* Lugh after his beheading, capering and dancing, grinning with delight. His warm lips had touched her unwilling cheek, the puff of his breath had brushed her neck. What more proof of life could there be?

Galena and Jason had started on some explanation when they reached the great hall, and Nerine had stopped them.

She didn't want to know. *Couldn't* know. Or she'd never manage the courtesy required in the morning when she bade Ard-cean farewell. In the morning, she'd pretend the beheading was a trick, even though she suspected it could not be.

In the meantime, she would sleep. Except she couldn't sleep.

She kept hearing the sound of the prince's blade cutting the air. The thunk of its metal slicing flesh and bone. The tumbling thump of a body falling into the pit. She kept feeling the drops of blood hitting the skin of her hands. Even though she had washed her hands – three times – while readying herself for sleep.

She turned from her right side to her left. Sleep was impossible.

After what seemed like three nights of darkness, rather than half of one, she heard servants stirring beyond the doorway of her room. She begged a rush light from one, and dressed by its dim and flickering illumination. Galena shifted under the blanket of her plaid cloak, but did not awake.

Nerine slipped out of the room and threaded her way through the sleepers bundled in their plaids on the floor of the prince's hall.

The wardens had already assumed their posts at the great doors to the outside, two within and two without, but they made no remark at Nerine's presence, merely returning her cool nod with mannerly ones.

The doors faced west and the sky was pale gray over the line of trees hiding the Pathissus. Nerine followed the terrace around the north side of the building to the east, where the horizon glowed lemon yellow, silhouetting the foothills and the more distant mountain ridges of the Karpathians.

An orange sliver of fiery brilliance appeared where sky met earth. The dome of the sky flushed turquoise as the blazing sliver grew larger, and its hue transformed from amber to gold, to the radiant white yellow of the daytime sun.

The flat black of the mountains kindled to folded green, and on a nearer hill a tangle of something at its crest grew visible. Nerine looked away. She knew what that tangle was. A net holding down a severed head, preventing the vultures from carrying it away.

She shuddered and looked to the north, where the lower ridges of the Karpathians beckoned. In a day or two, maybe three, she would be over those mountains and out of the lands of the Keltoi. She wished she could start for them now, this instant, running down the slope from Ard-cean's hall, across the fields of his people, and into the forest. Away from this place where severed heads were venerated.

But she couldn't. She must break her fast, wait while the Poniró Peltastés readied themselves for travel, and – worst of all – thank Ard-cean for his hospitality.

~

It wasn't as bad as she expected.

When Ard-cean emerged from his hall onto the western terrace, his entire retinue accompanied him, among them the young man who'd played Lugh.

The prince wore his customary plaids again – today's garments a brilliant clash of orange and turquoise – and his dignity was that of a ruler, calm and measured, not that of the priest of a bloodthirsty god, stained with death and violence.

He stretched his arms out, palms up, to speak the traditional blessing for travelers, only his naming of Nerine a divagation from the norm.

"May your path welcome your passage, may the wind be at your back, and may Ingeld himself hold you close to his heart, my daughter."

Nerine responded with the traditional blessing for one's host. She knew it now, quite well. "May the rooftree of your people be ever strong and unbroken, may the hearth of your heart be ever fiery, and may Danu herself raise you always to life. My father." Those last two words took effort, but she managed them.

Ulkos Ard-cean's face lit. Once again he seized her hands and kissed her cheeks. Nerine forced herself to stand serenely, not recoiling with her body the way her heart and mind recoiled.

And then it was done.

Jason boosted her onto Efyenés' back, and Nerine was riding down the switchbacks of the stone and wood road of the prince's hill, amidst the

Poniró Peltastés, listening to the sharp echoes of the horse sandals on the hard surfaces.

They did not return to the river, but followed a track through the prince's fields, with the blue, blue sky overhead, dotted by small puffs of cloud. Workers were harvesting the grain. The Lunasad celebrated the start of the harvest, after all. Beyond the fields stretched rolling meadows, pairs of oxen grazing in a few, more featuring goats or sheep.

Upon entering the woods, they were already climbing the slopes of the foothills. The Karpathians were closer than Nerine had realized, but she was not free of the Keltoi so soon as she might have wished. The southern foothills were extensive, and she found she must greet yet more Keltic chieftains each evening, when they stopped for the night in a small hamlet.

Galena and Jason made several attempts to engage Nerine in conversation, and each time she indicated that she preferred silence. She couldn't bear talking about what had happened on the Lunasad, but neither could she bear to ignore it, speaking of other things as though the festival had never happened.

She retreated into her letter to Altairos, pouring out her distress at the beheading. How she felt she had touched a murderer's hands in greeting Ulkos Ard-cean. How she wavered between deeming the beheading a trick, and knowing it was all too real. How she dared not yet face the truth, which she sensed Galena and Jason were waiting to give her. How foolish she felt, that she could not face the truth. And how she missed, missed, *missed* Altairos.

And then her thoughts went to even stranger places.

Was Lord Hermes a murderer, when he sanctioned his messengers to travel in lands where their safety might rest upon their skill at arms? Was Lord Poseidon one, when he stirred the ocean to a frenzy, and sailors died? Yet the natural world partook of violence as part of its essence. Were not deaths at sea or storm or fire part of life?

When she emerged from her preoccupation, they were high above the Karpathian foothills, climbing the flanks of the actual mountains that divided the lands of the Keltoi from the lands of the Gutones.

Nerine noticed that a few golden leaves fluttered amidst the green leaves of the beech trees. The season was turning, first noticeable in the heights. The air was cool, and she was glad of the warmth of her plaid cloak, now wrapped around her while riding – rather than merely serving as a blanket for her slumbers.

As they rode higher, the beech forest changed to spruces, with open glades where the soil was too thin to support anything but grasses and scrub. At the saddle of the first ridge, no trees grew at all, and Nerine could see ridge after ridge marching to the horizon. Gold-green beeches filled the lower valleys. Dark conifers cloaked the heights, with rocky outcroppings of gray studding the steepest slopes. The Karpathians were not tall peaks – at least not here – but they went on for league after league.

Nerine's heart lifted. She felt cleansed by the heights, as though she stood once again on Mount Olympus, although Olympus reached much higher, with rock alone at its peak in the warmest summers, and deep abiding snowfields in the winter. But the heights were sacred, filled with the divine, free of mortal concerns.

She remembered that she herself partook of the divine. How had she allowed herself to become so mired in the wrongs of a barbarian prince? He might claim her as daughter. She might permit his claim out of politeness. But she was *numeni*. And, as a *numen*, she was free as the sea itself, daughter only to the gods themselves.

Standing on the saddle of land while they paused for the horses to graze, Nerine drew in a deep breath of the keen air, and threw off her plaid cloak to fling her thin-sleeved arms toward the sky.

Ard-cean lay behind her in the past. She would look forward.

～

Traversing the Karpathian mountains presented far more challenge than had any earlier part of the journey across Európi.

Neither Keltoi nor Gutones dwelled in these steep lands, which meant progress was slow. The Poniró Peltastés halted even earlier for the night, both to ensure the horses adequate grazing time and to set up the three tents – two large, one small – carried especially for their time in the Karpathians.

Nerine discovered how much less comfortable was a drafty tent for sleeping, and a turn watching the roasting hares on a spit over a smoky fire, than a Keltic hall, with its matrons eager to serve her.

She didn't care. She felt free and clean, shivering in the small tent she shared with Galena, while cooking for the *peltastés* made her feel truly one of them.

One evening, as she buried wild tubers in the coals of the fire and turned on the spit two large fish caught in a mountain lake, she finally permitted Galena and Jason to tell her what they'd been aching to share, ever since the Lunasad and its beheading rite.

"He was a criminal!" burst out Jason.

Nerine looked at him cooly. "Who deserved death?" she queried.

"Yes!" Jason both looked and sounded angry.

Nerine poked the last plump tuber underneath the coals with a digging stick and raised an eyebrow. She was ready to hear the truth, but she was not eager for it.

Jason looked at Galena, who shrugged. Then he turned back to Nerine. "I'm not going to tell you what he did, but it was not mere thievery, I can tell you."

Nerine looked at Galena. "Do you know?" she asked.

Galena shrugged again. "No. Nor do I wish to know."

Jason continued, his words still heated. "But it was wicked and someone innocent died because of it."

Nerine studied the fish. The *peltastés* had cleaned and scaled them, but left the skins to protect the flesh from burning. A puff of smoke wafted across her face, and she squinted against its stinging.

"How then did he spring to life after Ard-cean struck off his head? And why should he live, when someone innocent" – and young, she guessed, maybe very young – "has died because of him?"

Galena laughed softly.

Nerine glared. How could she laugh?

"There were two young men, Nerine, very like in appearance."

Nerine sagged, staring at the fire. Of course there were two. Why had she ever thought that somehow the beheaded Lugh had survived?

Jason touched her shoulder. She hunched it away.

"They do it very effectively," he said. "The darkness, the torches, the build-up of the first drama."

Nerine whipped her head around. "You've seen it before?" she demanded.

Jason hunched his own shoulders uncomfortably. "I – I – Nerine you are not the first traveler the Poniró Peltastés have escorted along the Amber Way."

She bit her lip and looked down.

"All societies have ways and means for dealing with wrongdoers," came Galena's cool voice. "Even the Hellenes put the worst to death and rarely so cleanly as with the swift strike of a sword. The Athenians favor strangling crucifixion, you know."

Nerine looked up. Galena was calm, as always. Jason looked worried, also characteristic of him.

"Why didn't you warn me?" Nerine asked, a catch in her voice.

Jason's face pinched yet more wretchedly. "You were enjoying it. The Lunasad. I didn't want to spoil it for you."

"Spoil it!" Nerine stared at him. "A beheading?"

Jason flushed. "It's just part of it. Part of the whole night. Part of the celebration." He sounded miserable.

Nerine sighed. She could sort of see what he meant. She *had* been enjoying herself. Until that dreadful moment. And he was different than she. The sea peoples were at peace with themselves. The land peoples were not. She had never seen a battle. Jason had probably seen many, participated in all that he'd seen. The roads east to ancient Babylon or south to Aethiopia were not so bloodless as this one across Európi. Jason would look on bloodshed and death differently than did she.

Nerine spoke at the same time as he, the same words: "I'm sorry."

Galena sniffed. "There's really nothing to be sorry about, but if it makes you two feel better, then be as sorry as you wish." She stepped away from the campfire.

Nerine lifted her chin, ignoring Galena and addressing Jason. "I *am* sorry. I didn't understand that some of what I encountered on my journey would be so disturbing. And I'm sorry I expected you to judge what would disturb me, and what would not. That I expected you to shield me when it was disturbing." She firmed her lips. "I'm not a child any more. And you are younger than I. Are you not?"

Jason blushed. She could just see it in the fading light. "I have seventeen years," he admitted. "But I *am* sorry, Nerine. I would have warned you, if I'd only thought." He clenched a fist. "I think I know you well enough to know that . . . the Lunasad beheading would bother you. And I wish I *had* warned you."

She leaned away from the fish to kiss his cheek. "Shall we just forgive one another?" she suggested.

He blushed more furiously. "You've done nothing to forgive," he insisted, "but if you could find it in your heart to forgive me . . ."

The last bits of coldness in her heart melted. "Of course I forgive you, but I'm not convinced you've done anything wrong either."

They smiled at one another.

And then Nerine smelled the fish starting to char. She'd forgotten to turn the spit.

~

24 ~ Phlegm Versus Fire

THE SEASON HAD DEFINITIVELY turned when they came down out of the mountains.

The ash trees among the dark spruces on the northern slopes were flame red, and the beeches lower down were golden, their branches forming luminous vaults overhead and their fallen leaves cladding the forest floor with sliding brightness.

The day was gray with mists sifting through the boles of the trees, carrying the scent of woodsmoke. Had they returned to the haunts of men?

Nerine glanced aside, seeing something passing in and out of view, as Efyenés moved along the track.

Ah! A larger gap between two mature beeches afforded a clearer look. A rounded burial mound of turf lifted from the forest floor, with a great standing stone upon it and a ring of narrower stones encircling it. This was how the Gutones buried their dead.

Nerine shivered. She had had enough of death.

The land flattened swiftly as the afternoon wore on. The Karpathians rose more abruptly on their northern flanks than on the southern, and lacked the leagues of foothills that preceded them in the valley of the Pathissus. Nerine and her entourage passed by several more burial mounds and then arrived on the outskirts of the first Gutones settlement.

Like the settlements of the Keltoi, those of the Gutones featured outlying meadows for the grazing of stock and fields of flax or wheat or rye, but their buildings were considerably different. Oh, the walls were stacked logs – like the southern Keltoi – but far shorter, almost stubby, with great thatched roofs steep enough to shed the northern snows, with exposed beams emerging at the very peak to cross one another.

Nerine discovered why the walls were so short when she entered the chieftain's hall. It was sunken into the earth. Just inside the double doors, three wide and shallow steps led down to the floor.

The Gutones themselves possessed similar contrasts.

They were blond like the Keltoi, but shorter and more slender, less burly. The men's faces went clean shaven, and both men and women kept their hair very tidy, pulling combs from their belt pouches throughout the day as necessary. For they did not braid their hair, but wore it loose or held back from the face by a band, or neatly knotted at the nape of the neck.

Their treatment of their hair mirrored their temperament. Where the Keltoi were fiery and emotional, the Gutones were phlegmatic and taciturn. Nor did they wear plaids, preferring solid blues, reds, or especially yellow. Only at the edges of their garments – the wrist, the neck, and the hem – were there bands of colors mixed in glorious patterns.

And their clothes were fitted, rather than swirling, even their capes lying snug over their shoulders and along their arms.

Nerine found them very restful, a welcome quality following her disenchantment with the impassioned Keltoi. The Gutonic chieftains greeted her simply, "Gothis dags" – good day. And she replied with the same.

She did ask Galena if the Gutones also worshipped the Lord Hermes under another name – they did: Othinn, the spear carrier – but Galena held herself more aloof than before. Perhaps she sensed that Nerine, accustomed by the trek through the mountains to do for herself, needed less assistance. More probably, she understood that Nerine found Galena's detachment from her fellows more repulsive than before.

It was true.

Nerine's attraction to Galena, prompted by the scholar's superficial resemblance to her mother, Queen Ionia, was over. Their threeway confrontation in the Karpathians, in which Galena had laughed at the reconciliation between Nerine and Jason, had shown Nerine where coldness of heart truly led: the value of life held cheap. She could not condone it, even in service to scholarly impartiality.

The way to the Sea of Balder followed the river Istula. Its waters were a grayish green on fine sunny days, but the weather had turned along with the season and their increasingly northern location. Most days featured a gray overcast, if not a drizzling mist, and the Istula flowed as a glimmering slate gray between its autumnal forested banks.

Nerine, Galena, and the Poniró Peltastés traveled from one Gutonic settlement to another, just as they'd gone from one inn to another along the

Bardários, and from one Keltic hamlet to another on the Moirios and the Pathissus. But Captain Bartholomai pressed the horses more than before, starting on the trail soon after sunrise and stopping just before sundown, rather than in the afternoon.

One evening, while Jason removed Efyenés' sandals and checked her hooves for soundness, Nerine asked him why their time on horseback had been extended. "Surely the horses need their rest and fodder now just as much as before, don't they?"

Jason gave a short chuckle. "Oh, they'll get a nice long rest once we reach the sea and stable them with our hosts. The days are getting shorter, you know."

Yes, Nerine knew that, but she didn't see what it had to do with resting the horses. Or . . . she suspected, but didn't want to know.

Jason continued his explanation. "The norns live in the northernmost reaches of Scandia, and we must both reach their shores and depart before the ice closes the sea." He let Efyenés' hoof rest on the grasses and looked up. "The Gutonic rowers will not risk themselves and their ship for us."

Nerine's stomach sank. "Ship?" she questioned.

Jason frowned. "The Gutones along the coast are seafarers, and their ships rival those of the Hellenes. Just as the peoples on the shores of the Middle Sea conduct trade via water routes, so do the Gutones."

Nerine's face pinched. "And we will take ship across Balder's Sea." Her voice was flat.

"It's much faster than traveling overland," said Jason seriously.

"But – but – I can't – I," stammered Nerine.

"Why ever not?" He sounded puzzled.

Nerine felt herself blushing. "I get vilely ill," she confessed.

Jason burst out laughing. Nerine had never seen him so merry.

She glared at him.

"No kidding? Sea *numeni* get seasick?" he questioned. "How absurd!"

"Oh, be quiet! It's not funny!" she snapped.

He muffled his laughter and then grew sober. "You're serious?" he probed.

"Sea people swim through the water, not on top of it," she explained. "We cannot tolerate the continual rocking motion on the surface. I thought we would travel on the shores of Balder's Sea, not across its waves."

"Huh." Jason stared at her in consternation. "I am sorry for it, Nerine, but our way is indeed by ship."

Nerine shivered, in spite of her warm plaid cloak. "How – how long do we sail?"

Jason, checking the last of Efyenés' hooves, glanced up in surprise. "We do not sail. The Gutonic boats do not have sails. We row."

Nerine gritted her teeth. "How long, Jason?"

He let Efyenés hoof go and patted the mare's neck. "Fifteen days."

Nerine stifled a moan.

"We'll go ashore each night," Jason reassured her. "The Gutones follow the coast closely and only leave sight of land once, when they cross from the eastern shore to the western."

Nerine didn't stifle her moan this time.

"Um." Jason bit his lip. "I'll consult Captain Bartholomai. Don't worry Nerine. I'm sure he'll come up with something. It won't be so bad as you fear."

Nerine was not so sure as he was. What answer could there possibly be? She would go aboard that Gutonic ship. The waves would toss it around. And she would keep neither food nor drink down for the duration of the voyage. Would they arrive at that northern shore with an emaciated sea nymph or a dead one? Or was she exaggerating as Jason believed she was?

When she first set eyes on the sea, white capped waves surging under a gray sky beyond a dull sandy strand, she felt sick just looking.

～

Captain Bartholomai was reassuring, but Nerine was not reassured.

The *peltastés* and the Gutonic oarsmen were loading their ship in the thin dawn light prior to their immediate embarkation. The *Saiwsgaitsa* – drawn up on the pebbly beach – was a graceful vessel, long and slim, with prow and stern lifting in low, shallow curves. Unlike the river boats of the Danouvios, she had flat flooring, and the space down the middle between the rowing benches was wide enough for two to sit side by side. That was where the baggage and passengers would rest. The *Saiwsgaitsa* was much larger than a river boat, more akin to the merchant *Lily of Aegyptus,* on which Nerine had become so ill, although not quite as wide and nearly half again as long.

"You've sailed the Middle Sea?" questioned Bartholomai.

"Y-e-es," answered Nerine. "That is, no."

Bartholomai's eyebrows rose.

"I sailed from the harbor of Lapadoússa some ways out to sea," she clarified. "And it was awful."

Bartholomai smiled. "That's not sailing, Kríousa. That's not even a taste."

She renewed the argument she'd put before Jason. Sea people weren't meant for sailing. Or rowing. Or anything atop the waves.

Bartholomai shook his head. "No, no, Kríousa, the *numeni* are not so different from mortals as that. You will adjust in a day or two. The adjustment interval is unpleasant, yes, but then you'll discover how wonderful travel by sea is. We *peltastés* will take our turn at the oars, but you will have naught to do but savor the sea breeze, listen to the cries of the gulls, and watch the shore slip past. Glorious! Even those of us rowing will enjoy it."

He patted her on the shoulder and then threaded his way through the sea grasses to the beach, bent on helping his men with the stowage.

Nerine returned to the byre where Efyenés stood with the rest of the *peltastés'* mounts. The Gutones shared their halls with their animals, but also built shelters for stored hay, where the outside stock could browse when snow buried the meadow grasses. The byre smelled sweet and dusty at once, a safe smell, a land smell. Nerine pressed her face against Efyenés' warm neck and wished she could stay with her mount. Efyenés nickered and turned her head to see if Nerine might have a nice, crunchy apple for her. Nerine sighed and rubbed Efyenés' withers.

The Sea of Balder. Efyenés would avoid it. Nerine could not. She straightened, gave the horse a last pat, and walked back to the beach.

The *Saiwsgaitsa* was loaded now, her stern still resting on pebbles and sand, her prow already washed by the shallow waves of this nearly level shore. Several mounds of baggage were tied down in the aisle between the rowers' benches, and Galena was being helped aboard to sit in a space roughly amidships.

Jason strode forward to meet Nerine. "Ready?" he asked cheerfully.

She nodded, hiding her nerves.

They walked to one side of the stern. Jason steadied Nerine's arm while another *peltastís* made a step with his hands for her foot, boosting her up to climb over the chest-high gunwale. The wood of the vessel was very smooth and dark, well cared for. Nerine picked her way around the clumps of baggage to sit next to Galena. Jason had assured her that amidships experienced the least pitching.

Plus she'd have good access to the side, if she needed it. She was expecting to need it.

Galena smiled at her, clearly excited about the beginning of their sea voyage. Nerine's return smile felt like more of a grimace.

A few more *peltastés* hopped into the *Saiwsgaitsa*, and then the rest of the men – *peltastés* and Gutonic oarsmen – gripped the gunwales on each side and ran the ship the rest of the way into the water, leaping aboard the moment her keel floated.

The *peltastés* sought the center aisle. The Gutones seized their oars, fifteen to each side, and pulled. The *Saiwsgaitsa* slid easily through the waves, more like a bird in flight than a boat on water.

Nerine looked around for something to grip. The gunwale was out of reach, likewise the nearer benches and baggage. Galena's arm? No, Nerine refused to seek comfort from Galena.

She gripped her own knees instead and looked out at the water.

The waves were more frothy folds than anything, skimming smoothly across the vast gray sheen of the bay to make lace on the pebble-strewn beach. The sea bottom must drop far more gradually here than it did at Lapadoússa. Her stomach still felt fine. The ship was moving forward, not up and down. She could almost hope that the Sea of Balder was far milder than the Middle Sea.

Except she remembered very well the difference between the harbor at Lapadoússa and the open sea.

The transition between this northern bay and the wider waters of Balder's Sea was much more gradual. For a time she watched the oarsmen, the sleeves of their yellow tunics rolled above their elbows, as they leaned into a quick stroke that seemed comfortable to them. All of them wore their hair in a tight knot at the nape of the neck. No loose flowing hair at sea – likely they couldn't free a hand to comb it tidy often enough.

Nerine stifled a giggle. She still felt fine.

The distance from shore grew. Their departure point had been a clear stretch of pebbles and sand, but the curving arms of the bay featured wetland reeds and rushes, alive with long-legged wading herons, floating terns, and a diving osprey.

The *Saiwsgaitsa's* motion was increasing. The oarsmen were well into their rhythm and the ship sped ever faster, but the wave action was also growing; a smooth glide up, followed by a swooping slide down, onward and onward.

Nerine still felt all right.

She noticed Jason and Captain Bartholomai glancing at her and murmuring to one another. Were they wondering when her face would turn greenish? Or congratulating themselves on their prediction that she would be fine.

Galena was looking around and taking it all in as eagerly as Nerine. Had she never been at sea before? Nerine thought not. Would Galena also suffer sickness? Or not?

The arms of the bay were spreading wider; the sea ahead, broader; the waves surging higher. The glide and swoop of the *Saiwsgaitsa's* glide grew more pronounced.

Nerine's head swam. A faint ringing sounded in her ears. And then her stomach turned over.

No!

She lunged for the gunwale of the *Saiwsgaitsa* to lean her chin over it in misery.

Seasickness had arrived in all its full panoply.

ᴄᴏ

Captain Bartholomai continued to assure Nerine that she would feel better in two or three days. Jason pointed out that Galena was fine.

Of course Galena *would* be fine, thought Nerine viciously. She was too cold to have a stomach that turned over. The severed head of a beheaded young man hadn't troubled *her* innards. Why would a mere rocking on the breast of the sea? Fah!

Galena moved to sit nearer the prow, where she could delight in the fullest rush and swoop of the *Saiwsgaitsa*. Jason came back to tend to Nerine, huddling by the gunwale amidships. He insisted she drink small sips of water and nibble crusts of dry shipbiscuit. She argued that her stomach would just have more to empty itself of. He explained, patiently, that she would feel greater nausea on an empty stomach than one with a few crumbs in it.

Nerine was too weary to withstand him. She sipped. She nibbled. And both the water and the biscuit did banish the sickly sour taste from her mouth. But she wished she could swim fast enough to keep up with thirty men rowing. Then she could escape this suffering altogether.

As it was, now more than ever, she missed Altairos. If Altairos were here, he would wrap a comforting arm around her. He would sympathize with her most truly. He wouldn't be concealing amusement, as Jason was. And he would get her back to shore.

Oh, how she longed for land.

How ridiculous that she, a *numen* of the sea, should long for dry ground. But she did.

In the early evening, when the long rays of the setting sun illuminated the shore grasses, with their backdrop of velvety trees, to a brilliant green, the oarsmen turned the *Saiwsgaitsa* toward the coast they'd been paralleling all day, and then ran her up onto the sandy beach.

Jason lifted Nerine to the ground.

The instant her feet felt the firm sand under them, she felt better. By the time she'd walked up the beach to the grasses edging the woodlands, she was completely recovered. She turned to glare at the sea. It was beautiful. The overcast sky had cleared to deep turquoise blue, and the light struck facets of silver and cobalt from the tossing water, while the sun glowed like a bead of amber on the horizon.

It was beautiful, and she hated it.

Most of the men were setting up tents and gathering driftwood for a fire. A few were spearfishing in the waves.

By the time dusk turned the sky and waters gray – a mellow and welcoming softness, not the thin, slick gray of the dawning – and the shadows were deepening, their dinner of roast fish and tubers awaited them.

Nerine had never been so hungry in her life. Honeyed pears – brought in the baggage – provided a lovely finish to the meal.

Nor had she ever been so weary. The instant she lay upon the sheepskin cloak that served as her bedding in the tent – and would keep her warm by day as the weather cooled – she was asleep.

The Sea of Balder was beautiful again in the dawning. Clear, pale skies over the watered silk of gray sea and the long-stretching shadows of the trees reaching out across the beach.

Nerine ate – a warm fish broth that had simmered overnight, welcome in the morning chill – only because Jason insisted, and allowed herself to be helped back into the *Saiwsgaitsa*, merely because her pride wouldn't let her run away.

The second day was just as bad as the first. And the third.

Jason pressed crystallized ginger upon her, which did help. A little. But she nibbled on it so steadily that his small supply ran out before the noontide. He urged her to keep her gaze fixed on the horizon, and that helped too. But not enough.

It got harder and harder to make herself climb into the *Saiwsgaitsa* each morning.

On the morning of the fourth day, although Nerine walked toward the ship, her steps lagged.

"This is the day it will get better," Jason encouraged her. "I'm sure of it!"

She didn't believe him, but let him tow her forward. She needed towing. She would just stand still if left to her own will.

Once asea – with Nerine amidships as usual – the oarsmen headed them away from shore. This was the one interval of the journey when land would be entirely out of sight. Nerine was not looking forward to it. All sea, no land – she'd likely be worse than ever. They were crossing from the east coast of Balder's Sea to its west coast by way of the isle of Gutland, the motherland of the Gutones.

All of the *peltastés* sat at the oars, giving half of the Gutones a rest. They would need it. This was their longest day of rowing.

Nerine looked longingly back toward shore, over the shallow lift of the *Saiwsgaitsa's* stern – identical to the prow as it was, defined only by the direction the vessel moved. The rising sun made her blink and squint as she watched the land grow distant, become a smudged line on the horizon, disappear as the horizon became a mere line where sea met sky.

In every direction she looked, there was only sea and sky, a vast clear blue overhead and a vast shining blue below it. The worst moment, absolutely the worst moment, except . . .

Her stomach was fine. *She* was fine. And the world of water and air was more beautiful than ever before.

The *peltastés* in their pale plaids – the *linothorax* packed in the baggage – pulled their oars with an efficiency that reminded Nerine of the motion of dolphin flukes. The Gutones in their yellow tunics pulled *their* oars with a lazy power more like that of a whale. The *Saiwsgaitsa* cleaved the water like a bird, indeed, soaring fast through the medium in the skimming swoops of a swallow in springtime.

Nerine felt cleansed and free, as though *she* were that swallow, glorying in flight, glorying in a realm more limitless than any other. She could go anywhere, be anyone, think any thought, feel any feeling.

Jason smiled at her.

She smiled back, but didn't speak. She could say anything she wished, but she wished to say nothing at all. Let the creak of the oars, the breathing of the rowers, and the soft sound the wind made in her ears be all her conversation. A word from her own lips would spoil it.

The active rowers and those resting switched places several times. And there were conversations, but none that Nerine participated in. Jason seemed to sense her mood and respected it, offering her luncheon foods without speaking. But his eyes shone satisfaction.

The sky and sea took on more vibrant hues as the day passed, robin's egg azure and gleaming sapphire in the noontide, deepening turquoise and luminous lapis lazuli in the late afternoon, and then radiant cobalt above polished midnight when the west horizon grew amber and the smudged line of land appeared.

Nerine sighed.

A journey at sea was every bit as glorious as Captain Bartholomai had claimed.

She broke her silence when they made landfall and the Gutones of Gutland ran down to the beach to welcome them.

"You were right," she told Jason.

The islanders built a great bonfire. There was music – sweet, shrill ivory pipes – and dancing and feasting. Nerine marveled at how the solemnity at the heart of the Gutonic soul kept their merrymaking from wildness, yet infused it with a more essential joy. Their dances were all ring dances, with fun moments where the individual dancers spun in place, or when half the dancers circled in one direction, touching hands with the other half, who circled in the opposite direction.

Nerine watched, laughing merely because everyone was laughing, and perceiving an innocence in their celebration that seemed to echo an innocence in her own being. She fell asleep happy.

~

25 ~ Crisis at Sea

IN THE DARKNESS of the chieftain's hall, Nerine awoke for no reason at all.

Her sheepskin beneath her on the divan was soft and warm. Her plaid over her was comfortingly weighty. The dull glow of banked coals in the central hearth flickered slowly. Someone snored gently.

All was well. Why had she awakened?

She thought about the evening, convivial and lively.

She considered the day with its relief from her long illness and the exaltation of passing so freely across the waves.

She need not dread the morrow. Why was she worried?

For something worried her, gnawing at her like a pea crab burrowing in an oyster.

She turned to her other side, and then turned back again. Nothing was wrong in her surroundings, but something was wrong within her.

She fell asleep gazing at the glow of the hearth, hearing the muffled sound when a coal fell.

In the morning, her preparations for taking to the sea again distracted her. She couldn't wait! The overcast was back, looking white, it was so high, and the sea gleamed beaten silver with glints of gold, where the sun peaked through the clouds at the horizon. Traveling in the *Saiwsgaitsa* would be a different kind of adventure today – sharp and exquisite, rather than bold and vivid.

"I can't wait to embark!" she told Jason, as they walked across the strange spongy turf of the island, toward the low bluff overlooking its pebble beach. "Will I be alright today, too?" She couldn't imagine she wouldn't, but she was curious what Jason would say.

He looked serious. Did he have bad tidings for her? But, no, how silly. Jason always looked serious.

"Different ships have different patterns of motion," he told her. "You might be sick in another vessel, but never in the *Saiwsgaitsa*. Your body knows her now and won't forget."

"So when I travel to visit the Middle Sea in five years, you'll see that the *Saiwsgaitsa* brings me home?" she teased.

He blushed. "Lord Hermes has more than our cohort at his command, but you might request the Poniró Peltastés." His blush reddened. "If you wish for us."

She glanced at him curiously.

He looked away, and then she knew. Blessings great and little! How awkward. She should have realized . . . much sooner. She just wasn't used to being around young men who found her attractive. She'd kept to her family circle, for the most part, and then . . . it had always been Altairos, for her. But Jason was acting just like Altairos had. When she was just thirteen and he, fourteen. And she'd not guessed then. Not guessed until he returned from far Aegyptus, when she discovered she loved him and learned that he loved her.

What was she to do about this? Because, for her, it was still and would always be Altairos. But she wouldn't think about that now. Couldn't think about that now. She needed to figure out what to do about Jason.

He helped her into the *Saiwsgaitsa* as usual, and she pondered this new problem as the men ran the ship into the sea, and their Gutonic hosts onshore called blessings of safe travel.

Moments later they were afloat, skimming across the shining silver sea toward the scant line that was the western shore. They would parallel that shore for the next seven days, arriving on the seventh at the northernmost point of Balder's Sea. She drew very, very close to her ultimate destination. Was the flutter in her belly excitement? Or nerves? She couldn't be sure.

But Jason. What was she going to do about Jason?

There was no real answer, she realized. He would recover from his attraction to her once she was gone. And in the meantime, she would continue to be friendly and kind. But perhaps she should not rely upon him so much for companionship. That would be easier now that she was no longer ill.

She glanced at Galena, sitting near *Saiwsgaitsa's* prow and recovered from her initial excitement over a voyage by water. Her face remained still, unmoved by the beauty and wonder of the sea, as unmoved as it had been when the Keltoi severed Lugh's head from his body.

Nerine did not wish for Galena's companionship. No matter. Her long days on the beach awaiting Altairos' return from his mission of diplomacy had accustomed her to being her own best company. Seven days with no close confidant were nothing in comparison.

She shrugged.

And then the realization that had niggled at her in the night burst upon her.

Blessings and damnation! How could she have been so obtuse?

The *Saiwsgaitsa* swooped across a surging sea and Nerine felt not even a hint of nausea. None at all. She could be standing in the prow of a triaconter in the Middle Sea with Altairos at her side, looking forward to their next adventure together as husband and wife, the wind in her face, Oenotria or Aegyptus or Phoiníke ahead of them, Altairos' arm around her waist.

Ah! That it was not so, *hurt*.

It hurt like being slammed into the sand by a rogue breaker. It hurt like being scraped along the shingle by a riptide. It hurt like a dagger to the heart.

She had given Altairos up for *nothing*. There would have been no lonely years apart while she dwelt amongst his disapproving family. Or within her own disappointed one. Waiting, always waiting, for him to return. Until the call of the sea grew too strong in her solitude, and she melted into water to flow with the tides for millennia.

Her belly felt like ice. Was she crying? No, her eyes were wide, but dry, her face still. As still as Galena's.

She caught her breath, even though she had not been breathless. She looked out across the sea, turning leaden gray as the sun rose beyond the gap in the clouds at the horizon, its light eclipsed by the thick overcast. She shivered.

Jason touched her arm. "Are you cold, Nerine?"

She nodded. Her plaid mantle was not enough warmth for a sunless day. Nor enough to comfort her sudden sense of loss.

Jason pulled her sheepskin cloak from the baggage and wrapped it around her. It felt heavy on her shoulders, and the suede of its inner surface was soft against her neck, while the brown of its exterior fleeces cut the wind. Her body was warmed, but her soul was cold, oh-so-cold.

"What have I done?" she whispered, so softly that her lips moved without making a sound. Could she undo her mistake? Her very great mistake. Order the Poniró Peltastés to turn around? Carry her back to Olympus? Back to the Middle Sea?

And then what?

Nearly four moons had elapsed since she left the reef palace. At least that many more would pass before she could return. Altairos would not have been awaiting her on that beach for the better part of a year. And even if he had . . . even if he returned some indefinite time later, what then?

She had to *think* about this. She had not done so yet, she realized. She'd reacted, she'd felt, she'd acted. But not once had she paused and really thought things through.

And she should have. Altairos had been right to ask her to wait, to talk things over, to consult the wisdom of others. Why had she not listened?

She wished the answer to that question did not leap so readily to mind, but it was obvious. She was accustomed to find no answers to life's dilemmas when she consulted others. But she'd never really consulted very *many* before concluding that her own counsel was her only resource.

Who had she asked for help in her search for her vocation?

Her parents. Nurse. Calla. Altairos. And Altairos' pappa. Six. Six people and no more. On the issue that meant the most to her. Had she been insane?

No. But the limits had felt so . . . *limiting.* So immovable. So *final.* She'd just accepted them for how they felt, without really questioning that her feelings, while real, might not be accurate.

And she'd done the same when the next thing that she desired more than anything in the world – marriage to Altairos – had felt impossible.

She'd given up too soon. Immediately, really. She'd assumed the fight was hopeless and surrendered without assessing its necessity.

There'd been some excuse for her when she was a child. It was natural for a child to assume her parents were all-powerful and all-knowing. But not all children did assume that. Tyr hadn't. And, she suspected, Eilidh hadn't either. Why had Nerine been so . . . passive?

No, that wasn't the right word. She'd *not* been passive. She'd found her own solution: going ashore alone to find adventure. And she'd found it.

Had that been her defining moment? Her discovery that when her elders had no answer, either there wasn't one or else she, Nerine, must find it on her own?

It seemed so. Because she'd certainly approached her other problems in the same style. When the first few people she'd asked, about posts that would allow her to travel once she was grown, possessed no answers, she'd assumed she must find her own answer. And when she'd not been able to, she'd assumed there was none.

And she'd brought that learning into her betrothal. That *she* must have the answer, and that if she did not, there was none.

Blessings, Nerine! Have some sense, she thought at herself fiercely.

Well, she hadn't had sense. Maybe it was time to apply sense now. Could she work her current puzzle through more sensibly? What exactly was her problem?

She still wanted to marry Altairos.

The barrier of her seasickness had suddenly been removed. Or . . . not removed, but shown to be not a barrier. Well, so. That hadn't been the only barrier. What of the others?

Nerine's mother had lost her best friend – her cousin Hester – when Hester ran away to marry the land king Zeron, Altairos' pappa. And then Mother had lost her middle daughter, Xianthe, when Xianthe ran away to join Poseidon's harem.

Could Nerine really do that to her mother? Be the third beloved person to run away from home? Because she couldn't pretend that she would have returned home to inform her family of her decision to marry Altairos.

Ah, blessings! She was beginning to hate herself. She didn't trust herself to claim her betrothal and stick fast to it in the face of her family's disapproval. Even now, she didn't. Was she able to choose her own road only in secret? Because that was the way she'd always done it?

Fah! She *did* hate herself!

Stop it, Nerine, she admonished herself. Calm. Down.

So, the problems her family would have with her marriage – if it were even possible that her sundering of her betrothal hadn't made it impossible – still remained.

She bit her lip and looked out across the tossing gray waves. The wind had picked up, and the crests showed white, carrying the *Saiwsgaitsa* higher. While the troughs between waves were deeper, receiving the *Saiwsgaitsa* lower. Despite the increased motion, Nerine's stomach remained untroubled.

Jason had taken an oar from one of the Gutonic rowers, so she sat alone for the moment.

She wanted to watch the ripple of the muscles in the oarsmen's arms. *They* were not cold, despite the cold wind.

She wanted to listen to the cries of the gulls soaring out from the shore just off to her left.

She wanted to breathe in the clean, salt aroma on the wind.

She wanted to do anything but think about the things that needed her thinking.

So. Thinking. She refused to shirk it, now that she had come to it. What of the other side of the problems surrounding her renounced betrothal? What of Altairos' family?

King Zeron's wife and Altairos' mother had been a sea *numen*. Mother's cousin Hester, in fact. King Zeron had not seemed bitter. He'd even welcomed Nerine as his son's friend. But he'd asked her not to fall in love with Altairos. She could not imagine he would welcome her as Altairos' wife. How could he? No father would wish his son's wife to be someone whose very being might make her faithless, as Hester had proved faithless to Zeron himself. The servants in the land palace all hated the sea people because of Hester's desertion. Surely Altairos' brothers would feel the same.

The dissipation of Nerine's seasickness had changed none of the other barriers.

She could marry in the teeth of opposition from both her family and his, but was that wise? And even were she willing to do so . . . she had declared to Altairos that she would not. And then left him, even as he begged her to wait.

Gods! She was despicable!

She felt a sob working its way up through the frozen center of her and suppressed it.

She would feel later. Right now, she must stay cool and think this all the way through to the bitter end. She only wished she were not frozen. Cool was one thing, but icy? Was that any more conducive to clear thought than hot emotion? She suspected not, but it was all she had right now.

So. More thinking. As best she could manage it.

Suppose she were willing to marry in the teeth of opposition and she ordered the *Saiwsgaitsa* to be turned right now. Suppose their travel to reach Olympus was as unimpeded as their journey out had been. Suppose she returned to Lapadoússa and found Altairos awaiting her in the mild moons of the southern winter. And suppose he turned her down after the pain she had caused him.

What then?

She would then make this journey north all over again, assuming the norns still wanted her after such a delay. And if they did not, then she would be relegated to life at home with her family.

Nerine shuddered. That was one of the things she had run so fast and far from.

Consider the other option then. What if Altairos received her with open arms? What then?

He deserves better – that was her first thought. And her second. And her third. It was true. She was a girl who had always gotten her way by going behind others' backs, by being secretive. She'd never been able to stand up and claim what was most dear to her in the face of opposition. With *that* as her legacy, how dared she offer herself as wife to *any* man, let alone the one she loved most in all the world.

So. That was the bitter end of her thinking. And it was bitter. More bitter than even the bitterest of tough and bitter *thali* pods.

～

The *Saiwsgaitsa* surged over the leaden gray waves – swooping up and swooping down, with never a flutter in Nerine's stomach – racing north under the leaden gray sky. Captain Bartholomai had taken an oar, so Galena chatted cooly with a resting Gutone seated next to her at the ship's prow. The wind, strong on Nerine's face, sounded loud in her ears and flooded her nostrils with the salt smell of the sea.

Was she making the same mistake she'd made so consistently before? Consulting no one save herself?

But who was there to consult?

Galena? She'd as soon consult the Keltic Ard-cean who'd severed Lugh's head with his own sword.

Jason, who blushed at her every word? Captain Bartholomai? One of the other *peltastés* with whom she'd discussed horse sandals and currying? She'd barely met these people but three moons ago. How could she seek their counsel? Trust their counsel? She couldn't. And even if she could –

Abruptly it occurred to her that she needn't *take* their counsel. The idea was not to find someone else to tell her what to do. The idea was to talk over her own ideas with someone else. To test her ideas against those of others. To discover the flaws in her thinking, and then think again. And test the flaws in her next batch of thoughts. And to continue until her thinking was clear and, not flawless, but *less* flawed.

Now *that* was sensible.

And she couldn't do it.

Not here. Not now. Not with these people. She wanted to be able to do it. She wanted to be different than she was. But she wasn't and she couldn't. This was too big. And these companions were too strange.

If only she'd seen the necessity for this kind of sharing years ago. If only she'd practiced it with smaller things. With people she knew and trusted. Then she might be able to do it here and now, with something big, and with people she didn't know that well.

But if she'd managed to practice sharing, she'd likely not even be in this situation.

Oh, Nerine, you are pitiful, she told herself. It didn't feel good.

So. She'd made a great mistake. And now she was deciding on how to fix it, in the same poor way that she'd decided important things before. But she'd given herself no other options. And she'd never been one to shirk decisions, even if she'd always shirked confidence in others.

So she would decide.

And her decision was that she must let Altairos go. She'd decided that before, but she'd been fooling herself. All her long, long letter to her beloved – her "notes" about her travels – proved she'd not meant it. This time she would mean it.

She scooted closer to the pile of baggage near her, secured by rope and netting.

She reached through the narrow gap between the netting and the ship's decking to pull her satchel out. She stared at it. Within it rested one complete scroll of written papyrus – all her account of her experiences – along with enough blank papyrus, more cakes of dried ink, and extra reeds to carve into writing styluses, to inscribe yet another long, long letter.

No, she would not open the satchel to scrabble in its depths for her letter. This must be a complete break. With no possibility for going back. She stood abruptly, surprised at how well she could balance on the heaving deck of the *Saiwsgaitsa,* and swung her right arm, with the satchel gripped in her right hand.

"Nerine!" screamed Galena.

Nerine had everyone's attention now – everyone who wasn't rowing.

Nerine's arm reached the end of its swinging arc. She opened her clenched hand, and the satchel – her last connection to Altairos – flew out over *Saiwsgaitsa's* gunwale, out across the tossing sea, and sank beneath the waves.

⁓

The ship plunged down the slope of another wave, sea spray scattering from her prow.

Nerine's knees went weak and she plumped back down to sitting.

Galena was the first to reach her, despite the necessary scramble over men and baggage. She gripped Nerine's shoulders and shook them.

"You've just destroyed history!" Galena yelled. *Now* her face was not inanimate. "How could you? I *saw* all your notes on Keltic plaid patterns, on Gutonic tablet weaving!" Galena was crying, actual tears pouring down her face. "I'd planned to ask you for copies. The Muse of History would have blessed you for centuries. Oh, how could you?"

Nerine stared at her blankly. What?

"I'll never forgive you! Never! And neither will my lady Clio," sobbed Galena, allowing Captain Bartholomai – who'd given up his oar – to pull her gently away.

Then Jason was crouching next to Nerine, peering into her face, pulling her sheepskin cloak back around her shoulders.

"What happened, Nerine?" he asked. "Are you alright?"

She felt hollow. How could she answer him? What could she say? It was all too complicated to explain.

"Nerine?" He was barely audible over the wind and the waves.

"I'm – I'm – I just realized something," she managed.

His lips softened from worry to sympathy. "What did you realize?" His voice was so kind it made Nerine want to weep.

"I – I can't explain it. I'm sorry." She swallowed down the tears that were threatening. "I just realized that something I wanted is impossible – and I'm a fool!"

He pressed her hand. "Can I help?"

Ah, she wished he could. But he couldn't. Nor should he. She was regaining her senses, and remembering she'd just resolved to hold Jason at a greater distance. He was the last person she should allow to help her, to comfort her.

She shook her head, very slightly, shaking away inner pre-occupation, reorienting to the world – and the people – around her. "I'm sorry. I didn't mean to upset everyone. I'm alright." She wasn't okay, but there was nothing anyone else could do about it. She would need to recover on her own.

"I'd like to help," pursued Jason. "If I can."

"No, it's nothing."

"Oh, Nerine, I know it's not nothing. Not after . . . that!" He sounded very tender.

She mastered herself enough to meet his gaze, a smile trembling on her lips. "Nothing you can do anything about," she amended. "Truly."

His return smile was rueful. "If you change your mind, I'm here."

Managing her responses was helping her to manage herself. The hollow feeling was fading, yielding to a measure of calm. "I know." She glanced down at her lap, then up again. "Thank you, Jason. Perhaps you could –"

He looked appallingly eager.

"– could offer my apologies to everyone for alarming them?"

"Of course!" He nodded firmly. "I'll do it!"

And apparently he planned to do it immediately, because he left her, working his way along the crowded aisle, murmuring to each man seated there. Who knew what he was saying – Nerine couldn't hear his words – but they nodded or quirked an eyebrow, or snickered, accepting his reassurances in their own characteristic ways.

Back at the *Saiwsgaitsa's* prow, Galena alone repudiated Jason's explanation. She tossed her head, sniffed, and turned pointedly away. Jason shrugged, looking back toward Nerine.

Nerine shrugged back. Don't worry about it, she mouthed.

❧

26 ~ Water and Wings

OVER THE NEXT SEVEN days, Nerine learned the difference between Galena honoring Nerine's wish for solitude and Galena avoiding her. Where before Galena might visually check to see if Nerine wanted help with something, or whether Nerine preferred the right side or the left side of the tent, when they slept onshore, now she ignored Nerine completely.

Instead of consulting Nerine about which of them would gather kindling, or tend the supper, or bury leftover bones, she sought orders from Captain Bartholomai.

Nerine couldn't muster the energy to care. She had plenty of her own thinking to do, and being ignored by Galena fitted in perfectly with that. The greater challenge was dealing with Jason. He grew more attentive than ever, and while Nerine didn't want to hurt him by repudiating him, neither did she want to encourage him. Striking the right balance was hard. She needed to be *even*. Blowing hot and cold on the poor youth would be even worse than being too kind.

Assuring him that she'd thought through her problem and was fine seemed her most effective tactic. She could do it in such a friendly fashion, too, which set him at a distance without being cold. Thanking him cheerily for his sympathy also worked well.

She had to choke back laughter at the puzzled look she often spotted on his face.

He hadn't yet figured out that she'd substituted greater friendliness for intimacy. Which was just as well. He'd likely be over his infatuation, without ever realizing why, by the time he had to bid her farewell at the cottage of the norns.

At least she'd manage to spare *him* unnecessary hurt.

For herself . . . well, she wasn't really hurting either. She was thinking. Thinking a lot. About the same things that had prompted her to hurl her writing supplies overboard, but more calmly.

She'd been right that Altairos deserved a wife with more moral courage than she possessed, but renouncing him – permanently, as she had this time – was really only the first step. The next step was figuring out how to *grow* some of said courage. She refused to acquiesce to her own cowardice. And she was pretty sure she knew what she must do to change.

When she arrived at her destination, she must not only get to know the norns and learn how to fulfill her post skillfully, she must form a friendship with at least one of them that was close enough for confidences to be exchanged. And then she should practice sharing her closest concerns and talking them over.

That was her weak point, and a grievous one.

She was determined to change it.

In the meantime, she savored this last interval of her closely held privacy. For now, she need not share her concerns. For now, she need not open her inmost thoughts to the challenges of others. For now, she could be her old self, without stretching for the new.

And she would snicker privately at Galena's icy demeanor. She'd never guessed that even Galena possessed a weak point, although she should have. No one was invulnerable. But history as a weak point – *recorded* history – was unusual, to say the least.

Nerine controlled her outer smile.

Galena was not the only entity growing colder. The overcast weather continued, and the days never warmed, even at the noontide. The Gutones muttered about the possibility of ice forming early on the northern extremities of Balder's Sea, and insisted on taking to the water each morning before the sun was up, as soon as the sky lightened enough for them to see. And they rowed well past sundown, which meant setting up camp by the light of the fire – a clumsy and annoying process.

Captain Bartholomai did not complain. He knew as well as the Gutones did that the sea must remain free of ice, long enough for them to reach its northernmost shore, *and* safely return to the warmer southern waters, after escorting Nerine to the cottage of the norns.

～

The overcast broke on their last day at sea, the lowering clouds edging away toward the north at the noontide, revealing a clear windswept sky, pale blue and brisk. Dark pines fringed the shoreline, the land sloping gently upward as one gazed inland. Soon after the sun emerged, the shore bent away to form a deep inlet where a river entered the sea.

The *Saiwsgaitsa* turned to follow the line of the land and then approached a stretch of level sand. The Gutonic oarsmen splashed into the shallow water and drew their ship ashore.

Moments later, Nerine stood between two tall pine boles on the pale, soft reindeer moss of the Scandian forests. She'd arrived in Scandia at last. It seemed too soon, for all that she'd been traveling for nearly four moons.

Once the men had dragged the *Saiwsgaitsa* well clear of the water, Nerine stepped forward to help with the unpacking. Captain Bartholomai checked her.

"Are you ready for walking?" he asked, scrutinizing her boots.

She nodded, puzzled.

"Good. Let the *peltastés* gather your gear."

As she watched, a half dozen of them – not Jason – donned their *linothorax* armor and then loaded various bags into rucksacks, which they slung to their shoulders.

"Come," said Captain Bartholomai, "you must make your farewells."

Nerine frowned. "We leave so many behind?" she asked.

The captain merely nodded.

She chose to thank the Gutones first, telling them that she'd never imagined the glory of traveling over the waves instead of under them, and praising their strength and skill at the oars. A few joked about her initial sickness, more were taciturn – not unappreciative of her gratitude, but reserved in the manner of their kind. The eldest bade her find friends in her new home, which made her wonder if he were visionary, or merely well acquainted the travails of young women. Perhaps he had dozens of granddaughters.

Saying goodbye to the *peltastés* was harder – she'd traveled amongst them longest – and bidding farewell to Jason, hardest of all.

He had no reciprocal trouble, blessings be thanked. Her outgoing friendliness had done its work, and he was already wondering what task Lord Hermes would give his cohort when they finally returned to Mount Olympus.

Nerine felt oddly forlorn. She hadn't wanted him longing for her, but she'd expected the sadness of parting friends. And forgotten that young men longed for adventure more than for friendship.

"It was fun, Nerine," he said, grinning.

She sighed.

His smile faltered. That would never do.

"It was," she agreed, and cuffed him on the shoulder.

He perked up and wrapped an arm around her upper back – half hug, half buffet – then turned away. Maybe this was a little harder for him than he was letting on. Nerine felt better.

She glanced at Galena. They disliked one another equally at this point, but surely a civil goodbye was more seemly than a complete lack of notice.

It appeared Galena thought so, too, because she approached Nerine with a swift stride.

"I must apologize for my incivility, when you disposed of your scroll of notations," she stated calmly. "Perhaps you might forgive a passionate historian in the grip of her greatest love. If that is possible, I would be most grateful."

Blessings! Nerine had not been expecting that. And had prepared nothing to say in return.

"Of course I forgive you." The words fell out of her mouth before she knew if they were true. She took a breath, struggling to find what she *did* wish to express. Because Galena deserved something from her. She'd been a kind and helpful companion for most of their long journey together. "Indeed, I am most grateful for your attendance upon me. And for all your teaching of how to go on while traveling overland. I should have been very weary and bored without you."

Galena brightened, if such could be said of someone so serene. "You know that Lord Hermes will send his winged couriers to you twice yearly?" she queried.

Nerine nodded. She'd wondered at the outset why they could not have conveyed *her* to her destination. Until she'd compared the weight of herself and her baggage to that of an inked scroll or a memorized message. Winged sandals could bear only so much.

"I would beg a boon, then," continued Galena.

Nerine's eyebrows shot up. What was this?

"Should you find both time and inclination, I would treasure any notes on the Keltic plaid patterns, or the decorative bands of the Gutones, that you might pen for me and my lady Clio."

Nerine started to laugh and couldn't stop, even when Galena lifted her chin to look down her nose in astonishment. Only Galena would be indifferent to Nerine's dislike, but anxious for Nerine's observations about Európi and its inhabitants.

"If I find the time – though the norns will likely keep me busy – I will record my memories of such and send them to you," she promised.

Galena smiled.

Nerine touched Galena's forearm and turned away.

∽

Captain Bartholomai, and the six *peltastés* who would accompany him, picked up their crescent shields with the two javelins secured to their inner side. The captain motioned Nerine to take her place in their midst and led the way into the forest.

A generous path of dried pine needles – reddish brown – threaded through the pale reindeer moss carpeting the ground between the tree boles. Nerine's footfalls, cushioned by the pine needles, made little sound. Were Efyenés treading this route, she would not need the protection of her horse sandals.

Nerine smiled, surprised that she missed the mare. She wondered if the norns kept horses. She'd learned to enjoy riding on that long trek across Európi.

The path narrowed as it penetrated further into the woodland, and the *peltastés* rearranged themselves to walk in single file, with four ahead of Nerine and three behind her. The level pitch of the ground began to rise, gently but steadily. Nerine could feel it in the muscles of her calves.

No breeze stirred beneath the trees. All was silent, save for the puff of the *peltastés'* breaths, the faint creak of their *linothorax* armor, and the rustle of Nerine's garments. The resinous scent of the pines ghosted through the still air.

The sun disappeared behind the clouds again, and the gold speckles of light sifting through the tree canopy vanished, turning the cheerful mood of the forest to a foreboding gloom. Outcroppings of gray rock emerged from the slope and became more prominent as they continued to climb.

Nerine shivered.

Her plaid wrap was warm enough – she'd folded her sheepskin cloak in with the baggage – but the increasingly somber surroundings seemed an ill omen for her future. She tried to shake off the feeling. Surely she was foolish. The norns had *invited* her to the post of handmaiden. They were waiting to *welcome* her.

The way entered a narrow cleft in a rocky bluff, shallow stone treads twisting between rough walls of granite, the stone exuding a chill breath. Several dozen steps later, the path ended, where a smooth sheet of dark water poured over a lip at head height, to splash on a circle of round river stones, then disappearing into the ground through the cracks.

Nerine's shoulders tensed. Had Captain Bartholomai led them amiss?

He turned to address his men and her.

"Beyond this fall of water, the rules of the world do not apply. Some of you know this." He looked at the *peltastís* immediately before him. "Some of you have never passed this way before." He looked at Nerine and a *peltastís* standing behind her.

"Do not worry about the strangeness, nor about what it means, nor what rules do apply. Merely keep moving forward." His lips straightened.

"There will come a time when your limbs seem not to move, but do not attend to it. Set your will on moving forward, and move forward you shall."

His eyes met Nerine's directly. "Do you understand?"

She nodded.

"Good. Follow me!"

On those words, he turned and stepped through the glassy sheen of the falling water, disappearing from sight the instant his trailing arm passed through the uncanny doorway.

The second man in the file didn't hesitate, nor the third and fourth.

Nerine wanted to hesitate, but suspected it would only increase her reluctance.

She strode forward, and the water struck her brow and boot, cold – very cold – but, somehow, not wet. Then the rest of her passed through the gelid curtain into darkness.

～

She could see nothing, hear nothing, but the ground was firm under her feet and she sensed a vast space spreading around her. Hands held before her, she shuffled forward. No wall met her searching fingertips and no unevenness in the footing tripped her.

She grew more confident and increased her pace.

A glimmer of light shimmered to her right, as though a moon shone on the ripples of a black lake at midnight.

She walked onward, glancing often over her shoulder toward that rippling glimmer. Were her eyes adjusting? She could see that it *was* a lake, with white swans gliding across its black, mirrored surface and shadowy reeds or rushes fringing its margins.

Where the cool, dim light came from she could not see. There was no moon, no sky, not even a vaulted roof. The darkness hung impenetrably, hiding all but the lake, the swans, and the reeds.

A flapping of wings and splashing of webbed feet came across the water, as one of the swans took flight, lifting and disappearing into the darkness. Another bird soared downward – a loon – gliding long and low, before touching the lake in a gentle, curling riffle.

The reeds rattled where a small bird clutched one, swaying with it in an absent breeze.

Nerine kept walking, the lake always at her right, darkness everywhere else. There was no sign of the *peltastés*. Which would have alarmed her, had Captain Bartholomai not warned her that the normal rules of the world would not hold here, wherever here was.

On and on she went.

A new movement in the lake caught her eye – a beginning swirl, as though a giantess had dipped her great hand into the water and stirred.

Almost did Nerine pause, but Captain Bartholomai's other cautions came to mind, and she kept walking.

The swirl of the water grew more pronounced, faster. A whirlpool developed, its steep sides sliding down to some unknown destination within or below the water.

Nerine felt something cold touch her boot toes. A hopping frog? A creeping serpent?

She looked down.

It was the water. Somehow her steps had led her to the margins of the lake – a lake with water that was chill, but not wet.

She leaped away from it, back toward the dry ground that had supported her from the moment she entered this uncanny place, but it seemed the dry ground had disappeared. She landed with a splash amidst more reeds, floundering.

She broke into a run, but each splashing step carried her closer to the whirlpool.

She could feel the cold current, formidable, powerful, and still not wet – an inexorable force that drew her in like a funnel of wind, and then knocked her from her feet. She submerged, unable to breathe – with neither air for her lungs, nor true water for her spiracles – whipped around in a racing circle, and then swallowed down whole through the gullet of the whirlpool.

～

An instant later, the cold maw that had seized Nerine spat her out.

She stood panting on a slab of irregular granite, at the edge of a slanting Scandian meadow. Long golden grasses, wind-ruffled, lapped around brown-leaved shrubs and one scarlet clump of chokeberry. Blue spruces, glossy green hollies, and amber aspens skirted the open slope.

Nerine smelled woodsmoke.

Someone coughed.

Nerine looked over her shoulder to see Captain Bartholomai and three other *peltastés* – those who had entered the lake-realm ahead of her – standing behind her. Even as she stared, another *peltastís,* and another, blinked into being, followed by yet another. Their faces were pallid and strained. Had they, too, succumbed to the whirlpool? Or something worse?

"Good," pronounced their captain. "No complications, no delays. Well done!"

Nerine wished that he'd warned her in more detail. Although, if the experience were different for each person, how could he?

The captain entered the meadow and tramped up its slope, the dry grasses rustling with his passage, an occasional twig snapping under his step. Nerine and the men straggled after him in a loose clump. Nerine pulled her plaid wrap more securely against her to resist the wind. They rounded a thicket of tall hazel bushes, coming into a sheltered clearing of short turf, backed by a low pine-crowned bluff.

A stone cottage – creamy white and gray-veined, with a steep thatched roof and several smoke-spiraling chimneys – squatted before the bluff. A narrow slot of a wooden porch – roofed with wooden shingles – sheltered a two-part door, the lower half closed, the upper half slightly ajar. Square windows – with their casements of diamond-shaped, horn panes flung open – occupied the expanse on each side of the porch. A crimson-leaved vine climbed the stone, peeking in at one window before sprawling across the thatch of the roof.

It looked homey, welcoming.

The air stood very still. Nerine let her plaid wrap hang loose.

The *peltastés* and their captain paused.

In the pause, both halves of the cottage door swung open, and a diminutive old woman, cloaked in black, stepped onto the porch. With twisted, claw-like hands, she put the hood of her cloak back from her seamed face, revealing a scraggly halo of gray hair. She squinted, the lines around her dark eyes deepening, surveying the group standing in her front yard with the beginnings of disapproval.

Captain Bartholomai stepped closer to her and knelt.

"Eldest, I bring you the Kríousa Pelagieus at my Lord Hermes' urgent behest and confide her into your hands and safekeeping."

At the close of this formal greeting, the captain bent yet further to kiss the crone's skirt.

"Hmm," she answered, scrutinizing Nerine and frowning. Her crooked finger gestured sharply. "Too pretty." Her voice scraped, harsh on the ear. "Too young." Another slash by the denouncing finger. "And sneaky. Take her back."

Nerine's stomach sank all the way into her boots.

∼

The Cottage of the Norns

27 ~ Initiation Rites

FOR A MOMENT, they waited as though frozen by the norn's words. Captain Bartholomai knelt at the cottage porch in his red-trimmed, white *linothorax* armor, with the hem of the norn's black garment still between his lowered fingers. The six *peltastés* under Bartholomai's command stood motionless on the tree-guarded turf at Nerine's back.

And Nerine herself, shocked speechless by the repudiation expressed in place of the welcome she was expecting, knew not what to do.

So *this* was one of the three fates Nerine had promised herself that she would attempt to become friends with? Someone who rejected Nerine after a mere glance?

And how could she know that Nerine's specific weakness was holding her own in a disagreement? That Nerine then pursued her own ends secretly, rather than openly? Was Nerine *really* sneaky? She had not used that particular word in her negative judgment of herself.

Before anyone could respond to the norn's demand, a second norn stepped through the cottage door.

She was tall and queenly, her dark hood already lying on her shoulders to reveal her black hair – pinned up – her pale, patrician features, and deep violet eyes. The expression on her face was cold.

Nerine couldn't decide whether this norn reminded her of Mother – warm at heart, concealed by a cool demeanor; or of Galena – uncaring, also hidden by coolness.

"Do we send the kríousa home then, Orroch?" The queenly norn's voice was as stately as her appearance. "Tynghed has been overburdened all this half year while we awaited our new handmaiden."

"Ye see her!" Orroch gestured with her dismissive finger. "She'll get the threads wrong, at best, and deliberately when she has a mind to it. She'll be worse than useless!" Orroch snorted.

Captain Bartholomai let Orroch's hem drop from his fingers, and rose to his feet, stepping aside.

The queenly norn paced forward, skirting around Orroch, and then coming to stand before Nerine. Her cool, slim fingers tipped Nerine's face up so that she could study her.

"Do you lie?" she inquired politely.

The incongruity between her tone and the question would have made Nerine laugh, except that her shock was giving way to anger. She set her teeth and then answered, "I do not."

"Do you cheat?"

Nerine's breath shortened, hissing slightly as it passed in and out of her nostrils. She wondered, briefly, if they were pinched white the way her mother's were when she was furious. "I do not!"

"I am Eowys," the norn informed her, still utterly cool. "You may call me so. No honorific is necessary between a fate and her handmaiden. Do you steal?"

This was ridiculous! Even if the norns decided they wanted Nerine after all, Nerine did not want them. She drew herself up very tall. She could not match Eowys' height, but she could certainly match her demeanor. She was a princess and her mother's daughter. She knew how to counter rudeness.

"I am Kríousa Nerine Merenou Pelagieus, but you may call me Nerine. At my pleasure, no honorific is necessary." She nodded, every bit as stately as Eowys. The norn's fingers on her chin fell away. "And, no, I do not steal."

Eowys nodded back, not one wit discomposed. "Then why does Orroch call you sneaky?"

Abruptly Nerine's anger fled. Eowys and Orroch and – what was the other one's name, the third norn not yet present? Tynghed – yes, Tynghed, had a right to ask into Nerine's character. As handmaiden to the fates, she would occupy a position of trust and considerable power.

They had not possessed the opportunity to question her while she dwelt in the Middle Sea. And it was well that they should do so while they could yet dismiss her easily – while the Poniró Peltastés remained to convey Nerine safely home.

So how should Nerine answer Orroch's accusation of underhandedness? Honesty was essential. But airing her most personal concerns to . . . *nine* listeners, counting the *peltastés*, felt daunting. She could feel her escort at her back, growing indignant on her behalf. Their captain had circled around to stand with them.

As she considered her reply, the third norn arrived, hurrying from the door through the narrow porch and around Orroch to pause on the turf.

Tynghed was every bit as beautiful as Eowys, but in a warmer, approachable style. The way she moved showed she preferred to be engaged with the world and people around her, rather than reservedly observing. Even her hair – bright chestnut curls that resisted the pins confining them to Tynghed's head – fit her lively demeanor. She smiled, but her glance conveyed disagreement with her sister norns.

"For shame, sisters!" Tynghed's voice was musical and kind. "Is this how we welcome our young handmaiden to her new home?"

She rustled forward, and Eowys stepped aside to allow her room.

Tynghed took both Nerine's hands in hers and raised them to her lips, first one and then the other. "Be welcome by our hearth and in our hearts, Kríousa! I am so glad you are safely here." Her eyes were very bright, with unshed tears, Nerine realized. Tynghed really meant what she'd said and was ashamed of the repelling greeting offered by Orroch and Eowys.

"Did you hear . . ." Nerine faltered, and then pushed on, "what they said?" It was harder to maintain her composure in the face of Tynghed's sympathy than before Orroch's hostility or Eowys' formality.

"Not a word," answered Tynghed breezily, "but a mere look tells me *more* than enough!" She squeezed Nerine's hands. "We were at the loom, you know. Orroch could rise from her bench easily enough, and Eowys spring down from her perch on high. But I must order the shuttles and the silks before I let the weaving be, that nothing become confused by our hiatus."

Nerine nodded, although this explanation confused more than it enlightened. But she must not let Tynghed's kindness overwhelm the very reasonable point that Orroch and Eowys had raised. It felt odd how swiftly she passed from righteous indignation to championing the norns' concerns. She refused to allow the fact that she had the audience of the *peltastés* to deter her. This was too important. And . . . it was her first chance to practice straight forward dealing as she'd promised herself. In a more challenging environment than she'd planned, true. But she would begin as she meant to go on.

"My lady," she began.

"But no!" Tynghed let go of Nerine's hands to shake a finger mischievously. How odd that a shaken finger could be so different – Orroch's judgment versus Tynghed's good cheer. "I am Tynghed, an it please you, and I do hope it does!" She laughed.

"And I'm Nerine," Nerine interrupted. "But –"

Tynghed grew serious. "But what, child?"

Nerine swallowed. "Orroch declared that I am sneaky. And Eowys wished to know why. And I . . . found them discourteous, but I understand their concern." She felt a little breathless and lightheaded.

Tynghed's face softened. "Ah, you sweetheart. And you intend to answer, do you not?"

"Yes." Nerine dragged a breath into her constricted-feeling lungs. She'd just realized how Orroch would have knowledge of Nerine's shortcomings. The norns had been weaving Nerine's fate along with those of everyone else. Of course Orroch would know.

She bit her lip and looked at Tynghed, dredging for the courage to go on.

Tynghed smiled sympathetically and then surveyed the *peltastés* arrayed defensively behind Nerine. "Should you prefer more privacy, Nerine? Shall I dismiss your escort to their refreshment?"

Captain Bartholomai touched Nerine's shoulder. "I shall lead my men aside, out of earshot, Kríousa. There is no reason for your protectors to be privy to your intimate concerns."

Ah, how she'd love to accept his offer. She *would* prefer privacy. Which was why she suspected she must forego it on the present occasion.

"No, wait. Please." She swallowed again. This was *hard*. "Orroch has made an accusation before you all. And I should prefer to clear myself to the degree that I may."

Captain Bartholomai's jaw set, but he nodded. Evidently he felt the accusation should not have been made at all. Which was heartening – it was nice to have defenders – but she didn't want the Poniró Peltastés carrying away the impression that she might be sneaky. She still didn't see herself that way. Despite all the secrets she'd kept from her family.

She stepped away from both Tynghed and Captain Bartholomai, angling her stance so that she had her back to no one, so that she faced everyone. The bright clearing was very still around them.

She lifted her chin and raised her voice.

"Orroch has described me as sneaky, and Eowys has wondered if that means I've lied or cheated or stolen. I have not. But I have kept secrets from" – she gulped – "my mother and father."

She saw looks of understanding pass across the faces of most of the *peltastés*. Perhaps they, too, had withheld certain things from their parents. Orroch sniffed skeptically. Eowys gave no indication at all of what she might be thinking. And Tynghed's eyes were shining again with unshed tears.

Nerine forced herself to continue. That this was so difficult showed her how unpracticed she was. She'd *never* shared such raw stuff before.

"My secrets were only such as might hurt myself, none other. Although" – was she really understanding this only now? – "if hurt was done to me, then it would hurt Mother and Father as well. But . . . I could not bear to beg their permission. And . . . I'd hoped to beg their forgiveness, but the moment for that never came."

Nerine's knees felt weak. She stiffened them.

"And that is all the truth, although not all the details." Was it enough? She passionately hoped it was enough. She could not bear to share more than she had.

"Well said, Kríousa Pelagieus!" came Captain Bartholomai's strong voice. He set up a rhythmic clap – *clap . . . clap . . . clap . . . clap* – and the other *peltastés* followed his lead, ending with a chorused shout, "Hey!"

Tynghed stepped to Nerine's side and wrapped an arm around her waist. "Oh, my dear! Mere childishness. Who could blame you?"

"No," said Nerine. "It was more than that. It was a lack of strength on my part. And . . . I'd already realized, on my journey here, that I needed to grow stronger."

She saw Eowys give a restrained nod, but Orroch shook her head impatiently.

"Ye speak true," she said in her cracked voice, "but ye dinna estimate the effort properly, and ye dinna know our ways at all."

Nerine sighed. Well, she'd done her best, and it was too bad. In spite of Orroch's censure and Eowys' rudeness, Nerine had wanted a place serving Tynghed.

"Why did you send for me then?" she asked curiously.

Orroch cackled, throwing back her head with its thin tangle of gray hair. "To see if ye'd measure up in spite of thy sorry doings, girl." She pursed her withered lips and sniffed. "Which ye have. Just by the wee wit of a hair."

With a nod, she turned on the porch and retired into the cottage.

Nerine looked blankly at Tynghed and Eowys. "I'm to stay?"

Captain Bartholomai shouldered forward. "Only if you truly wish it, Kríousa. You have some say in this, too." He frowned at Eowys and the open door into the cottage, clearly still angry on Nerine's behalf. "You have a right to require real hospitality and consideration from those you serve."

Eowys looked down her nose at him, her violet eyes stern. "You would have us risk a dishonest fate?"

"That's not what this was about, and you know it!" he growled.

Eowys smiled, very faintly. "Very well, then it is for the kríousa to decide." She turned to address Nerine. "The place as handmaiden is yours, if you desire it. What will you?"

Nerine glanced from one to the other to the other.

Tynghed's eyes pleaded, say yes. Captain Bartholomai continued to glare at Eowys. And Eowys stood entirely composed.

What had Captain Bartholomai meant, that the confrontation was not about determining Nerine's probity? Would he say, if she asked him?

The ghost of Orroch's laughter echoed in her ears. Ah! They'd been testing her courage, not her honesty or her honor. How odd and how appropriate. It was courage she came here to develop. It seemed she'd begun with a vengeance.

She eyed Eowys steadily. "I accept," she said.

～

Captain Bartholomai was not ready to accept Nerine's decision, however. He drew her away, next to the hollies, to speak privately with her.

"The old one's a right griffoness, Kríousa, and the proud one not much better. Are you sure? I and my men would bring you back to Olympus happily enough." He put both his hands on her shoulders. They felt weighty and warm. "I cannot bear to leave you to distress, Kríousa."

Her smile at him turned watery. For all that his attention had rested primarily on his men, and rightly so, clearly he'd spared more thought for her than she realized. He was reminding her of her father just now, caring and protective.

"I know it will be difficult here, especially at the first, but I do want to stay," she said.

"Kríousa, we will be four moons returning to Olympus, and it would be four moons yet again to return for you. Can you stand nearly a year with two norns among the three as your enemies?" His voice was urgent.

"I am scared, a little," she admitted. "And without Tynghed, I could not dare it. But . . . I believe she will be a stalwart champion. And . . . what I said is true. I need to learn the strength to insist upon what I know is right for me, even when others disagree. And I think I can learn this more readily among those who dislike me than with those who love me. Like my family." She wondered if he could understand that. It sounded rather mad, said aloud.

But Captain Bartholomai nodded and took his hands from her shoulders.

"Very well. But when Lord Hermes sends one of his winged couriers, do you return word if you have need of us. I will personally beg a boon of the pegasi that they pass beyond the boundaries of their holy precincts to bring us to you quickly!"

Nerine was shaken by his earnestness.

"I shall do so," she promised, "but I hope that I will be able, instead, to send you word that I am well."

"I shall hope for that as well, Kríousa." He kissed both her hands. "May all blessings be yours!"

After that, Captain Bartholomai was swift to rally his men, order the bestowment of Nerine's baggage, and depart. The ice on the Sea of Balder would not await his convenience, so it behooved him to move efficiently. Nerine wondered how he would find the uncanny doorway back through the lake realm. No such portal had been visible behind her when she'd emerged from it.

Nerine shook her head. That was foolish. Of course, the captain knew where to find it, else he would have asked directions of the norns before he departed.

Tynghed drew Nerine toward the cottage.

"Orroch and Eowys have returned to the weaving, and I must join them shortly. Shall you mind if we wait until the evening to settle you in your chamber and show you the amenities of our home?"

It felt odd to have Tynghed deferring to Nerine's wishes. "No, my lady."

"Ah!" smiling, Tynghed raised her finger. "Not my lady. Say it, Nerine."

Nerine found herself smiling back. "Tynghed, then."

"That is right." Tynghed nodded.

She paused in the front room of the cottage, bright with red-orange window quilts pushed aside and an oval rug of sea colors – turquoise and blues and greens. A round table and chairs occupied the left portion of the room before a hearth of banked coals and a corner cabinet. The right side of the room was bare, with another window on its right wall and a closed door on the back one.

"Then this is what we shall do. I shall throw the shuttle for Orroch as is my duty, and you shall stand by me and observe. And it may be that Orroch will request an action from you sometimes, in which case you will do it, if you know how, and you will ask instruction if you do not. How does that sit with you, Nerine?"

"Very well, my lady. I mean" – she saw Tynghed's raised finger in time – "Tynghed."

Tynghed smiled and opened the closed door.

～

The room beyond occupied the full width of the cottage, with three windows on each outer wall, but the space was much deeper than the front room. It needed to be to accommodate the mighty loom on which the norns wove the fate of the world and all within the world.

Shelves full of large spools of thread and yarn occupied the upper portion of the walls all round, while doored and drawered cabinets filled the lower walls. The left half of the room was bare, but the loom in the right half dominated the space.

Were Nerine to lie full length on the floor beside the loom – not that she would have dared; an ominous shadow lurked below it – it would take more than three of her to reach from the nearer end, where Orroch sat at her bench, to the farther end, where the warp threads came up over the raddle. Even the loom's width was slightly greater than her own measure from head to foot.

Not only was the loom broad and wide, but it was tall, the center section where the elegant Eowys perched reaching nearly to the rafters overhead.

Yet the size of the thing was not the whole of its presence. A menace clung to it, much like the menace that Nerine imagined must halo the kraken of the sea's deeps.

Old Orroch, seated at the front of the loom, and queenly Eowys aloft, took no notice of Tynghed's and Nerine's arrival. Orroch chanted a series of strange syllables while she passed small flat spools of thread through portions of the warp. Eowys leaned to the left to pull up a collection of heddles there, and then leaned to the right, for a different array of heddles.

Almost as soon as Tynghed walked to the right side of the loom, however, Nerine in her wake, Orroch snapped, "Throw the shuttle of metallic bronze through the shed. Now!"

Tynghed picked up the boat-shaped wooden piece with bronze yarn wound in its center and tossed it smoothly along the warp threads, the bronze unspooling behind it. Orroch stretched out her left arm to catch it on the other side, shoved one of several peddles at her feet, which moved the warp threads, and then tossed the shuttle back to Tynghed, who caught it and set it down.

Nerine watched with interest.

Calla had used a ground loom. The servants in Altairos' palace had preferred vertical looms. This loom of the fates, a grander instrument altogether, worked along principles similar to the others, but with many refinements.

Nerine itched to try it herself – if only she could weave ordinary cloth, rather than the fate of the world. That was not possible, so she watched in fascination. Gradually she became aware that Orroch's chant informed Eowys which heddles to pull, and that these two – the Weaver and the Patterner – did most of the work. She wondered why Tynghed – the Shuttle-catcher – was necessary.

Then she noticed the tension that rose in all three norns when the moment for Tynghed to play her role approached. Apparently the timing of the toss and its speed could be as important as where it passed across the warp threads.

An inch of the tapestry fabric, the tapestry of the world – which amazed Nerine when she thought on just what was happening before her – was created while she watched. She'd fallen into thinking this first stint as handmaiden would be easy, despite its poor beginning, when Orroch's voice cracked.

"Come hold this, girl! Quickly now!"

Orroch had threaded a length of yarn through a button, pushed the button through to the underside of the warp just left of center, and handed the yarn to Nerine, who came around to Orroch's left.

"Not there, fool girl! I canna catch the shuttle with ye on my left." Orroch plucked the yarn strands from Nerine's hand and then thrust them at her again once she stood on Orroch's right. Nerine had to lean rather close in order to reach, and she wondered if Orroch would yell at her for that, too.

But Tynghed sent the shuttle across – one of a rich brown – three times, and Orroch wielded the beater between each pass and return, then declared the button fast.

"Fetch me a needle, girl," she demanded.

Nerine looked agonizingly at Tynghed, who nodded toward a tray on a nearby cabinet. A pebble, a rook's feather, and two needles lay there. Nerine brought both needles to Orroch, who frowned, seized the larger one, and bade Nerine return the smaller to the tray.

She saw that Orroch threaded one strand of the button's yarn through the needle's eye, and worked the yarn through a handspan of the woven fabric before snipping off the excess length. Then she did the same for the second strand of the button yarn, all with amazing speed, before she continued her chanting for Eowys and passing the many different flat spools of thread before her through the warp as the design of the tapestry required.

The rest of the afternoon passed in exactly this fashion, peremptory commands from Orroch punctuating the longer stretches during which Nerine pinched herself, because it seemed so incredible that she stood watching fate being created right before her wondering eyes.

As the daylight failed, Orroch demanded candles, and Nerine followed Tynghed's direction about where to find them and where to set them. It was full dark outside when they stopped at last.

Orroch stood rubbing her back and surveying their work. Then she glared at Nerine, emitted a huff of displeasure, and stalked toward the front room.

Tynghed was setting her multiple shuttles in order on a low table beside the loom. She glanced up at Nerine and smiled. "You did well."

Eowys, climbing down from her bench high in the loom, smirked, but said nothing.

Nerine met her deriding gaze steadily. If this was the result of her performing well, she shuddered to think what it would be when she performed poorly. Then she chided her herself for expecting anything different. She'd known full well when she said those words – *I accept* – that it would be hard. But she could do it. She would do it. She *had* done it, today. And she would get better with practice.

⁓

Tynghed settled Nerine in her room after a modest supper eaten at the table in the front room.

The bedchambers opened off a corridor leading from the back of the weaving room. Nerine's was second on the right.

Tynghed entered it first, lighting candles in the wall sconces from the taper she carried on a chamberstick, and then turning to see Nerine's reaction.

The sleeping couch with its embroidered aqua quilt and rose silk curtain, the cushioned armchair and dressing stool – both upholstered in silver-shot turquoise – and the convenient pine cabinetry would all become familiar and loved in time, but on this first night in the norn's cottage, they seemed especially inviting, offering her the welcome that the norns themselves – at least two of the three – had not.

"It's lovely!" she exclaimed. "Thank you!" She pointed to the tall, fat cylinder of blue and aqua tile that stood in the far corner. "What is that? I've never seen its like."

"Come feel," said Tynghed, leading her around the bed and placing her hand against the tiles. They were very smooth and warm, almost too warm to the touch. Tynghed let Nerine's hand go and trilled a laugh. "It is a tile stove to keep your chamber warm through the winter. Winters are very cold here in the north. Orroch and Eowys think it too early in the year to light the stoves in their chambers, but you are from the south. I felt sure you would be more comfortable with a fire in your stove."

Warmth stirred in Nerine's heart to match the warmth in the room.

"You planned all of this, didn't you, Tynghed? Just for me."

Tynghed's musical laugh sounded again. "Did I guess right? I had to guess what you might like, because I did not know."

Nerine turned impulsively and hugged her. Only when Tynghed hugged her back did she wonder if she'd been too forward. During this one afternoon she'd spent with the norns, she'd discovered that Tynghed possessed a certain dignity beneath her friendliness. She could easily have repudiated Nerine's embrace. But she didn't, and when her arms loosened, the norn kissed Nerine's cheek.

"Ah, you do like it! I'm so glad!"

Nerine had envisioned herself unpacking the few necessities she needed to prepare for bed, and nothing more, before she lay down to sleep. It had been such a long day, starting at sea and passing through that dark and strange lake-realm, then running aground on the horrendous accusation by Orroch, followed by the long afternoon's work at the loom. She was exhausted.

But someone had been before her, and all her belongings were bestowed in the two wardrobes and the bank of drawers between them on the wall opposite the bed. Perhaps the red-cheeked girl who'd brought the supper?

She didn't know, but she was grateful to be able to merely clean her teeth, wash her face, undress, and turn back the covers of the bed without more ado. Deciding that her hair could wait until the morning, she checked the contents of the drawers under the shelf along the windowed wall. The top leftmost held jewelry, most of it chosen by her mother.

But tucked in one corner lay a tangle of gold links with three teardrop beryls. Ah! She'd almost forgotten King Zeron's gift, so long had it remained hidden in her luggage. Smiling ruefully, she fastened the bracelet around her wrist. Perhaps it might help her again. She could think of Altairos' pappa without pain now.

It seemed a good omen.

As she drifted off to sleep, she knew she'd made the right decision – both to come here in the first place, and to stay even after she discovered two of the norns disliked her.

～

28 ~ *Snow and Swan*

NERINE'S CERTAINTY was tested – and severely tested – over the next many moons.

Orroch always spoke to her unkindly, she was usually impatient, and grew blistering every time Nerine moved clumsily. Which was often, because Nerine never stood and merely watched after that first afternoon.

Every morning she followed the norns to the well beneath the World Tree to observe the visions therein. For nearly a moon, Tynghed helped her to interpret which materials were required and to find them. But Nerine did the setting out of the threads and trinkets, and Orroch always had some fault to find with how Nerine had arrayed them.

When Nerine started choosing the thread colors and textures and the nature of the trinkets by herself, Orroch grew even more scathing. Yet, Orroch didn't require Nerine to change her choices. That seemed odd, until she asked Tynghed about it one evening by the hearth in the front room, after the other two norns had retired to their chambers.

The glow from the coals was softly orange.

"It's because you're choosing them rightly, of course," Tynghed answered.

"Then why...?" If Nerine were choosing rightly, shouldn't Orroch be satisfied?

Tynghed bit her lip. "Cinnisuent was Patterner before Eowys, and she was Orroch's especial choice." Tynghed sighed. "Orroch is angry, because she wants Cinnisuent to yet be her Patterner, Eowys to be her Shuttle-catcher, and me to be their handmaiden. It would not matter who had the post of handmaiden, Nerine. Orroch would still be angry."

That made Nerine angry. She could understand that her mistakes might stir Orroch to ire. Nerine's mistakes could mean that the Weaver wove the wrong fate into the tapestry of the world. It was a heavy responsibility. But that Orroch chose to simply take out her ill temper on Nerine for no good reason? *That* was unreasonable!

She said as much to Tynghed. For she'd made good on her promise to herself to learn to confide in one of the norns. And Tynghed was the only possibility – that much was clear.

But Tynghed – to Nerine's surprise – upheld Orroch.

"Cinnisuent left *because* of Orroch," said Tynghed seriously. "She felt that Orroch interpreted the visions in the well of destiny to liberally, too freely. That she found happy outcomes where there should be none."

Nerine stared at Tynghed. She couldn't imagine nasty-tempered Orroch choosing anything liberally.

Tynghed continued. "They'd been the best of friends since before I came here. I don't know how long. Perhaps a hundred years. Perhaps longer."

Nerine jumped just the tiniest bit where she sat on the stones before the hearth. She'd known the norns were *numeni* of time, just as she herself was a *numen* of the sea, but she'd not really thought it through. How old *was* Orroch? To look so old despite her immortality? A thousand years? More?

A coal fell in the hearth. Tynghed lifted the poker from where it was propped against the surrounding stonework and pushed the frontmost log back a little.

"As handmaiden and then as Shuttle-catcher, Cinnisuent never questioned Orroch. That's what Eowys tells me. But when Cinnisuent made Patterner, it changed her sensitivity to all patterns, and she could see where Orroch deviated from the more strict interpretation. They argued about it for all the years that I was handmaiden." Tynghed sighed again.

"And yet, Orroch still loved her friend. I don't think she saw how bitter Cinnisuent had grown, nor how deep their division was."

Another coal fell in the hearth, but the poker lay loosely in Tynghed's hand.

The warmth lapped Nerine round.

"The day Cinnisuent understood she would never change Orroch's mind, she left." Tynghed turned to look earnestly at Nerine. "Can you understand how that cut her to the quick? Please be patient with her, Nerine. She is utterly *un*reasonable to you, but there *is* reason behind her distress."

Then it was Nerine's turn to sigh. Tynghed had pleaded Orroch's plight well. But Tynghed didn't have to bear the brunt of Orroch's displeasure, and Tynghed wasn't afraid of Orroch. Nerine was.

The knowledge of what had gone before removed Nerine's puzzlement, but it couldn't remove the sting from Orroch's constant criticism. Nerine began to understand better why she'd been so secretive around Mother and Father.

Their disapproval – should they have felt any – would have been far milder than Orroch's. But it would have hurt even more, because Nerine relied on their love and approval. Perhaps bearing up beneath Orroch's lash would be good for her. Nerine touched King Zeron's bracelet, now always around her wrist. She could grow strong here – in exactly the one way she needed to.

That resolution did more for her patience than Tynghed's pleading.

It also helped Nerine to bear with Eowys.

For Eowys had her own ways of making Nerine feel inadequate.

In the mornings, when Nerine emerged from her chamber in a vibrant turquoise gown or a vivid chartreuse one, Eowys reached out to take the bright silk between her fingers, held it against her own linen sleeve of matte violet or soft periwinkle, and sniffed.

When Nerine burnt her lip on the unaccustomed hot oatmeal at breakfast, Eowys' lips turned down in a derisive sneer.

And every time Orroch reprimanded Nerine for a fault, Nerine noticed Eowys' ironic gaze upon her, approving Orroch's acrimony and condemning Nerine's inability to please.

Eowys' voice remained always cool and smooth, but her facial expressions conveyed her disapproval as thoroughly as did Orroch's more explicit complaints and harsh tones.

Nerine sometimes wondered that she herself was not miserable, but she wasn't.

The visions in the Well of Destiny were wondrous; the working of the great loom, fascinating; and Tynghed's warm approval dominated Nerine's awareness. As the autumn leaves fell from the aspen trees and the hawthorne bushes, Orroch's grumbles and Eowys' glares became an unpleasant background that Nerine largely ignored.

I don't need to be approved of, she realized. And the realization gave her yet more strength to enjoy her work – which she did – and to give no weight to the negative judgments of people who disliked her – in this case, two exceedingly powerful norns.

She felt she'd accomplished something.

And she had. But she also grew aware that her accomplishment was a private one. Her inner resistance to Orroch and Eowys was perhaps the necessary foundation for the moral strength she craved, but she would need more than that. One day Orroch would command her to replace a right thread with a wrong one.

What would Nerine do then? Would she obey Orroch? Or would she knuckle under?

Nerine was not sure she would have the strength to stand up for what she knew to be right, and she needed to be sure.

～

The first snow was a miracle of beauty to Nerine's eyes.

She'd never seen frozen water shaped as small bits of lace falling out of the sky to turn the ground white and load the spruces with white cloaks.

Tynghed took her outside at the noontide to play. They scooped handfuls of the snow, packed them into balls, and tossed them at one another, laughing.

Nerine tasted a mouthful: pure and cold and fresh, and melting on her tongue to taste like nothing, and – yet – tasting like a rainswept sky or a waterfall's spray. Glorious. Magical.

Tynghed showed Nerine how to slide down the slope of the adjacent meadow on a plain bronze shield rooted out of the garrett under the thatched roof. One sat cross-legged in the hollow of the shield, rushing faster and faster down the hill until – crash! – one ran against the bushes at the bottom to be tipped out into a snowdrift.

Nerine learned how to lie down in the deepening snow of the yard and sweep her arms to make pegasus wings. It was good she'd put on her traveling plaids – trews and tunic and cape – plus the sheepskin cloak. They kept her warm.

Even so, she was soaking wet by the time they came in to Eowys' frowns and Orroch's complaints that they'd be weaving until midnight.

Nerine noted that Eowys managed to frown at Tynghed with a laugh in her eyes, while changing that laugh to a dagger glare when her eyes moved to Nerine. Even Orroch's face, glowering while she castigated Nerine, softened when she switched to Tynghed. Of course.

Nerine hurried to change into dry clothes, but forgot the snow caught in her tied up hair. All through the darkening afternoon, it melted and dripped down her neck to soak the back of her silk gown.

The norns kept their cottage none too warm, and Nerine shivered while fetching a sewing needle and straight pins or holding a bell tether for Orroch to secure it to the warp and the weft threads. Once she dripped on the tapestry itself.

"Fool girl!" yelled Orroch, interposing her cupped hand before the drop could land.

They didn't work at the loom until midnight, as Orroch had dourly predicted, but they had to weave after supper for several hours, by which time Nerine's teeth were chattering, except when interrupted by yawns.

Tynghed bade her stoke the tile stove in her room high and put an extra quilt on her bed, but Nerine was too tired by the time she'd untied her hair to rid it of the last snowflakes. She didn't bother to brush it, merely throwing on a nightgown and diving between the sheets.

In the morning, she awoke hot and sweating, despite the chill in her room, and her throat felt scorched and sore. She wandered past the loom to the front room in her nightdress, hoping that Linnea had brought the breakfast tea early, so that she could soothe her poor throat before she readied herself for the day.

She was lucky. There was the teapot with steam curling out its spout.

Nerine poured herself a mug, ladling a generous dollop of honey into it. Honey would help, she felt sure.

When she took her first sip, the hot fluid was wonderful, but it hurt to swallow. And then she was coughing and coughing and couldn't seem to stop. Her tea mug fell from her hands, shattering on the hearth stones where she stood, hunched at the pain shooting through her chest.

Someone's gentle hands – Tynghed's – steadied Nerine's shoulders.

"Don't move," murmured Tynghed's kind voice. "You'll cut yourself." Nerine's feet were bare.

The scrape of wood on wood – chair legs on floorboards – came.

Then – "Sit," said Tynghed.

One of the spindle-backed chairs was there to catch Nerine as her legs abruptly gave way.

Nerine felt dizzy. She was vaguely aware of Tynghed mopping the spilled tea and sweeping up the broken crockery, Tynghed explaining to

Orroch and Eowys, and then more hands urging Nerine to rise and guiding her back to her bed.

After that, everything became a blur of sweating heat alternating with shuddering chill, bitterly vile liquids tipped into Nerine's mouth, wracking pain in her chest, and worried voices over her.

Orroch's irritable tones were inevitably present with the bitter draughts, Eowys' smooth ones with the soothing lavender water that cooled Nerine's brow when she sweated, and Tynghed's kind voice when Nerine sobbed in the increasing pain.

One night she dreamed. Or maybe it was not night. Nerine could no longer tell the difference between day and night.

Dreaming, she was a bird with white wings, soaring through the darkness and growing weary. If only she could alight somewhere. If only the sun would rise. If only she might rest in the dawn's healing rays.

But there was no rest, no light, no sun.

Her wings grew wearier, sluggish.

She caught a gleam of dark water below her. Ah! Now she would rest. The water would receive her, floating her buoyant body on its welcome surface, soothing away all her cares.

She angled down and down.

Just before she touched it, before her webbed feet felt its grateful caress, a gust of wind buffeted her, batting her upward, back into the dragging darkness.

A slap smacked her cheek, and Nerine opened her eyes – no longer a swan – to see Orroch hovering over her.

"Nid yw cwsg marwolaeth yn perthyn i chi. Byddwch yn effro! Wyf yn ei orchymyn i chi fyw!" Orroch exhorted.

Did Orroch sound worried? How odd. Surely Orroch would prefer Nerine to die of this awfulness, thus ridding Orroch of her annoying presence.

~

When next she slept, Nerine did not dream.

And when she awoke, she felt much better. *Much* better. No suffocating heat oppressed her. No icy shivers wracked her. She could breathe without pain. Her throat didn't hurt. And she could see daylight glowing through the horn panes of her bedchamber windows.

Once she was up and about again – the first two days, she was too weak to stand – Nerine asked Tynghed how the norns had managed to both nurse Nerine and get their work done. She knew absolutely that they would never neglect their weaving. The fate of the world depended on it.

Tynghed added a log to the hearth in the front room, drew up two of the spindle-backed chairs before the leaping fire, and pressed Nerine into one before she answered.

"Orroch and Eowys managed without me whenever it was possible," Tynghed said.

"But the full shuttle casts?" Nerine heard incredulity in her voice. "Orroch is the shortest of the three of you! Her arms simply don't reach that far."

"There's an alternate stitch for that," explained Tynghed. "Eowys plucks up a handspan of heddles in sequence, all the way across the warp, while Orroch passes the necessary thread through each bunch. And then they go back the other way, with the opposing heddles pulled."

"But the timing," protested Nerine.

"Yes, we had to make sure I was present for the shuttle casts when the timing required precision. And those events in history when the alternate stitch wasn't appropriate."

Nerine was still not satisfied. She patted her hair, now much shorter and pinned, not tied, to her head. It had grown too tangled during her long illness, and the norns had cut it to jaw length. The pins kept it out of her face as she reclaimed her duties.

"Eowys washed my face with lavender water. And Orroch – Orroch dosed me with horrid medicines." She couldn't bear to give voice to her other suspicions of Orroch.

Tynghed laughed. Nerine loved the sound of Tynghed's laughter, merry and bell-like.

"I took Eowys' place a few times," said Tynghed.

"You did?" Nerine couldn't imagine Tynghed as the Patterner.

Tynghed nodded. "You will see me as Patterner and Eowys as Weaver when the pattern is very easy. And you will cast the shuttle. We must learn, you know. Orroch will not be the Weaver forever."

Nerine's eyes felt so round, she wondered if they might fall from her eye sockets. Orroch seemed as old and unmoving as a mountain. She couldn't imagine Orroch ever deciding to depart her home, nor being subject to whatever ending a *numen* of time eventually came to. Did they circulate as patterns of shadow and light on the currents of time, just as sea *numeni* came to circulate within the currents of water?

"But when Orroch tended me?" probed Nerine.

"Then, indeed, the loom came to a halt, and we wove late into the night. Once, we wove all the way through to the dawning, stopping only to view the Well of Destiny, and then returning to weave again."

"Does not Orroch hate me? Why would she take so much trouble for my cure?"

Tynghed was silent for an interval. The firelight played on her pensive face. Nerine could hear Eowys putting fresh candles in the sconces of the weaving room. That was Nerine's task, but the norns were yet coddling her.

Orroch's cracked voice called something from the snowy dark outside. The hinges of a window casement creaked from the weaving room – Eowys must have opened one – and Eowys' cool voice answered, "Just an armspan."

Orroch's scratchy tones drifted back, "Aye, it's glad I be for wee favors. The snow be deep and that split holly a great scunner."

The hinges of the casement sounded again, Eowys closing it.

Tynghed sighed and answered Nerine's question with another. "Do you really believe that?"

"That she hates me?" Nerine gritted her teeth together.

Tynghed's mild face grew stern. "Well?"

Then it was Nerine's turn to sigh. "I suppose not, but it often feels like it."

"Be sure she does not," assured Tynghed. "You should know better."

"Should I?"

Tynghed just looked sad.

As the winter deepened, the tops of the spruce trees drooped in curling arches, so heavy was the snow frozen to their needles, and Linnea arrived each morning on a path delved deep between cliffs of packed snow towering to each side of her.

Tynghed commissioned Briallyn – another of the servants living near who provided various necessities for the norns – to sew woolen gowns with linen shifts beneath for Nerine. Nerine's bedchamber was warm enough (when she remembered to keep the tile stove stoked high), but the norns preferred cooler air and kept the rest of the cottage cold. Nerine was a good deal more comfortable in the woolen gowns, both because they were warmer and because the colors were softer than the bright silks of the trousseau sewn by the nymphs of Olympus. But she tried going barefooted indoors, and eventually outdoors, too, when the snow began to melt.

"The truth of the bare earth comes up through thy heels," declared Orroch, "when there's nae boot leather nor sandal sole tae interfere."

And Nerine found this to be so. The visions in the Well of Destiny shone clearer when the flesh of her feet pressed cold soil, and her intuition for the correct color and texture of thread proved stronger.

Her fear of Orroch transmuted from a personal anxiety to more diffuse horror. She'd connected her dream of flying as a swan to the lake-realm she'd traversed with the *peltastés*. A living mortal or immortal might walk the shores of that lake – or even pass through its whirlpool – without harm.

But to fly there as a bird, as a swan, the symbol of one's soul? Ah, then one skirted death. And Orroch presided over that realm – an anteroom to the kingdom of Lord Hades, Nerine felt sure.

She'd asked Orroch about it once, when Orroch dosed Nerine during her days of convalescence.

"Was I dying, when I dreamed I was a swan?"

Orroch stared at her, then let her eyelids blink slowly closed and open.

"Had the whirlpool sucked me down as a bird . . . ?"

Orroch's eyes shone very dark. Nerine thought she saw the lake and the white birds reflected in them.

"This mystery be not for ye," the norn stated. And that was the end of it. Nerine was still too weak to pursue it. When she was stronger, she was too wise to ask more. But she shivered whenever she remembered that she occupied the same room with Lord Hades' gatekeeper – gatekeeper to the land of the dead.

~

29 ~ The Gordian Knot

EARLY SPRING IN SCANDIA was a muck of sucking black mud, freezing rain, and gray skies. But then the days lengthened, and Nerine felt the magic in the land, as the aspens and hawthorne and birches put out new leaves of a green so bright it seemed flamelike against the dark pines and hollies. The meadow grasses flushed a green equally vivid, dotted over with flowers in every shade of the rainbow.

The chorus of birdsong at dawn reminded Nerine of the muses on Mount Helicon, singing in celebration of beauty and light and wonder.

Barefootedness in the spring felt utterly right, just as bare skin felt natural and right in the waters of the Middle Sea.

Tynghed requested linen gowns from Briallyn, so that when Nerine left off her woolen ones due to the increasing warmth, she need not return to wearing the Olympian silk that felt so out of place in the practical north.

Nerine's sight for the visions in the Well of Destiny grew keen. She often felt the hill around the enchanted spring – green and beflowered in the rising sun – fade before the force of the images of fate. Even the World Tree, potent and dominating, became – briefly – a mere anchor to the well's revelations. And Nerine's intuition for the materials to set out for the day's weaving felt unshakeable.

When Orroch grumbled that the red silk wasn't bright enough or the garnet-headed pin was too sharp, Nerine stared at the Weaver with her own brand of scorn. And when Eowys signified her support of Orroch with a sniff or an arctic glare, Nerine just shook her head in bemusement. Orroch's criticism and Eowys' contempt simply felt irrelevant. Their negative judgments might brush against Nerine's certainty, but they could not induce doubt.

Nerine found herself almost gleeful in the growth of her inner strength. So *this* was what it felt like to be unbothered by the dissenting opinions of others. It was marvelous. Now, if only she could develop some personal strength similar to her professional strength.

But her professional strength stood them all in good stead, one afternoon in the late spring.

The norns had flung back the casements of all six windows in the weaving room. The sun shone through those on the west, while the breeze brought the vanilla scent of the rosebay through the eastern windows nearest the loom.

The rhythm of the weaving had been easy, almost relaxed throughout the day. Orroch had bade Tynghed and Nerine depart for a time in the morning, and they'd repaired to the sloping eastern meadow to pick flowers and make them up into bouquets. When they returned to the loom, Tynghed sent the shuttle across the warp only twice, while Nerine fetched a chilled mint infusion to quench the thirst that the day's warmth induced in all of them.

As she perched on a stool near Tynghed, Nerine almost felt that she'd returned to her first afternoon in the cottage, when she'd merely observed. Except the spring day was delightful, and her knowledge so much more extensive.

"Trim quean burr," sang Orroch in her instructional chant to Eowys, who plucked up the heddles as instructed. Orroch passed a sand yellow strand of linen through and called again, "Neak fello thirk."

Nerine watched Eowys lean forward to pull the configuration of heddles that went with that call, and every hair on the back of her neck rose. She felt as though she floated in the lagoon of home while lightning struck the sea beyond the reef face. A strange needle-like chill ran all over her skin.

She leapt to her feet and cried out, "No, no, no! Ah, blessings, no! Do not!"

Eowys froze, staring at Nerine in surprise.

"It's not right!" exclaimed Nerine.

Orroch snorted. "Nonsense, girl! What do you know of it. *Neak fello thirk,* Patterner."

But Eowys did not move. "I should like to know what configuration Nerine believes is correct," she said.

Orroch growled softly in the back of her throat.

Nerine didn't need to touch the bracelet on her wrist. Not this time. She said, "I do not know the names."

Eowys' face was very still. "Show me," she said.

Nerine glanced at Orroch. Orroch glared back, but made no motion forbidding Nerine to approach the loom more closely.

Nerine walked to the loom's side at the center, the safest part – away from the mystical abysses that plagued the fore and aft – where the upright posts supported the superstructure of Eowys' seat and the yoke for the heddles.

Eowys still held the heddles for *neak fello thirk*. Nerine pointed to one of them. "Not this one, but this" – she pointed to one two over – "and not this one either, but that one" – more pointing to show exactly which heddles were the *right* heddles.

"Ah, yes, I see!" Eowys' voice had never before sounded so joyful, so open. Nerine was amazed. This was an entirely different side of the queenly norn.

Eowys' tone grew decisive. "Orroch, she's correct." Her fingers changed their grip to drop two heddles from the group and pick up two others.

Orroch stared at the change in the shed. "A nighean an diabhoil!" she exclaimed. *You daughter of a devil!* Then, "*Sirken nyl trask,*" a new call to match the heddles changed by Nerine's perception.

And they wove onward.

Nerine scarcely paid attention. *Eowys* had said *Nerine* was right. Eowys! It was unbelievable. And Orroch had admitted it to be so. *Orroch!* That was beyond unbelievable. More like impossible. But it had happened.

Nerine felt like she had passed over the brink of a colossal waterfall and survived the plunge into a rock-girdled pool below, swimming away freely in the gentle river beyond the rapid-tossed catch basin. The sunlight felt warmer, gentler. The breeze smelled sweeter. The tapestry on the loom looked more beautiful. And the norns at their rite were numinous.

The world wrapping Nerine round felt sacred.

That evening, when the light shone deep and golden and the shadows stretched long – the day's weaving complete – Nerine walked out onto the turf before the cottage.

A moment later, Eowys appeared on the porch with two bizarre contraptions under her arm and a different one held in her hand. Each of the paired devices was an oval wooden frame, with a net stretched tightly across it, and a short handle attached at the bottom of the oval. The other was a round cork, a little larger than the ball of Nerine's thumb, with a cone of feathers emerging from one side.

Eowys strode toward her and asked, "Should you like to play at Battledore and Shuttlecock? It's a fun game after a strenuous day."

Nerine studied her. Was Eowys serious? She looked just as stately as ever, but her eyes held a friendly light in them that Nerine had never seen before. Apparently Eowys wished to give up her vendetta. Would Nerine meet her halfway?

It wasn't really even a question. Nerine could discover no grudge within herself. Was that what inner certainty granted one? She wanted it even more.

"I should like that very much," Nerine answered.

It turned out that the goal of Battledore and Shuttlecock was to keep the cork in the air, no matter how difficult a trajectory the other player gave it. Nerine and Eowys dashed about the turf clearing, panting, yelling, and even giggling, rackets swishing and shuttlecock bounding.

When Nerine heard Eowys giggling, she almost missed the cork the next time it came to her. Queenly Eowys *giggling*? She would never have guessed that the Patterner knew how to have fun.

They played the game on other spring evenings, and sometimes Tynghed joined them. Evidently it was a game in which more than two could participate. Although it was easier with three than with two. Sometimes Orroch sat on the porch step and watched through narrowed eyes, but she never took a racket herself.

After that first game, on the night following Orroch's mistake, their supper of smoked herring, pea soup, and pancakes with lingonberry preserves came very late. Orroch herself said very little, but Tynghed and Eowys talked the mistake over thoroughly.

The dusk crept into the room through the open windows, where only the candles on the round table held the dark at bay. The day had been too warm to require a fire on the hearth. In the dim glow, Tynghed took a flask of mead from the corner cupboard and poured modest splashes into the bottom of their tea mugs.

Nerine tasted hers. The brew prickled on her tongue, piercing in flavor, yet sweet.

Eowys sipped delicately, looking particularly somber after her lightheartedness with her battledore. "Do you realize that Alexander's success in Gordium would have been affected?" she said.

"Would he have failed to solve the puzzle of the famous Knot?" asked Tynghed. "The one that foretells his kingship over Asia?"

"Of course we norns know that he is destined to reach the river Indus in the lands of the far Astakenoi, but had he failed to untie the Gordian Knot, his fate would be far different," answered Eowys.

Orroch's eyes glittered in the candlelight.

"Then we owe Nerine our very great thanks," exclaimed Tynghed.

"Indeed we do," agreed Eowys. Her calm gaze caught Nerine's. "Will you accept of my profound gratitude, Kríousa Pelagieus? A great wrong would have been done, had you not been so vigilant. Vigilant and . . . honorable and brave." She lifted her tea mug to Nerine.

Nerine pondered her answer in the warm silence of the night. She wanted to do more than accept Eowys' gratitude. What did she want? To intimate her willingness for true cordiality to exist between them. Could she find the words that would do so?

"I am happy to have earned your trust," she said after some moments. Would that be enough?

Eowys nodded and said, "You are one of us now."

"Indeed," agreed Tynghed.

And then Orroch herself lifted her mead and tilted the mug to spill a tiny splash of it on the floor. "On Woden's breast let it be felt."

As spring turned to summer, Orroch's crotchety manner changed not one bit. But Eowys' new respect for Nerine did not dissipate. Eowys did not unbend so far as silliness – the way she did when playing at Battledore and Shuttlecock; she remained cool and reserved. But friendliness underlay all her words and glances, and she endorsed Orroch's continuing criticisms no longer.

Eowys believed in Nerine's worth.

When Lord Hermes' herald arrived in early summer, Nerine was able to send a sincere message to Captain Bartholomai of the Poniró Peltastés that she was happy and content. Tynghed's warmth and kindness joined by Eowys' friendly support made the cottage of the norns feel like home – a home where Nerine not only belonged, but where her work had a larger purpose. Orroch's grumbles could not tarnish that.

Nerine also sent verbal messages to both her sisters on the Hellene peninsula and a written letter on the copper sheets of the sea for her parents and Tyr. Knowing that Eilidh and Agnippe had truly found their vocations had meant a lot to Nerine. She could only assume that Mother and Father would wish to know that Nerine had also. She wanted them to share her happiness.

She'd not seen the herald arrive, but she watched him depart. His bronze helm shone gold in the summer sun, and his short, white tunic – in the traditional draping folds of Olympus – did not hide his sandals as a longer tunic would have.

The sandals looked normal enough as he stood on the ground, although their straps and the edges of their soles gleamed with gold leaf. But when the herald leapt into the air, golden wings unfurled – one from the outer portion of each sandal and large as the wings of a pegasus. The herald pressed his legs together, and the wings hurled him high.

He was out of sight in mere moments.

The norns went back inside. No doubt the winged heralds were an ordinary sight to them. But the heralds of the sea – Poseidon's messengers – were altogether different, swimmers, not flyers. Nerine lingered in the clearing, a little stunned. No wonder Lord Hermes gave the most urgent messages to his winged couriers.

This one would likely be back on the slopes of Mount Olympus by sundown.

She shook her head in bemusement.

～

Later in the summer, Nerine went under the loom for the first time.

When she and the norns contemplated the Well of Destiny at the dawning of a clear day – the sky pale gold through the rustling leaves of the World Tree – they saw that Kleopátra, the Regent of Epirus, would receive a shipment of grain from Cyrene to relieve famine, passing along the excess to Corinth, where a shortage also threatened.

Nerine knew immediately that a child's bracelet of small gold beads, one of the trinkets stored in a fragrant cedar box in the weaving room, would be required.

The beads would represent the precious grain, while the circular shape of the bracelet would symbolize an aura of protection around the transaction and Kleopátra.

When Orroch seated herself before the great loom, her lips crimped at the sight of the bracelet on her tray of weaving supplies, but she said nothing. Only later did Nerine realize that Orroch was worried. At the time, it seemed merely more of Orroch's usual criticism, however uncharacteristically silent.

The weaving through the morning was easy and the norns, relaxed. Orroch even sent Tynghed and Nerine outside for a time to enjoy the sunlight on their bare arms and faces.

When they came indoors after the noontide, Orroch stopped her weaving altogether to instruct Nerine.

"What see ye when ye observe the fall of the world tapestry past my knee?" she asked.

Nerine looked once more. She'd already looked many times, but never been able to decide exactly what she was perceiving.

"I see a darkness, and I cannot decide whether it is a shadow from which all light is forbidden, or a great chasm into which the tapestry disappears. But it has a presence which" – she hated to admit this – "which terrifies me."

"Very good, child."

How strange to hear approval on Orroch's voice. Nerine studied the face of the eldest norn. Yes, Orroch really meant it. Very strange, indeed.

Orroch nodded. "It is the Abyss of Time, reaching into the past, all the way back to the very beginning, whatever that beginning may be." Orroch turned a little on her bench to grasp Nerine's wrist. "The abyss is dangerous, child. Your terror is apt."

More approval from Orroch. Why?

Orroch gathered the circlet of beads from her tray. "This bracelet must be sewn into the tapestry surrounding my rendition of Epirus."

Nerine could see it in the mirror that rested at an angle below the warp: a lovely shrine surrounded by an oak grove – the Oracle of Dodona.

"Ye shall hold the beads in place, Nerine, whilst I sew, but ye must creep beneath the warp threads to do so."

Nerine caught her breath, feeling the beat of her heart speed up. To hold the bracelet as Orroch described, Nerine would have to crouch very near to where the tapestry fell into the abyss.

"Will I fall?" she asked, almost involuntarily.

"Ye could, but ye must not," answered Orroch.

"I'll take great care," said Nerine.

"Ye must. But listen to me." Orroch waited until Nerine was looking at *her*, not the shadowy threat of the abyss. "The abyss is known to move. Ye must never place thy hand on the floor, nor thy knee, nor thy haunch without testing the surety of the boards before ye let them take thy weight. Do ye understand?"

"Like this," said Nerine, demonstrating, touching the floor ahead of her with her bare toes and then slowly transferring her weight to that foot.

"Exactly like that," agreed Orroch. "But every time. Ye know the boards be present as ye walk across the floors of the cottage. Under the loom, the floor that was strong but a moment before may be absent a moment later. Ye must test each time ye move."

Nerine nodded. "I understand, Orroch."

"Will the beads fit about thy wrist?"

They would not. Nerine's wrist was slender, but not slender enough.

Orroch insisted Nerine tie a pocket around her waist to hold the bracelet. "Ye must have both hands free whilst ye move under the loom."

This was done, and Orroch led Nerine to the side of the loom, her bony fingers once more clutching Nerine's wrist.

"Ye go under here, where it be safe. Then ye creep forward toward danger, one limb at a time."

Nerine started to bend. Orroch stopped her. "One hand and then one hand. And then one foot. Say it, Nerine!" Orroch's voice was less scratchy than usual, sterner.

"I will place one hand at a time or place one foot at a time. I will never move quickly or without thought." She understood the danger Orroch was attempting to convey.

"Now ye may bend," Orroch told her.

Nerine crouched down, peering under the loom. She was nearly at the heddles, and the strands of the warp made a flat roof overhead. Beneath, the floor stretched forward to an array of shafts controlled by Orroch's peddles. And to the abyss, an indefinite blur of darkness with confused edges.

Nerine crept beneath the warp threads, still crouching, shuffling her feet forward while helping her balance with her hands. Once she was all the way under, she shifted to her hands and knees.

She glanced aside to see Orroch's bright eyes watching her.

Nerine stretched her right hand forward, touching the pine floor with her fingertips, then slowly transferring her weight to her palm.

"That is right," said Orroch.

It still felt entirely unfamiliar to hear Orroch saying that Nerine had done *anything* right.

Nerine moved her left hand even with her right, again touching down delicately with her fingertips and transferring her weight slowly.

"Now thy legs," instructed Orroch.

Nerine moved her right leg, touching down with her toes, resisting the temptation to move a hand forward, then letting her knee come to rest. She was nearly crouching again, rather than resting horizontal.

"The other leg," Orroch ordered sharply.

When Nerine moved her left leg, she really was crouching.

"And now a hand again," commanded Orroch.

It was an agonizingly slow way to proceed, but Nerine had no desire to rush. Rushing might pitch her forward over that uncertain brink. Even as she drew closer to it, its edges did not resolve. She had the sense that, even though she could feel solid floor beneath her, she might fall.

When she was very close to the abyss, so close that the pounding of her heart thudded in her ears, Orroch told her to allow her left haunch to touch down. She did, and was very relieved to feel a solid floorboard under it and under the side of her bent leg.

"Are ye steady, Nerine?" asked Orroch. "Are ye balanced?"

"Yes," answered Nerine.

"Then take the beads from thy pocket, and hold them up to encircle Dodona within Epirus."

The instant Nerine did so, she could tell that her arms and shoulders were likely to get very tired. Holding something overhead was awkward.

Orroch slipped to her bench so fast, she almost scampered. And then her needle was dipping with equal swiftness, down between two beads, around the strand connecting the beads, and back up through the tapestry. Then down to catch the next chink between beads, and the next.

Nerine continued to be amazed at Orroch's speed with a needle.

Maybe Nerine's arms and shoulders would not grow tired after all. Orroch was half way round the bracelet already.

Except for puffs of breath coming from Orroch, the weaving room was utterly silent. Eowys sat without moving in her eyrie, tense. Tynghed sat without moving on her stool, equally tense. Nerine sat on one haunch beneath the warp and between two peddle shafts, her arms upraised and trembling just slightly. But her hands were steady, to aid Orroch in her task.

In and out the needle dipped.

The instant Orroch tied her knot, the floor . . . jinked.

Nerine's reflex was instantaneous. Her hands flew back from the finished portion of the tapestry to where the warp threads stretched free of the weft, and her fingers clutched even as her legs fell out from under her to hang in the abyss.

Tynghed shrieked. "Nerine!"

Nerine dangled, panting.

"Reach back with thy foot," came Orroch's calm voice.

Nerine tried. "I can't feel anything," she gasped.

"Try again."

Nerine tried. This time she felt floorboards and used her foot to haul herself backward onto that haven of floor. But she didn't let go with her hands. She couldn't without tumbling forward into the abyss that opened below her shoulders.

She hauled her other foot up and found solidity for it as well.

Then she worked her hands backward along the warp threads, until she crouched upright on her two feet.

Still she did not let go with her hands, working herself backward with her feet and then her hands, until she'd reached the heddles.

The abyss seemed very far away, but still she was scared to let go, and moved sideways with care. First feet, then hands on the warp threads, until she emerged altogether from the loom.

Tynghed was there, waiting. Nerine fell into her arms and burst into tears as the norn's embrace tightened.

She didn't know how long she cried. Not long, she suspected, but it was very intense. When she stopped, Tynghed tucked a handkerchief into Nerine's hands, and Nerine dried her eyes and cheeks.

"Are you alright?" asked Tynghed gently, looking very, very anxious.

"Yes," breathed Nerine.

"I do be so sorry, child," came Orroch's scratchy voice. "The abyss be always a danger, but had I known it would jump thy first time, I would I had sent Tynghed."

Tynghed's arms tightened around Nerine again. "And I would have gone. Gladly."

Eowys climbed down from her perch to add her arms to the embrace. "You were heroic, Nerine. You deserve a laurel wreath of the Olympiad. The bay laurel grows not in Scandia, but I shall make you one of hawthorn."

And she did, when they had finished the day's weaving.

For the weaving must be done, regardless of any crisis that might occur during the work.

As it chanced that day, the weaving was complete early, and Eowys sallied forth in the late afternoon to clip a very pliant branch of hawthorn, strip it of its sharp spines, and bend it to form a leafy wreath.

She set it on Nerine's head with great ceremony and insisted that she wear it all through supper and onward, until it was time for sleep.

Nerine felt honored. And grateful that the norns applauded her feat appropriately. She'd never been so terrified in her life.

It was not the last time that Nerine ventured beneath the great loom that summer, nor was it the only time the abyss moved. But it was the only time it moved so precipitously and dangerously.

Nerine understood deep in her bones that all Orroch's caution was justified. Not that she had doubted her before. The abyss *felt* perilous. Always.

Orroch herself seemed permanently changed by Nerine's misadventure. The approval and praise she'd spoken were not repeated, but neither was her previously unending criticism. Indeed, her criticism came entirely to an end, for Nerine could sense it in neither Orroch's manner nor her expression. Apparently Orroch no longer disapproved of Nerine.

Nerine almost missed the scathing remarks. Not only had they grown familiar, but they'd also masked something of Orroch's essence that Nerine found more troubling than her former angry contempt.

The same sense of terrible power and peril that leaked from the abyss hung around Orroch like a mantle: treacherous and deadly.

～

30 ~ Secrets Release

THE SUMMER IN SCANDIA was lovely, green and fresh compared to the hot months of the Middle Sea. And the days were so long, with the sun up early and down late, that there was plenty of time to wander in the afternoons and long, light evenings.

Tynghed took Nerine to visit with Briallyn the seamstress, Gwenedd the weaverwoman, and others who lived nearby. Himinlaeva the cook invited Nerine to learn how that specialty, pressed *sylta*, was made. Nerine had so much fun working alongside the serving maid, Linnea, that she was invited to participate in the concoction of several more delicacies.

When the leaves began to turn at summer's end, she was shocked to realize that she'd been living in the norn's cottage, fulfilling her duties as their handmaiden, for nearly twelve moons.

Lord Hermes' herald descended out of the blue sky in autumn on the exact day Nerine had arrived a year before.

He brought news of long-missing Xianthe.

Xianthe was well – very well – and not living in Lord Poseidon's harem after all. Had never even swum within its portals.

The blond girl in the harem – supposed by them all to be Xianthe – really *had* been the Duke of Liguria's niece. And it was in the Ligurian Sea that Xianthe had found an old crone who knew the way to the undersea sanctuary of Tethys herself, great mother of the oceans and all the water of the world.

Xianthe had persuaded one of the Duke's dolphins to tow her out through the Pillars of Herakles and into the far north of the World Ocean, where she was welcomed by the three thousand oceanids who were Tethys' daughters.

She dwelt there now, busily visiting all the trouble spots on the ocean floor at Tethys' behest, and working out solutions. She was gloriously happy and wanted her family to know.

Nerine's knees went weak with relief.

Xianthe, safe. Xianthe, happy. And Xianthe so changed – grown mature – as to send reassurance to her family. It was the best of news, beyond all hoping.

Tynghed noticed Nerine's wobbly legs and pale face, and dragged her over to the bench they'd placed in a sunny spot alongside the cottage wall beneath the eaves. The solidity of the weathered wood subdued her trembling.

"Disturbing tidings?" asked Tynghed.

"Oh, no!" How had the norn so misinterpreted Nerine's reaction? Perhaps shock looked the same, whether good or bad. "The best!"

Tynghed tilted her head, questioning.

"My sister ran away from home four years ago. She just sent word that she is safe and happy. With a post under Tethys. We'd all been so afraid for her."

"Ah, yes." Tynghed squeezed Nerine's shoulders. "Relief can be as shattering as loss, can't it?"

Nerine nodded and found herself telling Tynghed about how confined she herself had felt at home. How she'd escaped from the reef to the shore without ever seeking permission.

"That was why, a year ago, Orroch accused me of sneakiness. And this was the secret I kept from my family. But poor Xianthe never found a way to feel free at home. My youngest sister, Agnippe, said Xianthe almost *had* to run away."

"The women in your family need wide ranges, it would seem," murmured Tynghed.

Nerine hadn't thought about it that way before, but Tynghed was right. Agnippe in her sacred spring and Eilidh on Mount Olympus had not roamed terribly far, but neither were they a mere day's travel from Pelagie. While Xianthe had swum through many seas to anchor with Tethys, and Nerine had crossed a continent to reach the norns.

"Eowys asked me if I lied, and I said no. But I suppose I did, by omission." Nerine bit her lip. It didn't feel good to admit that. But it did feel right to take Tynghed more fully into her confidence. Sharing confidence was what Nerine had vowed she would do, here among the norns. Tynghed was the second person – after Agnippe – with whom Nerine had shared her old secret. A strange mix of regret and heady excitement intruded upon her relief.

Breaching her closely held privacy still felt risky, and yet it was freeing, too. And the larger freedom held the exhilaration of wider horizons, more engagement with the world and the people in it, the very essence of what Nerine loved about travel.

Realizing yet another personal fault – her lie by omission – made her feel unclean.

Tynghed's face showed only sympathy. "You lied only about that one sole thing, though, didn't you?" She smiled. "Never about any other disobedience or to gain unfair advantage over your brother and sisters?"

Nerine shook her head. Her secrecy had never been about gaining an advantage. She'd sought protection only.

"Don't you think you should forgive yourself?" suggested Tynghed.

Was that the missing piece? Nerine could accept what she'd done. She wouldn't have been able to tell Tynghed without that acceptance. But she still couldn't feel good about herself. Would forgiving herself make her feel better?

"No," she said slowly. "I think I need to resolve I won't do it again. *That* would make me feel better. I'm stronger now than I was then. If something is so important to me, I'll fight for it openly. Not grab for it secretly." Now she felt . . . lighter. "Thank you, Tynghed."

Tynghed laughed that musical laugh of hers. "You figured it out. I merely listened."

"No, it's more than that. This is the kind of strength I decided on my journey here that I needed to learn."

"Sharing your deepest concerns?" asked Tynghed, surprised.

"Yes! It's really hard for me, but you make it easier."

"Then perhaps I do merit your thanks, but it is still you who are finding the courage and doing the work. Will you do more of it?"

"I hope to." Nerine could see what the next bit of inner courage would require, but stood up from the bench in the sun to speak to the herald, who had finished his conversation with Orroch.

Nerine's message was short, merely reassurances to her family and to the *peltastés* that she now felt truly at home with the norns, and that her place with them was a blessing. She wished she could send a message to Altairos – although blessings knew what she would say – but the heralds of Olympus visited only immortals. Mortals were relegated to prayer and oracle when they wished communication with the gods.

Just before the herald departed, it occurred to her that she should make some mention of her reaction to the news he'd brought.

"Please tell my siblings and my parents that I rejoice in Xianthe's safety and contentment."

He nodded and leapt into the sky, flashing upward more quickly than anything Nerine had ever seen – save the herald himself on his previous visit. The image of a shooting star came to her, a flaring spark arcing downward to the sea. Ah, she'd forgotten; the meteors of Perseus darted as swiftly as a herald of Lord Hermes.

Later, in the evening, she tackled her next act of courage.

～

Supper had been eaten outside in the chill autumn air as shadow overtook the ground, and the sky shaded from blue into turquoise into gold, and then palest gray, luminescent even with the sun below the horizon.

They'd spread a wool blanket on the ground and circled it with lanterns, lighting them as the gloaming advanced. Sitting with her legs curled under her, Nerine drank in the magic of the northern dusk. The blanket itched her bare feet, and she didn't care. It was part of the wonder of the evening, along with the hint of woodsmoke on the faint breeze, the rustling of the curled leaves on the trees, and the eerie call of an owl.

The sky darkened to velvet blue, and the first star shone out.

"Come, sisters," whispered Tynghed. Was she unwilling to break the spell of the night? "We must go in."

In silence, they gathered the remains of their meal into a basket that Linnea would take away in the morning, folded the blanket, and carried both with them into the cottage.

Orroch lit the fresh kindling and logs waiting in the hearth. She and Tynghed moved the spindle-backed chairs from around the table to face the fire.

"Sit ye doon, sisters," said Orroch, suiting her actions to her words.

Tynghed sat next to her, leaning her head on Orroch's shoulder, like a daughter seeking closeness to her mother. Orroch stroked Tynghed's bright chestnut hair.

Nerine stilled the shiver that threatened her.

The mantle of power and peril that cloaked Orroch still terrified Nerine. She couldn't imagine how Tynghed could be so comfortable around the eldest norn. Yet Tynghed wasn't faking her ease – wasn't *lying* – Nerine corrected her thought. Tynghed really loved and trusted Orroch.

Eowys collected a chamberstick and lit the taper. "I shall be in the stillroom, if you need me. The borage tincture needs straining and refreshment."

Orroch nodded and Tynghed smiled sleepily as Eowys glided from the room.

Nerine stood behind her chair, grasping the curve of its wooden back, uncertain if she should take this opportunity. Or not. This was her chance to right her wrong done to Eowys. Dare she seize it?

She stepped away from her chair, but her fingers still clung to its back.

C'mon, Nerine, you can do this, she told herself. She touched King Zeron's bracelet, yet encircling her wrist.

The fingers of her other hand still clung to the chair back.

She unpeeled them, said, "I'll help Eowys," and followed in the Patterner's wake. Orroch and Tynghed scarcely stirred.

Nerine walked through the dim weaving room, lit only by the firelight glowing from the open doorway behind her, and then into the darker hallway beyond. The stillroom was the third door on the right. The door was open, and Nerine paused on the threshold.

Eowys had lit the candles in the wall sconces, and they shed a warm light on the central work table, the waist-high sideboards, the cabinets, the bunches of dried herbs tacked to the ceiling beams, and the diamond-shaped horn panes of the two casement windows on the far wall.

The large jar of borage tincture sat on the work table. The liquid had reached the stage where it possessed a lovely rose color, while the blue blossoms were translucent and blue no longer.

Eowys looked up to see Nerine.

"Will you fetch the bowl and sieve?" she asked, kindness in her face, overlaying her usual reserve.

Nerine treasured the fact that Eowys welcomed Nerine's presence now. A year ago, she hadn't.

The bowl and sieve were behind a door in one of the sideboards. Nerine bent to retrieve them, and a long-handled spoon, closed the door, and placed the sieve within the bowl on the table.

Eowys broke the seal on the cork closing the tincture jar.

Its cool, cucumbery scent filled the room.

Eowys poured the tincture into the sieve. Nerine lifted it, allowing the liquid to drain into the bowl, while the borage blossoms were separated out. They collected limply in the bottom of the strainer.

Drip, drip, drip.

It took a while for the last of the moisture to be released.

"That's enough," said Eowys.

Nerine set the sieve down, while Eowys climbed on a stool to reach two of the bundled herbs above – more borage.

Together, they plucked the dried flowerheads from the stems and cast them into the bowl, while pulling the dried leaves off and making a pile of them on the table.

Nerine had imagined herself talking to Eowys while they worked. But their silence felt so comfortable, so companionable, she couldn't bear to break it.

Her own soft footsteps, the chink of the spoon against the bowl, and the rustle of their skirts were the only sounds. And the cool scent of the borage limned all.

Eowys stirred the borage blooms into the tincture. Nerine put the dried leaves into two small glass jars and the stems into a third, then sealed all three with cork stoppers. She located the proper place to store them in a wall cabinet, and then fetched a wide funnel, a wide cork, and a fresh large jar for the tincture.

Eowys poured the tincture into the jar and sealed it.

Then she placed it within a cabinet, where it would be shielded from light, and started collecting the dirty implements for cleaning.

Eowys would be stepping through the door in a moment.

It was now or never.

Nerine touched King Zeron's bracelet yet again.

"I would speak with you," she said.

Eowys studied Nerine, a faint smile in her eyes. Then she placed the dirty bowl with the strainer and spoon within it back down on the table. "Tell me," she invited.

Nerine leaned against the table beside her.

"A year ago, you asked me if I lied, and I said no. But now I think my answer was not entirely accurate. I *had* lied. By omission."

Eowys looked merely interested, not condemning. She shifted from standing upright to leaning against the work table, apparently ready for more than just a brief confession.

Nerine allowed herself a small sigh of relief. And then embarked yet again on the story of how she'd gone ashore without her parents' permission or knowledge. And kept visiting the shore, still in secret, and knowing that she should be more open.

"But you told me this when I asked, a year ago," said Eowys.

Nerine worked to meet Eowys' calm gaze. "Not at the first, when you first asked."

Eowys smiled. "I was rude."

"But I was not accurate," said Nerine. "I said no. Not because I was lying then, but because I hadn't realized yet that my secrecy was a lie of sorts."

Eowys shook her head. "But, Nerine, you didn't leave your answer there. You expanded. You clarified. People often don't get the answer to a hard question right on the first try. And you kept trying. Until you did get it right. I respected you for it."

"Even then?" Nerine had certainly never guessed it.

"Yes, even then." Eowys reached out to tip Nerine's chin up. She'd been looking at the floor again. "I think you expect too much of yourself sometimes. Mmm?"

"I told all my old secret to Tynghed this afternoon, and she told me I needed to forgive myself. I knew she was right, but I also knew I needed to do two other things in order to feel comfortable."

"And they were?" asked Eowys.

"Resolve to fight for what I wanted in future, instead of stealing it. And to tell you all the details."

"Which you have done," said Eowys. "Do you feel better?"

Nerine checked inside herself. How did she feel?

Clearer. Brighter. Yes, much better. She could go forward from here with a clean conscience. And she'd succeeded one more time in unveiling her inner self. It seemed to get a little easier, each time.

She nodded.

Eowys let Nerine's chin go to touch her shoulder.

"But Nerine, I think you have another thing altogether to confess."

The sting of fear pierced her. It seemed Eowys was correct. But what else lay heavy within Nerine? She felt light, released. What could be the source of her alarm?

Eowys smiled, a tinge of humor in her cool eyes. "Come, let's clean up first."

～

Nerine trailed Eowys across to the scullery with its stone sinks and drainboards.

Eowys washed bowl and sieve and spoon. Nerine dried them. And then they returned the implements to their places in the stillroom.

"Where shall we talk?" inquired Eowys.

Nerine felt a sudden longing for the outdoors, cool and filled with the rustling of the breeze-blown autumn leaves, the dark sky overhead, spangled with northern stars that seemed brighter and sharper than those in the south. Under such stars, Nerine might find it easier to search herself for hidden truths.

"Could we walk in the meadow?" she asked.

"An excellent idea."

Eowys handled it all, shepherding Nerine to the front door, collecting their cloaks, and informing the other two that Eowys and Nerine were stepping outside for a bit.

They went to the sloping meadow to meander along the deer trails that crisscrossed it.

Nerine paused near its center to look up. The sky was very, very black and the stars, brilliant. She knew what she needed to confess now.

Turning to Eowys, she said, "I fell in love with my childhood friend, Altairos. We became lovers and betrothed." Next came the hard part. "But I renounced our betrothal, and left him hurting."

"It hurt you, too," observed Eowys.

"Yes, but I made the same mistake I'd been making all along."

"Protecting your privacy," guessed Eowys.

The same piercing pain she'd felt when Eowys suggested that Nerine had more sharing to do, stabbed again. "Oh, blessings, yes!"

She'd thought she'd been running from all the impossibilities that would attend their marriage. But that wasn't the complete truth. She'd been lying by omission again – to herself this time.

She'd run from Pelagie because she was scared of what her life would be without Altairos. But she'd run from Altairos, because she was scared of what her life might be *with* Altairos, and with herself as his wife.

Keeping secrets had become almost essential to her.

The secret she'd kept from her family had been deliberate. But she'd unwittingly possessed secrets from Altairos also. All her life under the sea was known to him only by what she told him. And no matter how honestly she spoke, the sea cloaked her from him. He could not see her there, hear her speak there, or witness the interplay between her and her family there. The sea kept her secrets for her.

Not that she was hiding anything from him.

It was just that standing fully revealed before anyone – Nerine entire, rather than merely sea Nerine, or land Nerine – scared her senseless. Even when the one who would see her was Altairos.

It hurt again to realize how right she'd been, there in the middle of the Sea of Balder, when she accused herself of lacking moral courage. Now she saw it all, the thread that ran through all her poorest decisions, a taint that had brought her to grief.

She was eradicating it now, with each confession she made.

The pain of seeing her flaws clear and whole was a good pain, she realized. But she felt cold. Was that why she'd sought the night? That its chill might mirror, or even bring out, her own?

"I thought I was protecting Altairos from the abandonment that his pappa went through, when his sea *numen* wife could no longer resist the call of her water form," said Nerine.

"But that is foolish," answered Eowys. "Your queen mother told you herself that your water gift would give you choice in that matter, where another *numen* would have it not."

"Yes," whispered Nerine. "I was protecting myself. My privacy."

"Which you cracked open on the day you came to us. And have cracked open yet more tonight," concluded Eowys.

"Too late for Altairos," countered Nerine.

"But not too late for you," answered Eowys.

"I never felt flawed when I was a child," said Nerine, "even when I knew that there was something wrong with my secrecy."

A slight lilt entered Eowys' cool voice. Was she smiling? "You were a child, Nerine. And largely a happy one. Is that not so?"

Nerine frowned. "Yes."

"Then how should you feel differently? It is as women that we achieve full awareness and choice. Don't regret your innocence, even in your mistakes."

"So I start over." Nerine sighed.

"No. You continue."

Eowys drew Nerine's arm through hers and set them walking again. The path of trampled grasses was wide here, and there was room for them to go side by side.

An owl hooted. The thrashing of brush marked that a deer leaped somewhere.

"It feels like starting over," said Nerine.

"Perhaps it is, but you don't start from scratch," said Eowys. "Starting afresh can feel good."

"Was I right to believe that Altairos deserved a wife with more courage?"

"Hmm." Eowys walked without saying anything. Considering her answer? "You were right and you were wrong."

Now it was Nerine's turn to walk in silence, pondering how her particular mistake might be both right and wrong.

Eowys continued. "You were wrong, because no one is flawless when making a marriage vow." A soft laugh escaped the norn. "There would be no weddings were that a requirement."

Nerine's stifled laugh turned into a snort. That made almost too much sense. Had Nerine imagined there existed some perfect woman who *deserved* Altairos as husband? It was a ridiculous notion. But she'd known that she herself might be too flawed for their marriage to be happy. Surely there was some bare minimum of virtues necessary, without which a marriage fell into indifference or, worse, dislike.

"You were right," said Eowys, "because *you* deserve to *be* someone who has courage. And you are making that wish come true right now."

Ah! Now there was a truth. Nerine felt it pass through her, from crown to heel, like a wave of blessing.

"I have more work to do," she said. Somehow that felt like a good thing.

"Yes," said Eowys. "Yes." Her simple affirmation felt more like celebration than mere agreement. Perhaps it was.

Nerine felt newborn.

～

As the autumn slipped into winter, with bare branches, cold winds, and then snow, Nerine revived her shoreside discipline of acceptance and awareness. She'd been using King Zeron's bracelet for courage as she tackled her quest to be more open to the people around her, less closed and private.

It seemed likely that he would have approved of that use.

But, just as surely, he'd intended his gift and his advice to address more than a particular problem. He'd hoped Nerine would practice tranquility and hope for a lifetime.

So Nerine began the attempt to mingle her two disciplines: sharing her secrets and appreciating the moment, even when it was uncomfortable.

Some of the things that were hard for her seemed ridiculous.

Why did the contentment born of the tick of falling snow against the closed shutters feel like it should be unspoken? Or the thrill that came of listening to the song sparrow's whistling call in the spring meadow feel private? Why did she want to keep her affection for Tynghed and her admiration of Eowys secret?

But she did.

And just as she'd found that her surrender to aching loneliness or piercing grief often eased the passage of those feelings, so she discovered that full acceptance of her discomfort at the opening of a private experience could also be removed or, at least, softened.

The one thing that did not change or ease was Nerine's awareness of the mantle of power and death that cloaked Orroch.

It seemed incongruous that slight, bent Orroch, with her bright eyes and wise face, should be the focus for a sense of doom. She *was* the eldest norn, a *numen* who had served the loom of fate when Mother Holle herself wove its threads. Perhaps, for that alone, Orroch had earned majesty.

But it frustrated Nerine that terror-tinged awe suffused her when Orroch's attention was upon her. She should, at the very least, make progress against it. But she didn't.

Despite this one recalcitrant flaw in her life, she was happy and content.

Each morning's visit to the Well of Destiny with its visions felt magical. Selecting the threads and ornaments that Orroch would weave into the world tapestry was satisfying. And passing a needle to Orroch, or catching the shuttle when Tynghed tossed it, Nerine felt purposeful.

The cottage of the norns was where she belonged.

Spring passed into summer, and summer into fall.

She couldn't believe she'd lived only two years in Scandia. This was her home, and the rightness of it spread to tint the past, as though she'd always been at home, within herself as well as within her surroundings. As though she had always lived *here*.

A third year passed, and then a fourth.

Nerine's contentment deepened.

She loved Tynghed and her joyous nature. She enjoyed Eowys' quiet respect. She even learned to savor the shudder of dread that Orroch's gaze upon her provoked. Although she still wished she could banish it.

And over it all, the tapestry of the world was so beautiful. It seemed to grow in beauty every year. Was that possible? Did the world itself grow ever more lovely, with the tapestry mirroring its transformation? Or did Nerine's perception merely grow more acute?

Howsoever that might be, bliss threaded Nerine's days.

She took to sitting in silence when the norns gathered around the hearth in winter evenings. Being quietly happy at a summer noontide when they picnicked out of doors. Walking in meditation when she and Tynghed tramped through the autumn woods to visit Gwenedd.

In Nerine's fifth year with the norns, something shifted.

She became aware of it, strangely, during her quiet moments. A shiver of unease, a flicker of discontent, a hint of restlessness.

She ignored it for a time. She would not let it disturb this safe harbor she had fought so hard to achieve. She would *be* content. She would *be* happy. She would *be* fulfilled.

But the more she fought her restlessness, the stronger it grew.

Then came a moment of revelation. Of course. That was the way of things. The harder you fought a feeling, the more powerful it grew. She *knew* this. How had she forgotten? She must surrender to it. Accept it. Let it flow through her and then away.

She tried her practiced discipline – sitting with restlessness, sitting with discontent, sitting with unease – and it failed her.

Then came a second revelation. Her restlessness had arisen first within her moments of quietude. Meditation had given it birth. Why would meditation then disperse it?

And then a third revelation: she was homesick.

She longed for the warm waters of the Middle Sea, for her past in the reef with her family – Father, Mother, and her brother and sisters all about her. She ached to revisit the shore. And to find Altairos awaiting her there.

Ah! That hurt.

All the pain of loving Altairos and renouncing him returned to her.

Had the years of her contentment and happiness been an illusion? Or merely a respite?

She didn't know.

Then, into this maelstrom of inner disturbance, came the fateful vision of the ship *Astiphílaka* going down in the storm, its timbers splintered by the violent water, and Altairos drowning in the deeps.

⁓

The Tapestry of the World

31 ~ Open a New Door

NERINE EMERGED FROM her memories with a feeling of surprise.

She'd not intended to delve so deeply into her past, but now that she had . . . she knew her own strength. The sense of restlessness that had plagued her for the last year intensified. She knew who she was and where she'd come from. She felt ready to turn the spindles of the scroll that was her life, to find the next adventure to write on the waiting papyrus of her future.

With that thought, she fell out of reverie and back into time, where both mortals and immortals career from blessing to disaster and back again.

Lying aslant across her bed, feet on the floor, Nerine stared over her knees at the armchair where Orroch had lately been sitting. It was a comfortable armchair, well upholstered in silver-shot turquoise. Nerine had curled up in it many a time over the last five years, cozy while she pondered or daydreamed or merely rested. It reminded her of the sponge circles in the reef palace of Pelagie.

But Orroch's aura of ominous power seemed to linger in it now. Even though Orroch had left the room.

Nerine imagined the norn's residue taking shape as courier's sandal wings – but black-feathered, not golden – rising to hover over Nerine, before sweeping her away to a dark lake where doomed swans flew.

She shivered, despite the warmth from her round tile stove in the corner. Stop it, Nerine, she told herself.

Orroch had given Nerine a respite in which to figure out what was missing from the materials she'd laid out for the day's weaving. Orroch had promised that they would light candles when the spring dusk arrived and weave until midnight – or past it – if they had to.

But there was a limit to the time even Orroch could grant. The day's weaving must be accomplished, even if they wove it wrongly, because one thread or trinket was missing.

Even if they wove Altairos' death, because Nerine could not find the one item that would save him.

She *had* to find it.

But she'd searched all the cabinets and shelves in the weaving room before breakfast. And hadn't found it.

She'd searched every nook and cranny of her own room after breakfast and not found it.

How long before Orroch returned to say that Nerine must come to the loom and perform her handmaiden's duty, missing trinket or no missing trinket?

Nerine had almost *had* it, too, right before Orroch knocked on Nerine's door. *Almost.*

She'd felt that looming, louring sense of destiny approaching – an inexorable power that could not be denied – advancing upon her, upon the present, and bringing both doom and salvation. Just another few moments more, and she would have known exactly how to divert the death fated for Altairos.

But Orroch had knocked, and the approaching revelation fled with her knock.

Nerine brought Altairos' dear face before her mind's eye. Not the very last time she'd seen him. Not when he shouted her name in desperation. That was too painful. But before that dreadful moment, when he'd gazed into her eyes, his own face tender and loving. And the moment before that one, when he'd laughed, throwing back his head in abandon, his black curls tossed by the motion, his mouth open and joyous, and his bright eyes crinkled in the way that they did.

She loved him.

Which meant she'd better cultivate whatever mood it took to inspire her with the knowledge of what item, sewn into the tapestry of the world, would save him.

How long had she been lying here while she roamed her past in hope of inspiration? From her first meeting with Altairos, when she was eight and he was nine, to now when she was twenty-three was a long span of years. But the mind was fleet and could compass even such a span quickly.

She didn't think she'd been too long about it. Surely she had still a little time left. She hoped so, because her trip through memory had not delivered the answer she was seeking. Should she get up and search her room again?

Somehow that didn't feel right.

Finding the right materials for the loom was something she did every morning after viewing the visions in the Well of Destiny. That was a mental puzzle more than anything else. Looking at the assortment of materials available could help. But Orroch had admitted in this very room that some of the threads or baubles needed were summoned from the past – or even the future – when the handmaiden envisioned them in her thoughts and knew them necessary.

What about Mother Holle's three questions that Orroch had just shared with her?

Nerine hadn't pondered them very carefully. She'd been too urgent.

She would review them calmly – *without* Orroch's looming presence – and see if she got different answers.

The first. Was she ignoring the still small voice of insight because she was afraid?

Oh, Nerine was afraid all right. Desperately afraid for what came to the one she loved. Was that the answer right there? That she must relinquish her fear? Which meant accepting it.

What would that feel like?

She cast herself into her future, imagining. Imagining herself at the loom. Imagining Tynghed tossing the shuttle of darkest blue – the deeps of the sea – across the warp. Imagining Orroch passing the green silks – entangling seaweeds – through the smaller shed created when Eowys pulled the requisite heddles. Imagining herself, doing nothing. Imagining Altairos' cold dead body drifting down through the waters to lie on the dark sea floor.

Imagining herself a year from now when the tearing grief had passed to leave her heart sore with a more lasting sense of loss.

Could she bear it?

She would have to.

But she was finding no freedom here, in this imagined acceptance. Perhaps the most advanced philosophers could meditate on death and experience bliss, but Nerine was not one of them. Her face was damp. She had wept again without knowing it.

She bit her lip and drew her handkerchief from her sleeve to dry her eyes and her cheeks.

Very well, what was Mother Holle's second question?

Did she feel wrongness, and if so, what was its opposite?

Nerine shook her head and sat up.

No. That was not going to be a helpful question.

It felt good to be decisive.

I can do this, she told herself again. She was handmaiden to the fates themselves, and through them, handmaiden to *fate* itself. What was that third question? She dredged her memory for the words Orroch had spoken.

Did anything unusual happen while she searched?

Yes! There was gold in that question. That was the question she needed to meditate on. Lightly. With trust. With *hope*. She grinned mentally, thinking of Altairos' pappa. With hope, indeed.

The armchair Orroch had lately vacated caught Nerine's eye.

There? Should she sit there? Cloaked by the remnant of Orroch's doom?

Without answering herself, Nerine stood and turned. But she did not sit. She stood staring at the built-in drawers flanked by her two wardrobes.

Her chest tightened with a feeling of anticipation.

That sense of something coming was present again! Not a heavy feeling of doom approaching this time, but a light flutter of possibility. Just. Barely. In. Reach.

Oh! Oh! Oh!

Her heart was beating fast, so fast.

The shelves. The wardrobes with their doors. Doors!

That was *it*.

A door! She needed a door, and not only for Altairos. For herself.

The answer lay in her earlier reverie after all. She'd walked in memory through her life, from an early age all the way to the present when her peace grew troubled by a restlessness without cure. A restlessness that demanded change. That begged for fresh opportunity. That longed for the opening of a new door in her life, the chance to walk through it toward something bright and challenging.

Could she knock on one of those wardrobe doors and have it swing open – not on the huddle of her dresses hanging within – but on a radiant landscape, beckoning with promise?

And then she had something more.

She knew!

She rushed forward and fell on her knees to pry at the drawer with one handle beneath the leftmost wardrobe. One of her fingernails – short as she kept them – broke. And then she got a crack open just wide enough to wedge her fingers inside it and pull.

The drawer shot into her lap, just as it had when she opened it in her earlier search, heavy on her thighs.

∽

Nerine studied the drawer's contents.

Those colossal calipers made of iron and intended to grip huge blocks of ice were what made it so heavy, but it was the other item – resting near the back of the drawer between two small bolts – she sought.

The rings on both small bolts had broken entirely the last time she wrenched the drawer open.

But the rings at either end of the hanging pull . . . were intact!

She seized the loose pull in both hands and clutched it to her breast. This – this modest piece of bronze – would save her beloved.

Nerine would crawl beneath the loom and hold it up to the tapestry. Orroch would push her needle and thread through each ring, sewing the drawer pull to the woven fibers. And Nerine would swing the hanging bronze to knock on the tapestry of the world, opening the door to her beloved's salvation.

Two more tears – of relief – slid down her cheeks.

Thank the blessings – and Orroch with her wise questions – that Altairos would not drown.

Nerine paused there, on her knees, in gratitude.

Then she maneuvered the heavy drawer back into its cabinetry, closed it, and stood. It was time to tell Orroch she was ready.

She looked around her room, almost as though it would be the last time she saw it. What a silly conceit. It was her room. She'd be sleeping in the bed tonight – or, more likely, in the early morning between midnight and dawn – and waking to visit the Well of Destiny for the next day's visions. Of course she would see her room again.

But still she looked.

There was her narrow bed with its aqua quilt embroidered with silver, rose, and green. And there the rose curtain she pulled around her when she slept. And there the shelf under the windows for her sundries. All just as

Tynghed had arranged it five years ago, in hope that it would delight her new handmaiden – Nerine – when she arrived. Dearest Tynghed.

Nerine glanced at herself in the bronze mirror on the wall between the two windows, her slim form gowned in soft golden wool. The white fichu around her shoulders was pinned with a gold brooch in the shape of an auger, slim and spiraling, like a narwhale's horn. Altairos' gift, so long ago.

Her hair had grown since the norns cut it during her long-ago winter fever, and she wore it loose as she had in the sea, the mass of its green-gold curls hanging down her back to her waist. Her spiracles made two tiny dimples between her eyebrows. They had not been open since her last dip in the Istula, the river running through the land of the Gutones of Európi, but she knew they would do so were she to brave the icy waters of Scandia.

Slight hollows graced the sides of her face below her cheekbones. She'd grown from almost a woman to fully one, here in the north. Were her hazel green eyes a little wiser? She hoped so.

She turned toward the door and then paused again, suddenly aware of a dilemma.

All this morning she'd indulged the fault that she'd worked so hard to overcome: her excessive reticence.

She'd watched Altairos drowning in the Well of Destiny and hidden her tears, standing well behind the norns so they could not see her silent crying. She'd kept her face calm when Linnea arrived with their breakfast, setting the table with good cheer while her heart was breaking inside her. She'd vowed to trick Orroch – Orroch! – when she evolved her plan to search a third time for Altairos' salvation.

She was wrong to seek in secret what she dared not seek openly.

She'd once vowed never to do so again.

And then! When Orroch came to her, when Orroch gave her guidance, when Orroch granted her yet another interval of time . . . still Nerine pursued her aim clandestinely.

She *could* not save Altairos *this* way. She must not.

Ah, blessings! How it hurt to let go of the prize she'd sought so desperately and succeeded against hope in finding.

But if Altairos could not be saved openly, then *she* could not save him.

She felt like she'd just shoved a dagger through her heart.

～

32 ~ Essence of Fear

NERINE STOOD A MOMENT more, there in her room, facing the door out, with her precious drawer pull in her hand.

Must she really confide her whole plan to the norns? Or one of them, at least.

Her held breath ran out of her.

Yes. Yes, she must.

But it would be Tynghed she would choose. Kind Tynghed who was merry and warm and would understand how Altairos deserved to be saved. Who surely knew how much a woman might love a man.

Except . . . Tynghed had already petitioned Orroch for Nerine. And for Altairos. That was what the three norns had been arguing about so bitterly when they entered the cottage to eat their breakfast. And Orroch had declared that Tynghed would forfeit her post as Shuttle-catcher, if Tynghed said one word more about it.

And . . . Nerine had already confided . . . much – indeed, everything – in Tynghed.

It could not be Tynghed to whom Nerine turned this morning.

Nerine straightened her shoulders and took a step toward her door, the floorboards chilly underfoot, despite the warmth in the room.

Very well, she would consult Eowys. Cool and queenly Eowys. Who carried understanding and compassion beneath her reserve. Who was *not* like Galena. Nerine sniffed, remembering how she had once wondered that very thing. How absurd! Eowys cared. Eowys cared about the whole *world*. One could not be a norn, sworn to create the fate of the world, without caring.

Nerine put her hand on the door latch.

And stopped again.

Orroch had not threatened Eowys. But Orroch had commanded silence on any further discussion of Altairos and his fate.

And – Nerine hated to admit this, but it was true – Eowys was not the norn in whom Nerine had never reposed confidences.

That was Orroch.

Oh, blessings!

Orroch. Nerine would have to confide in Orroch. Orroch, whose bright black eyes saw too much. Orroch, whose old criticisms of Nerine had only evolved into silence, never praise.

Except that was not true either. Orroch had praised Nerine the first time she ventured under the loom to dare the abyss. And Orroch had praised her this very morning for her accuracy in choosing loom materials.

Tell the truth – Nerine scolded herself – even if you tell this truth only to yourself.

She didn't want to confide in Orroch, because the chill of death hung about Orroch. If Nerine allowed herself to trust Orroch, then – in her trusting – Nerine would allow death to touch her. Touch her deeply.

But this morning . . . Nerine would have to trust Orroch. Trust Orroch with the heartfelt truth about Nerine. That was the only way. To save Altairos. And herself, although Nerine wasn't sure quite how her own fate was bound up in all this. Her thoughts had become too tangled for clarity.

She teetered there a moment more.

Would she go fetch Orroch and confide in her?

Or would she merely tell Orroch that she was ready for the weaving?

One choice . . . or the other.

A coal fell in the tile stove at the corner of her room.

~

Nerine pulled the door latch up, thrust the door open, and stepped out.

She swung left, striding through the short hall to the weaving room, which was empty. Strangely so. She'd expected to find the norns there.

The front room stood empty as well. She ventured out onto the narrow, unwelcoming porch that sheltered the front stoop.

Orroch sat on the left bench, in shadow and slightly hunched, staring at her bare, wizened feet on the cold flagstones. She looked up when Nerine opened the top and bottom halves of the front door.

"Ye've found it?" she asked, her eyes shrewd.

"Yes," answered Nerine, baldly. She gestured for Orroch to stay where she was and sat down opposite her, on the right bench, pressing her hands together – with the drawer pull – between her knees. "But I must ask you something."

"Aah," sighed Orroch, leaning back. "Now it comes."

Nerine frowned. Then asked – as baldly as she'd said 'yes' – "How much leeway do you have in the weaving of dooms?"

Orroch propped her chin on one hand, forefinger over her mouth, and said nothing.

Nerine huffed with impatience. "Tynghed said that your friendship with Cinnisuent broke, because Cinnisuent believed the Well should be interpreted strictly, while you chose to interpret it more flexibly." Nerine was aghast at her lack of tact. Was this any way to persuade Orroch? For she did intend to persuade. Had her urgency forfeited the only chance she had? "How much leeway do you have?" she demanded again, fiercely.

Orroch's mouth moved. Was that actually a smile? Orroch never smiled, if such a small stretching of the lips could be called a smile. And, if smile it was, it wasn't a nice one.

"Ye will have to tell me more than that, for any pliancy that I choose or choose not to exercise is found within the connections between each and every detail of an event."

Nerine sighed. She'd known it would come to this. She could not merely tell Orroch what she wanted and how it might be achieved. She would have to tell Orroch . . . everything that mattered most. Everything that hurt the most. Everything that made Nerine feel most vulnerable.

Very well. She'd already made this decision when she left her room. She would not shirk now. It wouldn't even take as long as when she'd told Tynghed the first part of her story. And Eowys the second part, all those years ago.

Nerine straightened on her bench, its seat hard and cold beneath her.

Opposite her, Orroch – despite her momentary smile, or was that because of her smile? – seemed to exude an icy mist, like the breath of a glacier when it calved, a vast bulk of frozen water falling to crush any creature in its way.

Nerine shivered.

"I fell in love with my childhood friend, and when he asked me to marry him, I said yes. But then I saw all the difficulties before us. I retracted my consent and said no. I pretended to him and to myself that the difficulties were too great." She hesitated. "There were difficulties. And they were . . . significant."

Memory brought before her King Zeron's prohibition, her own mistaken understanding of sea sickness, and Mother's probable disappointment. Nerine would never have found the courage to confess to years of illicit visits to the shore. Not then.

But more powerful than these external problems had been her desire for secrecy. What she'd begun naively, she'd continued in deceit, until it became necessary to her. The prospect of merging her two lives – that of land and that of sea – had felt too dangerous, too revealing.

She'd admitted as much, when she'd confessed to Eowys. Now, in Orroch's dread presence, another revelation came to her. There was another fear beyond her fear of exposure.

"The real reason I said no was because I was afraid of how vulnerable I would be, if I allowed his love to fill my heart. I dared not risk the agony that would come, if he or fate should ever take his love from me, after I'd come to depend upon it."

That was stating it baldly indeed.

Had she done so because Orroch encouraged truth without embellishment?

No, it was merely that Orroch required it. And so did Nerine. Now.

Merely was definitely the wrong word.

Orroch's hand fell from her predatory lips to her lap. "And . . . ?" she said.

She was correct. There was more. Nerine had known the eldest norn's wise old eyes saw too much.

"When the ship *Astiphílaka* goes down in the Middle Sea today, Altairos will drown. And I have discovered that even though I would not marry him, it does not protect my heart from grief, because I still love him. Even if I never see him again to tell him I was wrong, the way I want to, I would save him!" She gulped, then whispered, "Please, Orroch. Help me save him."

Orroch's not-a-smile glimmered again.

Nerine shuddered.

"And . . . ?" repeated Orroch. She looked like a crow on the battlefield, dark and hungry, eager to rend the flesh of the fallen.

Nerine's fingers trembled. She held out her drawer pull. "I found this. If you will sew it into the tapestry of the world, then Altairos will be saved."

Orroch held out her hand, commanding. She sat very straight now, no glimmer of a smile on her face, as though she were indeed the goddess of death, meting out dooms. Which – truly – she was. Nerine called Orroch the Weaver, but there existed another name for her. Morta. The Cutter. Death.

The norn's twisted fingers seemed a cage in which the curving drawer pull rested.

"I shall sew this into the fabric of fate, Nerine," said Orroch, "but there are a variety of knots I might use. Ye know this."

"Yes," whispered Nerine.

"Look at me!" cracked Orroch's voice.

Nerine looked up. Her gaze had dropped to her bare feet on the cold flagstones.

"One knot could make this the bronze fittings on a falling mast, mighty like a tree, a widow-maker." Orroch loomed larger than herself, the veritable face of a glacier.

"Yes," Nerine whispered.

"Another knot would make it the ramming prow of the *trieres*, slicing through the water, slicing through the body of a drowning man."

"Yes." Nerine's voice was less than a whisper.

"I might yet kill him with this thing ye have found to save him," said Orroch.

Nerine didn't say anything at all. What was there to say? She'd known that Orroch was no safe power to approach. She'd also known that she had to approach her. Orroch could have tied any of those lethal knots, even had Nerine stayed silent and secretive.

Two more tears spilled from Nerine's eyes.

～

Orroch loomed yet taller on her bench.

Nerine stared at her. She seemed to see two Orrochs, one superimposed on the other.

The Orroch Nerine knew wore black, and her face was cruel, her eyes pitiless. She was the fate who meted out dooms, the bringer of loss and grief, the one who made an end.

The Orroch Nerine knew not wore white, and her face was stern, but merciful, her eyes filled with compassion. She was the fate who granted boons, offered blessing, and brought rest to the weary.

Which Orroch would preside when she sat at the loom this time and wove the shipwreck of the *Astiphílaka*? The doom-sayer? The hope-giver? Or was there yet a third Orroch present?

Nerine looked more closely. What was she seeing?

As she gazed, her courage rose. She'd done the right thing. She'd acted as the Nerine she wanted to be. Not the cowardly, secretive Nerine she'd once been, but the Nerine who was willing to confront risk with strength and hope. The Nerine she'd become. The Nerine she'd nearly lost, here in this moment of crisis.

Curiously relaxed – even now, especially now, when Altairos' fate hung in the balance – Nerine studied the three Orrochs before her. The dark, deathly one. The radiant, merciful one. And the third who hid behind the other two. Who was that third?

Abruptly Nerine slid off her own bench to her knees, her hands still pressed together as though in prayer. Willing herself to see that third Orroch, Nerine knelt before her in supplication and placed her praying hands in that Orroch's lap.

"I trust you," whispered Nerine.

And then the third Orroch came clear. A wizened, old woman with a weary face and love in her eyes. Nerine's eyes teared up yet again. Why . . . Orroch loved her handmaiden, loved Nerine. How was it that Nerine had never perceived it before?

Because I was afraid, Nerine realized, and my fear clouded my sight.

As it had done on too many occasions before.

I will be afraid, even after this, thought Nerine, but I will know to look beyond the curtain of my fear. *That* is the essence of bravery.

Orroch's hands closed on Nerine's, palms pressing in a prayer of her own. "Together, we will save him, young Nerine. It will take the both of us."

"Yes," Nerine whispered, and buried her face in Orroch's lap.

One of Orroch's hands – twisted though it was – came to Nerine's head to stroke her hair.

∽

33 ~ Shipwreck

THE DARK LINEN of Orroch's skirt felt very soft against Nerine's cheek, and Orroch's fingers very gentle on Nerine's hair.

Orroch's other twisted hand came between Nerine's cheek and the linen, cool and knobby, but kind. She lifted Nerine's head to place a kiss on Nerine's brow with her pale, withered lips.

"Shall we, my handmaiden?" she asked.

Nerine nodded.

Orroch picked up the bronze drawer pull and pressed it into Nerine's hands. "Ye will need this."

Nerine smiled. She had procured Altairos' salvation, but it had required more than the mere finding of an elusive trinket. It had required that she secure Orroch's cooperation. An impossible thing that had proved possible after all.

Orroch led the way into the cottage, passing through the bright front room into the weaving room where the great loom reared its menace.

Eowys and Tynghed awaited them, the one already roosting high on her perch, the other seated beside the dozen shuttles required for this day's weaving.

Nerine went to stand at Tynghed's side. Tynghed turned to study Nerine. The Shuttle-catcher's normally bright face was worried.

Nerine shook her head, ever so slightly and smiled. It's okay, she wanted to say, but did not. That would be Orroch's privilege, not hers. But some of Tynghed's tension ebbed.

"Let us begin," commanded Orroch. "*Shent coren byatt,*" came her first instruction.

Eowys lifted the heddles, and Orroch pushed a gray silk through the shed.

Gray and black and lurid white, the clouds.

Dark blue and celadon green and foaming white, the waves.

The norns wove, the storm mounted, and the sea grew hungry. Hungrier. Ravenous.

Crack! Tynghed sent the metallic blue-white yarn across the warp, the wood of the shuttle hitting the frame of the loom at the start.

Crack! Orroch sent it back.

Lightning struck.

Then the brown wool and the black, the ship's timbers splintering.

The blue-black silk and the green, the swallowing sea and the entangling wrack.

"No!" cried Nerine.

"Get ye under the loom, girl," ordered Orroch.

Nerine scurried, bent, and scooted beneath the warp threads.

"With prudence, ye eejit!" Orroch screeched.

Nerine shuddered to a stop. Moving so swiftly that the abyss claimed her would do Altairos no good at all. She could hear the shuttle cross the loom again. And again. But she forced herself to move slowly. One hand and one hand, the drawer pull clutched in her left. One foot and one foot, groping forward while avoiding her ensnaring skirts.

"Endin wikker narl," called Orroch.

The heddles lifted, Orroch's hands moved, Tynghed cast the shuttle.

One hand and one hand. One foot and one foot. And then Nerine was there, perched at the brink of the abyss, its ravening dark reaching for her.

"Lift the bronze!" cried Orroch.

Nerine held the drawer pull up to the fearsome tapestry of roiling waves and foundering ship.

Orroch's needle dove and retreated, dove and retreated, binding the left ring into the maelstrom.

Nerine's arms trembled.

Orroch's needle dove again, binding the right ring of the curving bronze, tighter and tighter, tight enough to pull the curve out of Nerine's hands, making it lie flush against the fabric.

The bronze became an anchor, its broken chain winding Altairos round, its weight dragging him down.

"No!" screamed Nerine, "no!"

"Thy gift, Nerine," spoke Orroch's stern voice.

What? Nerine was panicking, and her thoughts slid greasily through her mind, all meaning gone.

Eowys spoke into the drumming silence. "You are a *numen* of the sea, Nerine, with special gifts. Use them!"

Oh, blessings! It had been years! And her gift required focus and composure. Nerine was anything but composed.

What had Mother said? "Relax your operculi, daughter. Let them move. Relax your spiracles. Let them widen. Your gills know how to breathe."

But gills and operculi and spiracles were no use in air.

Amidst her panic, quailing before Altairos' anchor, a different anchoring stole into Nerine's breast. Her ribs loosened. Her nostrils ceased their terror-stricken pinching. And her lungs remembered how to breathe. One breath. And then two.

She released her clutch on the mortal bronze.

Relax the fingers, and the wrists, and the forearms.

She closed her eyes and drew on her inner strength.

Water flowed, skimming across her palms and drenching the tapestry of the world.

Her eyes flew open to see her translucent hands and the fountain that sprang from her fingers, wetting the wool, easing it and easing it yet more.

Slowly, the arc of the bronze pull swung down to hang loose.

A piece of metal ready to grab and knock against fate's door.

～

Nerine stared at the vignette above her, woven with all Orroch's skill.

Ship and wreck and wave and storm, depicted in wool and silk. Sailors clinging to the broken and sinking spars, helmsman yet gripping the steering oar, and a robed man drowning in the sea. Oh, blessings!

But where was the striker plate against which to batter her bronze?

Doom would not hear Nerine knocking, if her knocking made no sound.

Nerine's cry was silent this time. She watched the tapestry grow dark with water as her gift strengthened in her despair, a current drenching the wool so thoroughly that it dripped and flowed in turn, pouring water into the abyss.

She would flood the abyss in her grief, and then a kraken could surface from its depths to drag her down where a narwhale would spear her heart.

A narwhale!

Nerine's hands turned from water to flesh and she grabbed at the brooch on her gown's neck, fumbling, fumbling, then slowing of their own accord. Carefully, carefully, she released the pin from its catch. Deliberately, she lifted it to the tapestry. One hand swung the drawer pull, measuring its reach, and let it go. Both hands pinned the brooch in the exact spot.

"Well done!" sounded Tynghed's merry voice. "Oh, well done!"

"Knock, Nerine," called Eowys.

"Thy hand guides fate itself," said Orroch. "Mete your doom an ye would."

Rap! Nerine struck the bronze pull against the gold shell.

Altairos was saved!

"Knock again for the sailors," commanded Orroch.

Rap! Nerine knocked.

And the sailors' spars floated, carrying them to the surface.

Oh, blessings! She'd done it. She'd done it *all*.

And yet . . . something felt unfinished.

"Ye may knock once more, an ye will it," said Orroch.

Oh, blessed be! For herself. Nerine could knock yet a third time. And then what would happen? A doom? A hope? A new door opening?

Did she dare?

Her fingers tightened on the bronze pull.

Rap!

And the abyss moved, moved as it had never done before, even that first time when Nerine climbed under the loom in the summer following her arrival.

Nerine fell, arms outstretched.

∼

34 ~ Darkness

SHE FELL TOO FAST to grasp the warp strings.

She fell too fast to call out.

She fell too fast to see the light slip away.

The darkness grabbed her, frigid and hideous, a kraken of time to devour her entire and never let her go.

Through the darkness she fell and fell, toward the icy heart of the earth, where Mother Holle would entomb her in time, neither to die, nor to live, nor to swim the sea's currents, as was her destiny as a *numen*.

The wind of her fall whipped the skirts of her dress and dragged at the curls of her hair.

Down and down she plunged.

Far below her, a warm smudge of radiance dawned in the darkness. Strengthening, it dove toward her. Or she dove toward it.

Brighter and brighter it shone. Greater and greater it grew, expanding to light the rough wall of the crevasse through which Nerine plummeted.

Nerine flashed through the most intense locus of the warm light – a red-orange glow – and then it was gone, a stolen moment of comfort in Nerine's endless fall.

And yet, that moment of vision lingered, bequeathing a strange vignette in her mind's eye.

Lit as though by a fire, a ragged opening in the wall of the abyss had revealed a cavern delved from rock. Within the cavern, the folds of the tapestry of the world were taken up, piled layer upon layer, by three crones older than Orroch. Their hair straggled white and uncombed, while their backs bent, hunched. Necklaces of bone hung round their necks, and deerskin cloaks hid their scrawny bodies.

These were the fates of an earlier age, storing the world, storing time itself, against some unimaginable ending – or was it a beginning? – when at last their terrible labors might cease.

And still Nerine fell, seeing the ravaged faces of those ur-hags in her memory, fading against the dark that reclaimed her.

What abyss could be so deep that it had no bottom?

For, still, she fell at a speed which should carry her through the earth's frozen heart and beyond.

What lay beyond the earth's heart? No legend told of it, if it existed.

And still she fell, heart hammering.

Could she fall so far that her fear ceased and boredom claimed her? If so, she had not fallen far enough yet.

Another glimmer of light teased her eyes. Something inky and fluid gleamed in the depths. Ripples of dark water spread out below her, to a dark shore where the reeds rustled, and a white swan flew up to greet her.

Ah, no!

Orroch's lake-realm awaited her at the bottom of the abyss.

Nerine screamed.

～

As the shrill echo of Nerine's scream faded, the flying swan veered near her.

"Fear not, dear heart," whispered Orroch's voice from the bird's open bill. "This be the mystery to which we bade ye not. Fear nothing."

And then the bird swerved away.

The waters of the dark lake drew nearer. Its ripples gleamed as it started to swirl, forming the whirlpool at its center.

An instant later, Nerine plunged into its liquid maw. The water took her.

She expected the water to spit her out in the norn's meadow, but it did not.

She wondered if it would spit her out in the rocky crevice where she and the *peltastés* had first entered the lake-realm, but it did not.

Water – well and truly water – held her. But it was not lake water or spring water or river water. Not fresh water at all. Her spiracles opened, the gate at the base of her throat moved, and her operculi unfurled. Nerine swam through sea water. She was home.

For this was not the icy currents of Balder's Sea. Nor yet the unruly ones of the World Ocean. These were the warm waters of the Middle Sea where Nerine had been born and lived. Her gown had vanished – when and where she knew not – and the salt waters of her home enfolded her, fluid caressing bare skin.

Ah! She felt healed.

This was where she belonged, where she felt at peace, where her future would unfold.

~

She looked around her.

The sea was dark and deep below her, dim around her, and lighter above her. She swam up. Would she have to swim up as far as she'd fallen down in the abyss of the norns?

But, no, there was the silver glimmer of the surface and the pale gleam of something else.

Suddenly anxious, Nerine kicked out, swimming frantically toward air. Not because she needed air, ah, no. But because she feared, feared –

– that the body she saw rolling in the waves above was her love, ah, no!

Robed no more – had the waves torn his garments from him? – his pale body floated, flaccid and tumbled by the sea in the wake of the storm.

He *could* not be dead. Orroch had *promised*.

In a fury of rage, Nerine's gift burst forth. A wave, a tide, a tide of a wave gathered on her will, rising toward the sky and carrying Altairos on its crest, higher and higher, roaring toward that unseen shore, heard not observed, in the dreadful vision that had started it all.

On water, she carried her love. In water, she followed her love. And in tumult they both came ashore, crashing down on a pillow of water, and then surrounded by foaming froth as the massive wave withdrew.

Nerine lunged for Altairos, wrapping her arms around his cold still body and dragging him away from the hungry sea.

"My love, my love," she wept, her hot tears falling on his chill face.

Black hair straggled away from his low brow and closed eyes, dripping water from the sodden curls. He lay so heavy in her arms, a dead weight. His arms trailed in the hissing sea foam. Bruises mottled his unmoving ribs.

Ah! She couldn't bear that he'd been battered before his drowning. How much had he suffered?

She pressed her cheek against his.

The tickle of a quivering eyelash brushed her skin.

She stiffened and straightened to see his eyes flutter open.

And then he was coughing and coughing and coughing. She helped him turn over as water poured from his lungs, while bile spewed from his stomach. And she held him all through his paroxysms, jolted by their fierceness, the wet sand gritty under her bare legs, and a chill wind hurrying under the cloudy sky.

He lived, ah, blessings, he lived!

～

35 ~ A Deserted Strand

ALTAIROS' SKIN PRICKED OUT in goosebumps under Nerine's arms, as he turned in her embrace, shivering, teeth chattering.

"N-n-nerine?" he said, barely able to speak for the shuddering of his body.

Still crying, but smiling through her tears, she choked, "Yes, oh, yes!"

He sat up and pulled her to him, enfolding her against his bare chest while he buried his face in the curls of her damp hair. "Nerine, oh, Nerine, my love."

He was crying, too. She could feel it.

They gripped one another frantically, there on the strand, until another large wave pushed a skimming of sea foam, hissing across the wet sand, to embrace their legs and haunches.

"Can you stand?" Nerine gasped.

He couldn't at first, too weakened by his ordeal to do more than get his feet under him. And then, when he rose, he almost fell again. Nerine grabbed his left arm and shoved herself under it, steadying him.

"Gods, Nerine! I'm feeble as a kitten," he wheezed.

Then his grin dawned – even as he swayed and wobbled, held on his feet only with her aid – and his eyes crinkled in that way she loved.

Together they hobbled away from the sea. Storm rains had dampened the beach, but beneath a wet crust, the sand was silky and dry. No dunes lifted along this stretch of shore. The beach simply leveled out and then met a low bluff – turf fringing its top – that rose just above their heads.

Nerine guided them to where the bluff formed a wide alcove, sheltering them from the wind, and allowed Altairos to sink down and sit. She crouched before him, gazing into his dear face.

"I c-can't b-believe you're here!" he stammered.

She shook her head, still smiling, and leaned in to kiss his cheek. "I can't either," she said, mistily.

Her hair – a sea person's hair – was nearly dry, as was her skin. But Altairos' black curls still dripped on his moist skin, and he shivered.

"I have to get you warm!" she declared.

He looked down at himself, apparently bewildered by his lack of clothing.

"Gods, Nerine! This wasn't how I wanted you to see me naked for the first time."

She giggled. She couldn't help herself. Such a mix of joy and relief and – *still* – fear for him surged through her, that she suspected she could laugh and cry and cling to him for a long time. But she mustn't. She had to go search for some way to get him dry and warm.

She kissed him again, aiming for his cheek, but he moved his head, and her lips – warm and soft – met his, cold and clammy. She didn't care. He was *here*, he was breathing, and he was hers – all hers – again.

His mouth tasted of sea water, and his lips warmed under hers.

"Nerine, Nerine," he mumbled.

"I love you," she whispered.

He drew back. "You do?" he demanded.

She nodded.

His eyes darkened, and his mouth drew straight. "Then, for the love of Aphrodite, why in Plouton did you run from me?" He sucked in breath to yell again, swallowed his words, and then shook his head. His gaze bored into hers. "Nerine, what in Hades was I to think, but that you didn't love me enough to face difficulty at my side? Gods!"

He looked away from her, studying the sand under his heels.

A chill passed through Nerine. Oh, blessings! She knew he loved her still. He couldn't kiss her like that and not love her. But was he free to do so? If he'd thought she didn't love him . . . had he married someone else? It had been five years – oh, gods!

Then his head came up – eyes blazing with a strange mixture of anger and mastery and love – and the chill in her soul ebbed.

"We're marrying," he declared. "I don't care who or what stands in our way. Do you hear me, Nerine?" His voice was hoarse and fierce.

She was crying again. "Yes, yes," she sobbed.

"And no backing out," he commanded. "I won't let you!"

"I don't want to," she said.

"You did before," he reminded.

"I was wrong." And she wrapped her arms around him.

Then he was kissing her again, tenderly at first, more roughly as the kiss lengthened.

She broke away gasping. "You're still shivering," she said.

He lifted an eyebrow. "This is warming me."

"It's not enough," she insisted.

"What do you think you will find on this deserted strand?" he asked.

"I don't know," she answered. "But let me look. Please, Altairos?"

He surveyed her a moment, then transferred his attention to himself, apparently taking in his damp and sandy state for the first time. "Gods, Nerine, I'm a mess! I'll come with you."

But when he tried to stand, once again his limbs betrayed him.

New fear surged through Nerine. Land people were far more vulnerable to chill than sea people. Mortals could die of cold – dear blessings! – and he had all the signs: stumbling steps, incessant shivering, and pale, chilled skin. She could still lose her beloved, if she couldn't find more shelter than the windbreak this bluff afforded them.

A line appeared in Altairos' brow as he frowned. "Hmm," he muttered in displeasure.

She skittered from one foot to the other, afraid to leave him, as weakened as he was, but knowing she had to find something more than what they had here.

"I'll be right back," she promised – to herself, as much as to him.

One side of his mouth curled. A reluctant acceptance, she deemed it. And then he nodded.

She hurried away.

The wind was strong outside their alcove, dashing the tossing dark waves in violent surf against the land, and blowing the gray clouds across the hurrying sky.

She found a pile of driftwood farther along the beach where the bluff grew lower – reaching only to her knees – and a scrap of torn sail half buried in the sand.

She looked inland across the slowly rising turf. No houses, no people, not even any trees. Just the empty land stretching up to meet the sky. An overcast sky with scurrying gray clouds beneath it.

But what was *that* – a strange wavery line – stretching up from the horizon? A thread, a filament, a ribband of *smoke*!

She took off running, leaping the low bluff, and then pounding across the damp turf.

⁓

Panting as she crested the rise, she could see in the distance the far side of the island they'd fetched up on. A spit of rocks protruded out into the sea, curling around a cliffed inlet to her right, while curving away from a long straight line of coast ahead of her and to her left.

Overlooking the inlet was a tumbledown stone cottage missing half of its turf roof. Next to it grew three stunted pines, deformed by the constant wind. Or *had* grown three pines. One of them had been struck by lightning in the storm. Its splintered trunk lay at an angle, that thread of smoke rising from its damp, smoldering wood.

Nerine ran down the slope. Fire, if only she could coax that smoldering to increase, rather than extinguish as it looked set to do.

Up close, the fallen trunk was blackened, but very wet. The lightning strike must have come before the rains and then been dowsed by them.

Nerine strode to the nearest companion tree. Its bark remained relatively dry, protected by both the needles clinging to its branches and its upright position. She stripped a few threads off and then returned to the stricken pine.

Ah, blessings! Was there any spark of fire left, a tiny coal, something?

A glimmer caught her eye, deep in a small cleft of the splintered wood.

She leaned near and sighed a soft breath over it. The orange glimmer flared brighter. She sighed again – blowing would be too strong – and held a thread from her handful of bark near that glimmer as she sighed again. Brightness sparked into a small flame and caught the bark, which flared higher. She added another thread of bark and another.

She had a fire! A small one, diminutive, but fire!

She dashed to the pine that had supplied her with bark, broke some of its twigs off, and then rushed back to her fire. She fed it one twig, carefully, carefully. She could still lose this precious source of heat. Then another twig and another.

She tore larger strips of bark from the donor pine, then small branches, and – finally – two large branches, their diameters as large as her wrists.

She needed more. More than these trees could supply her with. It had taken the full force of her weight to rip the larger branches from the tree. She would not be able to break the branches larger still without tools. She glanced back the way she had come. It wasn't that far. She could see the line where the turf gave way to sand – the short bluff hidden – and then where the sand met surf.

She looked at her fire again. Would it last?

It would have to.

She ran back toward the pile of driftwood on the sand, feet pounding, turf squelching, breath panting. Jumping down from the bluff, she thumped onto the sand, spraying it in the wind as she landed.

The biggest pieces of driftwood were too heavy for her. She collected an armful of the smaller ones and jogged back to her fire. She could see its flames, even from a distance, and it was burning well when she returned. She piled her driftwood nearby, and added one piece to the fire. When it caught, the flames burned blue and green along their edges.

She started to add another driftwood branch when an idea seized her.

The cottage featured a chimney. Even missing half its roof, its walls would provide better shelter than the alcove in the bluff on the beach.

Nerine peered in through the doorway.

The interior was paved with stone flags, and the hearth occupied the far end, where the roof was intact, its beams unbroken, and the woven wattle upholding the turf that served in place of thatch or tiles on this desolate isle.

Nerine moved quickly after that. Never mind the dirt, rubble, and broken beams littering the floor. The hearth was her focus. She laid her materials carefully, two short and thick pieces of driftwood perpendicular to the room, a fluffy pillow of shredded bark and pine needles and twigs between them, two larger driftwood logs braced over it, two more cross pieces, and a final log atop them.

Thank the blessings she'd learned to build fire properly from Linnea. The flow of air was key, or so Linnea had always assured her.

Transferring the flame would be tricky. If she simply plucked a burning brand from her fire outside, would the wind blow it out? She would have to try.

As it chanced, the wind did extinguish the flame when the branch was separated from its fellows and lifted. The wind was less nearer the ground. But Nerine could see the charred wood glowing and carried it inside, where it burst into flame once more.

She placed the burning branch alongside her pillow of bark and pine needles and twigs.

They caught!

And soon the logs caught as well, burning, burning, and throwing off heat.

∿

When she made it back to the shore, heading toward the bluff's alcove, she saw a staggering figure far, far down the beach.

Great and little blessings! Altairos!

She took off running again.

He grinned tiredly when she drew close enough to see his face.

"I told you to wait for me!" she exclaimed.

"I grew worried for you," he said, his voice mild, but a twinkle lurking in his weary eyes.

She huffed, irritated because his fatigued swaying worried *her*, and then hurried to brace her shoulders under his arm.

"I found shelter," she announced.

"Did you now?" He sounded impressed. "That's good. Very good."

They staggered forward, but saved their breath – he, for staying upright and walking; she, for supporting him.

At the driftwood pile, she rooted around until she found a long stick Altairos could use as a staff. She pulled at the scrap of sail, but it didn't come loose. She knelt to dig the sand, digging more and more, until at last, a huge width of canvas came free. She nearly lost it from her grip as the wind took it, flapping the vast expanse like a pegasus wing.

Altairos laughed, tottering there against his staff, while she battled the thing into submission, bundling it under her arm.

"Can you walk without me?" she asked.

"Just get me up the last of this bluff," he answered.

She weighted the sail canvas under the driftwood and helped him. Then she gathered up the canvas and as much driftwood as she could carry, and they started up the sloping turf.

"Wait!" she said abruptly.

He glanced at her.

"Just . . . wait a moment. I'll be right in sight. I promise."

She set the canvas down, driftwood piled atop it, and leapt down to the beach. She ran to the sea's edge and cupped her hands, skimming from the top of the water where it was less mixed with sand. Agnippe was better at this – much better – but Nerine had learned how to do it, too.

With the surf foaming around her ankles, she closed her eyes and focused, sending her awareness into the liquid held by her palms. Clear, cool, limpid, fresh.

She opened her eyes. A thin sifting of sand and salt coated her palms, but the water above it looked . . . inviting. A wave hissed in, boiling over her toes. She bent her head and drank from her hands.

Mmm. Fresh and welcome and wet, soothing to the mouth, wonderful in her throat.

She drank it all, and then scooped up another draught and prepared it for Altairos.

He'd been watching her all the while. Guessing, no doubt, what she was doing. She had to walk very slowly across the sand, trying not to spill her liquid gift. When she got to the bluff, she stopped. She could not make the knee-high step with both hands cupped and steady.

Altairos walked the few steps that separated them and knelt, using his staff to keep from falling.

She lifted her hands, just a little. He bent his head. And drank her hands dry. His lips kissed her fingers before he raised his face.

"Ah! That was good!" He sighed.

"More?" she asked.

He hesitated.

"You still thirst," she stated.

He nodded, looking uncertain.

"I can do it again."

And she did. Then they walked to the crest of the hill, he leaning on his staff, she carrying driftwood and the bundle of sail canvas.

When they saw the stone cottage with smoke threading from its chimney, a twin "oh!" broke from their lips. His in delighted surprise. Hers in relief.

Her fire in the hearth still burned!

The fallen pine continued to burn as well, the flames soaring high in the wind, now that the trunk was well and truly caught. Nerine was glad the turf was damp, and the cottage built of stone. She wondered if the other two trees would catch.

She broke another small branch from the nearer pine and used the fringe of needles to sweep the floor immediately before the hearth inside. She shook the canvas outside, gripping it firmly, and letting the wind whip the rest of the sand from its weave.

Altairos protested when she came inside and wrapped it around his shoulders where he sat by the hearth.

"It's big enough for the both of us and then some," he said.

"I have to get more of the driftwood," she explained.

He looked like he wanted to object. Then he scrutinized the fire – burning well before him – and sighed. It was obvious they needed more wood.

She brought it all, even the pieces that were too heavy for her. She found she could lever them up on one end, let that end flop down ahead of her, and then lever the closer end up and over. She was hot and sweaty by the time she'd collected a small pile in a corner under the cottage roof and a very large pile outside the door.

The burning on the fallen pine had subsided to coals while she worked, and by the time she was done, the setting sun shone on the horizon where there was a break in the cloud cover.

Leaning in the doorway against the stone of the thick cottage wall, she announced, "I'm going to rinse off."

Altairos was half asleep, warm and wrapped in the sail canvas, his head propped on his knees.

He started to object to Nerine's plans – "The sea is dangerous, no one should swim alone" – and then laughed at himself. "I've been living with landsmen these many years, and most of them can't swim," he explained.

She laughed with him, but couldn't forebear reminding him: "I'm a *numen* of the sea, silly!"

"I know," he answered ruefully. "Come here a moment, you."

She came, and he kissed her.

She smoothed his hair – now dry – out of his face. He smiled and rubbed the tip of his nose on her cheek. "Don't be long," he adjured her.

"I won't be." She was beginning to understand that he didn't want her out of his sight. She couldn't blame him. The memory of their last moments before their five years of separation lay heavily between them. She had some apologizing to do.

∽

36 ~ Shared Vows

NERINE RETURNED TO ALTAIROS just before the last sliver of sun disappeared below the horizon and the black night – unlit by moon or star – closed down.

The sea had been brisk and refreshing. The strong wind blew her dry, but hadn't time to chill her.

Inside the cottage, she put another piece of driftwood on the fire and stood looking down at her beloved. Despite his worry, he'd fallen asleep, curled on his side with one arm under his curly mop of black hair, and the sail canvas drawn over him.

His face had regained its color, tan and slightly flushed from the heat before the hearth. His forearm matched the brown of his cheek and neck, but his shoulder gleamed milky pale beneath the rosy gilding of the firelight.

Nerine seated herself beside him, content to simply gaze on him, his mere presence a benediction.

The stone floor was very hard under her sitting bones, and whipping air rushed in coldly through the doorless entrance and the one shutterless window. But the hearthstones threw out a generous warmth, and the cottage walls shielded her from the worst of the wind.

A log shifted in the fire, and Altairos opened heavy-lidded eyes.

Nerine smiled at him, happy, and he smiled back.

After a long moment, he pushed himself up to sitting, draped an extra fold of the sail canvas around Nerine's shoulders, and urged her to scoot over to sit on another fold. It was heavy and rough, but warm from his body heat.

She leaned her head on his shoulder, and he stroked her hair. His hand felt like a blessing, loving and gentle.

"Nerine," said Altairos seriously, "I cannot make all the difficulties before us disappear. I wish I could."

She hushed him, putting her fingers over his mouth. "Don't, don't," she murmured.

He frowned, puzzled.

"Those weren't the real problem," she explained. "It was me. I was afraid."

He kissed her temple. "And how should you not be? Your family might cast you off for following in your Cousin Hester's wake. Or my family might repudiate you for being *numeni* as was my mother, who abandoned her children and her husband."

He kissed her hand and then took it in his and pressed it against his cheek.

"There was much to fear, sweet Nerine. And there still is. But I'm asking you to bear it with me."

She was tempted to tease him. To say, "What happened to 'no backing out – I won't let you'?" But she couldn't. Not now, not before she'd spoken her truth.

"It wasn't *that* that I was afraid of." She gulped and went on, propelled by his confused look. Ah, blessings, but he was adorable. "Or not only that," she explained. "It was – it was –" She was having trouble admitting it. To *him*. She'd managed to tell Eowys. And then even Orroch. But neither of them were the person she'd wronged. Neither of them were the man she loved with her entire being.

She bent her head, then raised it again to cling to his eyes with her gaze. "I'd gotten too accustomed to secrets. My life on land was a secret from all my family. And –" this was the hardest part of all "– my life in the sea was a secret from *you*. Marrying you meant I wouldn't have secrets from anyone any more. I'd stand entirely revealed, and I . . . *couldn't*."

There. She'd said it. What must he think of her?

She almost expected him to recoil, but he didn't. His confusion had passed. Now he looked at her steadily, listening and receptive, with a thoughtful expression in his eyes. He gave a little nod, encouraging her to go on.

Very well. She would go on. There was a little bit more. The piece she'd understood only while confessing to Orroch.

"I love you so much. I was afraid to give in to it." She felt his hand, still holding hers, tighten. She whispered, "I was afraid to surrender to my love. Afraid to surrender to you." A tear dropped from her eye and trailed down her cheek.

His other hand swept around to grasp her free hand, and then both his closed on both of hers.

"But you are brave now," he said to her, half question, half certainty in his words. "Brave enough to be loved, and not just as sea Nerine or land Nerine. Brave enough to be loved as Nerine herself."

His brows drew down, ever so slightly, and then smoothed again. "Because," he said slowly, "loving is the truest kind of seeing there is. And only now have you courage enough to be seen fully."

Oh, blessings, he understood! Perhaps even more clearly than she. And he forgave her.

He lifted her hands in his, resting both on his knees, and continued. "You don't need secrets any longer. And you will let my love into your heart, there to dwell for as long as we both shall live."

"Yes," she said, her voice so faint it was not even a whisper. "Yes," she repeated, stronger. "I will."

He kissed her lips, very tenderly.

His forehead leaning against hers, he asked, "Will you wed me tonight, Nerine? Now?"

"How?" she asked.

"I know the words to the vows," he said, and then chuckled. "I stood with three of my five brothers as they said them, and then with my pappa."

"Oh!" This was the last thing she'd expected. It lifted her. She was flying, soaring, floating on happiness. "Yes! Yes!"

"We'll have to say them all over again before witnesses," he cautioned her.

"I want to say our vows tonight," she insisted. "With you."

He bent to kiss her brow and then settled back, composing himself, still holding her hands in his. He looked up from her hands to her face.

"I name you, Nerine Merenou Pelagieus, as blood of my blood and bone of my bone." His smile was more tender yet than any he had given her thus far.

"I give you my body. I give you my spirit. And I give you my faith."

He kissed the backs of both her hands. Her throat felt hot and aching.

"I pledge myself to you from now until I pass through Charon's gate, through the best and the worst that may come. I name myself your husband."

She leaned in to snuggle her head against the side of his neck. He kissed her hair.

"Now you, love," he breathed. "Repeat after me."

But she remembered it, all of it, as though his words still echoed in her ears.

"I name you, Altairos Zeronou Lamperieus, as blood of my blood and bone of my bone."

His eyes closed as gladness suffused him. She kissed each closed eyelid, and then continued when his glad gaze met hers again.

""I give you my body. I give you my spirit. And I give you my faith." Ah! She was his, now. His, and truly so. "I pledge myself to you from now until . . ." There she faltered.

"Say it this way, Nerine," he suggested, and then gave an altered wording for the phrase.

Her breath caught, but then she repeated him, word for word. "I pledge myself to you from now until you" – her voice trembled – "pass through Charon's gate, through the best and the worst that may come."

His hands firmed around hers, and she finished strongly. "I name myself your wife."

They stared at one another in wild joy, and then he swept her into his arms, kissing her lips, her hair, her neck, and then her lips again.

"My love, oh, my love," he murmured against her mouth. He drew her close and lay back, easing her atop him, caressing her body, worshipping her with his hands, and lighting desire within her. Her desire spiraled. Within the benison of marriage – this time – he gave her the gift of a husband for his wife. And allowed her – this time – to give him the gift of a wife for her husband.

Ecstasy twined through her, again and again, until they slept in one another's arms, wrapped in a torn piece of sail before their borrowed hearth.

∽

Nerine awoke first, ravenously hungry.

Even so, she lay still, savoring the feel of Altairos' warm body against hers, the comforting weight of his arm across her waist, and the softness of his sleeping breath ruffling her hair.

Her rumbling stomach urged her to move, as did the hardness of the stone floor under the sail canvas and the cool of the morning air. The clouds had gone in the night, and sunlight drenched the clutter of broken beams and fallen stones where the cottage lacked its roof.

Nerine tamped down her eagerness to get into the warm sun. Waking in her husband's arms was so sweet.

How would he look when *he* awoke? What would he say?

She didn't have to wait long.

Even as she wondered, his eyelids fluttered open, he smiled and drew her closer, murmuring sleepily, "Mmm."

She laughed and kissed his chin.

"I think I know where to break our fast," she said.

That brought him alert. "You do?" he exclaimed. "Gods, Nerine! I'm starving!"

She felt like her smile might stretch completely off her face, she was so happy.

He unwrapped himself from her and helped shove back the sail canvas from atop them. In spite of her vigorous shaking the day before, a few grains of sand sifted from its folds.

She noted that Altairos was greatly improved from the weakness brought on by his near drowning. Her breath caught in relief. He seemed a little stiff climbing to his feet, but once standing he stretched vigorously. She frankly stared, enjoying the sight of him.

His curly black head of hair and cheerful eyes were the same as ever, which gladdened her heart. But his face at twenty-four was firmer than it had been at nineteen, his square jaw more definite and his cheeks leaner. She observed the stubble there with inner amusement. He wouldn't be shaving this morning, alas.

His unclothed body had become familiar to her touch in the night, but now she feasted her gaze on it. His shoulders were broader than they had been, more muscled, and his torso narrowed from them to lean muscled hips and the core of his masculinity.

He was beautiful to her, all clean-limbed strength and vitality and latent power. She was almost tempted to forego the finding of food. And so was he, she could tell. He had been gazing at her in turn, seated naked on the rumpled fabric of their makeshift bed.

His eyes took her in, from her greeny-golden curls to the slightly rosy tips of her toes on her crossed legs, and everywhere in between: her breasts – still slight – her slim waist and flaring hips. And then back to her face, his own alight with tenderness. She felt utterly beloved and lovely in his sight.

Then his stomach growled, and they both laughed.

She scrambled up, holding out her hand and urging, "Come with me!"

Hand in hand, they jogged down the slope toward the spit of rocks extending into the sea, stopping briefly at a low-lying thicket of spurge olive for morning necessities, and then sprinting the rest of the way to the sea.

The water seemed a sparkling, laughing thing compared to its ominous mood of the day before. Its gentler waves, blue under the bright sunshine and clear blue sky, washed the tumbled boulders of the rocky spit. Nerine led Altairos into the shallows on its inlet side. A rugged, rumpled texture of pale tan and ivory – made up of bumpy ovoids with curving sides and sharp edges – clung to the rocks just below the water.

"Oysters!" exclaimed Altairos. "Perfect!"

They waded forward to begin plucking the shellfish from their attachments and tossing them up onto the dry rocks. It didn't take long to accumulate a modest pile. Nerine searched among the boulders, looking for a nice, palm-sized rock, but Altairos found one first.

"Now, wife of mine" – Nerine could see him practically bursting with pride as he called her 'wife' for the first time – "we shall eat!"

He smashed the first two oysters open and offered their innards to her. Soft, delicate, with a salty, buttery taste.

Altairos proffered her the third and fourth as well, but she insisted he take them for himself. After that, they shared, turn and turn about. When they noticed their thirst, Nerine purified handfuls of water, making it fresh and free of salt. Her skill improved rapidly. Drinking the fruits of one's gift was motivating that way!

Nerine grew sated first. She sat on the rocks enjoying the gentler wind, the sound of the waves, and the warmth of the sun on her skin. Watching Altairos all the while as he polished off another two dozen oysters.

They were both rather messy at the end of their meal, spattered with oyster juices and bits of broken shell. A quick dip in the sea solved that.

"Now what?" asked Nerine, when they walked out of the water to stand on the turf once more.

Altairos smiled and drew her into his arms. Their kiss lingered, and Altairos' hands wandered. After too short an interval, he sighed and drew back.

"I could do this all the rest of the morning," he said.

Nerine wanted that too, but . . .

"But," said Altairos, "I think we must prepare to be here some days. Many of my sailors will have survived. Most, I hope." A shadow of worry crossed his face. "Word of the *Astiphílaka's* sinking will go to Zakynthos, and my pappa will send ships to look for me. But, our rescue will not be immediate. I believe we have work to do, Nerine."

He grinned at her, and her heart turned over.

She kissed his nose. "Let's get to work then," she said.

And work they did.

She insisted that they tear a swatch from their bedding to fashion a rough tunic for Altairos – the sharp edges of the oyster shells helped with that task – tying the trailing threads to fasten it over his shoulders and around him.

"Much as I enjoy the sight of you naked, I won't enjoy you, with my eyes or with the rest of me" – she laughed as he blushed – "if you are burned by the sun, love."

"Then you need covering, too," he protested.

"But I don't, husband mine." Ha! That was her first turn at inserting that word – 'husband' – into her conversation. It felt wonderful to say it. She could understand why Altairos had beamed so dazzlingly when he'd said 'wife.'

"A *numeni's* skin is more resistant," she explained. "It has to be. The deeper waters protect us, but we often find ourselves swimming in the shallows. My skin will not burn. I promise."

He kissed her. That happened often throughout their labors. They'd found one another after grief and long separation. She longed for his touch as much as he clearly longed for hers.

They checked the banked coals in the hearth first, and added another log to smolder slowly. If they lost their fire, they wouldn't be getting another.

Then they set about clearing the cottage of its debris.

The beams went on a pile outside the back wall. They were heavy and unwieldy, but creating a clear path from the doorway to the hearth was worth it. Nerine had almost tripped and gone sprawling several times already. And their labors presented them with an unexpected bonus. The shutters for the window had been hidden under the mess, along with an intact waterskin still attached to its carry strap.

Altairos immediately set about refastening the shutters – gray and splintery – to the hinges protruding from the window opening. He was able to locate three of the metal shafts that passed through the hinge knuckles, but had to improvise with a tough pine twig for the fourth.

Their cottage would be less drafty when the wind picked up again.

Nerine took the waterskin down to the sea to fill it. She discovered her gift could generate a current that leapt like a fountain, and that she could purify the leaping water just as she might purify water cupped in her hands.

Altairos drank down nearly a quarter of the contents of the heavy bladder after she lugged it up the slope to the cottage.

Nerine tossed rocks from the floor out the window, while Altairos broke most of the smaller branches off the smaller of the unburned pines.

"What are those for?" Nerine asked him.

"Let's sweep out the cottage and I'll show you!" he answered.

Sweeping dust and dirt with needled pine branches, especially since they aimed to clean the entire stone floor, not just a spot in front of the hearth, wasn't easy. Nerine was wishing heartily for a broom by the time they finished.

"Help me bring a few of the beams back in," Altairos instructed.

She groaned. They'd lugged them all *out* not so long ago. But she soon understood what he intended. The beams created a rectangular frame on the floor before the hearth, two of the longer making the sides, and two somewhat shorter forming head and foot. Pine boughs, filling the frame and placed as evenly as they could manage, became a mattress. The sail canvas went over, folded in half to yield a bottom sheet and a top covering.

"Shall we try it out?" suggested Altairos, his eyes half-lidded.

Nerine laughed. "After luncheon," she insisted firmly.

The midday meal was oysters again. She wasn't yet tired of them, and hunger made an excellent sauce. But she hoped they wouldn't be stranded on this islet for too long. Perhaps she should try fishing for their supper.

But she was too weary by the time evening drew on.

They'd spent the afternoon exploring the rest of their small domain, rather than testing the comfort of their new bed. Nerine was relieved to discover several more piles of driftwood on the beaches – much needed fuel for their fire – as well as a clump of pines growing in a dip of land along the shore farthest from the cottage, and hidden from it by a rise so gentle as to go unperceived until they climbed it.

From the top, they could see the entire island, the cottage located on the second highest spot overlooking the cliffed inlet, with the land in one direction slanting gradually toward the beach where they'd washed ashore and more steeply in the other toward the spit of rocks.

"The real trick will be catching the attention of the next passing ship," stated Altairos. "But I have an idea."

"Good!" Nerine had been worrying about that as well. Their secluded paradise was paradise enough, so long as Altairos was in it with her. But she didn't want to live here forever.

The wind picked up and the sun set behind the island as they dined yet again on oysters and rinsed themselves off afterward. The first stars shone in the deep, translucent sky above them.

Altairos held out his hand to Nerine. "Shall we repair to our humble abode, my wife?"

She placed her hand in his and let him tow her up the hill.

∼

He built up the fire and closed the window shutters, then came to join Nerine where she sat on their bed. The air had stilled again. The snap and crackle of the pine burning amongst the driftwood sounded loud, and the flicker of the flames played across contentment on Altairos' face.

"Were you terribly angry with me?" Nerine asked. "When I left without listening to you?"

He sighed and drew her back to lean against him. "It hurt too much at first," he admitted. "I huddled there on the sands, almost numb."

That bruised her heart. She bent her head to kiss his upper arm where it crossed her breast. "And then?"

"I did get angry, eventually. When I was back on shipboard. I took to the oars, which the captain thought crazy, trying to row my way to peace. As though that could be done." His hand found hers in her lap and gripped it. "Mostly I ached for you and thought of how selfish I was to even think of dooming you to a marriage mostly lived without me, while I enjoyed all the adventures you longed to have for yourself." He dropped a kiss on her temple. "I'm still worried about how we'll manage, but we'll figure out something. Something better than you waiting ashore while I sail to foreign lands."

"Oh! But I'll come with you!" she exclaimed, turning around entirely in his arm.

"How is this, Nerine? You cannot!"

She blushed, ducking her head and bumping his nose with her forehead. Her "Oh! Did I hurt you?" overlapped his "Ouch!"

She kissed his poor nose and then, when he laughed, laughed with him.

"Nerine, you were so sick on that stupid harbor trip I arranged," he insisted.

"I know," she agreed, then argued, "but it wasn't stupid. It *wasn't*."

He tilted his head, reserving judgment, she suspected.

She continued, "I was sick again when I took ship to the norns on the Sea of Balder. But, Altairos . . ."

He gazed at her, intent.

"You were right. I acclimated. I was fine by the fourth day."

Hope flashed in his eyes before they closed, and he folded her in to hold her.

She leaned against him, enjoying his warmth and his strength. After a time, she murmured, "Can you ever forgive me?"

"There's nothing to forgive," he said.

"But there is. Please listen," she begged.

He listened much better than she had five years ago, quietly attentive while she shared more of her thoughts from her voyage on Balder's Sea and her determination to take her loved ones into her confidence.

"I said that I was afraid I might fall prey to the sea longing, the way Cousin Hester – your mamma – did, but it wasn't true. My mother had already told me, although I'd forgotten it, that because my first water gift was the water form, the longing would not take me."

She had to interrupt her confession to explain what the water form was, because he didn't understand.

"You mean you become water, Nerine?" he asked, awed.

She nodded. "Just my hands and arms now, but, in time, all of me."

"That's – that's amazing, Nerine!" He seemed enraptured, perhaps imagining her in that state, a woman formed of the lucent, glimmering sea.

She forged onward with what she felt she *must* say, *must* make clear. "But, Altairos, even if I'd been right about my vulnerability to the water longing – and I wasn't – I was wrong to shut you out from the decision of what to do about it. It was a decision that touched you just as strongly as it touched me. It should have been made by both of us, not by me alone."

His eyes narrowed just a hint, and his lips pursed, ever so slightly. Considering her words?

With effort, she met his gaze straightly. "I didn't succeed in foregoing secrecy the first time I tried to be forthcoming. It took me several attempts, over moons and years, and I still fall back into the habit sometimes. I know sharing decisions will take practice." She bit her lip, and then burst out, "Altairos, I don't want to do to you again what I did to you there on that shore when I left! But I probably will! I'll try hard to share the decisions that should be shared" – she suspected there were a lot of them, when you were married – "but I know I'll make mistakes. I'll probably even keep a secret or two, just from sheer inattention!"

He sat silent a moment. Then he gripped her hands, a serious expression on his face. "Nerine, I am not perfect either. And our marriage won't be perfect. But it's something we'll do together. And, I believe, gain much joy of. Even when we've hurt one another. Because we will, dear heart. You know we will. That's what worries you, isn't it? That you'll hurt me again?"

She nodded, fighting tears.

"I'm stronger now," he said. "And wiser, I hope. Next time I'll grab you when you jump up to run away!"

That made her laugh through her tears. She wanted to let him have the last word, but this didn't feel finished to her. She had something more to say. No. She had something more to realize. Probing for it, she found it: certainty. She wouldn't be running away again to solve her problems. Or sneaking. Or using secrecy.

She might want to run. She might want to fall back on old bad habits. She'd wanted to try to fool Orroch. But, when push came to shove, she'd done the right thing. The thing that was harder and called for courage. And she would do so again, when needed. She'd *learned* to be honest, and she would learn to share decisions. She could trust herself. And that felt very, very good.

Now she could give Altairos the last word. Even better, she could tease him.

"Would you really grab me?" she quizzed.

He laughed. "Never doubt it, love!" And then he pulled her down to lie next to him, kissing her and letting his fingertips drift along her neck to her breast, circling her softness in a way that called desire to coil within her.

She deepened the kiss, bringing her hands behind his neck to tangle in his curling hair.

Some time later, she insisted he doff his makeshift tunic, and then they discovered that their pine bough bed was much better than canvas-covered stone paving.

～

37 ~ Paradise

THEY STAYED NEARLY a full *déka*-day on the island, and Nerine did try fishing – successfully – when they tired of oysters, which was soon. Fish, thickly wrapped in seaweed and baked in the hearth coals, was delectable.

There wasn't much to do. A cottage with no furniture and no kitchen tools required little housekeeping. They had no garden to weed nor animals to tend. No loom to work at. No clothing to mend. Tickling fish and shucking oysters and purifying saltwater took little time.

But Nerine was not bored.

And Altairos seemed utterly content also.

They had one another to explore, new lands more enthralling than Aegyptus or even far Indus.

He told her all about his journeys from one king to another in the city-states adjacent to the Middle Sea, gathering together – with Lord Calix – a great fleet of warships from all the realms they visited, and then burning out two pirate havens.

He was equally interested in hearing of Nerine's journey across Európi, questioning her about the details of land travel – so different from sea travel – and listening in fascination to the customs of the Keltoi and the Gutones. If only she hadn't destroyed her notes! She felt sure she was forgetting some of the best details.

Nerine was more reticent concerning her duties under the norns. Oh, she told him about Tynghed and Eowys and Orroch, and what life with them was like. But the visions in the Well of Destiny and the actual weaving of fate felt too fraught, bore too much weight and significance, to be shared with anyone who had never dwelt in that Scandian cottage.

Altairos fretted about the fate of his shipmates from the wrecked *Astiphílaka*. Nerine tried to reassure him, saying she was certain they were safe and well, but he didn't believe her, until she ventured to broach her self-imposed reserve concerning the mysteries of the norns. When she told of Orroch weaving the sailors into the tapestry of the world, and her own second knock of the bronze drawer handle against her gold brooch to save them, he grew more sanguine.

Hand in hand, they strolled the beaches or swam side by side in the sea, usually in the morning. Roaming the island's slopes and stopping to sit and talk, at one spot or another, seemed more natural to their afternoons. They spoke not only of what they'd done while parted for those five long years, but also about what they'd thought and how they'd felt. Many comments about their present happiness interrupted their sojourns into the past. As well as silences when they simply smiled at one another.

Once, as they sat on the turf at the highest point of the island, bright air all around them, Nerine told Altairos about her conversation with his pappa. How King Zeron had taught her that present despair – if you fought it too hard – could sap future joy, memories from the wasted past overshadowing and weakening the completeness of present fulfillment.

"I think he's right," she said. "I have regrets that I maintained such secrecy from Mother and Father. I so much regret that I ran from you." She bit her lip and smiled ruefully at him. "But you know the time after Agnippe left for Mount Helicon?"

He nodded.

"I was bitterly lonely. All my siblings were gone. Calla –" she paused, missing Calla all over again "– had passed. And you were away. I . . . felt despair then."

Altairos took her hand and held it between both of his. She'd learned – during these days on the island – that accounts of her past pain bothered him more than memories of his own. But she wanted to share this with him. It felt important.

"I practiced believing in hope, even while I despaired. And I welcomed my despair in, without either feeding it or fighting it. Does that make sense?"

He sat still a moment. "I'm . . . not sure," he answered. "Tell me more about it."

"What I discovered," she continued, "was that when I was able to practice full acceptance of my grief and loneliness, at times they dissipated entirely to become bliss. But even when they remained, they didn't weigh me down as they had before. And, Altairos!" This was the important part, the part she really wanted to tell him. "Now, when I am so happy, I don't regret those despairing months at all. They seem to add to my present happiness. There is no possibility that they could detract from my joy! And that amazes me."

Altairos sat silent again. Was that awe she perceived in his eyes?

Finally he prodded himself into speech. "Pappa never told me . . . any of that. I wish he had, but I'm not sure when he might have. He was so busy, and I always felt so supported by my brothers. I felt no lack, and I think this counsel he gave you comes more naturally when there is need for it."

He fell into silence again, and she sat quietly, too, practicing the acceptance that had lightened her despair, curious how it might act on her present happiness.

The breeze lifted tendrils of her hair. The sun shone warm on her skin. The turf under her felt slightly spongy, and the soft purr of the surf on the island's shores calmed her. She felt perfectly balanced in the moment, aware of place, and aware also of Altairos' presence. Her happiness deepened into joy.

"Do you think I could learn this discipline of Pappa's from you, Nerine? Or are we too happy for it?"

She beamed at him. "Do you know, I was just wondering that very thing. Are we too happy? So I tried it. Just now."

"And?" His eyes were bright with hope.

"It was wonderful," she said.

"Teach me, Nerine," he appealed.

"I'm not sure it can be taught," she said. "But I think it can be practiced."

"Then let's practice it, the both of us. Shall we, Nerine?"

"Yes! I want to," she answered.

So they added the practice of acceptance and hope to their other pleasures of walking and talking, of swimming and silence. And their days together in that out-of-the-world island became a paradise. While their nights, when they spoke their love to one another with intimate touch and the delights of that touch, became bliss.

∽

On their ninth morning, just after a rinsing dip in the sea, Altairos straightened from donning his tattered tunic and spotted a sail on the horizon.

"Nerine! Dear gods, look!"

He didn't wait for her to look, however, grabbing her hand and running with her up the hill.

"What is it? Altairos, is it a ship?" she panted. She'd tried to glance out to sea, but been too hard pressed to keep his pace without stumbling.

"Yes! Quick!" He dove through the door of their cottage and started gathering logs from the stack in the corner. "Kindling, Nerine. And hurry!"

He piled their fire-making materials around the pine still retaining most of its branches, not the one they'd denuded for their bedding. First a fluffy mound of twigs and pine needles and shredded bark, then the smaller pieces of driftwood, and finally veritable logs.

Nerine seized a stick from their banked hearth, one end uncharred and safe for her grasp, the other end a glowing coal.

It burst into flame when she carried it out into the breeze.

She thrust it into the heart of the kindling under the pine boughs.

There was no need to fan the flames. The breeze did that. Moments later, the lower branches were afire and then the whole tree. Its wood was green and growing. Smoke poured from the torch it made, mounting into the cloudless sky.

Altairos ran around to the other side of the cottage, Nerine on his heels.

Now she could see the sail, square and filled with the wind. Its mast rooted in a triaconter – a warship – not a merchant's vessel, although the oars were shipped and at rest. And the flag of Zakynthos flew above the sail.

"Do they see us?" gasped Nerine.

Altairos had both his hands shading his eyes. "I think – I think – yes! They're readying the skiff."

As the vessel drew closer, Nerine could see the sailors adjusting the rigging, while others scurried on deck. They dropped anchor just where the inlet merged into the open sea.

"Get the bedding canvas, love."

She fetched it out, and together they waved it, a wild wing of white flapping against the sky and tugging at their grip.

The skiff had been launched. The oarsmen – their backs to shore – bent to their task, but the steersman lifted an arm and waved.

Nerine bundled their bedcover in her arms and carried it back into the cottage. She looked around briefly. They'd been so happy here, but there was nothing to carry away with them. Except, perhaps, the waterskin.

She shook her head.

No, her memories were treasure enough.

When she returned to Altairos' side, they joined hands and made their way along a narrow, switchbacking path from the clifftop to the sheltered beach below.

～

Epilogue

Six moons after their departure from paradise island – Ádionisí on the sea charts, as she learned later – Nerine stood in the prow of a *triaconter* watching the desert coast of Libúa slip by on her right. The ship was under sail – and the oarsmen at rest – for the wind was brisk behind them. The *Epaphéas'* prow surged through the waves, lifting on the crests and then plunging.

Nerine wore an elegant white linen gown in the draping Hellenic style, its edges embroidered pale green and fawn. A circlet of beryls and pearls adorned her green-blond hair, while matching brooches pinned the shoulders of her gown. The loose garment felt good after the snug fit of the frocks of northern Scandia, and after going entirely unclothed following her rescue of Altairos from the drowning sea.

She smiled as the ocean spray dampened her face, welcome in the heat of the strong sun of the southern summer. The sea shone intensely blue, contrasting with the yellow sands and orange rocks of the shore. There had been stretches of Cyrenaica where the desert gave way to green grasses and palms swaying in the breeze – and more fertile lands awaited them in Aegyptus along the great river Nile – but Libúa was a dry and barren place.

When the winds had failed yesterday, the oarsmen took to their oars most zealously, eager to reach a more clement locale for their night onshore and determined to make the next campsite with its reliable water source.

They'd achieved their goal, but everyone – except, perhaps Nerine – rejoiced in the reappearance of the steady air currents.

Nerine found herself able to enjoy every change in her circumstances. The starkness of the desert possessed a unique beauty. The palm studded enclaves felt exotic. The heat of the hottest days baked her body into a sublime languor. And the chant of the oarsmen on the windless days provided her a pleasant beat for meditation.

Practicing King Zeron's lesson with Altairos – the most distracting of companions, because she loved him so much – had given her the skill of using acceptance awareness almost anywhere. Sometimes she slipped into that soft focus when she should not – when a boring new acquaintance murmured courteous nothings and she missed the moment when that person switched to purposeful somethings.

It had happened once in the court of the suzerain of Cyrene. Fortunately Nerine's slip with the suzerain's consort went unnoticed, and she learned to be more disciplined with her awareness. Such mistakes would not make her diplomatic efforts at her husband's side the success she intended.

But on shipboard, she was free to indulge herself, and she did. This hot summer morning was glorious, and she gloried in it.

As the steersmen guided the *Epaphéas* a little father from shore – to avoid the cluster of jagged rocks protruding from the waves in the distance – Altairos joined Nerine at the prow, slipping his hands under her round belly and nuzzling her hair with the side of his jaw.

"Not sick?" he murmured in her ear.

Nerine smiled. "Not in the least."

She'd been sick on the ship that plucked them from tiny Ádionisí – their pocket paradise – and again in the first few *déka*-days of her pregnancy once they'd reached Zakynthos. But she was very well now.

Thank the blessings she'd not been sick past the time it took to plan their wedding celebrations. Because Altairos had been quite correct. Not only did they repeat their vows before their families, but they endured the full three-day ceremonial of *proaulia, gamos,* and *epaulia.* Although endure was probably the wrong word, despite the separation between them it entailed.

She'd been grateful – beyond grateful – that Mother accepted the news of her marriage – her consummated marriage – with every appearance of complacency, while Altairos' pappa – now her pappa as well – exhibited genuine enthusiasm.

⁓

Before Father journeyed with his retinue up the cliff from the sea to the land palace to make the *engysis,* the handshake with King Zeron – without which Nerine's and Altairos' marriage would not be valid – he drew Nerine into the old nursery garden to talk with her.

The water held that special clarity with a hint of blue that made the sea around Pelagie so lovely, and the spice from the bright quilt of reef plants scented it.

Nerine could almost imagine she was just eight years old and about to embark on the unimaginable adventure of breathing air and meeting a land dweller for the first time. Perhaps that was not so strange after all. Speaking her marriage vows before witnesses would transform her from a princess of Pelagie into a princess of Zakynthos. *There* was an adventure. And with this formal wedding, she would embark on the life of travel – Altairos at her side – that she had envisioned for herself when still so young.

But Father looked worried.

"Nerine, child." He seemed uncertain of how to begin what he wished to say.

Nerine smiled. "I'm not a child, Father, but a woman grown."

He sighed, water bubbling through his spiracles. "Indeed. Yet, I am still your father, and will be so forever, and I care for your happiness. Daughter."

She could sense that he'd substituted 'daughter' where he'd almost said 'child' yet again.

Nerine suppressed another smile. Instead of seeking Father's understanding and gentleness, she was hoping to be gentle herself.

"I will be happy, Father, incredibly happy. I have been happy, both on the tiny islet where Altairos and I were stranded, and during all ten years of our friendship as children."

"You've known the young man for fifteen years, Nerine?"

She'd told him so upon her return to the reef palace, but he'd not taken it in. Understandable amidst the hubbub of her unexpected arrival and the further commotion following her announcement that she was married and with child.

She'd not confessed all the details. Not then. But now was the time for it. Time for her to remedy the mistake she'd made as a child. An innocent mistake at the outset, but a grievous one when she'd kept her visits ashore and her friendship with Altairos a continuing secret.

Now was her moment to prove to herself that she possessed the courage she'd claimed.

"I dared breaching the water to breathe air two years before you and Mother decided to accompany me on that errand."

"What?!" Father almost roared the word. Then he swallowed, reining in his anger, and said more mildly, "You didn't."

"I did," Nerine assured him. "And I learned quickly enough of the dangers that entailed. But Altairos saved me."

"*Altairos* saved you?"

"That was when we first met, Father," she said gently.

"Great and little blessings, Nerine!" The water huffed out of his operculi as air might have huffed out of his lungs, if they'd stood on land rather than floating in the water of the nursery garden. "So that is why . . ."

No doubt he was putting together small anomalies that had never quite caught his attention during all the years of Nerine's growing up under his eye.

He became abruptly stern. "So that was why you rushed off to the norns in such a hurry! Because he went to pursue his diplomatic calling, leaving you forlorn and alone." His nostrils flared. "By the blessings, I'll – I'll – I'll have the scales off him before I shake hands with his father. How dare he –?"

Nerine wanted to laugh, but that would never do. Confusion would only hurt her father the more. He needed clarity and her help.

"Father," she said steadily. "No. That wasn't what happened."

His brow wrinkled in his darkened face.

"Altairos asked me to marry him."

"Then why . . . why in the sea didn't you, Nerine? You make no sense at all." His rage was ebbing into puzzlement. Understandably so. Looked at in retrospect, her actions were *not* sensible. At the time? Well, she'd been who she'd been.

"I felt sure that you and Mother would not approve. And that King Zeron would be truly opposed to our marriage." She paused. Some secrets just were not easy to speak of. Even now. "Because of Cousin Hester. Queen Hester."

"Aah," sighed Father. "Yes."

His anxiety and perplexity transformed to the benign sympathy that was his, that Nerine had always loved about him. Loved and depended on.

"My poor sweetheart." He looked at her very tenderly and drew her into a gentle embrace. "You believed it could never work, and chose the swift end rather than protracted and galling grief." He shook his head. "I am so very sorry."

She rested against his sheltering chest, once more remembering that comfort from her childhood.

"So what changed?" He released her from his arms, the better to see her face. "What happened that you spoke your marriage vows to one another, despite the barriers – the *perceived* barriers – to it?"

She'd already planned how she would explain this part of the chain of events without giving away secrets –the norns' secrets – that were not hers to share. "The gift of the norns reunited us. And I found that the courage I'd been cultivating had grown strong enough that even the barriers could not daunt me."

"Aah!" he sighed again. "That gladdens me." He looked her steadily in the eyes. "You know that you must not depend upon happenstance for virtue and happiness, child."

She could forgive him the 'child' now. It was endearment, not doubt. She lifted her chin. "I do know that, Father. It was . . . a hard-learned lesson. But I have learned it." She smiled and said more lightly, "Perhaps the hardest lessons learned are the ones that will not desert us when events press us most direly."

His face took on a quizzical expression, then he laughed. Some memory of his own? From youth? "I doubt I need worry for your choice, then, daughter mine. I shall go shake King Zeron's hand with a good will."

And he did just that. After kissing Nerine's brow, right above her spiracles.

～

Nerine's confrontation with Mother had come later.

She'd stayed with Mother and Father in the reef palace for a *déka*-day.

Both she and Altairos had agreed that springing changes on their respective parents too quickly after their startling news would prejudice land dwellers and sea dwellers alike against their union. But she had no intention of dwelling apart from Altairos the entire two moons it seemed the preparations for the triple wedding days would require.

After Father performed the *engysis* with King Zeron, and Mother visited Queen Briseis to discuss the details of the *gamos* itself – the ceremony with its procession and evening festivity – Nerine expressed her wish to retire to Calla's cottage.

"I'll be close by, Mother," she said, while they floated in Mother's dressing room, a lobe in the reef coated with pearly nacre and holding three great mirrors of polished bronze on the walls, as well as a collection of Mother's chests and jewel caskets.

"Nerine, really!" Mother looked down her nose. "It wouldn't be seemly."

Again, Nerine found herself hoping to be kind, rather than courting approval. Just as she had with Father. Perhaps this was what true maturity meant. Not that one ceased to care for the thoughts and wishes of one's mother and father, but that one had transferred authority from them to oneself.

"Mother, I understand that in order for the people of the reef and the people of Zakynthos to regard Altairos and me as married, we must perform the public ritual of marriage. Perhaps you feel this way, too. But –" she raised a hand as she saw her mother about to speak "– Altairos and I regard ourselves as married already. We pledged ourselves as husband and wife on Ádionisí and lived as husband and wife thereafter. I refuse to be separated from my husband for another two moons while all the planning and preparation goes forward."

"No." Mother took her most regal stance. "I won't have you running away, just like Xianthe when she went to Great Tethys." Her mouth straightened. Was Mother hiding tears and the trembling lips they engendered? "Or like poor Hester. I won't go through that again. I simply won't." Mother regained her poise with those last three words.

"But you won't be," Nerine pointed out.

"Indeed I won't," agreed Mother. "You'll be staying right here, in the parlor we gave you when you outgrew the nursery."

That wasn't quite how Nerine remembered that transaction. She'd claimed that parlor, not been granted it.

"I wonder if this ruby tiara would suit you. Such a shame that land-dwelling brides must wear red to be married in. Red just isn't your color!"

Nerine choked back a laugh and tried again to persuade her Mother. She would resort to insistence, if she must, but Mother would be so much happier if she were persuaded, not forced, that Nerine could not begrudge the effort.

"Mother, Xianthe ran away. With no notice of her intention, no reassurance for your worry, and no information as to her destination."

Mother sniffed. "And *you* are not yet a mother. *You* can have no notion of a Mother's fears."

Nerine didn't contradict her, but her sense of the baby growing in her womb grew stronger with every day, and her love for this yet-unknown son or daughter grew with it.

Mother tossed her head. "No, I won't have you wear rubies. I wonder if my carnelian hair brooch might serve?"

Nerine persevered. She could do this, despite Mother's determination to sidetrack her.

"When Cousin Hester ran away, I know it hurt you a great deal."

Mother stopped searching her memory for every jewel she possessed to stare keenly at her daughter.

"You never saw her again, did you?" said Nerine, softly.

Mother's face was very, very still. "No. I did not," she answered.

Nerine wanted to give her mother a hug, but that would be premature. Mother could not accept comfort when she was still barricading herself against hurt and thus against sympathy. How strange it felt to understand Mother so well. Understand her, and love her all the more.

How could she ever have thought that Galena was like Mother? Mother was cool, reserved, and haughty in her demeanor, yes. But *Mother* – could be hurt. Had been hurt. Half of her queenliness derived from some inner wound that Nerine had never fathomed. But only half. The other half came of Mother's strength. And Nerine would respect both Mother's hidden hurt and Mother's strength.

"Mother, had I married Altairos when I was eighteen, *then* I would have run away to do it. I hadn't the strength to do otherwise."

Mother's hand reached toward Nerine, but she didn't complete the gesture. She looked stricken.

"I am sorry for it," Nerine continued. "And I've paid for that weakness of mine. But I would have hurt you *then*" – 'yet again,' she thought, but did not say – "by running away. *Now*, I am stronger, and I am marrying Altairos twice over, *without* running away, precisely because of my strength."

Mother's eyes had softened, along with her expression. Perhaps now she might accept an embrace?

Nerine slipped an arm around her mother's shoulders and kissed her cheek. "I'll visit you nearly every day while I'm living in Calla's cottage with my husband. I'll be right here, really, and you may visit me also."

Her mother's head rested on Nerine's shoulder just an instant. Then she straightened suddenly and exclaimed, "I know! The circlet of tiger's eye will be just the thing! It should complement the red of the gown while also enhancing the hazel-green of your eyes. Perfect, child! I'll bring it to you tomorrow at Calla's cottage, so that we may check the effect."

Nerine did laugh at that point, and Mother laughed with her. Dear Mother! Only she would reconcile her perception of Nerine as a child with her acknowledgement of Nerine as a woman via jewelry. But that was Mother all over. How Nerine loved her, contradictions and all.

～

Eilidh, Agnippe, Rinara – Tyr's wife and still Nerine's dear friend – and even Xianthe returned to the reef palace to participate in the bride's privilege of a last day – the *proaulia* – spent entirely with her mother and sisters. Mother had been proud – which pleased Nerine as much as Mother's acceptance of Nerine's residing with Altairos in Calla's cottage during the wedding planning – and presided over the whole affair with an extra warmth to her graciousness.

Eilidh assumed a proprietary air, as though the marriage had been her idea in the first place, but her happiness for Nerine was real. Agnippe was soft and sweet, and couldn't refrain from kissing Nerine's cheek or touching her hand or leaning against her with an arm round her waist, all through the morning and afternoon, as though only touch reassured her that her sister had really returned safely from the north.

Xianthe proved astoundingly different from everyone's memory of her. All her wildness had been transformed into a quiet, contained strength. Nerine could see why Great Tethys sent Xianthe to the worst of trouble spots. Her discipline and focus would fix any problem that *could* be fixed, find any missing solution that might need devising, and overcome any adversary present.

Nerine faced no residual parental opposition – by the time Xianthe arrived – but if she had, Xianthe would have quelled it. Not with her old temper tantrums – those seemed entirely of the past – but with arguments so logical and persuasions so apt that no parent could have withstood her.

Nerine was happy she'd managed her own logical arguments and apt persuasions, however. It was good to manage for one's self.

Even with Xianthe before her, Nerine found it hard to believe that this was her next eldest sister. Xianthe's hair was the same curly green-gold, but cropped shorter even than Tyr's. Her face bore the same slightly aquiline nose and a hint of passion in the eyes. Xianthe at twenty-five *looked* very similar to Xianthe at seventeen. But her inner essence had changed. Truly.

Her main contribution to the *proaulia* – and, indeed, the *gamos,* and *epaulia* following – was a useful efficiency that prevented hitches before they happened. That and her composed wishes to Nerine for married happiness.

Rinara – in contrast to Xianthe – kept the proceedings lively and told bawdy jokes while the women were private, but (thank the blessings) curbed herself during the evening feast that took place on the beach where Altairos and Nerine had first met.

Nerine understood that usually the feast concluding the *proaulia* took place in the home of the bride's father, but Altairos' pappa and brothers and their courtiers required air to breathe. Thus the alternate choice. The land dwellers furnished the tables and seating, as well as the many torches that transformed the beach into a magical place. But the kitchens of the reef palace provided the food.

Nerine noted a few grimaces when the guests sampled the bitter *thali,* but most of the unfamiliar dishes provoked smiles, not frowns, from the land folk.

At the close of the evening, Nerine cut a lock of her hair and scattered it on the soft night breeze, praying that Queen Hera bless her marriage. A more usual petition would have been a plea that Artemis guide the bride through her transition from virgin to wife, but Nerine bore a child in her womb already.

Eilidh had asked Nerine if she were really ready to be a mother, intimating that the prospect should daunt her little sister. Mother had inquired if she had any particular concerns or worries. Only Rinara simply embraced the coming of a new niece or nephew.

That seemed the more proper attitude to Nerine. She was looking forward to the birth of her little one, and she'd said her vows to Altairos when there were no witnesses with the full expectation that she might conceive a child that very night. It was something she wanted. And she figured that the Nerine who had faced up to Orroch, who had grown courage out of cowardice, and who had fallen through the terrifying abyss of history could manage the challenges that would arrive with motherhood.

It might not be easy – all the experienced women seemed to think not – but Nerine was strong. She'd not have married Altairos without her conviction of it.

The day of the *gamos* was even more full than that of the *proaulia*. Altairos took a nuptial bath in his palace with water carried from a spring sacred to Aphrodite – and perfumed by crushed rose petals – while Nerine did the same in Calla's cottage. The rite symbolized fertility. Nerine suppressed a quick grin, when told of it. Yes, her union with Altairos was fertile, although only their immediate families knew of their coming child.

After Nerine's bath, she was garbed in a gown of carmine silk, sandals of scarlet leather were tied onto her feet, and a veil of sheerest white linen – woven in Aegyptus by the process known as water-mist, due to the translucency of its result – placed over her hair with its circlet of tiger's eye.

She met Altairos – also garbed in carmine, a formal robe – at the gate of the Mégaro Zakynthos, his palace home. Accompanied by a procession of kin and the nobles of both courts – land and sea – they visited each temple in the city and in the surrounding countryside, to make offerings and receive the blessing of the presiding priest or priestess. Evening had arrived by the time they finished at the shrine of Peitho – near the sacred spring that had provided the water for their nuptial baths – and could return to the courtyard of the land palace for the ceremonial removal of Nerine's veil and the repeating of their vows.

Another feast culminated the day, and then Nerine and Altairos were escorted to his rooms, where family members disrobed them, ushered them to the sleeping couch, and then departed, closing the doors behind them.

Nerine's memories of that night were every bit as sweet as those of her first night with Altairos, but quite different. For one thing, his brothers sang lewd songs outside their windows for half the night. Apparently that was the custom among the land dwellers.

She and Altairos had laughed and loved despite the serenade.

The next day's *epaulia* proved a less structured business, essentially a party in the public rooms of the Mégaro Zakynthos that lasted from morning into the night, during which each guest presented gifts to the newly married couple.

She and Altairos crept away from the festivities several times, longing for one another and no one else, after all the formality and continual presence of the crowd. A prince and a princess could not get married quickly – it seemed – unless they were alone on an island in the Ionian Sea.

But now they were married twice over, once on their own promises, and again in the traditions of Hellene culture. Did that mean their joining was twice as strong? Nerine's lips curved up.

⁓

The *Epaphéas* plowed through an especially tall wave, its spray more than a cooling mist on Nerine's face, leaving actual droplets of saltwater on her neck and gown.

The sea breeze fluttered a lock of her curling hair into her face, and Altairos' hands felt warm and anchoring beneath her rounded belly.

"Shall we linger in Memphis, after our negotiations in Alexandria with the Nomarch Cleomenes are complete?" asked Altairos. "The climate of Aegyptus is salubrious, and you might await the birth of our child in comfort there."

Nerine considered this idea and shook her head.

"The Nomarch is known to be a cruel, greedy ruler. I do not think our proposals will prosper with him. He is more likely to demand we pay him for lending his *triereis* to a continuing patrol against pirates than to see the advantage to his trading fleets," she said. "I would rather be on shipboard than anywhere within his reach."

"Shipboard?" echoed Altairos.

"Yes, why not? We have a midwife with us who trained under Agnodice herself. I shall gain no better attendant elsewhere, and I feel safe on the *Epaphéas*."

"You're amazing, love." She felt his lips kissing her hair.

A moment of dalliance with her husband tempted her, but the future also called her thoughts.

"Do you think the world too cruel a place for the rulers of mortals to place peace and prosperity ahead of their power to control and expand their realms?"

He didn't answer her immediately. She didn't wonder at it. Her travels across Európi had shown her how varied were the hearts of men. The Keltoi had offered her warm hospitality, and yet their high-prince exulted in the beheading of a youth. The Gutones seemed more rational, but she understood from the captain of the Poniró Peltastés that they regularly raided the villages along the eastern shore of Balder's Sea.

"Cleomenes will not aid us in stamping out piracy on the Middle Sea the way his predecessor did, but Azemilcus of Tyre will. Ebulus of Paphos, perhaps. Niketes of Messene, surely."

Altairos fell silent for another interval and then spoke again.

"I think . . . peace and prosperity are worthy aims. They *matter*. But the choice you and I have is whether we *work* toward what matters. The achieving of it?" He nodded. She could feel his face moving against her hair. "I would say that rests in the lap of the gods. You might say it is woven on the loom of your norns. But Pappa would say that the words and deeds of those who care the most will one day prevail. I choose to be one who cares."

"And I will stand with you," said Nerine. It felt good to know her resolve. Better to say it. Best of all to act on it. Together, she and Altairos would travel and negotiate for peace wherever they landed.

She wondered if there would ever be a golden age of accord, but suspected that peace would come in small flows, a drip here, a drop there. Between friends. Between kin. Between allies. And each small spring of peace would be blessed, just like the cultural one her sister Agnippe tended.

Nerine's own future, diplomacy and the tending of mortals and the agreements between them, beckoned her.

Altairos' hands, caressing her belly, brought her back from her contemplation of her future to the present.

"Tired?" suggested Altairos.

She swallowed a laugh.

Altairos advised her to rest due to his anxiety for her, which was sweet. He also proposed it in hope that he might retire with her to their curtained tent at the ship's stern and do anything but rest.

She covered his roaming right hand with her own.

"Shall we have a boy, do you think?" she asked.

It was his turn to muffle a laugh, in her shoulder as he held her close. "You'll never get me to express a preference, Nerine, no matter how cleverly you go about it. Whether we have six boys or six girls or some of each, I shall be well content."

"So many?" she murmured.

His left hand slipped under the top fold of white linen draping her dress from neck to waist, his fingers secretly encircling her breast.

"So few," he teased, "when we have so many joyful nights before us?"

She slipped a hand behind her to retaliate, sneaking in her own secret touch of him.

"Now I'm sure you need to rest," he declared, managing a calm tone, just barely.

"Mmm," she answered, smiling, glad in his embrace.

The End

Appendices

Who's Who in Fate's Door

The Three Norns in Scandia
Tynghed – the Shuttle-catcher
Eowys – the Patterner
Orroch – the Weaver

Neighbors to the Norns
Gwenedd – weaverwoman who creates the fabric for the norns' clothes and
    household linens
Briallyn – seamstress who sews for the norns
Himinlaeva – cook for the norns
Linnea – cook's helper
Eindred – handyman for the norns

The Royal Family of Pelagie
Nerine – a sea nymph who travels far
Eilidh – oldest sister to Nerine
Tyr – older and only brother to Nerine
Xianthe – older sister to Nerine
Agnippe – younger sister to Nerine
Meren – Nerine's father and guardian of the Middle Sea
Ionia – Nerine's mother and guardian of the Ionian Sea

Retinue at Pelagie
Nurse – constant and loyal attendant to the royal children
Philena – handmaiden to Queen Ionia
Rhaxmus – minister to King Meren
Spiro – minister to King Meren
Druma – tutor to the royal children
Panagiotas – taught their water gifts to Eilidh and Tyr
Sophronia – a storyteller who lives in the Singing Cave
Hester – long-absent, distant cousin and friend of Ionia's youth

Dolphins of Pelagie
Leem – a friendly dolphin
Mai'ip – Nerine's companion dolphin
Phorn – a strong dolphin
Pheep – a particular friend of Nerine's

Peers of the Middle Sea
Rinara – daughter of the Duke of the Gulf of Gallicus
Arius – Duke of the Gulf of Gallicus
Anstice – Duke of the Ligurian Sea
Pyralis – guardian of the currents in the Strait of Sikelia
Evander – guardian of the Aegean Sea
Sophelia – consort to Evander
Leukonos – son to Evander and Sophelia

Peers of Other Seas
Florian – March of the Marmara Sea
Ardashir – King of the Hyrcanian Sea
Torvald – Duke of Balder's Sea

Royal Family of the Mégaron Zakynthos
Altairos – youngest and sixth son to King Zeron
Zeron – king of Zakynthos, father to Altairos
Dardanus – eldest son, first minister to the king
Eridion – second son, captain of the Levantine warfleet
Corydon – third son, captain of the Aegean warfleet
Planos – fourth son, captain of the Western warfleet
Hilarion – wild fifth son
Briseis – step-mother to Altairos, second wife to Zeron
Hana – new half-sister to Altairos

Retinue at the Mégaron Zakynthos
Calla – Altairos' old nurse
Calix – diplomatic envoy
Sahar – maidservant to Altairos
Karim – manservant to Hilarion
Jasser – manservant to Hilarion
Jihene – maidservant in the land palace

Companions of the Road

Galena – a handmaiden to the Muse of History

The Poniró Peltastés – an elite cohort under Lord Hermes of Olympus

Jason – the *peltastís* charged with Nerine's comfort

Bartholomai – captain of the Poniró Peltastés

Sophé – Captain Bartholomai's horse

Efyenés – Nerine's horse while she travels through Európi

Therius – captain of the sea warriors who escort Nerine to Thérma

Heiro – flute player from the Levantine Sea, a warrior under Therius

Encounters Along the Road

Klanos oni Oletu – a chieftain of the southern Keltoi

Ulkos Ard-cean – high-prince over all the northern Keltoi

～

Places in Fate's Door

Ádionisí – a tiny islet off the west coast of Greece in the Ionian Sea

Aegean Sea – located to the east of Greece

Aegyptus – Egypt

Aethusa – Linosa, one of the three Isles of Pelagie, first mentioned by the ancient Greek philosopher and geographer Strabo

Alboran Sea – the westernmost portion of the Mediterranean Sea, lying between the Iberian peninsula and Morocco

Balder's Sea – the Baltic Sea

Balearic Sea – located between Mallorca and the coast of Spain

Bardários – the river Vardar that runs south through Macedonia to the Aegean Sea

Danouvios – the river Danube that runs east from the Black Forest in Germany to the Black Sea

Európi – Europe

Gulf of Gallicus – the Gulf of Lion, shaping a large portion of the southern coast of France

Hellas – Greece

Hesperia – the main peninsula of Italy

Hyrcanian Sea – the Caspian Sea

Istula – the river Vistula, which runs from the Carpathian Mountains through Poland to the Baltic sea

Karpathian Mountains – the Carpathian Mountains, south of Poland and north of Hungary

Kréte – Crete

Lamptír – Lampione, the smallest of the three Isles of Pelagie

Lapadoússa – the ancient Greek name for Lampedusa, the largest of the three isles of Pelagie between Sicily and Tunisia, nearer to the coast of Africa than that of Italy

Levantine Sea – the eastern portion of the Mediterranean

Libúa – Libya

Ligurian Sea – located north of Corsica between that island and the Italian Riviera

Marmara Sea – connects the Black Sea to the Aegean Sea

Mégaron Zakynthos – the palace where King Zeron conducts his governance and where he and his family live

Middle Sea – the Mediterranean Sea

Moirios – the Great Morava River which runs north from the Black Mountain, near the border between Macedonia and Kosovo, to the Danube

Oenotria – southernmost Italy

Pathissus – the river Tisza, which runs from the Carpathian Mountains south through Hungary to the Danube

Pelagie – the area of the sea holding the three islands: Lapadoússa, Aethus, and Lamptír (Lampedusa, Linosa, and Lampione)

Phoiníke – Phoenicia

Pieria – a region near Mount Olympus

Pillars of Herakles – the Strait of Gibraltar

Karasoúli – a city in ancient Thrace, now known as Polykastro

Prásino Shallows – fun place to visit within the lagoon of Pelagie

Sedes Fountain – a gushing spring of fresh water mounting from the floor of the lagoon of Pelagie

Sikelia – Sicily

Thérma – a port on the coast east of Mount Olympus

Thoúle – the far north

Tyrrhenian Sea – located off the west coast of Italy

World Ocean – the Atlantic Ocean

Zakynthos – the city-state located on Lapadoússa and ruled by King Zeron, pappa to Altairos

~

Languages in Fate's Door

Aramaya – Aramaic, spoken in Syria and Mesopotamia

Celtiberian – spoken in central Spain (Hispania)

Galatian – spoken in Persia (Anatolia)

Iberian – spoken along the coast of Spain (Hispania)

Ionikós – Ionic, the dialect of Greek that was spoken in Athens and Attica and eventually became the lingua franca of the Hellenistic world (eventually changing to be called Koine)

Lepontic – spoken by the Keltoi

Metremenkemi – Delta Coptic, spoken in ancient Egypt

Punic – spoken in Carthage

Timeline for the Ancient Mediterranean

382 BC – Philip II of Macedonia is born

359 BC – Philip II takes the throne of Macedonia, frees the kingdom of invaders, and strengthens his armies

356 BC – Alexander the Great is born in Pella, capital of Macedonia

354 BC – Philip II adds Thessaly to his realm and then turns his military attention east, away from the Hellenic peninsula

352 BC – Nerine is born in the reef palace of Pelagie

346 BC – Alexander the Great, aged ten, tames the horse Bucephalas; his father declares that Macedon is too small a kingdom for him and that he must find another big enough for his ambitions

344 BC – Nerine meets Altairos; she is eight years old; Altairos is one year older

338 BC – Philip II of Macedonia defeats the allied forces of Thebes and Athens; he forms the League of Corinth, getting the city-states of Hellas to stop fighting one another; a time of peace ensues there

336 BC – Altairos begins his apprenticeship in diplomacy; Philip of Macedon is assassinated; the nobles of Macedonia and the army proclaim Alexander king; he is twenty years old

335 BC – Alexander marches into the Hellene peninsula to contain the rebellion that occurs when the news of Philip's death arrives; while in Corinth, Alexander asks Diogenes what he wills; Diogenes gives a curmudgeonly reply – "Stand a little out of my sun" – which delights Alexander; having consolidated matters at home, Alexander focuses his military attention east toward conquest and is across the Hellespont by the next year

334 BC – Nerine turns eighteen and travels across Európi during the summer and early autumn months; she arrives at the cottage of the norns by mid-September

333 BC – After conquering the Phrygians, Alexander the Great spends three months in their capital city, Gordium, solving the puzzle of their famous knot while there

332 BC – Alexander adds Egypt to his empire and founds the great city of Alexandria, capital-to-be of the Ptolemaic kingdom in future years

331 BC – Alexander conquers Persia and then marches on toward victories on the Indian subcontinent, only turning back toward Macedonia and home in 325 BC

329 BC – Nerine returns to Pelagie and begins the true work of her adult life

323 BC – Alexander the Great dies in Babylon; the League of Corinth dissolves with Athens declaring war on Macedonia

∼

Translations of Foreign Words and Phrases

a nighean an diabhoil – you daughter of a devil

aftí ínai i dikí mou patrída – that is my home

agoraki mou – my little boy, a term of affection used for any male, regardless of age

ard-cean – high-prince, a Lepontic word

asterías – starfish

astiphílaka – peacekeeper

basileus – king

byddwch yn effro – you will awake

cean – prince, a Lepontic word

efyenés – noble

egó tha sas glitósi – I will save you

ekteléste grígori – run fast

éna, dío, tría, téssera, pénte, éxi – one, two, three, four, five, six

epaphéas – one who contacts

gnorízo óti tha prépi na prokhorísete – I know you must go

i kimatomorphés ínai megáli – the waves are big

i palírria ínai pou érkhetai – the tide is coming in

ikía – home

íkosi pénte, íkosi éxi, íkosi eptá – twenty-five, twenty-six, twenty-seven

ínai éna kavoúri – it is a crab

ínai éna kavoúri apó tin thálassa – it is a crab of the sea

íste ipérokhi – you are wonderful

kaliméra – good morning

kitáxte – look

kitáxte to – look at this

kríousa – queen or princess

kyría – missus or lady

kýrio – mister or lord

lamptir – lantern

lemonáda – lemonade

mana mou – my mother, a term of affection not reserved only for one's mother

mikroula – my little girl, a term of affection used for any female, regardless of age

naïáda – naiad

nid yw cwsg marwolaeth yn perthyn i chi – the sleep of death does not belong to you

nosokóma – nurse

oni – of, a Lepontic word

penteres – a quinquereme, a warship (plural: pentereis)

periménete edó – wait here

pétra – rock

prásino – green

prépi na páo tóra – I must go now

scunner – an irritating person or thing

tetreres – a quadrireme, a warship (plural: tetrereis)

téssera, pénte, éxi – four, five, six

tha ímai philí sas píso – I will race you back

tha sas vithísoume – shall I help you

triánta – thirty

trieres – a trireme, a warship with three banks of oars (plural: triereis)

ulkos – wolf, a Lepontic word

wyf yn ei orchymyn i chi fyw – I order you to live

~

Glossary

Agnodice – the first female Athenian physician and midwife; possibly a mythic figure, rather than a living woman

auger – a small, narrow seashell with a shape and a spiraling pattern resembling the horn of a narwhale

belt – a land person would merely mean a strap of leather or fabric that wrapped around the waist; a sea *numen* means a more elaborate accessory, often jeweled, that encircles the waist or hips, but also passes between the legs, attaching to the portion around the torso

chamberstick – a candlestick is a device with a cup or a spike on which to secure or "stick" a burning candle; chambersticks are shorter than candlesticks and possess a wide pan in which to catch dripping wax; they are used specifically for carrying a lit candle to one's bedchamber

chitin – forms the exoskeletons of crustaceans such as crabs and lobsters, as well as of other creatures in the natural world

Cleomenes – appointed by Alexander the Great to be nomarch of the district of Egypt that included the city of Alexandria; he was rapacious and used his office for his own benefit

déka-day – the equivalent of a week in the culture of the ancient Greeks; they divided their months, or moons, into thirds; the first twenty days of the moon were counted one through twenty; the last ten days were counted in reverse order from ten down to one; the first ten days were called 'moon waxing,' the second ten days were 'moon full,' and the last ten days were 'moon waning'

engysis – the formal betrothal of a Hellene maiden, in which her father shook hands with the bridegroom or his father

epaulia – the third day of the celebrations comprising a Hellene wedding; friends of the bride and groom bring gifts to supply them for their life together as husband and wife

gamos – the second day of the celebrations comprising a Hellene wedding; the bride and groom and their family members made processions to the various temples of the gods to leave offerings and make petitions for good fortune; in the evening, they repaired to the groom's home for feasting and the exchange of their pledges to one another

gladius – a short sword, two-edged for cutting, with a tapered point for stabbing

ground loom – a primitive loom in which stakes are pounded into the ground to hold the bars to which the warp threads are tied; nomadic peoples often use this type of loom, because it is very portable; the weaver must either sit beside the fabric being woven or on it

heddles – the parts of a loom that move the warp threads up and down, separating some portion of them from the rest, allowing the weft threads to weave in and out between them

Kleopátra – sister to Alexander the Great, she married the king of Epirus and became regent of the kingdom when her husband went to war in aid of an ally; he was killed in battle, and she ruled for ten years; the more famous Cleopatra of Egypt was born nearly three hundred years after Kleopátra of Epirus

kvass – a lacto-fermented beverage created from beets or fragments of rye bread, often flavored with raisins; uses principles similar to making yogurt

linothorax armor – armor worn by the ancient Greeks; it was made of layers of linen laminated to form a thick barrier, nearly a centimeter thick; it wrapped around the torso; wide shoulder straps helped protect the upper body, while an attached skirt of flaps protected the thighs; the armor was white or beige in color with trim of bright red

Lunasad – a Celtic festival said to have been begun by the god Lugh in honor of his mother; it consisted of athletic contests, feasting, and a dramatic rendition of Lugh's battles with the demons of blight and famine

Mother Holle – an ancient Germanic goddess, a Great Mother, who was worshipped long before the pantheon that included Woden, Thor, Loki, and other familiar Norse gods

nålbindning – the earliest form of knitting, used even by the ancient Egyptians; it is done with a single needle, passing the yarn around a base circle of yarn in a sequence that produces a tube or a length of stretchy fabric

norns – the mystical beings in Norse mythology who ruled the destinies of gods and mortals

operculi – the cartilaginous flaps that cover and protect the gills; located
over the ribs of a sea *numen*

pandourion – a forerunner of the lute with a teardrop-shaped body, a long
neck, and three strings to be plucked or strummed

papyrus – this paper, made in Egypt by pounding strips of the papyrus reed
together, was used throughout the ancient Mediterranean world

pectoral – a necklace worn by the ancient Egyptians, suspended from the
neck, but lying on the breast; the pectorals of sea *numeni* are larger and
generally fastened at the back, as well as the neck; they cover most of
the chest and ribs

peltastís – a lightly armed warrior who carried a crescent-shaped shield
(called a *pelte*) of wicker covered with sheepskin; he was armed with
three javelins, often stored in straps on the inner side of the shield, and
a short sword; plural: *peltastés*

penteconter – an early warship rowed by fifty oarsmen, twenty-five on each
side manning single banks of oars

penteres – a quinquereme, a warship with three banks of oars, two rowers
on each oar in the top two banks, one rower on each oar in the bottom
bank (plural: *pentereis*); quinquereme is later Latin term used by the
ancient Romans; the ancient Greeks called these ships *pentereis*

peplos – the draping gown, with graceful folds and criss-crossing sashes,
worn by women in Hellenistic cultures; its basic shape is a long tube,
the top quarter or third folded over, with the fold then pinned or sewn
at each shoulder; the elegance of the garment is achieved by the tied
sashes to give it form and beautiful drapings

proaulia – the first day of the celebrations comprising a Hellene wedding;
the bride spent the day with her mother and sisters, preparing for the
change in her estate; the day ended in a feast for the families of both
bride and groom

shed – the space created, in weaving, when a portion of the long warp
threads are raised, while the rest remain in place; the shuttle carrying
the weft thread is passed through the shed

shuttle – a boat-shaped piece of wood with a spool at its center, around
which is wrapped the thread for weaving; the shuttle is tossed across
the warp threads, the weft thread unspooling behind it

spiracles – two small, dimple-like openings just above the nose and between the eyebrows of a sea *numen* that help supply the gills with water; sharks and other marine creatures also have spiracles that lie just behind the eyes

surging closet – a small chamber in the reef palace where a continuous flow of water is channeled strongly from an opening in the ceiling through an opening in the concave floor; it acts as a water closet on land does, carrying wastes away

sylta – a traditional preparation of veal and pork that is time-consuming to make

tetreres – a quadrireme, a warship with three banks of oars, two rowers on each oar in the top bank, one rower on each oar in the bottom two banks (plural: *tetrereis*); quadrireme is later Latin term used by the ancient Romans; the ancient Greeks called these ships *tetrereis*

trews – loose-fitting trousers worn by the Keltoi

triaconter – the earliest warships with thirty oarsmen, fifteen pulling single banks of oars on each side of the vessel; triaconters continued in use after the *trieres* came to be the dominant warship in the Mediterranean, because they were lighter and less expensive to maintain and made excellent scouting or courier vessels

trieres – a trireme, a warship with three banks of oars (plural: *triereis*); trireme is later Latin term used by the ancient Romans; the ancient Greeks called these ships *triereis*

vertical loom – a loom in which the warp threads hang from a crossbar supported by vertical posts; weights hold the warp threads taut; the fabric is woven from the top down toward the ground; these looms were common in Hellene culture

warp – the longest threads on a loom, stretching from the warp bar at the back, all the way to the front bar where the weaver sits

water gift – the sea *numeni* possess a special magic with water that allows them to create currents, change the temperature or salinity of water, or accomplish other useful feats

weft – the threads that pass across the warp threads, over and under, to create fabric

∿

Author's Note

Fate's Door is fantasy blended with the ancient world of our own Mediterranean Sea. Most mentions of real historical events within my story are brief and tangential, but I did my best to make them accurate. Although history fascinates me, I am not a scholar of history. I researched many of the specifics of the ancient world – such as horse gear and the Hellene term for a warship (*tireres*) versus the Roman term for such (*trireme*) – but my research carried me only so far as an interested layperson might go. My aim was to knit my story into the fabric of history, not to write a treatise on the times of the ancient Greeks.

I took one deliberate liberty with history and geography. There is a real island in the Ionian Sea, called variously: Zycanthos, Zakynthos, or Zante. While there is archeological and historical evidence that the island of Lapadoússa (or Lampedusa, one of the three Isles of Pelagie) served as a landing place and maritime base for the ancient Phoenicians, Greeks, and Romans, I could not find any details about it. I have posited that its favorable location allowed a trade-based city-state to develop there, and I named this city-state Zakynthos. My fictional Zakynthos is an utterly different entity from the Ionian island off the west coast of Greece.

～つ

J.M. Ney-Grimm lives with her husband and children in Virginia, just east of the Blue Ridge Mountains. She's learning about permaculture gardening and debunking popular myths about food. The rest of the time she reads Robin McKinley, Diana Wynne Jones, and Lois McMaster Bujold, plays boardgames like Settlers of Catan, rears her twins, and writes stories set in the magical realms of myth and fantasy.

Look for her novels and novellas at your favorite bookstore – online or on Main Street.

J.M. Ney-Grimm maintains a blog featuring flash fiction from her North-lands and other tidbits unearthed by her ever-active curiosity.

Visit her at http://JMNey-Grimm.com.

www.ingramcontent.com/pod-product-compliance
Lightning Source LLC
Chambersburg PA
CBHW020825030726
47496CB00001B/92